An encoun... ...ith a sexy,
seductiv...

Date w...
DOCTOR

Three sensational novels from
Melanie Milburne, Alison Roberts
and Lucy Clark

Special treats for February.
Want a date with a gorgeous man?
Look no further!

Date with a
DOCTOR

MELANIE
MILBURNE

ALISON
ROBERTS

LUCY
CLARK

MILLS &
BOON

Mills & Boon, an imprint of Harlequin (UK) Limited, Eton House, 18-24 Paradise Road, Richmond, Surrey TW9 1SR

DATE WITH A DOCTOR
© Harlequin Enterprises II B.V./S.à.r.l 2013

A Surgeon Worth Waiting For © Melanie Milburne 2005
The Italian Surgeon Claims His Bride © Alison Roberts 2008
City Surgeon, Outback Bride © Anne Clark and Peter Clark 2008

ISBN: 978 0 263 90281 5

010-0213

Harlequin (UK) policy is to use papers that are natural, renewable and recyclable products and made from wood grown in sustainable forests. The logging and manufacturing processes conform to the legal environmental regulations of the country of origin.

Printed and bound in Spain
by Blackprint CPI, Barcelona

A SURGEON WORTH WAITING FOR

MELANIE MILBURNE

From as soon as **Melanie Milburne** could pick up a pen she knew she wanted to write. It was when she picked up her first Mills & Boon at seventeen that she realised she wanted to write romance. Distracted for a few years by meeting and marrying her own handsome hero, surgeon husband Steve and having two boys, plus completing a Masters of Education and becoming a nationally ranked athlete (masters swimming) she decided to write. Five submissions later she sold her first book and is now a multi-published bestselling, award winning *USA TODAY* author. In 2008 she won the Australian Readers Association's most popular category/series romance and in 2011 she won the prestigious Romance Writers of Australia R*BY award.

Melanie loves to hear from her readers via her website—www.melaniemilburne.com.au or on Facebook—www.facebook.com/pages/Melanie-Milburne/351594482609.

CHAPTER ONE

'WHERE the hell is the anaesthetist?' Jack Colcannon growled as he looked at the clock on the wall for the fifth frustrating time. 'I have a huge operating list and I don't want to start late yet again.'

'Becky should be here soon,' Gwen Taylor, the scrub nurse, said. 'Anyway, if there was a problem she would have phoned in by now.'

Jack grunted as he turned towards the theatre tearoom. Rebecca Baxter might be his best friend's younger sister but working with her was proving to be a nightmare in more ways than one. Sure, she was a good anaesthetist—in fact, probably one of the best he'd worked with during the whole time he'd been at St Patrick's—but something about her always seemed to get under his skin.

He poured himself a cup of coffee and, taking it across to the window, looked at the view of the Sydney skyline in the distance. The summer sun was beating down relentlessly, and with only three weeks to go until Christmas he could almost feel the hectic pulse of the city as swarms of shoppers went about their frantic business.

He shifted his gaze and looked down to where he'd parked his new car earlier that morning. He'd taken delivery of it the week before and couldn't help a small smile of satisfaction as he thought of the power and thrust under the bonnet, the surge of speed that sent him backwards in the leather-clad seat as soon as his foot hit the throttle.

He took another sip of his coffee and was just about to turn away from the window when he saw a bright pink Volkswagen Beetle swing into the car park and begin the hunt for a parking spot.

5

Rebecca Baxter tried to nudge between two cars in the shade of a spindly tree, but after three attempts to reverse, she gave up and chugged a little further along to where Jack's car was parked. Putting on her indicator, she began to reverse into the tight space behind.

His fingers automatically tightened around his cup, his breath stilling in his chest as he watched her manoeuvre the car into position, the relief when she did it without touching the immaculate paintwork of his car sending his halted breath out on a whoosh.

'So there is a god after all,' he murmured as he began to turn away from the window.

The sound of metal crunching against metal made him swing back so quickly his coffee went in a dark brown arc across the floor, and his mouth dropped open as he looked down below.

'Oops!' Becky winced at her misjudgement of the clutch release, quickly scanning the car park to see if anyone had witnessed her error. To her immense relief no one had appeared to notice.

She got out and inspected her car. Thankfully there wasn't a single scratch.

But as for Jack Colcannon's car...

She bit her lip, took a calming breath, and turned around to look at it. She knew how particular Jack was over things, and not just his car.

His brand-new car, she reminded herself with a sinking feeling in the pit of her stomach as her eyes went to the nasty dent in his bumper. She bent over to peer at it. Was that a tiny bit of pink paint?

She sensed him coming before she heard him, which was saying something for her sixth sense, as he was practically bawling her out from the front door of the hospital, way across the car park.

'What the hell do you think you're doing?' He strode towards her angrily, his theatre gear plastered to his tall muscled frame by the hot stiff breeze that was coming in from the west. 'Who in God's name taught you how to park?'

Becky lifted her chin and faced his furious green gaze with an equanimity she didn't quite feel. 'My brother Ben did, and, if I remember correctly...' she gave him a pointed little look from beneath her lashes '...you even once took me out for a quick park yourself.'

Jack set his jaw.

How like her to remind him of the one time he had lost all control with her. More than a decade had passed since that sweltering afternoon when he'd looked down at the full curve of her pouting seventeen-year-old mouth and...

'Anyway,' she continued before he could think of a suitable retort, 'it's the tiniest, weeniest little dent. Nothing to make such a fuss about.'

He sent her a withering look and squatted down in front of his car to inspect the damage, running his long tanned fingers over the bent metal.

Becky felt her stomach muscles instinctively tighten. As much as she hated to admit it, Jack had the most amazing hands. She watched as they moved over the bumper, trying not to think of how they would feel moving over her skin, over her face, tracing the line of her mouth.

She had felt his mouth on hers—just the once, but the memory of it had stayed with her as if it had happened yesterday. Sometimes she felt as if she could still taste him when she swept her tongue across the surface of her lips...

He straightened to his full height and turned to look down at her, his mouth tight with tension.

'The whole thing will have to be replaced.'

'What?' She stared at him in heart-tripping alarm. 'The whole *car?*'

He rolled his eyes heavenwards, his tone clipped with biting sarcasm. 'No. Not the whole car, Rebecca, just the bumper.'

Becky hated the way he made the full use of her name sound like an insult. No one else did it, just him.

She would have hitched her chin up another notch but she

was already craning her neck to maintain eye contact as it was. He was taller than her six-foot-one brother by about three inches and, no matter how often she wore heels to work, her five-foot-five frame still barely came up to his broad shoulders.

'You know something, Jack?' she said with a cutting edge to her voice. 'You really should have booked in for that emergency personality bypass by now. You're really starting to annoy me, and that is not a good thing.'

'Oh, really?' He gave her a glittering look. 'Well, for your information, Dr Baxter, you rate pretty high on my annoyance Richter scale, too. My operating list is now going to be at least an hour late because of you breezing in here like this. What were you doing to make you so late? Your Christmas shopping?'

Becky glared at him, her mouth thinned out with anger. 'I had a flat tyre.'

'Another one?' His expression was disbelieving. 'That makes—let me see now…' He held up his hand and counted on his long fingers as if speaking to a small child. 'One last week, one on Monday and now another one today.'

She pursed her lips and folded her arms without answering.

'Come on, Rebecca,' he said. 'Can't you think of something a little better than that? What about a granny's or distant great-aunt's funeral or something?'

'I told you the truth.' She bit the words out hard. 'I have had three flat tyres in six days. It's costing me a fortune to have them fixed.'

'Yeah, well, it's costing the government a packet to keep this public hospital up and running, and if we don't get this list started immediately the CEO will be on my back yet again about the ever-increasing waiting list.'

Becky turned away to get her bag off the front seat, her teeth catching her bottom lip momentarily. She had never had car trouble before, but now it seemed as if something was going wrong every single day. Even the brakes had felt a little spongy when she'd pulled into the car park, though she'd had the car serviced less than ten days ago.

She hoisted her bag over one shoulder and flicked the remote to lock the car, turning back to glance up at Jack, who was watching her silently.

'I'll pay for the damages,' she said, brushing past him to make her way towards the entrance. 'Just send me the bill.'

Jack frowned as her heels click-clacked across the car park, her small figure disappearing through the automatic doors of the hospital as if the building were swallowing her whole.

He gave a rough-edged sigh, ran a hand through his dark hair and followed her into the building.

It was going to be another one of those days, he was sure.

'Betadine prep, Gwen, please,' Jack said, once the first patient was anaesthetised. Gwen handed him the Betadine and he applied it to the abdomen liberally before handing the dish and applicator back. The patient was draped and the diathermy and sucker set up.

'Scalpel.'

He made a midline incision in the abdomen of sixty-five-year-old Hugh Williams, who had a sigmoid colon cancer.

'Rebecca, the usual antibiotics and heparin, please,' he said.

'Already given,' Becky answered. 'Can we tip him a little head down, please? He's a vasculopath and a little hypotensive at the moment.'

'Yes, all right, head down a bit. Diathermy, Gwen,' Jack said as he completed the opening of the abdomen.

He inserted a Balfour self-retaining retractor and carried out an exploration of the abdomen to assess the extent of the cancer, his frown behind his protective mask deepening as he concentrated.

'No liver metastases but the primary is stuck to the left pelvic wall.' He addressed his registrar assistant, Robert Caulfield. 'It's going to have to be dissected off the iliac vessels and ureter.'

Half an hour later Jack spoke again. 'This tumour is very adherent, Robert—I'm taking it off the iliacs now… *Shoot!* Vascular clamp, Gwen. The tumour is into the common iliac and we have a hole in the artery. Robert, compress the bleeding with packs till we clamp the artery.'

'What are you guys doing down there?' Becky asked, her eyes still on the monitor. 'His BP has dropped right off.'

'We're into the common iliac artery and losing blood fast,' Jack answered. 'Where's that clamp, Gwen?'

'Coming, Jack,' Gwen said. 'We weren't expecting to need vascular extras.'

'Mr Williams has got marginal cardiac function,' Becky informed them. 'Either you stop the bleeding or we're going to be in trouble soon. I'm putting in an extra IV line and starting colloid. Did you cross-match blood, Rob?'

'Just grouped and held, Dr Baxter,' Robert answered. 'We don't normally cross-match for a sigmoid colectomy.'

'Right, then, I'm taking blood for an urgent cross-match. Jack, I'm getting in O-negative blood. I can't hold him on crystalloid any longer.'

'Whatever,' Jack said tightly. 'Just keep him in there till I can clamp this artery.'

'The Satinsky vascular clamp is here, Jack,' Gwen informed him.

'Hold back the sigmoid mesentery and get that sucker in there to clear the field while I clamp, Robert. Ready. Now, suck, retract.'

Jack applied the clamp to the common iliac artery and the bleeding stopped. He allowed himself a small sigh of relief and addressed Becky. 'Bleeding has stopped, Rebecca. How is he?'

'Hypotensive but holding in there. I've got O-negative blood pumping in, looks about two and a half litres of blood loss, but if you've got the bleeding stopped we can manage it.'

'Good. Vascular suture, Gwen.'

Jack repaired the hole in the common iliac artery, taking care not to damage the left ureter. The sigmoid colon was then freed and resected.

'Blood supply to the bowel ends looks good. I'm doing a

hand-sewn anastomosis. Gwen, outer 2/0 black silk and inner 2/0 chromic catgut.'

'No stapler, then?' Gwen queried.

'No, the anastomosis is too far from the rectum.' Jack went on to complete the anastomosis and close the mesenteric defect.

'You can close up, Robert, no drains,' he said, stepping away from the patient. 'Everything all right your end, Rebecca?'

'He's stable and good BP,' Becky said, exchanging relieved glances with the anaesthetic nurse beside her.

Jack left the operating theatre to write up his operation notes on Mr Williams as the registrar completed the closure of the abdomen.

'What's eating Jack this morning?' Julie, the anaesthetic nurse, asked the rest of the theatre staff. 'He came in growling like a bear first thing.'

'He was on call last night,' Gwen said, handing Robert a skin stapler. 'A twenty-year-old road trauma victim died in Theatre. He did everything he could but it wasn't enough. The kid bled out.'

Becky felt a wave of shame go through her for the way she'd spoken to him in the car park. She of all people knew the stress of losing a patient, how it ate at you in the middle of yet another sleepless night as you agonised over what could have or should have been done, even if there had been a chance.

She looked at the still unconscious Mr Williams and sighed. He was one of the lucky ones. His family would see him in a few hours, a little worse for wear but hopefully with a good few more years left to live, thanks to Jack's meticulous skill and care.

She followed the orderlies as they wheeled the patient out to Recovery, checking that Mr Williams was responding to voice before returning to Theatre to get ready for the next case.

'What was that ruckus about in the car park this morning?' Gwen asked once Becky came back.

'You *heard* that?' Becky gave her a startled look.

Gwen smiled as she stripped off her sterile gown and stuffed it in the laundry bin. 'What is it with you two? That stunt you just pulled off with Mr Williams proves just how well you can work together. Why can't you bury whatever hatchet there is and kiss and make up?'

'It would take an entire peace congress to sort out the mess,' Becky answered ruefully. 'Jack's had a chip on his shoulder about me for years, which up until this morning was the size of the Sydney Cricket Ground, but it has now just grown to include Centennial Park and Fox Studios as well.'

'Uh-oh.' Gwen's face screwed up in an I-know-this-is-going-to-be-bad grimace. 'Whatever did you do?'

'I ran into the back of his car. His brand-new car.'

Gwen whistled through her teeth. 'Not good.'

'Definitely not good,' Becky agreed.

'Why were you late in the first place?' Gwen asked.

'I had another flat tyre.'

Gwen's brows rose. 'What have you been doing, girl, parking on pins and needles?'

'Not that I know of.' She sighed as she looked at the wall where the patient list was situated. 'But I do seem to be having a run of bad luck.'

'Have you heard from your parents?' Gwen tactfully changed the subject.

'Not by phone but I've had a few emails,' Becky said, turning back to face her. 'They're doing a Greek Island tour and once that's finished they're moving on to spend Christmas in Prague.'

'What about your brother Ben? What's he up to?'

Becky wasn't sure how to answer. She hadn't heard from her older brother in weeks, which, considering his line of work as a special operations cop, wasn't all that unusual, but somehow just lately she'd felt increasingly uneasy, as if she could sense he was in some sort of danger.

'He's away on some assignment or other,' she said somewhat evasively. 'You know what thirty-four-year-old men are like. They don't like to be tied down for too long.'

'Speaking of thirty-four-year-old men...' Gwen's voice dropped to an undertone as she nodded towards the doctors' room where Jack had gone earlier. 'Has Mr Grumpy got himself a new girlfriend yet? It's been months since he broke up with Marcia.'

'I'm not sure...' Becky answered, shifting her gaze.

'That's probably why he's so out of sorts,' Gwen said reflectively. 'All those surging hormones of his are all dressed up and have nowhere to go.'

Becky was quite relieved when it was time to prepare the next patient. She was sure Jack wouldn't appreciate her discussing his hormones with the theatre staff.

'That was good work with Mr Williams,' Jack told her as he came in scrubbed up for the next procedure. 'I thought we were going to lose him.'

Becky wasn't used to his praise, and even though it had been handed to her somewhat grudgingly, she still felt a warm wave of something indefinable pass through her at his words and brief glance in her direction.

'Thanks,' she said, and turned to the patient she was monitoring.

'Right,' Jack said, turning to the rest of the gathered staff, 'let's get this mastectomy under way.'

The rest of the list passed routinely, the mastectomy followed by a laparoscopic adrenalectomy, thyroidectomy and two laparoscopic cholecystectomies before theatre management pulled the plug on the last case. No time overruns were being permitted, and any cases left over had to go onto the next scheduled list.

Becky could see the frustration on Jack's face as he stripped off his protective gear. He was a hard-working surgeon who hated the bureaucratic red tape that tied up the public operating system into neat orderly nine-to-five working days.

She'd often wondered why he didn't shift his skills to the

private sector, where the financial gains were far more substantial. His father, Emery Colcannon, was one of Sydney's best-known private cosmetic surgeons and it had always seemed a little strange to her that Jack, his only child, had chosen to become a staff specialist in a cash-strapped public hospital.

But, then, who was she to talk? Here was she, a twenty-nine-year-old staff anaesthetist who hadn't quite made up her mind whether to take the step into a lucrative private practice arrangement or continue as she was.

Maybe she and Jack weren't so different after all, she thought as she followed the last patient out to Recovery.

'Jack?' Becky entered the doctors' room half an hour later.

He looked up, closing the folder he'd been writing in and pushed it to one side as he leaned back in his chair. 'Yes?'

She closed the door softly behind her, trying not to be put off by his curt and dismissive attitude as her eyes met his.

'I'm sorry for being so rude to you this morning,' she said, looking down at her hands resting on the back of the chair she'd instinctively grabbed for support. 'I didn't realise you'd had a bad night and I wanted to—'

He got to his feet in one fluid movement, which seemed to instantly shrink the size of the room. She lifted her head and encountered his hard green gaze, her stomach doing a little reshuffle in the process.

'If you think you're going to get out of a damages claim then you are very much mistaken,' he said. 'I've already contacted the assessor. I'll post you the bill as soon as I receive it.'

'I wasn't apologising about the car,' she said. 'That was truly an accident. But I am sorry about the way I reacted. You were upset and I didn't think—'

'Leave it, Rebecca.' He picked up the folder from the desk. 'I don't need your apologies or your excuses. What I need right now is the flat surface of a bed for at least six hours— seven would be heaven.'

'I—I didn't really mean the bit about the personality by-pass,' she said as he strode towards the door.

Jack turned around to look at her, his hand still on the door-knob, his expression cynical. 'Didn't you?'

But before she could answer the door had opened and closed, and all that was left of him in the room was the faint trace of his aftershave lingering in the air that she began to draw somewhat raggedly into her lungs.

CHAPTER TWO

BECKY wasn't sure what woke her during the night. She wasn't normally a restless sleeper but she hadn't really settled all that well into the rented flat in Randwick. It was on a noisy street, and late-night revellers often wandered past, kicking over bins or vandalising cars.

She'd been saving for her own property but real estate was expensive in the inner suburbs, and she'd been hesitant about committing herself to borrowing such a large sum of money until she finally decided what career direction to take.

She lay listening for a moment without moving a muscle, doing her best to keep her breathing steady as she strained to hear whatever sound had woken her.

There it was again—the sounds of stealthy footsteps coming down the hall towards her bedroom, making every single hair lift up on her scalp in fear.

Becky didn't like to think of herself as a coward, but her level of expertise in terms of self-defence was of the vase-and-baseball-bat type. The only trouble was that her one and only vase was full of bright yellow roses in the kitchen, and she didn't, and never had, possessed a baseball bat.

She slipped out of bed as quietly as she could and, scrabbling around in the dark, picked up one of her shoes off the floor, holding the four-inch heel poised as she waited by the side of the door, her heart pounding like a hammer behind the wall of her chest.

Her breath stalled when the bedroom door was slowly pushed open. She flattened herself against the wall, wishing she could see through the darkness properly, but she'd pulled the blind down before going to bed in order to block out the streetlights. The tiny finger of light that found its way underneath the edge of the blind was only enough to fill the room with leaping shadows, which did absolutely nothing to ease her terror.

She clutched her shoe a little tighter for reassurance but her hands were damp with increasing panic and she knew it wouldn't take much for her drop it and run off screaming like the coward she was.

Ben would think it pathetic of her, of course. When the bravery genes were handed out in the Baxter family, her big brother had turned up first and taken the lot.

She watched in silent horror as a tall dark figure approached her bed slowly, cautiously, as if expecting her to leap out of the jumble of bedcovers and fire a weapon at him. The intruder switched on a tiny torch about the size of a pen and shone it over the bed and bedside table before turning around and training it right on her face.

'G-get out of my b-bedroom or I'll shoot,' she said, holding her shoe out like a pistol.

She thought she heard a snicker of laughter but her heart was making such a racket and there was a heavy roaring in her ears, so she wasn't sure if she imagined it. The intruder wore a full balaclava and gloves, his tight-fitting dark clothes making him appear all the more menacing.

'W-what do you want?' she asked, desperately hoping he wasn't the serial sex offender the police were searching for.

The intruder didn't answer but stood with his torchlight trained on her eyes so she couldn't see. Becky could feel herself cracking. She wasn't used to this amount of adrenalin flooding her system. Give her a flat line heart monitor any day. She could deal with that. But this was something else. Her legs were giving up on her and her hands were shaking so much the shoe dropped to the floor at her feet with a soft little thud.

The intruder turned off the torch and melted away in the darkness, closing the bedroom door with a tiny click as he left. Becky stood for endless seconds, unable to believe he'd gone without harming her, relief flowing through her like a tidal wave when she heard the front door open and close on his exit.

She lunged for the phone by her bed and pressed in the emergency code, her heart ramming her breastbone as the operator answered.

'Police! Get me the police!' she cried.

She was switched through to the local police and as soon as the officer on the end of the line spoke she blurted out her story. 'There was a man in my bedroom! You have to get over here and catch him.'

'What is your name, ma'am?' the officer asked.

'My name is— Hey, didn't you hear me?' Becky said. 'There was an intruder in my bedroom! He's probably still in the area!'

'What's your address?' the officer asked in the sort of bored tone that suggested he'd had one too many of this type of call that evening.

She forced herself to take a calming breath, answering in a controlled tone, 'I live at 4/56 Marigold Place, Randwick.'

'And your name?'

'Beck—Rebecca Baxter,' she said. 'Dr Rebecca Baxter.'

'I'll send a car as soon as one is available,' the officer said. 'In the meantime, is there anyone you could call to stay with you until we send someone over to take a statement?'

The only person Becky wanted to call was her brother, but when he was on assignment he was unreachable even by email. During those times it was like he had completely disappeared off the face of the earth. Her parents were on the other side of the earth, which left her with the last man on earth she wanted to call. But he lived close by, and her parents and brother had always insisted he was just like one of the family…

'Yes,' she answered a little lamely.

'Call them now, and hopefully our guys will get there before he or she does,' the officer said.

Becky stared at the phone for a moment before pressing in

Jack's home number, which she knew by heart from all the times she'd had to call him on patient-related matters.

'Colcannon,' Jack said somewhat groggily.

Becky glanced at the bedside clock and winced when she saw it was just after three a.m.

'Jack? It's me, Becky.'

She heard him smother a groan and the protest of the bed as he repositioned himself.

'Rebecca. I take it this isn't a social call?' She heard the sound of his hand scraping over the unshaven roughness of his jaw. 'Please, don't tell me one of today's patients has had a major bleed or—'

'There was a man in my bedroom,' she interrupted him bluntly.

There was a tiny silence.

'And you felt the sudden need to confess that to me?' There was more than a hint of satire in his tone.

'He was wearing a balaclava,' she bit out, stung by his mockery.

'Kinky.'

She let out her breath in a hiss. 'Will you listen to me, for God's sake? I told you there was an intruder in my flat and you're making a big joke out of it and I...I...' She gulped back a sob.

Jack bolted upright, brushing his hair out of his eyes, his hand tightening on the receiver. 'An intruder? What sort of intruder?'

'T-the usual s-sort, dressed all in black with gloves and—'

'Hell, Becky,' he said as his gut clenched painfully. 'Are you all right? Did he hurt you, or—?'

'I—I'm fine,' she said. 'The police are on their way.'

'I'll be right over,' he said, reaching for his neatly folded trousers. 'Stay there and don't answer the door unless you are sure it's me or the police, got that?'

'Y-yes.' She gave him the address, and put down the phone, and chewed her nails and waited.

* * *

She wasn't all that surprised when Jack arrived before the police. She heard his car roar up the street and watched as he parked behind her Beetle with the effortless ease she'd always envied.

She opened the door to his knock and stood before him uncertainly.

'You called me B-Becky,' she said and, stepping towards him, promptly burst into tears.

Jack held her trembling form against him without speaking. He knew she wouldn't have called him if Ben or her parents had been in town, but somehow knowing she'd thought of him as next in line made him feel inexplicably warm inside.

He'd always done his best to keep her at arm's length, not wanting to compromise his relationship to her brother with an affair with her that would have no future. He wasn't planning on getting married and Becky was nothing if not the marrying type. She'd already been engaged three times as it was. He'd seen the magazines she pored over during long operations where the monitors did half the work for her. Brides and babies were her thing. She even had names picked out, for heaven's sake!

No.

He wasn't going down the same pathway of his parents who, even twenty-four years after their acrimonious divorce, were still not on speaking terms. For years they had used him as a go-between until he'd finally put a stop to it by limiting his contact to birthdays and Christmas. Thank God he was on call this year, which meant for once he wouldn't have to choose between them.

The police announced their arrival and Jack eased Becky out of his arms to answer the door. He stood to one side as Becky gave her statement, his blood chilling as he heard the details.

'Did he say anything to you?' the female officer asked, pen in hand.

'No.'

'Nothing at all?'

'I thought I heard him laugh.'

The officers exchanged glances.

'What sort of laugh?' the male officer asked, looking at her intently.

'A sort of little chuckle.' She gave them a grimace of embarrassment. 'I might have imagined it. I was very frightened…'

'How long have you lived here?'

'About four months,' Becky said. 'I used to live in Mosman but my flatmate got married. I had to find somewhere else to live in a hurry.'

'Have you any known enemies?' the female officer asked. 'Perhaps an ex-boyfriend or partner who might have found it hard to let go?'

If only, Becky thought wryly. Every one of her ex-fiancés had had absolutely no difficulty whatsoever in letting her go. Two of them hadn't even waited around long enough for her to return their engagement rings.

'No.'

'What about through work?' the male officer asked, glancing at his notes. 'You said you're a doctor. Have you ever had a patient who was overly interested in you?'

'I'm an anaesthetist.' Becky's mouth twisted ruefully. 'Apart from my initial assessment before surgery, my patients are all asleep.'

'What about a colleague?' the female officer asked. 'Anyone you don't particularly like?'

Becky was very conscious of Jack's silent figure standing close by. She shifted from foot to foot and ran her tongue over her lips, but she had difficulty locating her voice.

'Dr Baxter?' the officer prompted, watching her closely.

Becky shook her head. 'No, there's no one I don't get on with.'

'Do you have anything of particular value in your flat that the intruder might have been after? Drugs or cash, or a prescription pad or jewellery?'

'I have a prescription pad in my bag but no cash or jewellery of any value. He didn't seem to be looking for anything. He just stood there, looking at me.'

'Do you think you'd recognise this man in a line-up?' the female constable asked.

Becky caught her lip between her teeth for a moment as she thought about it. 'I'm not sure.'

'Did he have any distinguishing features?'

'He was tall,' Becky said.

'How tall?'

'Six foot or so.' She looked at Jack briefly. 'Not as tall as Jack but similar build. It was hard to see—it was dark—and he was dressed in black clothing, including gloves and balaclava.'

'Yes, we haven't got any prints off the doorknobs so he certainly knew what he was doing,' the female constable said. 'Does anyone apart from you have a key to this apartment?'

Becky shook her head. 'No, not that I know of.'

'You haven't given anyone a set of keys at any time?' The constable flicked her gaze in Jack's direction before returning to look at her. 'Perhaps when someone was staying over for the night?'

'No.' Becky felt her cheeks grow warm with embarrassment. She hadn't even had a girlfriend stay for a sleep-over, let alone a man. Hell, how desperate and dateless had she become?

'Well, if you think of anything else, please don't hesitate to contact us,' the male officer said. 'And, of course, always lock your door and windows. We're still hunting for a serial sex offender and until we find him you can't be too careful.'

'Right.' Becky gave them both a weak smile as she led the way to the door. 'Thank you for your help.'

'No problem.' The male officer met Jack's eyes. 'It might be an idea if you stayed the rest of the night with her, just to be on the safe side.'

'Sure,' Jack found himself agreeing.

'And it would be a good idea to get the locks changed as soon as possible,' the female officer advised. 'There was no sign of a forced entry so unless you inadvertently left the door unlocked, this guy probably has a key.'

The door closed on the officers' exit and Becky turned to look at Jack, her chocolate brown eyes still shadowed with residual fear. 'You don't have to stay. I'll be fine.'

Jack drew in a breath of resignation. 'Your brother would kill me if I let anything happen to you in his absence.' He scraped a hand through his dark hair, leaving finger-sized comb marks in the shiny black strands. 'Not to mention your parents.'

Becky felt a little resentful that he was only offering to stay on behalf of her family. Why couldn't he be doing it for his own reasons?

'I'm sure you have much better things to do than babysit your best mate's kid sister,' she said, folding her arms across her chest.

'As long as I can lie flat and sleep, I don't care if I'm babysitting Godzilla's god-daughter.' He looked around the room, his gaze coming to rest on her small sofa. 'I don't suppose you have a spare bedroom in this matchbox of an apartment, do you?'

'I have one bed,' she said, her mouth pulled tight. 'Mine.'

'Want to toss for it?' he asked, taking a coin out of his pocket and turning it over in his fingers.

Becky's mouth tightened even further.

'I'll take that as a no,' he said. Glancing at the sofa, he added over one shoulder, 'Have you got a spare pillow I could borrow?'

She went to her room, snatched one off her bed and brought it back to him, shoving it at his chest. 'Here. Sweet dreams,' she said. 'I hope you don't snore.'

'I haven't had any complaints so far,' he said. 'What about you?'

'What about me?'

A small smile lurked around the edges of his mouth. 'Have any of your previous partners complained about the noise you make in bed?'

She forced herself to meet his glinting green gaze, even though her cheeks felt as if someone had blowtorched them from the inside. 'No complaints so far.'

'Well, then…' He started to unbutton his shirt. 'Do you think we should leave a light on in case Mr Balaclava thinks about returning?'

Becky suppressed a gulp as he shrugged off his shirt, the smooth tanned muscles of his chest making her eyes widen to the size of dinner plates. She'd thought Ben was fit, but Jack had obviously been working out. His pectoral muscles looked as if he'd been bench-pressing an entire road train with a couple of Hummers thrown in for good measure.

'I…I don't know…' Her gaze dipped to the flat plane of his stomach, the ripple of abdominal muscles making her instinctively suck in her tummy. She raised her eyes back to his with an effort. 'What do you think?'

Jack glanced at his watch. 'Lights or no lights, I think if we don't get to sleep within the next twenty minutes it won't be worth going to bed at all. I have a gym session at six a.m. and residents' rounds at seven-thirty.' He took off his shoes and socks and began to undo his belt when he suddenly thought better of it and let his hands fall away.

'You must be so tired.' She gave him an apologetic look, her hands twisting in front of her. 'I shouldn't have called you but you live the closest…'

'Don't worry about it,' he said lying down on the sofa, his long trouser-clad legs hanging over the end. 'As I said, Ben would lynch me if I didn't stand in for him as honorary big brother.'

She gave him an imitation of a smile. This was probably not the time to tell him she had never quite seen him in a brotherly light. That one kiss twelve years ago had changed that—permanently.

'Well, goodnight, then,' she said, turning for the door.

'Goodnight, Rebecca.'

She swung back round to face him. 'Becky,' she said insistently.

'Mmm?' Jack nestled into the pillow, his eyes closed. 'You say something?'

She drew in a stiff breath. 'I don't like it when you call me Rebecca.'

He lifted his head off the pillow to look at her, his greener-than-green gaze meeting hers. 'It is your name, isn't it?'

'That's not the point,' she said. 'You only do it to annoy me. I know you do.'

He gave the pillow a soft thump and, settling back down, closed his eyes once more. 'You're imagining it. I have no intention of annoying you. I just don't like abbreviated names.'

'You abbreviate yours,' she pointed out. 'Jackson Colcannon is your full name.'

He opened one eye to look at her. 'I hate the name Jackson. It always reminds me of one or both of my parents being angry with me.'

'Now you know how I feel,' she said. 'No one ever called me by my full name unless they were cross with me, which means I can only assume from your persistence in calling me by it that you are always angry with me.' She gave him a probing look. '*Are* you angry with me?'

Jack wasn't sure how he should answer. Anger wasn't exactly the primary emotion he felt when around her, although it was certainly way up there. She made him feel edgy and uncomfortable at times, as if she could see things in him he didn't want her or anyone else to see. He assumed it was because she had known him so long, watching him reaching adulthood alongside her brother. But he wasn't really angry with her, or at least not right now. If anything, he was angry at himself. He had no business thinking about her in any other way than as a surrogate sister. And right now, with her soft pouting mouth and fluffy blonde hair, she didn't exactly look all that sisterly.

'Can we just go to sleep?' he asked, flinging a hand over his eyes.

Becky came over and pulled his hand away from his face. 'Not until you promise.'

He eased his hand out of the warm curl of her small fingers and stuffed it down by his side, not trusting himself not to tug her down on top of him on the sofa. He could already smell her perfume on the pillow under his head, the exotic fragrance filling his nostrils until he could barely think.

'Promise me, Jack,' she insisted, her breath brushing over his face.

His eyes met hers in the soft light of the lamplight.

'Becky, then.' His voice, to his annoyance, came out on a croak. 'There—I said it. Satisfied?'

Her soft mouth curved upwards in a smile. 'You see? That didn't hurt a bit, did it?'

He scowled at her as he thumped the pillow once more. 'Will you, please, go to bed and let me sleep in peace?'

''Night, Jack.' And on an impulse she couldn't stop in time, she bent down and pressed a soft, barely there kiss to his stubbly cheek, her silky blonde hair falling forward to caress his bare neck. 'Thanks for coming to my rescue tonight.'

He grunted something inaudible in response and covered his head with the pillow.

Jack listened to the soft pad of her bare feet as she made her way to her room, heard the rustle of the bedclothes as she slipped back into bed. After a few moments he heard the click of the bedside lamp going off and another soft rustle as she shifted in the bed to get more comfortable.

He gave a silent groan as his lower body sprang to life at the thought of her lying within a few feet of him, the pulse of blood thickening him almost painfully.

'Damn you, Rebecca Baxter,' he growled in a deep undertone.

'Did you say something, Jack?' Becky called out from her bedroom.

Jack gritted his teeth. 'Goodnight, Reb—Becky.'

After a few short moments he heard her bedclothes being

pushed aside, closely followed by the pad of her footsteps as she came back out to the sitting room.

'I just thought of something.' She shifted from one bare foot to another, her chocolate gaze a little reluctant to meet his. 'Were you…with someone tonight? I mean…you know, sleeping with someone?'

'Sleeping with someone?' He almost laughed out loud. The last time he'd slept with someone had been— Hell, had it been *that* long ago?

'I mean having sex with someone,' she said, her cheeks tinged with pink.

'I don't think I have to answer that question,' he said firmly. 'For a start it's none of your business, and secondly I—'

'It's not like I'm jealous or anything.' Becky quickly cut him off. 'I just thought it was highly presumptuous of me to assume you'd drop everything and come over here.' She inspected her hands for a moment. 'I didn't want there to be any trouble… I mean, you having to explain to a girlfriend that you'd spent the night with me.' She raised her eyes to his. 'I wouldn't want there to be any misunderstandings.'

'Trust me,' he said with a touch of wryness. 'There will be no misunderstandings. Apart from the police, no one knows I'm here.'

'You won't tell anyone at work, will you?' she asked after a little pause.

'Hell, no,' he said, laying his head back on the sofa.

She pursed her lips for a moment. 'You make it sound as if it's some sort of terrible punishment to spend the night with me.'

You're not wrong there, baby, he felt like saying, but didn't.

'You didn't have to stay,' she went on. 'I can look after myself.'

'Yeah, right, armed to the hilt with a pair of stilettos,' he muttered as he recalled her statement to the police. 'I'd be absolutely scared spitless if I encountered you in a dark alley.'

'You think you're so funny,' she bit out resentfully.

'I don't want to think anything right now except about how

many minutes I can shut my eyes before I have to open them again,' he said. 'Now, will you go back to bed or do I have to carry you?'

Becky did her best to hold his determined look, but in the end it was too much for her. She was overtired, overwrought and overcome with emotions she couldn't control any longer.

'I—I'm scared.' She waved a hand in the general direction of her bedroom. 'He was in there. I can still see him when I shut my eyes.'

Jack swore under his breath as he got off the sofa. He came across to where she was standing, putting his hands on the top of her slim shoulders, his eyes holding hers.

'I know I'm going to regret this, but do you want me to sleep in your bed with you just for tonight?' he asked.

'You'd *do* that?' she asked, her eyes wide with amazement. 'You mean you wouldn't mind?'

He gave her what he hoped was a carefree smile. 'It'll be a piece of cake,' he said. 'Which side do you want, right or left?'

She smiled up at him. 'Let's toss for it.'

CHAPTER THREE

JACK hadn't expected to get to sleep at all, so when he woke at sunrise to find Becky lying on her side, looking at him, it took him a moment or two to gather himself. Her shoulder-length blonde hair was all tousled, her full mouth soft and her pink satin pyjamas clinging to the curves of her body in all the right places.

'Did I snore?' he asked, trying not to stare at the tempting shadow between her breasts.

A small smile tugged at her mouth. 'No, but you do talk in your sleep.'

He stiffened. 'What did I say?'

She gave him a wouldn't-you-like-to-know wink and got out of bed. 'What would you like for breakfast?'

Jack swung his legs over his side of the bed and grimaced at the rumpled state of his trousers. 'I haven't got time for breakfast but can I borrow your iron?'

He left soon after his clothes were pressed, extracting a promise from her to get the locks changed before she came in to the hospital.

Becky watched him drive away and once his car had turned the corner she picked up the phone book and began to flip through the pages, looking for a twenty-four-hour locksmith.

Jack finished his round with the residents and entered the operating theatre where Gwen Taylor was setting up with two other nurses.

'Has Becky arrived yet?' he asked.

Gwen's eyebrows rose just a fraction at his use of Becky's preferred name.

'Becky is it now?' she mused. 'Wow, what brought that on?'

He gave her a quelling look. 'Can we bring in the first case now, Gwen? Time is getting on.'

'David Barker, the new orderly, has gone down to get her. Don't be so impatient, he's still learning the ropes,' Gwen said. With a twinkle in her eyes she added, 'You just do the surgery and I'll run the theatre.'

'Fine,' he said, 'but let's have none of that tea and scones routine this morning. I want these three cases done before lunch. Lately my lists seem to be turning into a list of meals interspersed with the occasional operation.'

'How very amusing you are this morning.' Gwen gave him a droll look. 'Here's the patient. Why don't you go and scrub while we get things organized?'

Jack rolled his eyes and shouldered open the scrub-room door. Gwen Taylor was a good scrub nurse but she had a tendency to try and matchmake, which irritated him intensely. If word got out that he'd spent the night at Becky's place, he'd never hear the end of it.

Becky watched as David, the orderly, and Susie, the anaesthetic nurse on duty, slid the patient from her bed to the operating table.

'Just feel the edge of the table, Mrs Oakland,' Susie said. 'It's pretty narrow. We don't want you to fall off so make sure you're settled in the middle.'

'It is narrow,' Mrs Oakland said as she settled herself. 'How's that?'

'Fine, that's perfect,' Susie said. 'I'm just going to cover you with a warm blanket while Dr Baxter puts in your IV line.'

Becky put a tourniquet on Mrs Oakland's arm, inserted an IV cannula and started the drip while Susie held an oxygen mask over the patient's nose and mouth, encouraging her to take big breaths.

'The mask smells a bit rubbery, Mrs Oakland,' Becky said, 'but this is just oxygen to make you nice and ready.' She began to inject propofol into the IV line. 'You'll start to feel a bit sleepy now; you'll just drift off to sleep.'

Betty Oakland murmured something about feeling light-headed but her words soon began to slur and she drifted off into unconsciousness.

'Size 6 reinforced tube, please, Susie, with the introducer in. Thanks. She has a very small larynx,' Becky said.

She put the laryngoscope into the patient's mouth and elevated the tongue, taking care not to chip the teeth as she inserted the endotracheal tube. She connected the patient to the anaesthetic machine and started the volatile agents just as Jack walked in from the scrub sink. He dried his hands on a sterile towel before donning his gown and double gloves.

'Right to prep, Dr Baxter?' he asked.

Becky caught the tail end of Gwen's speculative look.

'She's asleep, *Mr* Colcannon,' she said with a hard little glance his way. If he was going to go all formal on her then she would do the same to him.

'Can you give a gram of cephalosporin and 5000 units heparin?'

'Already done,' Becky said.

Jack prepped and draped the abdomen with the registrar's help, applying a steridrape and setting up the diathermy, positioning the scratch pad and sucker.

'What do you think the splenic mass is, Mr Colcannon?' Robert asked.

'My guess is lymphoma. The spleen is so large that it's causing pain and thrombocytopenia. That reminds me, Dr Baxter, we've got platelets available if we run into bleeding. I'll give you warning if we need to access them.'

'Right, I've checked myself and they've already been brought round to the blood fridge in case,' Becky said.

'Prepared for just about anything, aren't you, Dr Baxter?' His eyes met hers for a moment.

'I always try to be prepared,' she answered. 'I don't like nasty surprises.'

He held her challenging look for a single heartbeat before holding out his gloved hand towards Gwen. 'Scalpel.'

He made a long upper midline incision and completed the abdominal opening with diathermy.

'That's one hell of a spleen,' Robert observed.

'Yes, and adherent to the diaphragm, too,' Jack said. 'I'm going to have to take the vessels first. At least this is a controlled splenectomy, not like that last ruptured spleen that bled out a couple of litres.'

'What a night that was,' Robert recalled with a visible shudder.

'That's the splenic artery clamped now,' Jack said. 'The spleen should shrink a bit through the splenic vein. Let's start to mobilise it while that happens, then I'll take the vein.'

'She's oozy, Mr Colcannon,' Robert said. 'What about the platelets?'

'Yes, I agree. Can you give the five packs of platelets, Dr Baxter?'

Becky turned to Susie. 'Get the platelets now, please. We'll run them through a side line with the normal saline.'

Susie returned with the bags of platelets which she and Becky checked, then started to administer one by one, each over about ten minutes.

'The spleen is freeing up everywhere but the diaphragm, Robert,' Jack said. 'I'll take the splenic vein now then sharp dissect it off the diaphragm.' He clamped and divided and ligated the splenic vein, freeing the spleen from its vascular pedicle.

'She's getting a few ventricular ectopic beats, Jack, I'm not sure why,' Becky informed him, momentarily forgetting her determination to address him formally.

'I've just got to get the spleen off the diaphragm and then we're through,' he said. Taking long dissecting scissors, he started to free the spleen from the diaphragm. 'There's no plane between spleen and diaphragm, Robert.'

'I think there's a hole in the diaphragm,' Robert said.

'Yes, it's plastered to the spleen. Dr Baxter, I'm going to

have to create a diaphragmatic defect to get this spleen out. I'll repair in the end. How's the patient?'

'VEBs all over,' Becky said. 'PO2's OK, we can oxygenate her fine. I'm not worried about the diaphragm, but this dysrhythmia's worrying. Susie, set up a Xylocaine infusion and I'm taking bloods for electrolytes and cardiac isoenzymes. Maybe she's had a silent infarct, although the ECG trace looks OK.'

'Diaphragm's repaired,' Jack said after a few more minutes. 'We're putting in a suction drain to the splenic bed and we're out of here.'

'The sooner the better,' Becky said, watching the monitor closely. 'I want this patient in the cardiac unit and a cardiologist on board. Susie, can you get me Dr Lockney on the phone in Cardiology and tee up a bed with the coronary care unit?'

'Sure,' Susie said, picking up the phone.

Jack lifted out the massive spleen, inserted the drain and closed the abdomen. He stepped away from the table once he'd finished, while Robert and Gwen dressed the wound and attached the drain to the suction bottle.

Jack stripped off his gown and protective head gear as he left Theatre to write up his notes on the operation.

'What's next on the list?' Robert asked as he took off his gloves. 'Have we got time for a quick cup of coffee?'

Gwen shook her head. 'Jack is in one of his let's-work-right-through-no-breaks moods.' She flicked her gaze to Becky, who was reversing the anaesthetic on Mrs Oakland. 'What's with all this Dr Baxter stuff, Becky? I thought him calling you Rebecca was bad enough. Don't tell me you ran into his car again.'

'You know what Jack is like,' Becky said, trying her best not to colour up. 'He likes to keep his distance.'

'He must have a new lady in his life,' Susie said. 'One of the nurses on Surgical A told me she was trying to track him down about a patient's pain relief during the night and he didn't answer his land line or his mobile.'

'That's probably why he wants to speed things up around here,' Gwen said with a mischievous little smile. 'He's in a hurry to get home to offload some of those hormones of his.'

Becky was relieved she had to accompany the patient out to Recovery. She'd had one too many of Gwen's speculative looks cast her way and didn't want to encourage any more.

The rest of the morning's list passed without incident and although Jack maintained his cool formal distance, she'd caught him looking at her once or twice, a small frown settling between his dark brows. She imagined he was regretting his offer to stay over the previous night, silently dreading it leaking out into the hospital gossip network.

It wasn't as if she was under any illusions as to her supermodel potential, and she was the first to admit she didn't even come close to his ex's designer elegance, but did he have to make it so obvious he wasn't interested?

Although she knew it was petty of her, she couldn't help feeling a little disappointed he hadn't even tried to make a move on her while they'd shared her bed. Most men would have had a quick grope at the very least, but not Jack. He had kept his trousers on and his hands to himself all night.

She peered at herself in the female change-room mirror and grimaced. She had surgical-cap hair and not a scrap of makeup on, not even lip gloss.

She ran her hands over her hips and sighed. She hadn't been to the gym in months and it was starting to show, and with Christmas just around the corner she knew it could only get worse.

'Right, my girl.' She addressed her reflection with determination. 'You are going on a diet and exercise programme, effective immediately.'

Her car was hot from being parked in the sun all day but Becky refused to be daunted. She drove to her flat and, after cautiously checking each room, quickly changed into running gear, scooped up the new keys she'd had cut that morning and jogged outside into the golden light of the evening.

She was ashamed of how breathless she was after simply running to the corner of her street. Ben had been telling her for years how important it was to get and stay fit but she'd never made the time to do it properly. He'd even suggested self-defence classes but she'd laughed at him, telling him the only wrestling she wanted to do with a man was the type that led to marriage and kids.

She knew it was probably terribly old-fashioned of her but all she had really ever wanted was to settle down and bring up a family, the way her parents had done for her and Ben. In her hurry to achieve her dream, she had blundered into three disastrous relationships, each one ending sourly. It still made her cringe to think of how she'd acted so impulsively, hurting three quite decent men in the process.

It wasn't that she didn't love her career—she did, and had even chosen it for its practicality—but she still secretly longed for that once-in-a-lifetime connection with one special person. What was life about if not companionship and intimacy? She didn't want to spend the rest of her life putting people to sleep during the day and coming home to sleep alone at night. Last night had shown her that, if nothing else. Waking up next to Jack had been so special, even though he hadn't touched her.

She'd watched him for ages before he'd woken up, studying his features, wishing she'd had the courage to reach out and trace her fingers over the dark shadows under his eyes which always seemed to be there...

She stopped running and took several deep breaths as her thoughts caught up. What was she thinking? That Jack was that special person she'd been waiting for all her life?

No!

Not Jack Colcannon.

She choked back a laugh. She couldn't possibly fall in love with her brother's best friend. Ben would be appalled. Her parents would be...

No.

Jack wasn't marriage material. He was more the date-them-and-drop-them type. She couldn't imagine him allowing himself to feel anything but disdain for her. He couldn't even bring himself to call her by her preferred name.

Besides, he was practically an honorary brother. He'd seen her with braces and break-outs on her skin, for heaven's sake!

Except there was that one time twelve years ago, when he hadn't acted quite like a brother…

'I haven't got time to take you for a driving lesson,' Ben had said. 'Ask Jack. He won't mind.'

Becky had pouted at her brother. 'Jack is a guest, I can't ask him.'

'Jack is practically a member of our family. He's been here for the last four weekends in a row. Surely you don't have to be shy around him now.'

'I'm not shy!'

Ben had given an amused chuckle as he'd spread out the weekend paper. 'No, that you're not. Go on, get out of here, brat, and ask him to teach you to reverse park. I'm resigning.'

She'd swung away in resentment. How like her brother to remind her of her failure to grasp the basic skills of reverse parking. So, she'd run into a few cars. So what? How else was she going to learn how to do it?

'Jack?' She found him under the shade of one of the elm trees in the garden, reading a medical journal. 'Can I ask you something?'

Jack put the journal down and lifted his head, his green eyes meeting hers. 'Sure, Rebecca. What's on your mind?'

She shifted from foot to foot like the awkward schoolgirl she was. Something about Jack always made her feel a bit self-conscious. She knew his father was a cosmetic surgeon and she couldn't help wondering if Jack thought she could do with some work herself. A little liposuction wouldn't go astray, and as for her breasts, which had been a bit slow on the uptake…

'I was wondering if you'd take me for a driving lesson,' she said. 'Ben has given up on me and my test is next month and—'

He got to his feet, his tall lean body casting a shadow over her five-foot-five frame.

'I guess I've got nothing better to do,' he said.

'Thanks,' she said, and added under her breath, 'I think.'

'Which car?'

'Can we take yours?' she asked, suddenly beaming up at him. 'I think I need to practise on a manual. Mum's is automatic and it's just not the same.'

She followed him out to where his car was parked and, after positioning her learner plates on the rear and front of the car, slipped behind the wheel.

'Wow,' she said, running her hands over the shiny dashboard. 'This is so cool. A real sports car!'

'Where do you want to drive to?' Jack asked.

She swivelled in her seat to face him. 'I would *love* to drive past Amelia Brockhurst's place out on the Ridgeway road. She'll be green with envy when she sees me driving this.'

A few bunny-hopping minutes later Becky felt as if she'd more or less got the hang of the gears and drove with increasing confidence out towards the Ridgeway road.

'Driving in a straight line is no real test of your ability,' Jack said. 'You need to practise some of the manoeuvres the examiner will be looking out for, like parking and hill starts.'

'OK,' she said, 'I'll do a hill start on the next hill we come to.'

Within a few minutes they came to an intersection with a stop sign and a steep incline.

'Will this do?' she asked, swinging a glance his way.

'Show me your stuff,' he said, bracing himself.

The car coughed and jerked as she let out the clutch, but somehow she managed to get over the hill without stalling, although there was a slight smell of burning clutch-plate lingering in the air.

'Hey! Am I good or what?' she crowed delightedly. 'Wait till I tell Ben. He thinks I'm hopeless at hill starts.'

'Let's do a reverse park,' Jack suggested. 'Drive on a bit until we come to somewhere suitable.'

'Somewhere suitable' turned out to be an old quarry where some forty-four-gallon drums had been left abandoned. Jack got out of the car to position them the approximate distance so she could practise.

'Turn the wheel now,' he directed, but she hit the drum regardless.

'I can't do it!'

'Yes, you can,' he said, getting back into the passenger seat, making an obvious effort not to notice the scratch on his paintwork. 'Now, try once more. Put your indicator on and swing the wheel to the right.'

She did as he instructed and managed to position the car without touching the drum.

'Did I pass?' She looked at him hopefully.

'Not until you do it on the other side,' he said.

'*The other side?*' She gaped at him. 'But I can't do it on the other side!'

'You have to be able to do it on both sides,' he said. 'What about one-way streets? You have to prove you can do it no matter what direction the traffic flows.'

She bit her lip in concentration and started to reverse, but the drum connected with the bumper bar and toppled over.

'Oops!'

'Try it again,' Jack said.

She tried it again but this time she almost flattened the drum. She bent her head to the steering-wheel and groaned in despair. 'I'm going to fail. I just know I am.'

'No, you're not,' Jack said, touching her on the shoulder to bring her gaze back to his. 'You can do this. I know you can.'

Becky could feel the warmth of his long fingers through the thin cotton of her top. Her eyes flicked to his mouth, her tongue snaking out to moisten her lips.

'Do you really think I can do it?' she whispered into the air that separated them.

'Yes. Now, try it again,' he said, letting his hand fall away.

'Run alongside the drum as if it is a parked car and now swing your wheels to—'

Crunch.

'You're not concentrating, Rebecca,' Jack said, gritting his teeth.

'I *am* concentrating!' she flashed back in frustration.

'No, you're not,' he said. 'You're going at it like a bull at a gate. Take your time and—'

Becky flung open the driver's door and slammed it behind her, stomping off in a temper fuelled by repeated failure and embarrassment.

'Rebecca.' He got out of the car to stride after her.

'Don't call me that!' She swung back to face him. 'No one but you ever calls me that.'

He set his jaw and eyeballed her determinedly, his hands tightly clenched at his sides.

'Get back in the car and try it again.'

'No.' She folded her arms across her chest, glaring back at him with spirited defiance. 'You can't make me.'

Two beats of silence passed.

'You think not?' he said, reaching for her, and pulled her towards him ruthlessly.

She stared at the grim line of his mouth for a moment, her stomach hollowing out at the determined glitter in his gaze as it collided with hers.

'*Get in the damn car,*' he ordered, his fingers tightening on her upper arms.

She lifted her chin, her chocolate brown eyes issuing an irresistible challenge. 'Make me.'

Becky brought herself back to the present with a jolt. She didn't want to recall that bruising kiss that had led to the stiff unbroken silence as Jack had driven them back to her parents' property. She didn't want to remember how his mouth had felt against the softness of hers, how her body had pressed itself against the solid hardness of his as if looking for a lifetime anchor.

She ran all the way back to her flat, gasping for breath as

if all the hounds of hell and purgatory and the council dogs' home were after her, coming to an abrupt halt as she came to the door of her flat.

It was swinging open.

CHAPTER FOUR

BECKY sucked in a breath and stared at the open door for a few moments, weighing up her options. She could call the police but her mobile was on her bed where she'd flung it earlier in her hurry to get changed. The landline was within reach but she wasn't sure she wanted to enter her flat if there was an unknown assailant inside.

'Hello?' she called out in a somewhat forced light breezy tone, as if expecting a long-lost friend to greet her. 'I'm home!'

She pushed the door open a little further, her eyes widening in shock at the disarray of her flat. Books and papers were scattered and most of the furniture overturned, as if someone had been intent on searching through her possessions for something important.

She stepped over the mess and moved through to the bedroom. She bent to pick up one of her dresses off the floor, a lightning bolt of alarm rocketing through her as she looked at the slash that had rent it in two.

Her eyes went to the mirrored doors of the built-in wardrobe, her heart coming to a complete standstill when she saw what was scrawled across it in one of her blood-red lipsticks.

GET OUT OR DIE BITCH FACE

Becky allowed herself one small swallow, doing her best to keep her head, as icy fear crawled like a long-legged insect right up her spine to settle amongst the fine hairs on the back of her neck, lifting each one in turn.

She reached blindly for the phone and dialled the emergency code.

'Colcannon,' Jack answered his mobile as he ran the last block back to his house near Bondi Beach.

'Jack, it's me, Ben.'

Jack stopped running. 'Hey, mate, long time no hear. How are you go—?'

'Listen to me, Jack.' Ben cut him off, his voice low and urgent. 'I can't talk for long, this call might be traced. I'm in trouble.'

'What sort of trouble?' Jack frowned.

'I can't tell you all the details,' Ben said. 'I'm on a big undercover assignment. The biggest of my career. But someone is trying to flush me out.'

'Who?'

'Someone on the inside of the operation is acting as an informant.' He took a ragged breath and continued, 'I can't let this operation slip. It's at a crucial stage. It'll be the biggest criminal bust we've had in years. It's vital my identity isn't revealed.' He paused for a moment and added, 'I need your help.'

'Anything, Ben,' Jack said. 'What do you want me to do?'

'I need you to look after Becky. She's in danger. Big danger.'

Jack felt a chill pass through his body and for some reason he couldn't get his voice to work immediately.

'They know her brother is in the ring, but they don't know which one of us it is. There are a couple of us working undercover. They're trying to flush me out by targeting her. It'll blow the operation if I break my cover now. That's what they want.'

'They?' Jack finally managed to croak.

'It's a drug operation,' Ben said. 'They know someone has infiltrated them but they're not sure who it is. This is like a process of elimination. A few buttons are getting pressed to see who responds.'

Jack wondered if he should tell Ben about Becky's intruder the night before, but decided against it. His friend sounded stressed enough as it was, without him adding to it.

'You've got to keep an eye on Becky for me,' Ben said. 'I need to know she's safe at all times.'

'What about the police?' Jack suggested. 'If you're so worried, shouldn't she have some sort of official protection?'

'*No!*' Ben's tone was insistent. 'We can't involve the regular force. We have to handle this by ourselves. You're the only one I trust, Jack. I think someone on the force is feeding this informant. I'm not prepared to take any risks.'

'You're starting to really scare me, mate,' Jack confessed.

'I'm sorry to involve you, Jack.' Ben's tone was hollow with anguish. 'But you are the only person I know I can trust and who's in a position to protect Becky.'

'I'm not sure I'm the right person for the job,' Jack said after a small but telling silence. 'Becky and I don't always see eye to—'

'If they have to kill her to get to me, they won't think twice about it,' Ben interjected bluntly. 'My parents are overseas and hard to trace, but Becky is a sitting duck. You've got to get her out of that flat, Jack. I don't care how you do it, even if you have to pretend to be in love with her to get her to come and live with you. You can explain it all to her later, but for now the word out on the loop has hinted if she stays in that building another night she'll be in the morgue by morning.'

Jack felt his stomach give a sudden lurch and was surprised his voice came out at all, let alone calmly. 'Should I tell her she's in danger?'

'No…don't do that,' Ben said after a short pause. 'If she knows it's to do with me, she might do something to lead them to me, something stupid. Just stick like glue to her outside work hours. That's what a man in love does, right?'

'She'll never fall for it,' Jack warned him. 'How am I going to convince her to spend time with me when we've been at each other's throats for years?'

'I'm sure you'll think of something,' Ben said. 'You'll have to. I don't think anyone will try anything inside the hospital—they probably wouldn't get back out past Security if they did. But after hours…' He let his trailed-off sentence say the rest for him.

'I'll do what I can,' Jack promised.

'Thanks, mate,' Ben said. 'I knew I could call on you. Just don't let anything happen to her. She's my kid sister and I love her, brat that she is.'

'How can I contact you?'

'You can't,' Ben said. 'I'm taking a risk now in calling you.'

There was a small silence before Ben added, his voice rough with bitten-back emotion, 'Jack...if anything was to happen to me...you'll tell my folks I love them, won't you?'

'Yes, of course, Ben, of course I would.' Jack swallowed the restriction in his throat.

'If I don't come out of this, don't let Becky throw herself away on some creep,' Ben added. 'She has terrible taste in men. I don't want to see her get hurt.'

'I'll do my best but—'

Ben broke off the connection without saying goodbye, which Jack somehow knew had been deliberate.

He stared at the mobile in his hands for some time, wondering if he'd just imagined the conversation he'd had with his best mate. He knew Ben's work was dangerous—every cop lived with the threat of death hanging over them in the line of duty—but this time his friend sounded as if he was in well and truly over his head.

The phone began to ring in his hand and he almost dropped it in surprise, his fingers fumbling to answer it.

'Colcannon.'

'Jack. It's me, Becky.'

Jack's hand tightened on the phone. 'Becky, are you—?' He stopped in mid-sentence, recalling Ben's insistence she wasn't to be informed of the danger she was in. 'I mean, how are you?'

'I've been robbed,' she said. 'The police are here and—'

'*The police!*'

Becky frowned at his tone. 'Yes, they're still here taking photos and so on.'

'I'll be right over,' he said. 'Don't go anywhere until I get there.'

'But I'm on call at the hospital,' she said. 'I have to go in right now. I had a call a few minutes ago. I have to assess a patient in A and E.'

'Right…' Jack forced his brain into gear. Ben had said he thought she would be fairly safe at the hospital so maybe that was the best place for her right now. 'I'll meet you there in a few minutes.'

'But you're not on call tonight, Brendan Fairbrother is.'

'I'm covering for him from nine this evening,' he lied.

'That's funny, he didn't mention it to me and I was just talking to him.'

'It was arranged weeks ago,' he said, privately amazed at how easy lying was once you got used to it. 'I'll ring him and remind him. It's his anniversary, he's probably forgotten. See you soon.'

Becky didn't get a chance to respond as he cut off the call. She turned to the police officers who were just finishing up their crime scene investigation, wondering how in the world her life had suddenly become so frighteningly complicated.

'Dr Baxter,' Constable Daniels addressed her solemnly. 'It might be a good idea if you stayed off the premises for a few days until we catch this guy. This doesn't look like a prank. Until we know for sure, it might be best to stay somewhere else, preferably with someone with whom you feel safe.' He handed her a card with his name and contact numbers on it. 'Call me at any time if you think of anything else that might help us in our investigation.'

She nodded in agreement, tucking the card away as she picked up a few items of clothing that hadn't been slashed, wondering who amongst her friends she could ask to use a spare bedroom for a few days.

If only she could contact Ben! He was the one and only person who made her feel safe.

Well…maybe not the only person…

* * *

Not long after she'd done an anaesthetic preassessment on a nineteen-year-old girl with acute appendicitis, Becky received a call from A and E informing her that a motorbike accident victim was on his way. As part of the trauma team she was required in A and E to manage IV and airway for trauma cases.

She ran into Jack on her way through to the resus room, where the ambulance officers were transferring the patient on a spine board from the ambulance trolley to the resus bed.

She began her assessment as Jack got a rapid history from the ambulance officers.

'We picked him up half an hour ago, Mr Colcannon. He'd been on a high-powered motorbike and impacted with a steel pylon holding a guard rail, obviously at high speed.'

'What was his GCS at the scene?' Jack asked.

'Unresponsive to anything,' the ambulance officer informed him. 'Totally unconscious. We extracted his helmet and stabilised his neck with a hard collar, got in an IV line and bagged and masked him to here.'

'Good work, guys,' Jack said. 'We'll resuscitate him and then I'll catch up with you before you go for any other details.'

Becky looked up as Jack approached the patient.

'I've intubated him, Jack. He's deeply unconscious and has a difficult airway to maintain. He didn't need any drugs. I just put the endotracheal tube down.'

'Primary survey first,' Jack said. 'Airway is secured.' He listened with a stethoscope before percussing the patient's chest. 'Resonant on both sides and good air entry. No visible chest injury. Pulse and BP?'

'Pulse 120, BP 80 systolic,' the nurse on duty informed him.

'Get in IV lines, Dr Baxter, and start colloid and O-negative blood fast, and get some blood off for cross-match, haemoglobin, electrolytes and amylase.' He examined the patient's abdomen by inspection first, then palpation and percussion, and after that listened with his stethoscope.

'Abrasions and bruising extensively over the left flank and a large haematoma. His abdo's distended and tense, dull to percussion and no bowel sounds. He's clearly got major intra-abdominal bleeding.' He turned to the nurse. 'Can you put in a urinary catheter and nasogastric tube? Dr Baxter, how are those drips going?'

'Both in and running full bore,' Becky said. 'He's getting hard to ventilate, his abdomen looks distended and is compressing his diaphragm.'

'Shall I get CT organised so we can see where his bleeding's coming from?' Robert asked.

'There's no way this guy's going to CT. He's in hypovolaemic shock, class 3 at least, we're barely keeping up, and his ventilation's going off because of intra-abdominal tension. He doesn't need a CT, he needs surgery, and now. Get the emergency theatre on line right away. Dr Baxter, are you right to get him to Theatre now?'

'The sooner the better, Jack,' Becky said. 'We need that abdomen opened and decompressed so I can ventilate him.'

'Good, get the orderlies in now, and you go up with him in the lift. Keep that O-negative blood going in fast while I get up to Theatre and scrub.'

The orderlies wheeled the trolley into the emergency lift from A and E straight up to the theatre complex, with Becky and Robert continuing resuscitation on the way.

Jack was already scrubbed with the theatre team by the time the patient was wheeled through the emergency theatre door. The patient was slid onto the operating table and Jack prepped and draped the abdomen rapidly.

'Don't worry about a steridrape, Sandra,' he said to the emergency scrub nurse. 'And I want two sump suckers on board and diathermy up to 50 coag. Robert, get scrubbed and in here and call the intern—we need an extra pair of hands.'

As Robert gowned and gloved, Jack made a long midline abdominal incision. A huge fountain of dark blood gushed from the wound over the side of the abdomen and onto the floor.

'Suck, Robert, with both suckers. Packs, Sandra.'

Jack scooped out three litres of blood and clot from the abdomen and identified the source of bleeding.

'Give me a long artery forceps. Pull hard on that retractor, Robert, I've got to see the splenic pedicle.' He applied a nine-inch artery forceps to the splenic artery and vein, then individually clamped the artery and vein and lifted out the spleen.

'Heavy catgut, Sandra,' he instructed. 'Full length, don't cut it, I've got to tie down deep.' He tied off the splenic artery and then tied off and oversewed the splenic vein.

'Looks like we haven't damaged the pancreatic tail in those ties, and stomach looks OK. One of the short gastrics is still bleeding.' Jack tied off the remaining bleeders and then carried out a thorough laparotomy to exclude any other intra-abdominal injury. Confident there was none and after sucking out any residual blood he closed the abdomen.

'That was amazing, Mr Colcannon,' Sandra said. 'I have never seen so much blood before.' She looked down at the floor and added, 'Or so well controlled.'

Jack grunted something in response and turned away to strip off his gown and gloves, catching Becky's look on the way past.

'She's right, Jack,' Becky said. 'We were sailing pretty close to the wind but you pulled it off.'

He gave a little shrug as he shouldered open the door. 'I'm sure Brendan would have handled it just as well.'

The door swung shut behind him and Becky looked down at the still unconscious patient. Brendan Fairbrother was a competent enough surgeon, but he wasn't as skilled at handling trauma as Jack was. In fact, there were few surgeons at St Patrick's who could match him for a cool head under pressure.

'He's one hell of a surgeon, isn't he?' Sandra said as she stripped off her gloves, sidestepping the massive pool of blood on the floor.

'He certainly is,' Robert agreed. 'But I thought Brendan Fairbrother was on call this evening. Did they do a last-minute swap?'

'It's Brendan's anniversary,' Becky said as she and the anaesthetic nurse began to transfer the patient to recovery.

'Anniversary?' Robert looked at Sandra. 'I didn't even know Mr Fairbrother was married.'

Sandra waited until Becky had left Theatre before responding, 'He's not married and as far as I know he hasn't got any anniversaries to celebrate.'

'So what gives?'

Sandra gave him a speculative little smile. 'I think our Mr Colcannon is developing rather a soft spot for Becky Baxter.'

'No way!' Robert said disbelievingly. 'He hardly even looks her in the eye.'

'You need to be a little more astute, my boy,' Sandra said, poking a playful finger at his chest. 'That man is on a mission, you mark my words.'

'What sort of mission?'

'He wants to be with her as often as he can,' she said. 'Why else would he offer to be on call two nights in a row?'

Robert rolled his lips for a moment. 'Maybe you're right. Who wants to be on call two nights in a row?'

Sandra gave him a knowing wink. 'Who indeed?'

Becky did her best to settle the young appendicectomy patient who was nervous about having her very first general anaesthetic.

'You won't remember a thing,' she assured her. 'As soon as I inject the drug into your IV line you'll start to feel sleepy. Next thing you'll be in Recovery and feeling a bit sore but it will all be over.'

'Will it hurt?'

'You'll be a bit uncomfortable for a few days after surgery but nothing a couple of painkillers can't handle. You'll be back out partying before you know it.'

'I'm missing three parties as it is,' Emma Stockport said, wincing as Becky found a vein.

'You and me, too,' Becky said with a smile. 'The lead-up to Christmas is a bit full on, isn't it?'

'Tell me about it,' Emma said, looking at the cannula Becky had inserted into the back of her hand. 'Eeuuw, that looks totally gross.'

'Start counting, Emma,' Becky said, feeding the propofol into her line.

'One…two….thr…'

Jack came in scrubbed and took a sterile towel off the trolley to dry his hands before putting on his gown and gloves.

'This will be a cinch after the last case,' he said, addressing Robert who had gowned alongside him. 'Want me to talk you through it?'

'Thanks, yes, that would be good. My logbook's looking pretty bare at the moment. None of the other consultants seem to have time to take me through cases.'

'Well, now's the time. Robert, start prepping and drape the patient.'

Robert prepped the abdomen with Betadine and draped the right iliac fossa with green drapes.

'Make your incision in the skin crease two thirds the way out along a line from the umbilicus to the anterior superior iliac spine. About 5 centimetres long,' Jack coached as Sandra handed Robert the scalpel in a yellow kidney dish.

Jack talked Robert gently through each step of the procedure, correcting Robert's technical uncertainties and guiding him to complete an uncomplicated appendicectomy.

'Good work. Close the skin with a subcuticular vicryl. Make sure she gets a stat dose of cephalosporin as wound infection prophylaxis. You can write up the op notes, and put yourself down as the primary surgeon and me as the assistant.'

'Thanks, Mr Colcannon, that was great,' Robert said with a grateful smile.

Becky was just coming out of the change room when Jack stepped forward from where he'd been leaning against the wall of the corridor, seemingly waiting for her to appear.

'I'm just on my way home,' he said. 'I was wondering if you wanted to grab a bite to eat somewhere.'

Becky stared at him blankly for a few seconds without responding. Jack ran a hand through the dark silk of his hair and shifted his gaze a fraction to the left of hers.

'I've been thinking about your flat,' he said. 'You probably don't want to stay there right now.' He glanced up and down the corridor before adding, 'I have a spare bedroom you could use for as long as you need to.'

Becky wasn't sure why he was issuing the invitation. His body language was giving off totally confusing signals. He looked distinctly uncomfortable, as if he was only offering out of a sense of duty.

'I wouldn't want to inconvenience you in any way,' she said crisply, making her way past him to the front exit.

'Hey.' He caught one of her arms on the way past and turned her around to face him. 'It's not an inconvenience. Really.'

She locked eyes with his. 'What's all this about, Jack?'

He let her arm go, his expression instantly guarded. 'What's all what about?'

She gave him one of her you-can't-fool-me looks. 'Come on, Jack, back in Theatre it was ''Dr Baxter'' this and ''Dr Baxter'' that, now you're offering me room and board. What's going on?'

His eyes fell away from hers. 'You've had back-to-back scares with an intruder and a robbery. I thought you might like some company for a few days until things settle down a bit.'

'Maybe you should define exactly what you mean by ''company'',' she said. 'You can barely be polite to me at work—how much worse would it be at your house?'

'Look, I know I haven't been all that friendly towards you, but I have my reasons.'

She rolled her eyes and swung away to the exit. 'Please, spare me your stupid reasons. Do you think I give a termite's toenail if you can't even get my name past the hard line of your lips?' She pressed the night button to release the front door and glared back at him over her shoulder. 'I'll book into a hotel until I get my place sorted out. Thanks for the offer but, no, thanks. I can look after myself.'

She was quite proud of her exit line, it suggested confidence and an assurance that she was still in control of her life no matter what red herrings were dished up to her. It was only when she got to her car at the far end of the hospital car park that she realised her confidence was really all a sham. She stared down at the shredded tyres on her car, and the cold long-legged insect of fear returned to tiptoe its way back up her spine.

Jack came to stand beside her, looking down at the viciously slashed rubber, his expression grim.

'Jack?' she whispered, blindly reaching for his hand, curling her small fingers around its solid warmth.

He squeezed her hand.

Just once. Briefly.

But it was enough.

'Let's go home to my place,' he said, and led her towards his car.

CHAPTER FIVE

BECKY sat in the passenger seat of Jack's car in silence. Fear had leaked into every layer of her skin until she felt as if she could even smell it. Her palms were sticky, her heart tripping erratically, her bent knees in front of her finding it hard to keep from knocking against each other.

'I wish I could talk to Ben.' She tied and untied her hands in her lap in agitation. 'He'd know what to do.'

'He'd want you to do what you're doing right now,' Jack assured her. 'To stay with me until the dust settles. I'll have your car delivered to the mechanic tomorrow. In the meantime, you can travel to work with me.'

'Who is doing this?' She swivelled in her seat to look at him. 'Who can possibly be doing this, and why?'

He stared straight ahead at the traffic lights while he waited for them to change to green. 'I wouldn't take any of this too personally. People get robbed all the time.'

'Are you for real?' Becky stared at him incredulously. 'I wasn't just robbed! I had a man in my bedroom, shining a torch in my face, for God's sake! Now my tyres have been slashed...' She stopped and gave one quick convulsive swallow. 'The three flat tyres.' Her eyes were wide with increasing fear.

'People get flat tyres all the time,' he said.

'That wasn't what you were saying the other day,' she pointed out, resentment creeping into her tone. 'You thought I was making it up.'

'All right, so I was wrong.' He sent her a quick unreadable glance. 'Anyway, you're nearly always late for work. You know how it gets on my nerves when I can't start my lists on time.'

53

'Well, bully for you, Mr Punctual,' she bit back. 'But, unlike you, other people have a life that occasionally gets in the way of being at work a whole hour before they need to.'

'I do not get to work an hour before I need to.'

'Yes, you do. You're always there early, champing at the bit, biting everyone's head off.'

'You make me sound like a complete tyrant,' he said. 'I just want to get the job done. I hate wasting time, and sometimes the under-funded public system can be frustrating.'

'Then why stay? Why not move over to the private sector and make a mint instead of the house-staff wage you're currently on?'

'I have my reasons.'

'Oh, yes.' Her tone was deliberately scathing. 'Those little reasons of yours.'

'Look, Rebecca…' his fingers tightened around the steering-wheel '…I have more than enough money. Besides, someone has to do something about the waiting lists. If every specialist bails out of the public hospital, the uninsured public they cut their teeth on in training will be left abandoned. Someone has to stick in there and solve the problems, not walk away.'

'If you call me Rebecca or Dr Baxter once more, I'll scream.'

'Oh, for God's sake,' he muttered as he turned into his street.

'I mean it, Jack.' She faced him determinedly. 'Do it one more time and your ears will suffer. Don't say I didn't warn you.'

He stabbed the remote control and drove into his garage, his jaw tight with frustration. *So help me, God, I'll kill you myself, Ben, for getting me into this,* he thought as he wrenched on the handbrake.

Becky followed him into his house, looking around with undisguised interest. It wasn't quite the 'Home of the Year' showcase mansion his father and current stepmother resided in, neither was it the comfortable, rambling family homestead where she and her brother had spent their childhood, but for all that it was spacious, if a little formally decorated for her taste.

'There are three spare rooms,' he informed her. 'You choose which one you'd prefer.'

Becky decided right then and there to choose the one closest his room just to annoy him.

'Why don't you give me a little tour?' she suggested.

He gave a grudging nod and showed her through the house, hurrying through it as if he couldn't wait to get away from her. Becky deliberately asked questions to prolong his agony.

'What's this cupboard for?'

'It's the linen cupboard,' he said, gritting his teeth. 'See?'

She peered inside and gave an inward smile at the neat piles of folded sheets and colour-coordinated towels. So, Mr Punctual was super-tidy as well.

'And which is your room?'

'That one there.'

'Where?'

'There.' He pointed vaguely to a room down the hall.

'Show me.'

'Whatever for?'

She folded her arms across her chest and tilted her head at him. 'Because I want to know the *real* you. I read this book once which said the way to truly know a person's personality is to meet their family of origin, go for a drive with them in their car and take a peek inside their bedroom.'

'I can't believe this,' he muttered. Striding down the hall, he opened the door for her. 'There. Analyse this.'

Becky inspected the neatly made bed, the spotless wall of mirrors on the inbuilt wardrobes, the neatly placed book by the bedside with a bookmark inside it instead of a dog-ear. Not a thing out of place and everything in its place.

'I knew it! You have obsessive-compulsive disorder,' she said, turning back to look up at him. 'I bet you wash your hands a hundred times a day, too.'

His green eyes went heavenwards in search of renewed patience. 'Of course I wash my hands a lot. I'm a surgeon, for heaven's sake.'

'You have issues of control.'

'Oh, for—'

'And you don't like disruption to your routine,' she said. 'It really gets under your skin. That's why this is really hard for you having me here, isn't it?'

You don't know the half of it, he thought with an inward grimace.

'I don't mind you being here,' he lied.

'What will we tell everyone at work?'

'Nothing,' he said. 'No one needs to know.'

'I'll have to let the hospital switchboard know,' she said. 'Otherwise how will they contact me when I'm on call?'

The line of his mouth tightened even further. 'Tell them you'll be only contactable on your mobile until further notice.'

'You see?' She gave him a triumphant look. 'You *are* uncomfortable with me being here. You don't want anyone to know about it. If you were at ease with it, you wouldn't give a damn who knew.'

'Listen, if my mother finds out you're staying here she'll have invitations in the mail by morning,' he said dryly.

'Invitations?' She looked up at him in confusion. 'Invitations for what?'

He gave her a grim look. 'Our wedding.'

'Oh.'

'"Oh" is right.' He rubbed his unshaven jaw. 'Come to think of it, if your parents hear about this…'

'They won't hear it from me,' she said.

'What if they ring you at your flat? Won't they worry when you don't answer?'

'They usually call or text me on my mobile, or send me emails, which I can access here or at work. Anyway, I can access my landline phone messages from off site.'

He gave a sudden frown. 'What about your clothes?' He glanced at his watch. 'I know it's late but perhaps we should go to your flat and get them.'

It was Becky's turn for displaying the grim look. 'The only clothes I have that are decent are the ones I'm wearing now. The rest have been hacked to pieces.'

'Oh.'

'I need to do some urgent shopping, but in the meantime do you have a T-shirt I could borrow to sleep in?'

He went to his wardrobe and pulled back one of the mirrored doors.

Becky peered around his shoulder, making *tsk tsk tsk* sounds in her throat.

'What?' He swung around to look at her.

She shook her head at him in mock despair. 'You are really anal.'

'Here.' He thrust an ironed and neatly folded T-shirt at her chest. 'And will you quit it with the character analysis? You're really starting to annoy me.'

She gave him a teasing smile. 'You are *so* uptight, Jack. You need to chill out a bit. You're acting like someone who was potty trained with a stun gun.'

'You know something, Rebecca, you are one of the most irritat—'

'Aaarrgghh!' Becky screamed at the top of her lungs, even going as far as plugging her own ears to escape the shrill, teeth-jarring sound.

'*Shut the hell up!*' Jack grasped her by the upper arms and gave her a little shake. 'Shut up! The neighbours will hear you!'

'I told you not to call me that. I warned you.' She took a big breath and squeezed her eyes shut. 'Aaarrgghh!'

'Damn it! If you don't shut up I'll do something we'll both end up regretting.'

Becky drew in another quick breath and opened her mouth for another good bellow, but before she could get the sound out Jack's mouth came down on hers and blocked off all sound except for the one tiny whimper that escaped from her lips before she could stop it. His mouth was hard and insistent, determined and ruthless in its mission to stop her from screaming.

As silencing methods went, it certainly worked, since she was so shocked she didn't even put up a fight. She felt herself weaken in his tight hold as his mouth changed its pressure, her stomach giving an unexpected somersault as his tongue flicked against hers, the heat and probe of it demanding a response from her she was in no way able to hold back. His tongue mated with hers, curling around hers intimately, the dart and retreat action stirring deep longings in her that she could feel reverberating in his hard body where it was pressed so insistently against hers.

Searing heat coursed through her from hips to breasts. She was aflame with a need she hadn't known she'd felt until his mouth had connected with hers. Her whole body was on fire, flames licking along her flesh until she thought she was going to explode with the sheer force of it.

His hands left her arms to grasp her head, angling it for better access, his long fingers buried in her hair, his lower body grinding into hers.

She felt every hard ridge as if they were standing together naked, the heat of his growing erection burning a pathway to her soul, melting her from the inside out. She could feel her body preparing itself, the liquid silk of desire swamping her, the delicate but intoxicating scent of mutual arousal rising upwards to tantalise and tempt.

She felt the sweep and plunge of his tongue, felt too the rasp of his unshaven jaw as he plundered her mouth even further, the scrape of masculine flesh on hers a delicious reminder of all that set them apart as man and woman.

Jack dragged his mouth off hers and stared down at her, his green eyes glazed with a combination of unrelieved desire and blistering anger.

Becky was the first to find her voice. 'You really shouldn't have done that,' she said.

A tiny nerve pulsed at the side of his mouth as he held her reproving look. 'You asked for it.'

Her brown eyes defied him. 'You called me Rebecca.'

He stepped away from her as if she'd burnt him.

'I must say, you've improved on your technique,' she added when he didn't respond. She ran a finger tip experimentally over her swollen lips. 'Only marginally, of course, but probably worth noting.'

He swung back to glare at her. 'You are the most annoying woman I've ever met, do you know that?'

She lifted her chin. 'Why? Because I won't let you walk all over me? That's your beef, isn't it, Jack? You can't control me. You can't put me in one of your neat little boxes like your stupid towels or T-shirts.'

'I don't know what you're talking about.'

'Yes, you do,' she insisted, coming up close to invade his personal space, pressing a finger to his chest. 'You hate the fact that I see through your keep-away-from-me mask. You've been doing it for years. You don't want anyone to get too close in case you start to feel something for them you just won't allow yourself to feel.'

'I don't feel anything for you.'

She gave him a narrow-eyed look. 'Then why did you just kiss me?'

'I wanted to shut you up.'

'You could have gagged me.'

His green eyes went to slits as he looked down at her. 'I could have strangled you too, but unfortunately there's a law against it.'

'Do you want to know what I think?' she asked.

'No. I do not want to know what you think. But no doubt you're going to tell me anyway.' His tone positively dripped with sarcasm.

Her mouth tilted in a knowing little smile. 'I think you wanted to kiss me.'

He didn't answer, but she could see that tiny, almost imperceptible pulse still leaping at the side of his set mouth, which indicated he wasn't as in control of his emotions as he would have liked.

For some reason Becky felt a tickle of excitement run over her for cracking his normally iron-clad control. She enjoyed teasing him, pushing him to the edge. She'd been doing it for years, although she wasn't entirely sure why.

'You wanted to kiss me, Jack, just like you did twelve years ago.'

'You were a spoilt brat twelve years ago,' he bit out. 'I shouldn't have kissed you then either, but it was either that or shake you till your teeth fell out.'

'Well, since you dislike me so much, I think it might be best if I call a taxi and go to the nearest hotel,' she said, picking her handbag up from the floor and taking out her mobile phone.

'*No!*' He snatched the phone out of her hand and held it out of reach.

Becky's eyebrows rose in twin arches. 'You know, Jack, along with strangling, holding someone against their will is also against the law.'

'I want you to stay with me,' he said from between clenched teeth.

'Why?'

'It's three a.m. I don't like the idea of you trawling the city for a hotel at this hour.'

'How terribly chivalrous of you but, really, I'm a big girl now and can quite easily find myself somewhere to stay.' She made a grab for her phone but he held it even further out of her reach. 'Give me the phone, Jack.'

'No.'

'Give me the phone or I'll scream again.'

'You scream again and I won't just kiss you this time,' he threatened darkly.

She let her arm drop by her side, her eyes widening at the look in his eyes. She couldn't make him out. He gave every appearance of being uncomfortable with her around, but as soon as she offered to leave he refused to let her go. What was going on?

'I see,' she said, even though she didn't.

She watched as he dragged a hand through his hair for the second time, giving him an out-of-character tousled look. She couldn't help noticing the dark bruise-like shadows beneath his eyes. He looked exhausted, as well he should considering he'd been on call two nights in a row, each of them stressful and technically demanding.

She suddenly felt ashamed of the fuss she was making. After all, he was only doing what any decent person would do, offering her a place to stay until things were sorted out at her flat. Most of her friends lived too far away from St Patrick's for it to be convenient, especially for her on-call shifts, and with Ben and her parents out of reach Jack was as close to family as she could get at short notice.

He handed her back the phone, his eyes avoiding hers. 'I'll organise to have your car fixed first thing in the morning. You should get some sleep—it's been a long night.'

She took the phone and stared at him for a moment or two, her fingers feeling where the warmth of his hand had been.

She was still trying to think of something to say when the telephone beside his bed rang.

He moved past her to answer it, turning his back to her. 'Colcannon.'

'Mr Colcannon,' Robert said. 'There have been a couple of admissions since you left. Sorry to call you so late but while they're not urgent, I just need some advice.'

'Of course, Robert,' Jack said. 'What have you got?''

'There's a Mrs Ryan who's had vomiting and pain in the right upper quadrant, going through to the back. She's tender in the upper abdomen, more on the right, but no mass, normal bowel sounds, slightly febrile. I think it sounds like acute cho-lecystitis. I've ordered an ultrasound.'

'Good, that's fine. Make sure you get bloods, including liver function tests, amylase and lipase, and start her on IV ceph-alosporin. What else have you got?'

'A male, mid-forties with suspected pancreatitis. He's a heavy drinker and presented with acute epigastric pain through to the back. His lipase is off the scale.'

'OK. Order a CT scan for the morning, put him in HDU for the rest of tonight, get him catheterised and make sure he's producing at least 30 mls an hour urine output. Repeat all his blood parameters and blood gases, and get a chest X-ray,' Jack advised.

'Thanks, got all that,' Robert said. 'The last one is an is-chiorectal abscess in a seventy-year-old male. I've organised Theatre and the anaesthetic registrar is available, but if you want Dr Baxter to be called in...'

'No,' Jack said. 'The registrar can handle that and so can you. You've done enough draining of abscesses now to do that with one hand tied behind your back. Anything else?'

'There's a suspected appendix but we're going to sit on it till the morning. The patient isn't febrile and the symptoms are a bit vague. He's also been on a bit of a bender so it's hard to make a proper diagnosis.'

'Friday nights are like that,' Jack said, running his hand along the side of his jaw. 'Call me if there's anything urgent. I'll be in around eight for a quick round. Thank God I'm off for the rest of the weekend.'

'It's certainly been a big week,' Robert agreed.

'Tell me something I don't know,' Jack said, and rang off.

'Do you have to go back in?' Becky asked, hovering at the end of his bed.

He returned the phone to its cradle before answering. 'No, there's nothing urgent going on. I'll check things when I go in in the morning.'

'The night isn't over yet,' she said, smothering a yawn.

'It is as far as I'm concerned.' He sat on the edge of the bed and began to untie his shoe laces. 'Besides, Robert's turning out to be quite a good registrar. He'll let me know if anything needs my attention and he'll deal with the rest.'

Becky watched as he methodically placed his shoes side by side, his socks neatly folded, not scrunched up as she or Ben would have left them.

'You look tired,' she said after a small silence.

'Yeah, well, that's just how it looks on the outside.' He rubbed his hand over his eyes. 'You should feel it from where I'm feeling it.'

'Why do you work yourself so hard?'

He lifted his bloodshot gaze to her, his expression becoming distinctly exasperated. 'Why don't you go to bed like a good little house guest and leave me in peace?'

Becky sent him an arctic look, wishing she hadn't tried to be nice to him. 'You can be such a jerk sometimes.'

'Only sometimes?'

'All of the time.'

He got up and began unbuttoning his shirt.

'What are you doing?' She stared at him, her heart doing a little kick-start in her chest.

'I'm getting undressed, so if you want to see the rest, stick around,' he said, his hands going to his waistband to unbuckle his belt.

Becky wished she had the courage to call his bluff. It wasn't as if she hadn't seen the naked male form, she had—hundreds, if not thousands, of times—but Jack's was something else.

She turned on her heel and left his room, the sound of his laughter incensing her even further.

She locked herself in the bathroom and, rummaging through her hastily gathered toiletries, washed her face and cleaned her teeth. She changed into the T-shirt Jack had given her, looking at her reflection with a rueful grimace as she saw how the soft fabric outlined her figure rather too closely.

She sighed and turned on the taps to rinse out her lacy knickers and bra before hanging them over the shower cubicle to dry.

The spare room was decorated in the sort of everything-matching-nothing-out-of-place way she'd come to expect from Jack. With a mischievous little smile playing about her mouth, she went through the room and deliberately put things out of place, ruffling the perfect curtains, scrunching up the spare pillows and leaving her clothes and shoes in a scattered pile on the floor. She tilted the gilt-edged mirror above the antique dressing-table at a crazy angle, making sure her recently mois-turised fingers left a decent-sized smudge.

She bounced on the bed a couple of times, knowing he

would probably hear it in the room next door but way past caring.

'Will you shut the hell up in there?' Jack's deep voice came through the wall. 'I'm trying to sleep!'

'Did you say something, Jack?' she cooed back, stretching languorously on the bed, one of her hands inadvertently knocking the electronic bedside clock to the floor. The radio came on at high volume, the shrieking of violin strings filling the silence with nerve-tightening sound.

'Oops!' She rolled off the bed, trying to find the 'off' switch, but all she managed to do was change stations and increase the volume. This time instead of violins the mind-numbing sound of techno music filled the room.

She was on the floor, still fiddling with the buttons, when Jack came bursting into the room, his face contorted with fury.

'What is it with you?' he growled, coming over to scoop the radio out of her hands and snapping it off.

Becky got up off the floor and straightened the T-shirt over her curves. 'I didn't mean to knock it off the table.'

He glared at her. 'And I don't suppose you meant to use the bed like a trampoline either?'

'I was checking the mattress,' she lied.

He gave her a disgusted look. 'And I bet you've tested a few of those in your time.'

Her mouth dropped open in outrage. 'You sexist pig! I bet you've dented a few as well!'

His jaw tightened. 'That's none of your business. Now, get in that bed and go to sleep before I—'

'Before you what, Jack?' she cut in before he could finish. 'Kiss me again? I know you want to. I can see it in your eyes.'

Jack held her taunting look for as long as he dared. He should never have kissed her. What the hell was Ben thinking? This was never going to work.

'You're imagining it,' he said, stepping away from her. 'I want nothing to do with you.'

He strode over to the door and slammed it shut behind him, the noise of wood and lock connecting making her flinch.

'Fine,' she muttered under her breath. 'I don't want anything to do with you either.'

She flopped back down on the bed and shut her eyes but, exhausted as she was, it took ages before she could relax enough to sleep.

CHAPTER SIX

JACK put down his cup of coffee as soon as Becky entered the kitchen the next morning. 'I was thinking about doing a quick ward round,' he said. 'Why don't you come with me for the ride?'

Becky gave him a quelling look as she picked up the coffee-pot. 'I can think of a hundred things I'd rather be doing than following you around the hospital while you check and double-check every patient's file, as if the only person who knows what they're doing in the whole hospital is you.'

'Yeah, well, I'm the one they sue if anything goes wrong,' he reminded her with undisguised bitterness.

'Don't you ever take a day off?' she asked, leaning back against the counter with her coffee cradled in her hands. 'You know, kick back and relax and forget all about being a surgeon for a while?'

Jack shifted his gaze from her scrutiny. 'I have time off.'

'When?'

'Tomorrow.'

'Well, bully for you, a day off,' she said with a curl of her lip. 'I wonder how you'll manage to fill in a whole twenty-four hours.'

Jack silently ground his teeth. This wasn't going to plan. He didn't want to leave Becky alone but neither did he want her trailing after him at the hospital, making her snide remarks on his working habits for all and sundry to hear. Ben had said to keep her with him at all times outside work but Jack knew she would be highly suspicious if he pressed her to join him on a ward round that he could just as easily get out of the way within minutes if he left now. If he waited for her to have a shower and do her hair, half the day would be over.

'I won't be at the hospital any longer than an hour,' he said. 'Don't answer the door.'

'I won't,' Becky promised. *Because I won't even be here,* she added mentally, smiling sweetly at him as he picked up his keys.

Once she was sure he was gone she went back upstairs to have a quick shower before throwing on her clothes. She gathered her few things together in a carry bag, turned off her mobile and made her way outside to wait for the taxi she'd called earlier. She asked the driver to drop her off in the city and went into the first reasonably priced hotel she came to.

'How many nights would you like to check in for?' the young woman at Reception asked.

'Um…the weekend to start with.' Becky did a quick mental tally of her credit-card account and crossed her fingers behind her back.

'Will anyone else be joining you?' The young woman handed her the registration forms to fill in.

Becky hated this part. It never failed to make her feel spinsterish and left on the shelf.

She gave the woman a little smile. 'I'm not sure, but who knows? A girl can get lucky in a big city.'

The receptionist smiled politely but it didn't reach her carefully made-up eyes. 'I hope you enjoy your stay with us. If there is anything we can do to make your time more comfortable, please let us know.'

'Thank you.'

'I'll get the porter to take your luggage to your room.'

'I don't have any luggage just yet,' Becky said. 'I'm going shopping right now to get some.'

The receptionist's eyebrows went up just a fraction but to her credit she didn't respond. Becky pocketed the swipe card key and left.

The shops were clogged with Christmas shoppers, which made the task of replenishing her wardrobe all the more time-consuming. The queues were interminably long, the staff considerably stressed and the spirit of Christmas nowhere to be found in the sticky heat that infiltrated the stores in spite of air-conditioning.

By midmorning Becky only had a couple of changes of clothes, some overpriced-but-to-die-for underwear and a pink and white bikini she couldn't resist buying on impulse. She stopped to have a manicure because of the free offer of hand lotion and lip gloss, and as she walked past the cosmetics counter she agreed to have a mini-facial in order to get the special deal on moisturiser.

At two p.m. she had a double caramel lattè and a slice of raspberry cheesecake in a café and turned on her phone to check for messages. The first three were from Jack but the other number she didn't recognise. She pressed the replay buttons and listened to each message in turn.

'Rebec..Becky, where the hell are you?' Jack's tone was clipped with anger. 'Call me immediately.'

She deleted it and pressed for the next message to play.

'So help me, God, if you don't tell me where you are, Rebecca Baxter, I won't be answerable for the consequences. *Call me now!*'

She deleted it with considerable relish and pressed the next one.

'Right.' Jack's tone was now livid. 'I don't know what game you are playing at, young lady, but when I find you I'm going to make you regret it big time. If you don't call me in the next hour I'm going to hire a bloody private investigator to find you. *Do you hear me?*'

'Loud and clear.' Becky grinned as she pressed the 'delete' button.

The fourth message was from the police officer who had attended her call about the burglary.

'Hello, Dr Baxter, this is Constable Matthew Daniels. I was wondering if you could give me a call at your convenience. There are a few questions I'd like to ask you about the robbery investigation. My mobile number is as follows…'

Becky saved the message and pressed 'recall'. It answered on the second ring.

'Constable Daniels.'

'Hi, this is Becky Baxter here. You called me earlier?'

'Hello, Dr Baxter,' he greeted her warmly. 'Thanks for getting back to me.'

'No trouble,' she said pleasantly. 'What can I do for you? You said you had some questions for me about the investigation.'

'Yes. I was wondering if I could meet you later this evening to go over them with you, what, say, about seven? Would that be convenient?'

'Sure,' she said. 'I've got nothing planned.'

'I'll pick you up,' he offered politely. 'What's your current address?'

'I'm staying at a hotel in the city,' she told him. 'The Principal On The Park. Room 1205.'

'That was good thinking on your part,' he said. 'Twenty-four hour security.'

'Yes…' She gnawed her bottom lip for a moment. 'Have you got any leads on the case, Constable Daniels?'

'Please, call me Matt.'

'Only if you'll call me Becky,' she said. 'Everyone else does.' *Well, almost everyone.*

'Becky, then,' he said. 'As to the case, I'd rather discuss that with you in person.' There was a small pause before he added, 'Off the record, so to speak.'

'Oh.'

'Will I meet you in the bar or in your room?' he asked.

'The bar will be fine.' She had a sudden thought and added, 'Unless you'll be in uniform? Maybe you'd prefer…'

'I won't be in uniform and the bar is fine,' he said. 'See you at seven.'

Becky had her finger poised over the turn-off switch when her phone began to ring. Jack's number flashed on the screen and her finger hovered for a moment in indecision. Several people looked up from their tables to glare at her and she turned her back and answered it, knowing she was probably going to regret it.

'Could you hold for a moment?' she said, hastily clutching the phone to her breast to smother Jack's cursing protest.

She scooped up her things and quickly left the café, leaving some money for her snack on the counter on the way past.

She stood to one side of the busy pavement and held the phone up to her ear. 'Hello, Becky here.'

'*Where the freaking hell are you?*'

'Shopping.'

'Shopping?'

'Yes, you know that activity that women love and men hate? The one where lots of money changes hands in exchange for the latest fashion and accessories?'

'If you had *any* idea of how furious I am with you right now you wouldn't be able to stand upright for the quaking of your legs,' he ground out.

'Ooh! I am *so* scared,' she goaded him.

His one sharp swear word made her eyebrows lift momentarily and a funny sensation flickered between her thighs, making her legs feel a little unstable all of a sudden.

'I've been out of my mind for the past six hours!' he went on heatedly. 'You didn't even leave a note. I had no idea what had happened to you.'

'Why should you care?' she said. 'It's not as if you really want me staying at your house. You've made it more than clear I'm just a total nuisance.'

'You're not a nuisance, you're a bloody nightmare,' he muttered darkly.

'Well, lucky for you I have somewhere else to stay now, so you can keep your pathetic attempt at hospitality and shove it down your—'

'Where are you staying?' he barked at her.

'Wouldn't you like to know?' she tossed back.

'Tell me where you're staying,' he demanded, his voice rising.

'Stop shouting at me.'

'I am *not* shouting at you!' he shouted. 'Tell me where you are, for pity's sake!'

'I'm staying at a hotel.'

'Where?'

'I'm not telling you.'

Jack gritted his teeth in frustration as he tried to calm down. No one, but no one, made him as angry as Becky. His blood virtually pumped with it, making him as tense as a tightly stretched wire. He could barely think straight when she was around, and when she wasn't…well, he couldn't think at all.

He'd promised Ben that he'd look after her but he was doing a poor job of it so far. She'd slipped out of his sight, totally unaware of the extreme danger she was in. He'd thought of warning her about it on one of his messages but decided Ben was probably right. It would only frighten her and she'd already had two terrifying episodes to deal with as it was.

'Look…' He tried another tack. 'Can we have dinner tonight?'

'*Dinner?*' Her tone was incredulous.

'Yeah,' he said dryly. 'That activity that couples do from time to time, where large amounts of money are exchanged for a meal you could have cooked for a fraction of the price at home.'

'We are not a couple,' she said. 'And, besides, I'm already busy tonight.'

He frowned. 'Doing what?'

'I'm going on a date.'

'With whom?'

'A man.'

'What man?'

'No one you know.'

Jack's stomach gave a disturbing clench.

'Is it someone from the hospital?' he asked after a short silence.

'No.'

'How well do you know this guy?'

'What is this?' she asked disdainfully. 'Twenty Questions?'

'Who the hell are you going out with?' His voice rose once more.

'He's a cop.'

'*A cop?*' he choked.

Becky rolled her eyes and stepped out of the way of a determined shopper. 'What's the matter with you, Jack? He's one of the good guys.'

'How do you know?'

'Oh, for God's sake!' she said in exasperation. 'I already have a father and a big brother so quit it with the protective male relative routine, OK?'

'I can't help feeling responsible for you.'

'I can't imagine why.'

'Well, for a start, you're a walking, breathing disaster,' he said. 'Apart from when you're at work, where you are surprisingly highly competent and professional, but for some reason once you leave the premises you turn into an airhead.'

'Has anyone told you lately how much of a pain in the butt you are?' she snapped.

'I think you were the last person to do so.'

'I'm hanging up,' she said.

'If you hang up, I swear to God I'll—'

Becky hung up and switched off her phone, stuffing it in her bag with a determined shove of her hand.

She strode off into the nearest boutique and bought an outfit that cost a fortune, and didn't even blink an eye when the transaction was processed. With the rest of her purchases in each hand she went back to her hotel, ordered a hot snack from room service and ate it while she lay in the spa, using a host of free samples she'd been given at the cosmetics counter.

'I hate him,' she addressed the fragrant bubbles in front of her. 'He's a complete and utter Neanderthal.' She popped another French fry into her mouth and chewed it savagely. 'I hate him for being such a control freak. I hate him for being so…' She choked back a tiny sob. 'I hate him for being so…so damn un-hatable.'

Jack had a gut feeling she was in the city. Although there was a huge shopping complex at Bondi Junction, he thought he'd heard the distinctive whirr of the city's monorail among the sounds of carol singers and the general hustle and bustle of the busy crowds as he'd been talking to her on the phone.

The only problem was, the city was full of hotels. It would take him hours to call each one and even then privacy protocol was such that they might not tell him her room number.

He decided to think like a cop. Ben would be good at this, he thought as he walked the length of the city. He would narrow it down to the area he thought she would be most interested in shopping in. Not only that, city hotels were not cheap and she was a staff anaesthetist after all. She wouldn't be throwing money away unnecessarily, particularly as she had just been robbed and needed to replace what she could, and it could take weeks before the insurance claim was processed.

He decided she would most probably choose a hotel a couple of blocks from town, maybe somewhere up the far end of Hyde Park. The lush green of the trees along the Walk of Remembrance would appeal to her sense of sentimentality, not to mention the Pool of Reflection near the War Memorial. He decided she probably wouldn't go for harbour views as it would push the price up too much, although one could never be too sure with Becky. As far as impulsiveness went, she more or less took the cake.

At the first three hotels he drew a blank. But he got lucky on the fourth.

Becky gave her freshly dried hair a last quick pat and reapplied her new strawberry lip gloss. She sprayed herself liberally with her new perfume, which had been on sale with a bonus gift of a make-up travel kit. She ran her hands down her slinky hot-pink dress with the diamanteé shoestring straps, her heels giving her some of the height Ben had selfishly stolen from her at the Baxter genetic door.

Matt Daniels rose from his seat in the piano bar as she approached, a smile spreading over his face as she slipped her hand into his.

'You look completely different without your uniform,' she said.

His warm brown eyes swept over her in undisguised male appraisal. 'You're looking pretty good yourself.'

'Thank you.'

He held out a chair for her in a quiet corner. 'What would you like to drink?'

Becky really had no head for alcohol and as a general rule avoided it, but somehow tonight she felt a little bit more daring than usual. Although she had absolutely no idea what it contained, she asked for the first cocktail she saw on the list above the bar.

'I'll have an Abracadabra,' she said.

The drinks waiter took Matt's order for a light beer and discreetly moved away.

'So.' Matt leaned forward, his arms resting on his knees. 'How are you holding up?'

Becky gave him a wavering smile. 'I'm doing OK.'

'No panic attacks or sleepless nights?'

Her expression instantly became rueful. 'My bank manager would probably prefer it if I did, but, no, my number-one coping mechanism is to shop. It works every time.'

He smiled, his eyes crinkling in the corners. 'I have a sister just like you.'

'You do?'

He nodded and leaned back as their drinks arrived. He paid for them and waited until the waiter had left before continuing, 'My sister Penny has a black belt in shopping.'

Becky grinned and reached for her drink. 'Yeah? Well, I'm working my way up to a PhD in purchasing. After today I figure I'm almost there.'

He gave her an amused smile and took a sip of his beer. 'Do you have any family?'

'My parents are overseas just now,' she said, twirling her straw. 'They're celebrating being married for thirty-five years with a six-week cruise and a white Christmas in Europe.'

'Wow, that's some innings for a marriage these days.'

'Yes.' She gave him another little smile. 'I have a brother, too.'

'What does he do?'

'You're not going to believe this, but he's a cop.'

'No kidding?' He took another swig of his beer. 'What branch?'

Becky always found it hard to exactly describe what her brother did. He was guarded about the details, as if by telling his family what he did was going to somehow compromise him.

'He moves around a bit,' she hedged. 'He's been in traffic, then accident investigation and now I think he's doing a stint in the drug squad.'

'Tough call,' Matt said.

'That sounds like the voice of experience,' she observed.

He gave her a twisted smile. 'I've moved around a bit, too. You see it all eventually.'

She gave her straw another twirl. 'It's not an easy job, being a cop.'

'No, but sometimes you get results and it makes it all worthwhile,' he said.

She set her drink to one side, not sure she really liked the taste of it in spite of its colourful umbrella and little kebab stick of tropical fruit.

'So.' She met his eyes once more. 'What did you want to ask me?'

He leaned forward in his chair. 'There's something about the robbery and the intruder that doesn't quite add up.'

'What do you mean?'

He glanced around the bar as if he expected someone to be listening in. Becky couldn't help noticing the likeness to Ben. Once a cop always a cop, she thought as she leaned in closer to hear.

'I could be wrong, but I don't think the robber and the intruder are the same guy,' Matt said in a low voice.

Becky reached for her drink, for something to do with her suddenly twitchy hands. 'You don't?'

He shook his head.

'Who do you think it is?'

He pursed his lips for a moment. 'I'm not sure.'

She swallowed. 'You mean *two* people are after me?'

'I wouldn't go as far as saying someone's after you. The two incidents could very well prove to be totally unconnected.'

'If that's supposed to give me peace of mind, let me tell you it hasn't quite done the job.'

'No, I imagine not,' he said. 'Being burgled is a violating experience but having an intruder looking at you in the middle of the night is something else again.'

'Tell me about it.' She suppressed a shudder and took another sip of her drink, doing her best not to screw up her face at the taste.

'I had an unmarked car drive by your place a few times last night but so far nothing has come up that's in any way suspicious.'

'Thank you,' she said. 'I really appreciate it.'

'There's been a spate of burglaries in your area lately,' he said. 'It's not always the case, of course, but as a general rule we often find the same gang is responsible for each of the break-ins. They do an area and then move on to somewhere else.'

'You think my break-in was the work of a locally operating gang?'

He gave her a lengthy look. 'On first appearances it would appear to be a straightforward forced entry and quick grab for goods, but...'

'But?' she prompted.

'That scrawl in lipstick on the mirror.' He gave her an unblinking look. 'Is there anyone in your life you suspect of ill feeling towards you? I know you've been asked that before but sometimes it takes a while for it to sink in.'

A vision of Jack flitted into her mind but she just as quickly dismissed it.

'No.'

'Are you sure?'

She met his concerned gaze and was again reminded of her brother. It seemed as if cops were all the same, no matter what their rank.

'Look, I'm the first to admit I don't have the best track record where relationships are concerned,' she confessed with a little grimace. 'I've been engaged three times, but I'm absolutely sure none of my ex-fiancés would hold anything against me. Believe me, revenge would be the last thing on their minds. All they wanted was their freedom. I haven't heard from any of them for years.'

'Have you had anything else happen to you lately that could be considered a little suspicious?' he asked.

She chewed her lip for a moment then told him, 'I've had three flat tyres over the last week, and my tyres were slashed yesterday in the hospital car park.'

'Did you report all that?'

She shook her head. 'I was going to, but…'

'But?'

'I didn't want to face it, I guess,' she said. 'I'm not used to thinking of myself as a victim of crime.'

'You're not alone in that,' he said. 'No one wants to face such a prospect, but it happens all the same.'

'Yes, I know.'

'Does anyone else know you're staying here?'

She lifted her gaze to his. 'No. I haven't told anyone but you.'

'Good.' He looked relieved. 'Let's keep it that way for a while. I'm working on a few leads and it would suit me if no one knows where you are spending the night. If anyone needs to contact you, let them do it via your mobile.'

'But I gave my name at Reception. If anyone asks…'

'Put a block on it,' he said. 'Tell Reception you don't want your details handed out. I can do it for you on my way out if you like. You'd be amazed at what a flash of a badge can achieve.'

'Oh, would you?' She gave him a grateful look. 'I'm pathetic at all this cloak-and-dagger stuff.'

He gave her a reassuring smile. 'Let's hope none of this turns out to be in that category. For all we know, this is probably a simple case of mistaken identity or at the very least a straightforward break and entry.'

'I certainly hope you're right,' she said, taking another sip of her loathsome drink. 'I don't like to think of myself as somebody's target practice.'

'Random acts of violence are thankfully very rare. Statistics show that most victims of violent crime have known the perpetrator in some way.'

'So what you're saying is I'm somehow connected to these people?'

He gave her a brief look as he set his empty glass down. 'Suffice it to say I'm not ruling it out.'

'Great,' she said wryly. 'And I just sent off all my Christmas cards, too.'

'Want me to run a check on all the names?' he offered.

'No,' she said. 'But I'm going to have a serious rethink about my Christmas shopping.'

He stood up to leave, offering her his hand with a friendly smile. 'You really should meet my sister,' he said.

She returned his smile with one of her own. 'And you definitely should meet my brother.'

'You never know,' he said with an inscrutable little smile. 'Maybe I already have.'

Becky opened her mouth to respond but he'd already turned and slipped away.

CHAPTER SEVEN

BECKY swiped her card key and opened the door of her suite only to come up short when a tall dark figure rose from the sofa as the door closed behind her.

'How did you get in here?' she gasped as Jack stepped towards her.

He held up a swipe card in two long, tanned fingers, his green eyes locking on to hers.

'I told the person at Reception I was your husband.'

'*What?*'

He smiled a self-satisfied smile. 'I don't think they believed me at first—they weren't too keen to let me in—but I managed to convince them in the end.'

'How?' She eyeballed him suspiciously, wondering what he had done that could have gone beyond the authority of Matt Daniels's police badge.

He took out his wallet and waved a hundred-dollar note in front of her nose.

'You bastard!' She slapped at his hand in anger. 'How dare you invade my privacy? You had no right!'

He captured her hand and tugged her towards him, his eyes glittering dangerously. 'I told you I'd track you down and now I have.'

'Let me go!' She pulled against his hold but it was so firm she could feel the steady beat of his heart underneath her flattened palm, making her pulse kick up to a breakneck pace.

'Why did you disappear like that?' he asked.

'It's none of your business.' She gave him a glare. 'I don't have to answer to you.'

'I beg to differ, young lady,' he said, his fingers tightening a fraction around hers. 'Don't forget you still owe me for the replacement of my bumper, not to mention the renewal of your four tyres, which I paid for this morning, as well as the towing fee to the repair shop.'

She felt her stomach drop as she thought of her credit-card limit, and wished she hadn't been quite so reckless with her purchases that day. The dress she was wearing was worth at least two of his stupid bumpers, and just one of her shoes would have paid for a tyre at the very least.

'I'll pay you back every cent,' she said. 'Now, get out of here before I call the police.'

'Ah, yes.' His top lip curled back in scorn. 'That reminds me. How was your little date with the man in blue?'

She clamped her lips together, refusing to answer him.

'I must say he didn't stay long,' he mused. 'One drink and he was gone.'

Her mouth dropped open and her eyes widened in affront. *'You were watching?'*

The self-satisfied smile returned. 'I was expecting you to bring lover boy up here. What's wrong, Becky, losing your touch?'

Her eyes flashed at him in fury. 'Do you know how much I loathe and detest you?'

'I have a fair idea, but quite frankly it doesn't bother me all that much.'

'I don't think there is a single thing you could do either now or any time in the future to make me hate you more than I do right at this moment,' she said through tight lips.

'Good,' he said, suddenly pulling her even closer. 'Then you won't hate me any more for doing this.'

His eyes held hers for two or three heartbeats, which should have been enough warning but somehow wasn't. Her startled gasp disappeared into the warm cave of his mouth as it connected with hers with bruising force, her limbs going to water at the first determined thrust of his tongue as it arrogantly hunted down hers.

Becky felt the draining away of her resistance as if someone had suddenly pulled a plug within her, leaving her totally at the mercy of her urgent, desperate need for the sensory overload his hard, angry kiss was stoking within her. She could feel it flying with scorching heat along the pathways of her veins, the deep heady throb of it coming to a pulsating point of aching pressure between her legs where one of his hard muscled thighs had moved in to separate them.

His kiss became all the more determined, leaving no corner of her trembling mouth unexplored. She felt herself being swept away on a great wave of feeling, the pressure of his aroused body on the soft yielding of hers too much for her to withstand. She felt the sag of her legs even as he half lifted, half pushed her towards the bed behind her, the collapse of their combined weight on the mattress sending her breath out of her lungs in a startled gasp of pure pleasure as his hard frame moulded itself to hers, his angles fitting neatly into her curves while his tongue duelled hungrily with hers.

Jack wasn't sure exactly who was kissing whom. He had started this in anger but he wasn't feeling angry any more. What he was feeling now was a need so strong it was threatening to take over every moral boundary he'd constructed in the past to keep him from putting his hands on his best friend's little sister. She was in his arms and responding to him in a way he had not realised he'd wanted until he'd felt it again, just the way he'd felt it twelve years ago, just the way he'd felt it when he'd kissed her to shut her up—had it really only been yesterday? He didn't know or care. All he knew was that his body wanted her with a fierce, out-of-control desire, and nothing could stop him from consummating it right here and now.

With his mouth still locked to hers, he shifted the tiny sparkling straps of her dress to one side, his hand covering her revealed breast, his lower stomach tilting in sharp pleasure at the feel of her soft perfection, the tight bud of her nipple driving into the bed of his palm.

He felt her squirming beneath him, her body's instinctive movements thrilling him in a way no one had ever done before. He'd always kept himself slightly aloof from the emotional aspect of physical union, seeing it as something that could only complicate and blur the edges of reason in a casual relationship. But with Becky in his arms it felt different, as if she had somehow crawled under his skin and made it feel alive in a way it had never felt before. He felt it when her hands skimmed the muscles of his back, he felt it when her fingers dug into his buttocks to bring him even closer, he felt it when she undid his waistband and freed him into her hands.

'Oh, no,' he groaned, placing his hand on hers, the pulse of his erection still beneath her fingers.

She blinked up at him with wide uncertain eyes and he gritted his teeth and rolled off her, keeping her hand on him as consolation to his untimely overactive conscience.

'This is all wrong.' He put his free hand up to his eyes to cover them.

She splayed her fingers, which produced another deep agonised groan from his throat, but his hand kept hers in place regardless.

He uncovered his eyes and turned his head to look at her. 'Do you realise how close I am to following through on this?'

Becky moistened her lips with her tongue, not sure what to say. A few moments ago she'd been furious with him, but now…

'Becky…' He hitched himself up on one elbow and turned his upper body toward her, leaving her caressing hand where it was.

Becky moved her fingers once more, stroking the hard pulsing length of him, revelling in the dark glitter of desire her actions produced in his eyes as they held hers.

She traced her fingertip over his moistened tip, watching in awe as his features contorted with pleasure at her touch. He was like silk-encased steel under her caress, his body totally under her command, her feminine power apparent to her in a way it had never been before.

She knew then, as if someone sitting on her shoulder had just whispered it in her ear. She had been waiting for this moment ever since she'd been seventeen when his hard mouth had crushed down onto hers in a kiss of hot fire and frustration.

No wonder her three attempts at being engaged had failed! How could she fall in love with another man when all this time she'd been in love with Jack Colcannon?

In love with Jack...

She drew in a tiny breath as her fingers curled around him, the realisation of her feelings making her glow inside with liquid warmth.

She loved him.

'We have to stop this right now.' Although Jack's tone was determined, he did nothing to move out of her reach. 'It's total madness.'

She slowly lifted her luminous eyes to his. 'Why do we have to stop?'

His dark brows drew together momentarily. 'What are you saying, Becky—that you want to continue?'

She let her fingers do the talking and he sucked in a prickly breath, his body as tense as a tightly bound spring.

'Wouldn't it be nice if just for once we stopped arguing and tried another way of communicating?' she said softly, her caresses becoming bolder.

He ran his tongue over his dry mouth, staring at the fullness of hers as his blood charged through his body at turbo speed. He could almost feel her mouth on him, her little cat-like tongue...

With a strength he'd not known he'd possessed he wrenched himself out of her hold and got off the bed, tucking himself back into his trousers, his breathing still choppy as he put some distance between them. He scored a pathway through his hair with one hand and began to pace the room agitatedly, rubbing his jaw, cracking his knuckles, all the time avoiding her eyes.

Becky felt his rejection as if he'd slapped her with it. Shame ran like a hot red tide through her, completing its journey by settling in twin circles on her cheeks. She could see the undisguised distaste for her etched on his features. Even the line of his mouth was grim.

She got off the bed and straightened her straps with as much dignity as she could gather. It was spread pretty thinly.

'OK, so it looks like we continue with the arguing,' she said dryly. 'Where were we? Was it my turn to throw a verbal punch or yours?'

He stopped pacing to look at her. 'If it's any salve to your pride I *was* going to sleep with you. I've never been that close to losing control before.'

'Well, congratulations for withstanding the temptation,' she bit out. 'You really know how to make a girl feel irresistible.'

He frowned as she stalked across the room to pick up her shoes, her movements stiff with injured pride.

'Look, I don't want you to think I'm not attracted to you.'

She turned back to face him, shoes in hand. 'What are you scared of, Jack, that I might ask you for an engagement ring?'

'No, of course not, it's just…difficult.'

'Look, why don't you just leave right now before you make it any worse? I get the message. You don't have to wrap it up to make it more palatable.'

'Becky.' He turned her around to face him, his hands on her upper arms, his eyes holding hers. 'Believe me, you'll thank me for this in the morning. You've been under a lot of strain and you're not thinking clearly right now.' He gave her arms a little squeeze. 'You hate me, remember? What sort of guy would I be if I slept with you, knowing that?'

It was on the tip of her tongue to vehemently deny it but she stopped herself at the last moment. It was clear he felt nothing for her, so what would be the point of revealing her feelings for him? For years she'd actively demonstrated her dislike of him, had practically made it her life's work to annoy him. Telling him she loved him now would be nothing less than emotional suicide.

'You're right.' She gave him a self-deprecating smile. 'I'm not myself right now. God, what was I thinking? You are *so* not my type.' She eased herself out of his hold. 'Under normal circumstances you are the very last man on earth I would ever think of sleeping with.' She forced a laugh and moved her shoulders in what she hoped looked like a physical cringe. 'I wonder what was in that cocktail I had downstairs. Ben's always saying how alcohol impairs one's judgement. It must have been totally loaded.'

Not as loaded as the gun he'd just shot himself in the foot with, Jack thought wryly as he watched the relief wash over her features.

'It can get expensive, staying in hotels for extended periods,' he said, finally finding his voice. 'Wouldn't it be better to stay at my place until your place is cleaned up?'

She gave him one of her you've-got-to-be-joking looks. 'I'm only staying until I get another flat. I don't think I want to live in that one any more.'

Jack knew it wasn't exactly ideal, but at least the hotel had twenty-four-hour security, and another hundred bucks should keep the front desk silent over her presence in room 1205. And maybe another hundred would get them to call him if she happened to mention where she intended to go on her day off tomorrow.

'Your car won't be ready until late next week,' he informed her, handing her a card with the workshop's address and phone number. 'The mechanic wanted to check a few things first.' He didn't tell her he'd had to insist on the mechanic keeping it longer than necessary, but until he ruled out foul play he wasn't going to take any chances.

'Thank you,' she said, lowering her gaze a fraction. 'I don't know how I'll ever repay you.'

'Well…see you later, then,' he said, his hand hesitating on the doorknob.

She plastered a bright smile on her face. 'See you, Jack. And thank you for not…taking advantage of me. I really appreciate it. You don't know how much.'

He left without another word, somehow feeling she'd got the last one in anyway.

* * *

Becky tucked her sunscreen back in her tote bag and surveyed the sparkling ocean in front of her, her skin still tingling with the feel of the salt water after her short dip to christen her new bikini.

Bondi Beach had more than its usual Sunday-in-December crowd, the intense heat wave bringing in even more from the outlying suburbs.

She lay back on her towel and turned her head, squinting against the sunlight. She'd hardly slept last night after Jack had left, and the sun was so warm and the sound of happy bathers so soothing she closed her eyes and let the delicious warmth dry up the sea's moisture on her skin and seep right into her bones...

'Help! Help, somebody, please!'

She jerked upright at the sound of the desperate plea coming from a few feet away.

A little girl of about ten or so was shaking in terror as she stood over the convulsing form of her mother in the sand.

Becky sprang to her feet and ran to the terrified girl. 'What happened?'

'My mummy. She's a diabetic. I think she's got her insulin dose wrong. She's fitted once before,' wailed the distraught child.

Becky turned the woman onto her side into the coma position and pulled her jaw forward to help clear her airway.

'Can someone call triple 0?' she called into the gathering crowd.

The woman began convulsive fitting again, becoming cyanosed, with frothing saliva and a little blood from a lacerated lip, while her daughter sobbed in distress in the background, answering Becky's quick questions through tears.

'Can anyone here get a first-aid kit from the lifeguard station?' Becky shouted into the sea of fascinated faces.

In front of her the crowd started to separate as a dark, tall figure in black bathers pushed through with a plastic medical kit and an air of confidence she had seen many times before.

'Jack!' She stared up at him with a combination of relief and surprise. 'Are you tailing me or something?'

'Don't be ridiculous. I always swim here. What's wrong with this patient?'

'She's hypoglycaemic—too much insulin, no food and a little dehydrated.'

'There's IV gear and glucose in here,' Jack said as he opened the lifeguard's medical bag.

'Hold her arm still while I get in a cannula,' Becky instructed one of the lifeguards, who had accompanied Jack.

She inserted the only size cannula present in the kit, drew up 20 ml of ten per cent glucose into a syringe and injected it into the cannula. She repeated the manoeuvre three times until about 80 ml had been given. Suddenly the convulsions ceased, and after a few minutes, much to the relief of the onlooking crowd, and the sobbing thankfulness of the young daughter, the woman regained consciousness.

Within a few minutes an ambulance had picked up the patient and her daughter for transport to the local district hospital, the crowd dispersing back to their beach towels and umbrellas and the lifeguards returning to their lookout point.

Becky waited until the ambulance had gone before turning to Jack. 'I suppose you're going to tell me it's just a coincidence you were here this morning?'

'I told you, I often come down for a swim on Sundays,' he informed her evenly. It was more or less the truth, but the tip-off from the bell boy at the hotel had been a godsend, and well worth the expense. He gave the crowded beach a sweeping glance before coming back to her suspicious gaze. 'Along with the rest of the population.'

'I don't need a bodyguard,' she said, spinning on her heel to make her way back to her towel and bag. 'And even if I did, I don't think you're the person for the job.'

She shook off the sand on her towel and carefully straightened it before lying back down, closing her eyes, effectively shutting him out.

'Have you got sunscreen on?' he asked.

She opened one eye at him. 'I have all the protection I need.'

'If you ask me, you're starting to look a little pink.'

'I didn't ask you.' She flopped over onto her stomach and buried her head under her hat.

'Just here…' One of his fingers traced a light-fingered pathway over the top of her left shoulder.

'Stop it.' She wriggled under his touch. 'That tickles.'

'You shouldn't overdo it, you know,' he cautioned. 'A few minutes too long and you'll burn to a crisp.'

She angled her head to meet his eyes. 'Why don't you go and pick on somebody with fair skin?'

He smiled, his white teeth standing out against his deep olive tan. 'You might tan easily enough but it's not wise to try and do it in one day. I think you should reapply some sunscreen. I've taken off enough melanomas to know.'

'I think you should leave before I stuff the aforementioned sunscreen right down your throat.'

He threw back his head and laughed, bringing her head up off the towel to gape at him. When was the last time she'd heard him laugh? Truly laugh? Her stomach quivered at the sound of it, her legs feeling squishy all of a sudden.

'Here.' He reached for her bag. 'Get it out and I'll do your back, then I promise I'll go away and leave you alone.'

She rummaged in her tote bag and grudgingly handed the sunscreen to him, knowing she wasn't going to get rid of him any other way.

Jack looked down at the bottle, turning it over in his hands to see what exposure time the brand recommended.

His fingers stilled on the bottle as he read the handwritten label which had been placed over the manufacturer's directions.

YOU ARE GOING TO NEED MUCH MORE PROTECTION THAN THIS BITCH FACE

Becky swivelled her head to look at him, wondering why it was taking him so long to get the lid off.

'What's the matter? Isn't 30 plus enough to satisfy your perfectionist standards?'

He covered the makeshift label with his hand and squeezed out some of the lotion into his palm.

'No tan is a safe tan,' he said, absently smoothing some of it over the curve of her spine while his eyes quickly but thoroughly scanned the crowded beach.

Becky could sense his aversion to touching her and after a few moments slapped his hand away. Rolling over to sit up, she snatched her sunscreen out of his hand, glaring at him in affront.

'I wouldn't want to put you to any bother. I can see you've got much better things to do than…' Her words trailed away as she saw how his eyes dropped to the bottle in her hands as if it were a bomb waiting to go off.

She looked down at the label and froze.

CHAPTER EIGHT

SHE gulped back a swallow and looked up at Jack, the bottle falling from her fingers to the sand. 'He's here?'

Jack's eyes quickly scanned the beach on both sides, his stomach tightening at the thought of Becky's stalker hiding among the massive crowd.

'I'm not sure,' he answered, and turned to look at her, his eyes narrowed against the sunlight. 'When was the last time you put sunscreen on?'

She chewed her lip for a moment. 'I put it on before I went for a swim. I didn't reapply it after I came out. I was going to but then the little girl cried out for help.' She stared at her tote bag. 'I left my things here. Anyone could have come up and taken them, tampered with them...' She moistened her dry mouth as she reached for her bag to find her phone. 'We'd better call the police.'

'No!' His hand came down over hers.

She looked up at him in confusion. 'No?'

He removed his hand from hers, his eyes determined as they held hers. 'I don't think there's anything they can do. It's not as if they could identify anyone's footprints in this crowd.'

She looked at the stirred-up sand around her. Just to add credibility to Jack's statement, a teenage boy suddenly lunged right in front of them for the Frisbee his friend had thrown, stirring up a cloud of sand.

She dusted it off her legs and ankles and turned to look at Jack once more. 'I'm sort of over the whole beach thing right now.'

'Come on.' He hauled her to her feet with a strong hand. 'How did you get here? By bus?'

90

She nodded, looking away in embarrassment. 'I couldn't afford a taxi.'

'No problem,' he said taking her hand. 'We can walk to my house and I'll drive you back to the hotel.'

She curled her fingers into his and followed him without a word, somehow feeling relieved that he was by her side and in control.

They were silent in the hotel lift as it took them up to her room. Becky stared at the sand between her toes and wondered what had happened to her life. A couple of weeks ago she had been planning for a quieter than normal Christmas, now she was planning on staying alive.

'I'm scared,' she announced into the silence, still staring down at her scarlet-painted toenails.

Jack put an arm around her shoulders and drew her close. 'I know.'

Becky nestled into his solid frame, her head turning into his chest as she breathed in the familiar scent of him.

'You'll get through this, Becky,' he said into her hair. 'I know you will.'

'I wish I had your confidence,' she said, fingering one of the buttons on his casual surf shirt.

His hand went to the back of her head, his fingers burying into the silk of her hair. She felt his indrawn breath against her breasts as he pressed her even closer, close enough to feel the growing pulse of his arousal where it pressed against her stomach.

'I think we should empty out your flat this afternoon and move you temporarily into my place,' he said, easing himself away from her.

'Do you think that's such a good idea?' She looked up at him. 'We'll argue all the time. You know what we're like.'

'Then we'll have to call a truce,' he said.

'How long do you think that will last?' She gave him a sceptical glance as she stepped out of the lift on her floor.

'Look, once all this blows over you can get another apartment somewhere and things will go back to normal. I'm not asking you to live with me forever. Heaven knows, if I did, one or both of us would go stark raving mad.'

She swiped her card in the lock with unnecessary force and shoved open the door, tossing her wet sandy towel to one side and her tote bag to the other.

'OK, so maybe I could have put that a little better,' he conceded as she stalked off to the bathroom. 'What I meant was—'

'You know something, Jack?' She swung round and stood with her hands on her hips, glaring at him. 'Whatever charm school you enrolled in ripped you off. You don't know how to open your mouth without an insult falling out.'

'How have I insulted you?' He gave a look of exasperation. 'I'm doing my level best to help you.'

'Yeah, well, I'd really like to know what your motive is,' she said, scooping up her cosmetics and stuffing them into a carrier bag. She pushed past him at the bathroom door and haphazardly threw the rest of her things together.

'What do you mean by that?' he asked, turning around to follow her jerky, agitated movements as she packed.

She sent him an icy stare over one shoulder.

'You're only offering to help me as long as it doesn't inconvenience you. You don't want anyone at the hospital to know about us living together, albeit temporarily, and now you don't want me to call the police even though I've quite obviously been threatened again. What's going on?'

'Nothing. Nothing's going on.'

Her brown gaze glinted at him with growing suspicion. 'You know something about this, don't you?'

'Don't be ridiculous, Becky. You're imagining things,' he said, looking away. 'I'm just doing what your family would expect me to do in their absence.'

She narrowed her eyes. 'Have you talked to any of them about this?'

Jack hated lying to her but knew he had no choice. It wasn't just her life that was in danger, but Ben's as well.

'Talked to them? I don't even know where any of your family is right now.'

'You'd better not be lying to me, Jack, because if you are I'm going to be very, very angry.'

'I can deal with your anger,' he said, turning back to look at her. 'I'm more or less used to it. Now, let's get moving. I have to go in to the hospital this evening to check on a patient in HDU.'

He heard her mutter something under her breath about him being a workaholic but he chose this time to ignore it. There was something about this last threat to Becky that made him feel uneasy. It was clear someone was following her movements very closely. How else had they known she'd be at the beach, sitting in that particular spot among a huge crowd? Jack knew the sooner he got her out of the city and into his house where he could keep an eye on her, the better. He also knew it would take every iota of self-control he possessed to keep his hands off her, but he'd never forgive himself if anything happened to her. If only Ben would contact him again! He wanted his advice on the cop Becky had met for a drink. What if *he* was the informant Ben had alluded to?

They drove to her flat in Randwick. He took her key to open the door, his eyes widening at the mess in front of them.

'It's not pretty, is it?' she said, giving one of her torn books a despondent kick with one foot.

'I think it might be best if you just take what you value for sentimental reasons and the rest can be replaced through insurance,' he said. 'Got any garbage bags?'

She nodded and went to get them out of the small kitchen, bending down to the floor where they'd been strewn along with all the rest of the items in the drawers. But before she could straighten back up a missile came crashing through the kitchen window, shattering the glass and landing right in front of her.

'Becky?' Jack rushed to the kitchen and saw her on the floor, her face totally white as she held a rock in her hand.

'What happened?' He stepped over the glass and helped her to her feet. 'Did that just come through the window?'

She nodded and silently handed him the piece of paper that had been attached to the rock with an elastic band. He looked down at it, his stomach tightening as he read what was written there.

GET OUT OR DIE

'Right,' he said, taking her hand and pulling her out of the room. 'Forget your stuff—we're leaving.'

'No!' She tugged on his hand. 'I'm sick of being terrorised. I'm going to get my things and if anyone wants to take a potshot at me, let them.'

'Are you *mad?*' He tightened his hold. 'You don't know who's behind this.'

'I don't care. I want my things and I'm not leaving until I get them.' She extracted herself from his grasp and dug into her bag for her phone.

'What are you doing?'

She gave him a determined look. 'I'm calling Matt Daniels, the cop who is working on the investigation.'

Jack felt sick. He watched as she dialled the direct number she read off a card but he couldn't think of a way to stop her that wouldn't make her even more suspicious.

'Constable Daniels.'

There was the sound of scuffling in the background but in her rush to speak to him Becky ignored it. 'Matt?' She turned her back towards Jack. 'It's Becky Baxter.'

'Hello, Becky.' There was the sound of a male grunt before he added, 'How are things?'

'I need to talk to you. I've had a couple of weird things happen just lately.'

There was a tiny pause before Matt spoke. 'Why don't we meet some time tomorrow? I'm a bit tied up today, but what about tomorrow evening? Can it wait until then?'

Becky worried her lip before answering, 'Sure, it can wait.'

'Are you still at the hotel?'

'No. I'll be staying with a family…er…friend.' She gave him Jack's address.

'I'll pick you up about seven, if that's all right. Maybe we could have dinner?' Matt said.

'Dinner would be very nice,' she answered with a defiant glance in Jack's direction. 'And seven is perfect.'

'Great, see you then.'

'Bye.'

Jack made a sound of disgust in the back of his throat.

'What?' Becky spun around to glare at him.

'If he's such a great cop, why isn't he high-tailing it round here right now instead of taking you out to dinner tomorrow?'

'You shouldn't listen in on other people's conversations,' she reprimanded him coldly. 'Anyway, I like him. He reminds me of Ben.'

'Anyone in police uniform reminds you of Ben. It doesn't mean they aren't corrupt.'

'Corrupt?' Her mouth dropped open. 'What makes you think Matt Daniels is corrupt?'

'He hardly knows you and here he is, taking you out.'

'Maybe he's seriously attracted to me.' She gave him a pointed look and added in a breathy little tone, 'Maybe he even wants to have sex with me.'

'Oh, for God's sake, you're surely not thinking about jumping into bed with him? You don't know anything about him!'

'I intend to get to know him,' she informed him determinedly. 'I haven't been on a proper date in ages and I'm looking forward to it.'

Jack closed his teeth with a snap and watched as she sorted through her things, his gut clenching at the thought of her going out with a man who might very well have murder on his mind.

It wasn't that he was jealous…

Of course he wasn't.

He wasn't the jealous type. He had never felt anything more than a casual interest in any woman so he didn't see why he should be feeling so edgy about Becky getting involved with a man who could after all be a nice enough guy. He had no proof that Constable Daniels wasn't above board. All Ben had said was to trust no one.

It had nothing to do with being jealous.

He clenched his jaw.

OK, so maybe he was a little bit jealous.

But it was just because he didn't like to think of her throwing her life away on someone not good enough for her. As Ben had said, she had lousy taste in men; she could easily be hoodwinked into yet another disastrous relationship.

It wasn't that he thought of her as a potential partner for himself...

He gave himself a mental shake but no matter how hard he tried he couldn't quite forget the feel of her mouth, not to mention the caress of her busy little fingers on his—

'I'm all done,' Becky announced, jarring him out of his reverie. 'Let's go.'

He looked at her blankly for a moment or two.

'Hello?' Becky waved her hand in front of his face. 'Anyone home in there?'

'What?' His throat moved up and down in a convulsive swallow.

'What planet were you just on?'

'Planet?'

She rolled her eyes at him. 'Earth to Jack, can you read me?'

'Yeah...go...sure, let's go.' He took the garbage bag and held open the door, his movements mechanical.

It came to him then as if he had indeed been occupying some other planet, where the truth had been concealed from him all this time. He had feelings for Becky Baxter that had absolutely nothing to do with his promise to Ben. Feelings that he'd spent most of his adulthood avoiding.

He drove back to his house in a shell-shocked silence. He was conscious of Becky sitting within touching distance but she may as well have been sitting on the other side of the earth. She had told him so many times how much she disliked him, and even though she'd obviously been tempted to sleep with him the evening before, he knew the alcohol she'd consumed had coloured her judgement. She'd told him as much.

He helped her inside with her things, keeping conversation to an absolute minimum. Once she was more or less settled back in the spare room he made some vague excuse about going to the hospital which he knew could have waited till morning, but he felt in dire need of some breathing space. He reassured himself that after this latest scare she wouldn't do another disappearing act, and if he was super-quick he'd be back within forty minutes, maybe before she even got out of the shower.

'Shall I organise something for us to eat for when you get back?' Becky offered as he made his way to the door.

'Not for me,' he said. 'I'm not hungry, but you go right ahead. Help yourself.'

Becky frowned as she watched him leave. There was something about Jack that didn't quite add up. He was all protective and concerned for her welfare one minute and the next he looked as if he couldn't wait to get away from her. She gave a dispirited sigh and looked at her things sitting on the bed, waiting to be unpacked.

Temporarily, she reminded herself with a sharp pang of regret. Jack didn't want her in his life on a permanent basis, and if it hadn't been for his friendship with Ben and her parents, she wouldn't be in at all.

HDU was full that night, all eight beds occupied with post-op cases, some elderly and frail and struggling to recover from routine surgery, others recuperating from major surgery. Jack had two patients there, a severe pancreatitic and the splenectomy with diaphragmatic repair from his recent list. Cindy Jones was special-nursing both his patients and as Jack arrived, Robert greeted him in his usual formal manner.

Jack gave a brief nod in reply and reached for the first patient's notes.

'How are they doing, Robert? Any major issues?'

'Mr Pearson, the pancreatitic, is oliguric, despite pretty vigorous fluid resus. His urine output is under 10 mls per hour. His Ransom criteria are poor, he's not doing too well.'

'Have you got the CT report?'

'That's what I wanted to show you. They did fine slices through the pancreas with IV contrast. Most of the pancreas doesn't show up—I think he has major pancreatic necrosis.'

'Do they report any collection?'

'No collection, but a lot of peripancreatic oedema.'

'We may have to debride the pancreas. Can we get a Swan Ganz in and add in IV frusemide to try and up his urine output?'

'He's too much for us in HDU, Mr Colcannon,' Cindy Jones put in. 'Can we get him transferred to ICU?'

'I'm inclined to agree with you, Cindy. The last lot of blood gases makes it look like ventilation is going to be needed. Can you speak to ICU, Robert? Get him transferred round there, involve the intensivists, and we'll review the likelihood of surgery in the morning.'

'I'll get on to it now, Mr Colcannon. The splenectomy is fine, needing a lot of physio on his left chest, but OK.'

'Thanks, Robert. You're doing a great job with these difficult cases.'

'Thanks, sir. I'll see you in the morning. Have a good evening.'

'Right,' Jack said, glancing at his watch. If he put his foot down he'd be home in record time.

Becky had finished a simple meal of cheese on toast and had not long stepped out of the shower when she heard the sound of Jack moving about downstairs.

She towelled her hair and called out to him, 'How were things at the hospital?'

He didn't answer and she sighed as she reached for the hairdryer and gave her head a quick blast.

OK, so he was still annoyed with her for arranging to meet Matt Daniels the following evening. She couldn't understand why he was being so dog-in-the-manger about it. Even though he'd kissed her he'd made it perfectly clear he had no interest in her personally. He even avoided looking at her unless he absolutely had to. She'd seen the way his green eyes flicked away whenever she asked him something lately.

She turned off the dryer and peered at herself in the mirror above the basin and sighed. Was she *that* unattractive? Sure, she had a couple of pounds to lose, but what girl with an incurable sweet tooth didn't? So, she didn't quite meet his exacting standards. So what? His ex-girlfriend Marcia hadn't exactly been an oil painting.

Actually, she had, Becky conceded with a twist to her mouth as she unplugged the dryer. Marcia was a hospital physiotherapist who had the sort of face and figure that made most women envious and all men drool.

But that was beside the point.

She put the hairdryer down with a snap. She had the right to date whoever she liked and if she wanted to go out with Matt Daniels then she would go and enjoy herself. It wasn't as if she was going to let it go any further. How could it, when she was in love with Jack?

There was another sound of movement downstairs and, tucking the towel around her chest sarong-wise, she opened the bathroom door and called out once more.

'Jack?'

The house was quiet.

Too quiet.

Becky felt the sharp edges of fear claw at her insides as she strained her ears, her heart starting to leap about in her chest.

Was that a footstep on the stairs?

A creaking floorboard?

She spun around for a weapon, her eyes going to the still warm hairdryer. She grabbed it in both hands, holding it in front of her like a gun.

This had gone on long enough.

She wasn't going to be found cowering behind the bathroom door, waiting for her attacker to seek her out. No way.

She was going to come out fighting.

She took a steadying breath and pushed open the bathroom door.

CHAPTER NINE

'WHAT the—?' Jack stumbled backwards in shock as something caught him a glancing blow to his head. White spots of light flashed before his eyes and he clutched for the wall to keep himself upright.

'*Ohmigod!*' Becky stared in horror at the blood spurting from a gash just above Jack's right eye. 'It's you!'

'Yeah, it's me.' His words came out sounding a little woozy but his tone was still unmistakably dry. 'Or at least it was until you half brained me.' He lifted his fingers up to inspect the damage, wincing as they came back down covered in blood. 'But who knows? This could bring on that personality bypass you've been insisting I need.'

'I think it needs stitching.' She caught her lip between her teeth.

'Well, you'd better do it,' he said, brushing past her to enter the bathroom. 'I have a weak stomach when it comes to blood.'

'Very funny.' She spun on her heel to join him in the bathroom, meeting his eyes in the mirror where he was examining the wound. 'D-does it hurt?'

'Only when I breathe.' He held a facecloth to it and turned around to look at her. 'What made you do it? I thought we'd agreed to call a truce.'

'I thought you were an intruder.' She suddenly realised she was still holding the hairdryer and put it down with a little clatter on the vanity top. 'You didn't answer when I called out to you.'

'I called out to you three times, but you had the dryer going,' he said.

'Oh.'

101

He turned back to the mirror and checked the bleeding. 'Can you get my doctor's bag? It's in my study downstairs. I don't want to drip blood all over the carpet.'

She made a quick detour to her room, tossing the towel aside as she slipped on her bathrobe, before going for his bag and bringing it back up.

'You'd better sit down on the toilet seat while I do this,' she instructed.

He did as she said and she opened the bag, conscious of his long legs right behind her. She rummaged in the kit and found some steristrips and dressings, and gave her knuckles a mental crack or two.

'Maybe I'll just steristrip it,' she said somewhat nervously. Treating a highly skilled surgeon when you didn't have any major surgical skills except for anaesthetic procedures was not to be recommended, Becky thought ruefully as she leaned forward.

Jack removed his hand from the facecloth he'd been pressing to stem the flow of blood, but there was still a significant trickle from the wound.

'It's still bleeding. Put some pressure on it for five minutes and it should stop.'

'Lean back a bit so I can push on it.' Becky grabbed a pad of gauze she'd found in the medical kit.

After what seemed like five hours instead of five minutes with his body so close to hers in the tight space, she removed the gauze, relieved the bleeding had stopped.

'It's dry. I'll steristrip it now.'

'I can do it myself by looking in the mirror.' Jack started to get up off the toilet seat but she put a hand on his shoulder and pressed him back down.

'I know it's been a while since I've done this,' she said, 'but surely you trust me?'

He gave her an ironic glance from beneath his lashes. 'I don't trust you at all, but I'm too embarrassed to rock up to A and E and tell whoever's on duty that I've been assaulted with a hairdryer in my very own house.'

Becky felt the colour surge in her cheeks as she reached for some antiseptic, soaking a pad generously before turning to apply it to his wound.

'*Ouch!*'

'Don't be such a baby,' she chided him, stepping between his spread thighs to get closer to his wound.

She was intensely conscious of her nakedness beneath her worn bathrobe, her skin suddenly feeling overly sensitive where it brushed the cotton with each tiny movement she made.

She took a prickly sort of breath and added, 'I would have thought you'd be a little braver, considering the amount of pain you inflict on some of your patients at times.'

He grunted something under his breath before grumbling, 'I hope you're not going to leave me with a Dr Frankenstein scar.'

'Will you shut up and let me concentrate?' She put the antiseptic to one side. 'I'm not used to patients speaking to me while I tend them.'

'Just as well.'

'Hold still,' she said. 'I don't want to make a mess of it. Is it still hurting?'

'Not really, but I've got the mother of all headaches.'

'You might be a little concussed.' She carefully applied the steristrips, making sure the edges of the wound were close together. 'You might also end up with a black eye but hopefully you won't need plastic surgery.'

'Thank God.'

'Want to have a look before I dress it?'

He got up from the toilet seat and looked at the row of neat butterfly strips over his eye. 'Not bad.'

'Wow, a compliment from Mr Perfect himself!' She unpeeled a sterile dressing and reached up to apply it to his head. 'Bend down a little,' she said. 'You're too tall… There, that's it.'

'Don't you think you should check my pupils for any ir-regularities?' Jack said.

She stood on tiptoe and peered into his eyes. His pupils were dilated, but evenly, his green eyes glittering with something…was it pain, or maybe something else?

The silence seemed to stretch like a piece of elastic that had been under too much pressure for too long.

Becky felt the magnetic pull of Jack's gaze and suddenly found it hard to breathe. The air felt too thick. It dragged at her chest and throat until she was sure she was going to pass out with the effort of inflating her lungs enough to speak.

'I—I'm so sorry.' She stumbled over her apology. 'I didn't expect you back so soon. I really thought you were an intruder.' She twisted her hands a little bit and went on to explain, 'I didn't want to hide away like a coward, waiting for him to strike me down. I thought I'd get in first.'

He gave her a look of incredulity. 'So you thought you'd take him on all by yourself with a *hairdryer*? What were you thinking?' He gave a snort of derision. 'You wouldn't stand a chance defending yourself.'

She lifted her chin. 'I caught *you* off guard. You went down like a ton of bricks.'

'I did not!'

'Yes, you did.' Her mouth kicked up in a tiny smile. 'You didn't even block my hit.'

He gave her a disdainful look. 'That's because I knew it was you.'

'Then why didn't you say something and stop me?'

'How could I? You came at me like a bull at a gate. Besides, I didn't want to hurt you. One decent block from me might have broken your arm.'

Deep down Becky knew he was right, although the very last thing she wanted to do was admit it. She'd flown at him in such a rush, not even stopping to check his identity. If he'd so much as put up his arm to block her attack, she would have bounced off him like a rubber ball off a brick wall. Her brief bout of bravery seemed rather pathetic now she looked back at it with hindsight.

'I'll get you some Panadeine,' she mumbled and started for his bag.

'I don't need them,' he said. 'I think I'll lie down for a while with a cold pack. I have a full list tomorrow and I don't want to be drugged up to the eyeballs.'

He moved past her and she began clearing away the mess, grimacing at the amount of blood on the pads she threw in the bin.

'How are you feeling this morning?' Becky asked the next morning as she came into the kitchen where Jack had his head bent over the newspaper.

He lifted his head to look at her.

'Oh, my God, your eye!' she gasped. 'It's totally black!'

'As you see,' he said, his tone clipped.

'The cold pack didn't work?'

'Apparently not.'

'I don't know what to say.'

'It's been my experience with you that least said is soonest mended,' he commented dryly as he reached for his coffee.

Becky pursed her mouth in sudden anger. How like him to want to make her feel even worse.

'I'm going to work,' she announced tersely.

His glance went to the clock on the wall before returning to her flashing eyes.

'A whole hour early?'

'Why not?' She folded her arms crossly. 'You do it every day.'

'How are you intending on getting there?' He quirked one dark brow at her over the rim of his coffee-cup.

'I—' She snapped her mouth closed. She'd forgotten all about her car.

'Come on,' he said, pushing his cup aside. 'I'm ready to leave now anyway.'

'I'd rather walk.'

He gave her one of his don't-push-me-too-far looks as he scooped up his keys.

'Want to have a rethink on that, Becky?'

She pushed past him in the doorway, her colour high and her temper even higher.

'I should have hit you harder when I had the chance,' she snapped at him spitefully.

'Just try it, sweetheart, and see how far it gets you.'

Becky didn't answer. That funny flickering pulse had settled between her thighs once more, making her feel as if he had reached out and touched her intimately. She swung away and stalked out of the room, but even twenty minutes later as they drove in to the hospital in a mutually agreed stiff silence, she could still feel it beating within her.

Becky had the first patient—Mr Bamford, for an incisional hernia repair—on the table and asleep before Jack had even emerged from the change room.

'What happened to you?' Gwen gaped as Jack pushed through the theatre doors, arms upturned after his first scrub.

'I ran into something in the dark last night,' Jack mumbled from behind his mask. 'Just a little cut but the bruising has given me a black eye.'

'Gosh, it looks gross.'

Jack sent Becky a speaking glance before turning to Gwen. 'Thanks, but it looks much worse than it feels, I can assure you. Prep, please.'

He prepped the abdomen, applied the steridrape and set up the diathermy and sucker while Robert gowned.

'We're using mesh, Dr Baxter. Can you give a gram of cephalosporin?'

'Yes. I've got it mixed, it'll go through in a sec,' Becky answered, without looking at him.

Jack made a vertical incision and freed up and reduced the hernia.

'Let's have the 12 by 12 centimetre polypropylene mesh, Gwen, please, and lots of one-nylon sutures.'

'Do you want me to clip those, or cut as we go?' Robert asked.

'Cut, thanks, Robert, about a centimetre long. We need big bites and no tension.'

For the next twenty minutes Jack sutured in the mesh patch, trimming it to match the size of the hernia neck as he went.

'One-sixty milligrams gentamicin for the wound please, Gwen.'

'Will you use a drain, Mr Colcannon?' asked Robert.

'No, I don't use drains in this situation. Seroma formation is common, but there is no evidence that drains prevent it.' Jack suggested a couple of reviews for Robert to consult as he closed the wound with staples.

Jack was just finishing up the next routine case, a laparoscopic gall bladder, when Robert's page went off. 'Unscrub, Robert. I'll put in the skin sutures. You'd better get that page,' he said as he removed the last of the laparoscopic ports.

'Thanks, Mr Colcannon, I think that's a code blue for an emergency in A and E.'

Robert moved to the back of the theatre to use the theatre phone, but within a couple of minutes he was back at the operating table, looking a little pale.

'What's the problem?' Jack asked as Becky accompanied the patient out to recovery.

'There's a ruptured triple-A downstairs, confirmed on CT. He needs Theatre now. They want to break into our list—all the other theatres are in the middle of cases,' Robert informed him.

'*Shoot!*' Jack gritted his teeth in frustration. 'That's going to take three hours at least. We may as well forget about the rest of our list.'

'I'm afraid that's not the worst news, Mr Colcannon.'

'I can't imagine what's worse than having my elective list screwed up with a ruptured triple-A. Some of these patients have been waiting months for surgery, now I have to hand over my valuable theatre time to the vascular guys.'

'Well, actually...' Robert said with a grimace. 'All three vascular surgeons are away at a conference, and general surgery is covering vascular cases.'

'Oh, great,' Jack said darkly. 'I didn't get a memo from Admin about that. I wonder who the poor guy on call is who's going to have to deal with that?'

'Yes, well, that's the rest of the message,' Robert said.

Jack gave him a narrow-eyed look. 'You're kidding me, right?'

The registrar shook his head. 'You're on call for general surgery today.'

'I can't be on call again. Triple-A? I haven't done an elective triple-A since my registrar training, let alone a ruptured triple-A.'

Robert's pager beeped a text message and he read it out loud, '"Patient's in the lift, on his way up, with eight units of blood."'

'This is totally ridiculous!' Jack raised his voice. 'I'm being shafted into doing an operation I'm not properly trained for because the idiotic administration let all three vascular surgeons go on leave at the same time, and then tell me at the last minute that I'm covering.'

Becky could hear the shouting from the recovery room, where she had just taken the last patient. She had just been told of the situation by the recovery staff, and as she was the only free anaesthetist right now, she knew she was going to have to anaesthetise the triple-A. Theatre staff had already moved into action and were quickly setting up for a vascular case.

The lift doors burst open and two nurses and the A and E senior resident wheeled the desperately ill patient straight down the corridor toward Theatre.

Becky took over bagging and masking the patient and proceeded into Theatre, the orderlies transferring him across to the operating table. She administered high-flow oxygen while the anaesthetic nurse continued to pump in blood through the drip. Becky injected and intubated the patient, and connected him to the anaesthetic machine. She helped pump in blood through two drips as the monitor warned her of hypotension.

Jack burst through the theatre door, having scrubbed and

rapidly gowned while Gwen had set up the vascular instrument pack.

'You've got to clamp that aorta, Jack,' Becky said urgently. 'I've got no blood pressure up this end.'

'Rapid prep and drape, Gwen,' Jack said tightly.

Robert assisted with the set-up, and Jack made a long midline incision in the abdomen. The distended abdomen suddenly exploded with a gush of several litres of bright red blood.

'Aortic clamp!' Jack shouted, as he positioned Robert's hands with packs. He rapidly positioned the clamp across the aorta and squeezed hard on the handles, but the massive blood loss continued unabated.

'What the hell? The aorta won't clamp. It's rigid with calcification!'

Becky's anaesthetic machine gave a long monotonous beep.

'He's arrested, Jack. I've got no blood pressure and he's in asystole.'

In desperation Jack opened the aneurysm sac, scooped out plaque and clot from the calcified aneurysm sac, and shoved his left index finger into the lumen of the aorta. But the brittle vessel simply split further, releasing a final few surges of bright red blood before even that stopped, Becky's machine screaming the message that the patient had bled out and had no more blood to pump around.

In spite of twenty minutes of external cardiac massage, intracardiac adrenalin and massive volume replacement, with Jack finally managing to clamp the aorta, but above the renals, Becky gave the bad news.

'I'm stopping resus, Jack. He's gone, and nothing's going to restart this heart.'

Becky watched as Jack stood perfectly still for a moment or two, his gloved hands and gown covered in the patient's blood, his eyes behind his protective shield staring down at the lifeless body on the table.

'It was calcified,' she said. 'No one could have clamped it.'

Jack stripped off his gloves and gown and tossed them aside, his head gear soon following, his expression grim.

'You did the best you could do,' she added to fill the awkward silence. 'No one can ask more than that.'

Jack's hard green gaze hit hers with the full force of his bitter disappointment. 'Somehow I don't think that's going to comfort this man's wife and family, is it, Dr Baxter? That I tried my best?'

Becky opened her mouth to respond but closed it when she saw the rigid set of his jaw. He was upset, and rightly so.

No one wanted to fail in an emergency, especially an emergency that had been thrust upon him with no time for him to prepare. And now he had the unenviable task of going out and meeting the patient's relatives to deliver the bad news, a task no doctor ever felt up to no matter how many years of experience he or she had gathered over their career.

Becky had seen it so many times it made her feel ill to think of what he had to face—the sea of expectant faces, small bright fragments of hope shining among the shadows of their eyes as they rose from the edges of the waiting-room chairs, the smell of half-drunk tea and coffee lingering in the air, along with the scent of gut-wrenching fear.

CHAPTER TEN

THE rest of the list resumed after the theatre was cleaned, but the usual conversation among the theatre staff gradually ceased as they witnessed Jack's brooding silence as he worked his way through the routine cases.

Becky felt sorry for Robert, who had a tendency to try too hard at the best of times. Now, with Jack's added tension, it seemed the registrar couldn't do a thing right.

'Robert, I'm off the screen. I can't do laparoscopic surgery unless you hold the camera on what I'm doing,' Jack clipped out tersely.

'Sorry, the other instruments seem to be clashing with the camera.'

'Look, just hold it still. If I knock the camera, just keep watching the screen and keep me in the middle of it,' Jack snapped back.

Robert kept trying to point the camera where he thought Jack wanted to look, but in the end Jack pushed and pulled the camera into position himself, telling the registrar in a hard tone to just hold the thing still.

Becky gave Jack a reproving look as a cowed-looking Robert left the tearoom after the list was finished.

'You didn't have to be so hard on him. I think he's doing a good job, considering the piecemeal cases he gets from the other surgeons,' she said.

Jack thrust his coffee-cup down with a sharp crack on the table.

'He needs to toughen up or he'll never survive the training scheme. He simpers about, showing no confidence at all. No patient is going to take to him unless he demonstrates his ability to think and speak clearly, take some initiative and show some confidence.'

'You're hardly helping the process if you have him on tenterhooks all the time,' she pointed out. 'Everyone understands this afternoon's death was difficult, but I don't think it's fair to take it out on him.'

Jack's eyes glittered with sparks of anger as they pinned hers. 'What would you know? You weren't the one who had to face his wife, two daughters and three young grandchildren.'

'That must have been awful.'

He sucked in a ragged breath and turned away from her empathetic gaze.

'They had such hope in their eyes.' He moved across to the window and stared out over the hospital car park, his back turned towards her. 'I hate that—the way they look at you as if you are coming to tell them everything's gone well and he'll be up and about in a couple of hours for a cup of tea and a plate of sandwiches. Everyone expects miracles.' He swung around to look at her, his bruised eye looking all the more obvious with the shadows of disappointment in his gaze. 'It really gets to me. I always feel like the bloody Grim Reaper.'

'Jack—'

He held up his hand. 'No, don't insult me by saying it again. I don't need to hear I did my best, because you and I both know my best wasn't nearly good enough.'

'I wasn't going to say that.'

He gave her a long, hard look. 'What were you going to say?'

She stepped towards him and took one of his hands in hers, her small fingers stroking the long tanned length of his as she looked up into his face.

'I was going to say you are one hell of a surgeon and that if I ever had a surgical emergency you'd be the only one I'd want to help me.'

He held her look for a long time before speaking, his eyes, slightly misted, holding hers.

'Let's hope you won't be ever needing me that way,' he finally said, his tone a little rusty.

'I'm not planning on it, but I guess you never know, do you?' she said.

He didn't answer. Instead, he lifted his hand and traced one long finger down the curve of her cheek in a caress so soft Becky thought she must have imagined it.

'What was that for?' she asked, her voice a soft thread of sound.

He held her gaze for a long moment.

'Jack?'

He stepped back from her, his expression closing over, effectively shutting her out. 'I'll be ready to drive you home in about ten minutes. I just want to speak to someone first. I'll meet you at the front desk.' He turned and left the room, the door swinging shut behind him.

Becky turned and stared at his discarded cup on the table, and before she could stop herself she reached for it, running her fingertip around the rim where his lips had been, her mouth tingling in remembrance of how it had felt to have those lips pressed hard against hers.

Jack found Robert in the change room, gathering his things from his locker.

'I'll do a ward round now, Mr Colcannon, and ring you at home if any more emergencies come in.'

'No, you won't. Robert, you've got the potential to make a good surgeon. You did well this afternoon to cope with my mood after I lost that patient. I hope you're never in that situation but the odds are at some time you will be. It goes with the territory, I'm afraid, especially in the public system. But you look tired, and you should go home. I'll see the post-ops myself. Let A and E know they can reach you at home, and go get a break. I won't be far behind you. I'm more than a little bushed myself.'

'Thanks, sir.' Robert gave him a grateful glance. 'I was beginning to doubt myself this afternoon.'

'Don't be crazy, Robert. You're fine, just lacking in experience, which can easily be remedied. Now, get out of here. The place won't fall down without you.'

Jack allowed himself one small inaudible sigh as the registrar left the change room a short time later.

In some ways Robert reminded him of himself when he'd first started out—eager to please, wanting to learn as much as possible and be the sort of surgeon everyone had full confidence in. It only took a few losses to erode that growing confidence and he knew some trainees never quite recovered from it.

Losing patients was part of the cycle of a surgeon's life; even routine operations could go wrong. The human body, for all that science had discovered about it, still held some surprises. All one could hope for was that the cause of death was brought on by natural causes as the result of a disease going too far before treatment had occurred to try to stall the process. That was often true in the very elderly who had left things a little too long before having checks carried out. By the time they came to see him he had the loathsome task of offering them an operation that would very likely kill them or suggesting doing nothing, which would achieve exactly the same end. There had been some talk of rationing care in the public system—that expectations were too high, and that it couldn't provide maximal care to everyone.

Trauma, of course, was different. That was when good technical skill and a perfectly clear head in the 'golden hour' were vitally important. You still had your losses, inevitably, and often the recovery of those who did actually make it was long and arduous, some never making it back to full health.

It was times like these that he truly envied his father. Emery Colcannon hadn't lost a patient in the thirty years or so he'd been operating as a cosmetic surgeon, and never missed an opportunity to remind Jack of it. Jack had to make himself refrain from chipping back with some pithy comment about the dangers of getting it wrong with a Botox injection or eyelid lift hardly comparing with category-one trauma surgery.

Jack often wondered how his mother had survived living with his father as long as she had. He could stand about five minutes; she had survived eleven years, although she had barely spoken a word to her ex-husband since their divorce when Jack had been ten.

Jack knew his relationships with women were directly influenced by the bitter interactions between his parents. He hated feeling vulnerable in a relationship and had never allowed himself to feel anything other than physical desire with any of his previous partners.

But Becky was something else.

For years he had seen her as the kid sister of his best mate, almost wilfully blocking out the attraction he felt for her, in case he was tempted to act on it.

Damn it, but he was tempted.

Had been since that day he'd hauled her young supple body up against his and kissed her. And it hadn't been just a simple exploratory kiss, but the full works. The whole tongue routine, the pelvis against pelvis thing, and his hand on the soft budding breast, which he could still feel against his palm even after all these years.

He closed his hand into a fist a couple of times but the sensation was still there, as if the essence of Becky had eased itself beneath the surface of his skin, never to come out.

Even his house felt different now. He could sense her presence in every room and not just from her natural untidiness, which drove him crazy. It wasn't just the squashed cushions on the sofa where she'd been curled up or the damp towels hung up crookedly in the bathroom, or the scattered cosmetics containers with some of the lids still off. It wasn't even her perfume, which lingered in the air long after she'd left a room.

It felt to him as if by simply entering his house her lively personality had invaded the austere formal décor and somehow rearranged it permanently.

She was waiting for him at the front desk, chatting with the woman on duty as if they were old friends. Jack deliberately slowed his steps so he could watch her undetected. Her laughing brown eyes were sparkling with amusement, her soft mouth smiling, but her smile instantly faded when she turned her head and saw him. Jack couldn't help feeling annoyed, and to disguise his hurt he adopted a gruff demeanour as he led the way out to where his car was parked.

'What were you talking to the switchboard operator about?' he asked.

'Nothing.'

He gave her a disbelieving look as he unlocked his car. 'I would prefer it if you wouldn't discuss me with the hospital staff.'

'I wasn't discussing you,' Becky said. 'I was telling June about my date tonight.'

Jack's stomach gave a painful lurch. With all the stress of the day he'd forgotten all about her date with the cop. He drummed his fingers on the steering-wheel, wondering if he could come up with a good enough reason to get her to change her plans.

'And don't even think about trying to talk me out of it,' Becky said, giving him a warning glance. 'I've been looking forward to it all day.'

Jack didn't trust himself to respond. Instead, he concentrated fiercely on driving home, his mouth set in lines of tension as his mind raced with a thousand gut-wrenching scenarios.

'Jack, can you help me with my zipper?' Becky came bursting into the lounge room half an hour later. 'I think it's jammed or something.'

Jack sucked in a breath at the sight of her. She was dressed in a close-fitting ice-blue sheath that brought out the sun-kissed perfection of her skin and showcased her cleavage a little too well. She turned her back and his eyes widened at the slim length of her back, his fingers aching to trace a pathway down the delicate vertebrae.

'Can you see what's wrong with it?' she asked. 'Matt will be here any minute and I haven't even done my hair.'

'Um…' Jack's normally rock-steady hands started to tremble as he worked on the zipper, his knuckles brushing against her warm bare skin.

'I think I can see what's wrong,' he finally managed to say. 'It's caught on a little thread. Hold still while I unpick it.'

The doorbell sounded just as he slid the zipper up the length of her spine.

'Oh, no!' she gasped, spinning around to face him. 'Will you be a honey and let Matt in while I rush upstairs to do my hair?'

Jack grimaced as she bolted for the stairs. He drew in a breath and made his way to the front door, suddenly feeling about a hundred years old.

'Hi, I'm Matt Daniels.'

'Jack Colcannon.' Jack shook the other man's hand and in doing so tried to assess his character. The cop's grip was firm without being aggressive, his eye contact comfortably at ease, not in the least furtive or hesitant.

'So you're the family friend,' Matt said pleasantly.

'Yep, that's me.' Jack's tone was wry as he closed the door once Matt had entered the house.

Jack waited until they'd both moved through to the lounge before asking, 'Would you like a drink? Becky is probably going to be ages.'

'No, no drink, thank you.' Matt smiled and added, 'You know her very well, don't you?'

Jack found himself checking to see if the cop's smile made it the full distance to his eyes. It did.

'Yeah, you could say that.'

'You know her brother?'

Jack couldn't really tell from Matt's tone if he'd stated a fact or asked a question. It was a little disquieting, but cops were cops and he'd seen the same trait in Ben a thousand times.

'We were at the same boarding school,' he answered after a tiny pause. 'I used to spend a lot of holiday time at the Baxters' property in the southern highlands.'

'Mr and Mrs Baxter are currently overseas, aren't they?'

'Yes.'

The cop's eyes never once wavered from his, making Jack feel as if he was being cross-examined.

'What about her brother?' Matt asked casually. 'Any idea of where he is right now?'

Jack could feel his hackles rising and did his best to settle them back down.

'No.'

'So you haven't had any contact with him recently?' Matt's gaze seemed very direct and cop-like.

'No.'

'What happened to your eye?'

'I ran into a door.'

Jack could tell Matt didn't believe him but was saved from having to continue the conversation by Becky's arrival.

'I'm so sorry to have kept you waiting, Matt,' she said as she came into the room.

Both men turned to face her and she saw the male appreciation in both gazes as they swept over her, Jack's eyes in particular widening as they came to rest on the upthrust of her breasts.

Good.

It gave her a delicious feeling of power to know she affected him even though she could see he was doing his level best to hide it.

'Shall we go?' She hooked her arm through Matt's and turned towards Jack, sending him an arch look. 'You don't have to wait up. I'll let myself in.'

'I have some paperwork to see to anyway,' he said stiffly. 'I won't be going to bed early.'

'We won't be late,' Matt said. 'I have an early shift in the morning.'

Jack stretched his lips over clenched teeth. 'Have a wonderful time.'

'We will,' Becky said, and ushered her date to the door.

Jack waited until they were in the car before slipping out

to the garage to his own, starting it as quietly as he could and nudging it out to follow the cop's car at a discreet distance.

'I can't believe I'm doing this,' he muttered as he shifted through the gears. 'You owe me, Ben Baxter. Big time.'

As Matt drove to the restaurant strip of Glebe, Becky yet again couldn't help noticing the similarities he shared with Ben. He drove exactly the same way, his eyes repeatedly flicking to the rear-view mirror before darting to the right-hand driver's mirror.

'Jack seems to take his family friend status quite seriously,' Matt observed as he checked the mirrors again. 'Are you two involved in any way?'

'No, not really.' Becky fiddled with the strap of her evening purse.

'But you'd like to be?' Matt guessed, swinging a quick glance in her direction.

Becky gave him a shamefaced look. 'You must think I'm awful, accepting a date with you when I'm in love with someone else.'

Matt gave her a reassuring smile as he parked the car. 'You are one hell of an attractive lady, Becky, but to tell you the truth, every time you bat your eyelashes at me, you remind me of my kid sister.'

'That's really spooky,' she said. 'I was just thinking of how much you remind me of my brother.'

She stepped out of the car onto the pavement as he opened the door for her. 'So you don't mind if we just have dinner?' she asked.

He gave her another one of his easygoing smiles. 'That's fine by me. Come on, I'm starving.'

Once the waiter had left with their orders Matt leaned forward in his chair so that his forearms were resting on the table.

'So what did you want to tell me when you called yesterday? I'm sorry I couldn't speak to you right there and then but I was in the middle of something a little tricky.' His mouth tilted upwards in a dry little smile as he explained, 'I was handcuffed to a suspect, actually, and he wasn't too keen on being up close and personal with me.'

'Oh.' She recalled the scuffling sounds and gave a mental grimace.

'You said some weird stuff had happened,' he prompted.

Becky gave the straw in her glass a little twirl as she told him what had happened at the beach and later at the flat when the rock had come through the window.

'So both notes were handwritten, right?' Matt queried.

'Yes, black felt-tip pen, sort of smudged as if it had been scrawled in a hurry.'

'Do you still have both items?'

'Yes.'

'And you're positive you didn't see anyone loitering around your bag on the beach?'

'I was too busy with the woman who was having the hypo. There were people everywhere—you probably know what it's like when something like that happens. Swarms of people hang about, getting in the way.'

'Yes, unfortunately, I'm all too familiar with the pattern.' Matt took a sip of his drink before continuing, 'What about Jack? Did he see anything?'

'No.' She gave her straw another twirl, her eyes downcast for a moment. 'Actually, he didn't even want me to call the police.'

'Oh, really?' Matt's tone had gone all cop-like again. 'Do you have any idea why he would react in that way?'

She shook her head, raising her eyes to his once more. 'No. He's been acting so…so…' She hunted vainly for a word to describe Jack's behaviour of late.

'Weird?' Matt offered.

'Not really, just sort of more uptight and edgy than usual.'

'Have you considered the possibility that Jack might be in some way involved in the things that have been happening to you?' Matt asked.

Becky gaped at him for a moment. 'You can't be serious!

I admit Jack doesn't like me all that much but I hardly think he wants to bump me off.'

'He was the one who found the note on the sunscreen, right?'

She nodded.

'Where was he when the rock came through the window?'

'He was in the next room.'

'Are you absolutely sure about that?'

She gave another nod.

'He could easily have slapped the note on the sunscreen and arranged for a local kid to send that rock through the window,' Matt said.

'But why?' she asked. 'What possible motive could he have?'

'Maybe he fancies you. You'd be amazed at the lengths some men will go to get the woman they want to move in with them if other attempts have failed.'

She gave a rueful little smile. 'Jack would rather die than admit he needs someone. I don't think he's ever had a relationship that lasted longer than a month or two. He just won't allow anyone to get close to him.'

'So as far as you know you're the first person who has ever moved in with him?'

'Yes…although he doesn't want anyone at the hospital to know about it, which kind of dismantles your theory,' she said.

'I'm just trying to look at this from a few different angles,' he said. 'But as you say, if he's not the commitment type he'd hardly go to those sorts of lengths. It does seem strange he didn't want the police to be involved.' He gave his fingers a quick drum on the table. 'Very strange.'

Becky thought so too but didn't voice it. So much of what had happened over the last few days seemed totally surreal, she hardly knew what to think any more.

After they'd finished their meal Matt began the drive back to Jack's house, his eyes doing the whole mirror routine all over again.

'Can I ask you something, Matt?'

'Sure.' He flicked his gaze to the right-hand mirror and frowned.

'Why do you keep looking in your mirrors all the time? My brother does it, too.' She rubbed her hands up and down her arms a couple of times, suppressing the urge to shudder. 'It gives me the creeps. It always makes me feel as if we're being followed.'

Matt's gaze met hers for a brief but disquieting moment.

'We *are* being followed,' he said.

CHAPTER ELEVEN

BECKY felt her heart leap from her chest to her mouth and drop back down again.

'I'm going to pull over,' Matt said.

She swivelled in her seat, her eyes wide with alarm. 'Are you completely nuts? What if he's got a gun?'

He gave her a little smile as he killed the engine. 'Of course he's got a gun. He's a cop.'

'A *cop?*' Her heart did another somersault, this time with relief.

'Unmarked police car,' Matt said. 'He's been on our tail for several blocks. I'll go and see what he wants.'

Becky turned in her seat and watched as he got out and spoke to the plainclothes officer who had pulled up behind them. The streetlight partially illuminated the officer's face, which Becky found vaguely familiar. Perhaps he'd been a patient some time in the past—it wouldn't be the first time she'd come across someone she'd anaesthetised at St Patrick's. Literally thousands of patients came in and out of a hospital during the course of year, so it was reasonable to expect to run into one on the street occasionally.

Matt returned a short time later and got back behind the wheel. He snapped on his seat belt, his eyes checking his mirror as he did so.

'What did he want?' she asked. 'You weren't speeding, were you?'

He started the car and re-entered the traffic before answering. 'He gave me a caution about my brake lights. Apparently one of them isn't working.'

'Nice to know even cops get pulled over by the more petty members of the force,' Becky said, thinking of the array of minor traffic offences which had trimmed the points scale of her licence to an all-time low.

'He's just doing what he's paid to do.'

Becky turned to look at him as he brought the car to a halt in Jack's street. 'Are you *sure* you haven't met my brother? Or is there some sort of police handbook with a list of stock phrases all cops have to learn off by heart?'

He gave her an unreadable smile as he opened her door for her. 'There are some things the handbook can never teach you. You have to learn as you go.' He closed the door and escorted her up the path. 'Call me if you're worried about anything suspicious. I'd better take the sunscreen and the note for Forensics to examine, but they might not be able to tell us much.'

Becky led him to where she'd left them on a shelf in the laundry, giving him a plastic bag to put them in.

'I'll let you know if we come up with anything like a match on the handwriting, but the sand on the sunscreen bottle will make fingerprints hard to trace,' Matt said at the door.

'Thanks for tonight,' she said. 'I really appreciate the way you're taking a special interest in this.'

'Just doing my job,' he said with a grin. 'By the way, you might want to tell your friend he needs to brush up his skills on surveillance.'

Becky gave him a puzzled look. 'What are you talking about?'

Matt nodded towards the garage where the sound of Jack's car could be heard as he parked it. 'He's been tailing us all evening, and doing a pretty amateur job of it.'

'Jack was following us?' Her mouth fell open in shock. 'You mean, along with the other guy?'

'Tell him he should keep his day job,' Matt said.

'I will,' she said. She waved to him as he left but it was only as he braked at the corner that a little flutter of unease settled in her stomach. As far as she could tell both of his brake lights were working...

'How was your date?' Jack spoke from just behind her.

'What?' She looked at him for a blank moment, while her brain tried to make sense of Matt's deliberate lie.

'Your date with the cop,' Jack said, adding with a curl of his lip, 'Did he make a move on you?'

She glared up at him. 'Why don't *you* tell *me*?'

'What do you mean?'

'You were following us. Matt saw you.'

'So?'

'So you're a lousy private eye.'

'I don't trust him and neither should you,' Jack said.

'Oh, really?' She put her hands on her hips and faced him. 'Well, here's the irony—he doesn't trust you either.'

'What?' He frowned down at her.

Becky tilted her chin at him. 'He thinks you put the note on the sunscreen and organised for someone to toss the rock through the window to convince me to live with you.'

Jack stared at her for several moments. 'Well, that just shows what a dumb cop he is.'

'Meaning?'

'If I wanted a woman to live with me, I'd just ask. I wouldn't have to terrorise her into it, for heaven's sake.'

'But you *don't* want me here.'

'I didn't say that,' he said.

'I don't get this.' She gave him a long contemplative look. 'You do the whole rescuing knight routine but you act as if the armour's choking you. What is it with you?'

'You aren't the easiest person to have around,' he said.

'You have such a way with words,' she sniped resentfully. 'No wonder you have no social life, not to mention any sex life.'

'You know nothing about my sex life.'

'There's nothing to know,' she said. 'You haven't had a date in months. What did Marcia do to you, make you feel something you didn't want to feel?'

No, that's your job, Jack felt like saying, but he couldn't get his mouth to work. He could already feel the stirring heat of his body at her close proximity, the flash of her angry brown eyes reminding him of how much fiery passion her small body contained, a passion he'd experienced twice too often, making him want more and more.

'I really don't understand you, Jack,' Becky said. 'As soon as I get in from my date you're making nasty little cracks about me being involved with someone else, as if you're jealous.'

'I am not jealous.'

'Yes, you are. I saw the way you looked at me tonight. I can recognise attraction when I see it and you had it written all over you. Why else would you follow me all evening?'

'All right,' Jack said stiffly. 'So what if I'm attracted to you? It doesn't mean it has to go any further.'

'Why don't you want it go any further?' she asked.

'You know why,' he answered. 'Neither of us are long-term people. You flit from relationship to relationship and I...' He paused, searching for the right words, but couldn't come up with anything at short notice. The truth was he wanted a relationship with Becky, but on his terms, not Ben's. Ben had asked him to keep her safe, even if he had to pretend to be in love with her to do it. It seemed ironic to be doing the opposite—pretending to *not* be in love with her, in case she ever found out the promise he'd made to Ben.

In love with Becky. The words rattled inside his brain, looking for a place to settle, but he wouldn't allow them to. He didn't want to be in love with anyone and certainly not Becky, who drove him nuts most of the time. How long would such a relationship last—a few days, a few weeks, maybe a few months? What then?

'And you what, Jack?' Becky prompted when he didn't finish his sentence.

He met her eyes once more. 'I don't want to get involved with anyone just now.'

'All right, then,' she said. 'Why don't you prove it?'

'I don't have to prove any—'

She grabbed the front of his shirt and pulled him closer, her soft, warm breath brushing over his face as she issued him a challenge. 'Kiss me and let's see who's telling the truth here.'

'I don't want to kiss you.'

'Liar.'

'Rebecca, this is crazy.'

'Do it, Jack.' She twisted his shirt in her grasp a bit more. 'I dare you.'

Jack held her gaze for several heartbeats before pressing a quick chaste kiss to her cheek, then straightened again, his hand determinedly removing hers from his shirt.

'You call *that* a kiss?' Her tone was deliberately mocking.

'You told me to kiss you and I did.'

She narrowed her eyes at him. 'What are you afraid of, Jack? That you might not be able to stop once you start? That the steely control you're so proud of will tumble down as soon as your mouth touches mine, the way it did twelve years ago, the way it did the other night?'

Jack clenched and unclenched his fist, trying to remove the sensation of her breast beneath his palm, but it was no good, he could still feel her softness. His body was alive with its need of her, his blood already pumping with turbo-charged speed, thickening him almost painfully.

His eyes locked on hers, the air between them crackling with the passion that had taken a grip in the past and never quite let go.

His hands reached for her almost before his brain registered the command, hauling her up against him so her breasts were crushed to his chest, her mouth beneath his.

He was going to kiss her once and let go, he told himself as he tasted her sweetness. One thorough kiss and he would step back from her and walk the short distance to the stairs, delivering a curt goodnight over one shoulder. He swallowed her soft sigh of pleasure as his tongue snaked around hers, and forgot all about stepping back.

Becky felt the full force of Jack's need pushing against her belly, its hardness against her softness making her pulses instantly soar. Desire leapt from its secret hiding place deep within her and raced along her veins, bringing heat and fire to every layer of her skin. She felt alight with her need of him, burning inside and out for his scorching, thrilling touch.

His kiss deepened and her stomach did a free-fall at the sweep of his tongue above, below and around hers. She felt its smooth glide over the surface of her teeth before it dipped back to connect with her tongue once more, the blatantly sexual action making her legs weaken until she was barely able to stand.

One of his hands slipped down to shape her breast, his palm warm and possessive, his touch somewhere between a caress and a hungry grasp of tightly reined-in need. She dragged in a scratchy breath as his mouth left hers to blaze a trail of drugging kisses along the bare skin of her neck and shoulders, making her almost scream with the need to feel his warm lips on the aching points of her breasts.

He shifted the strap of her dress so that the upper curve of her breast was revealed to his burning-gaze, and her ragged breathing halted as his head came down. She felt the rasp of his tongue stroking over her, tantalisingly close to where her tight nipple was pushing against her dress as if in search of his mouth.

She felt the soft slip of fabric against her skin as it fell away from her, and then the hot sucking moistness of Jack's mouth as it finally claimed its prize.

He surged against her, her hips locked to his as she arched her back instinctively to bring him where she most wanted him. She whimpered as he ground hard against her, the silk of desire anointing her between her thighs, reminding her of how much her body ached for him, how it had ached for him for years.

She pressed her hand down between their tightly locked bodies, her fingers shaping him through the tented fabric of his trousers, her senses skyrocketing at the way his body leapt at her touch.

She could sense Jack was trying to dredge up the willpower

to step away from her. She quickly unzipped him and pushed his underwear out of the way to hold him firmly.

'You want me.' Her words came out in a wondering sort of whisper.

'I don't suppose there's any point in denying it when you're holding the evidence in your hand.' His voice had a rough sexy edge to it that sent her senses into another spinning overload.

She caressed him some more, letting her fingertip linger over the moistened tip as she watched the expression on his face contort with pleasure.

'Becky…' he groaned, and leaned into her touch, his hands tight on her shoulders as he tried to anchor himself.

'You don't really want me to stop, do you, Jack?' She held his glittering gaze while her fingers worked their magic.

'I can't give you what you want.'

'Right here and now, all I want is you.'

'You're probably premenstrual or something.' He stared down at the soft bow of her mouth, fighting for control. 'You've been under a terrible strain and your emotions are all over the place. You'll regret this tomorrow, I guarantee it.'

'I won't regret it,' she said. 'I've wanted this for years. Ever since that day you kissed me.'

'That was a big mistake.' He drew in another quick breath as her fingers tightened around him. 'I should never have done that.'

She smiled as she saw his struggle for control under the ministrations of her hand, the deep throb of his blood pulsing through the pads of her fingers.

'You have to stop doing that or I'll…'

'Or you'll what?' she asked softly.

His eyes held hers for a single heartbeat, the air between them heavy with the humidity of need.

'Or I won't be able to control myself.'

'I don't want you to control yourself,' she said. 'I want you to let yourself go and do what you want to do without restraint.'

'You don't know what you're letting yourself in for,' he said, running an exploring finger over the curve of her breast.

'I have had sex before, you know,' she said, sucking in a breath as his mouth moved down to close over her nipple.

He lifted his head after a few deliciously sensual moments, his green gaze meshing with hers. 'Maybe, but you've never had it with me.'

'You think you've got something up your sleeve that none of my ex-fiancés had?' she asked with a teasing glint in her eyes.

He slowly but determinedly backed her up against the wall, his eyes glinting dangerously as his heaving chest moved in time with hers, his aroused body jutting against hers.

'Well, for one thing, sweetheart,' he said dryly, 'it's sure as hell not up my sleeve.'

'It's still not quite where I want it,' she said, pressing even closer, her eyes never once leaving the heat and fire of his.

'Then let's see what we can do about that,' he said, and brought his mouth back down to hers.

This time his kiss was slow and deliberately provocative, drawing from her a response she had not thought herself capable of. Her hands clawed at him to get closer but he captured both of her wrists and held them above her head while his mouth moved over her breasts with devastating thoroughness.

She had never experienced anything so erotic in all her life. Her dress slipped to the floor in a pool around her feet, her lacy panties following when he hooked a finger in them to remove them.

She was standing naked before him, shivering with need as his eyes roved over her hungrily, one hand still firm about her wrists.

'We can't go any further,' he said, his breathing uneven.

Becky felt disappointment hit her like a hammer blow, her whole body sagging with the crushing weight of it. 'Why ever not?'

'Unless we move upstairs where I have a supply of condoms,' he added, his eyes still holding hers.

Her mouth stretched into a tiny seductive smile. 'Then what are we waiting for?'

He let go of her wrists and picked her up and carried her to his bedroom, each step he took towards the bed stirring her into a frenzy of anticipation.

He laid her on the bed while he removed his clothes, not stopping to fold or hang them. Becky smiled as she watched, her stomach fluttering with excitement when she saw how very aroused he was as he came down to join her on the bed.

He reached across her, his chest brushing across her breasts as he opened the bedside-table drawer and took out a condom. He sheathed himself and came back over her, his weight pressing her down until she felt as if she was melting from the heat of his body.

His mouth captured hers as he settled between her hips, the hard probe of his erection searching for her liquid warmth. She wriggled beneath him and he surged forward with a groan against her mouth that echoed throughout her body as her muscles gathered around him. He drove forward and retreated, his movements slow at first then gathering momentum until she was riding the crest of a giant wave that threatened to crash around her at any second.

Her back arched as he sought the point of her pleasure with his long fingers, caressing her, coaxing her towards the release she was craving.

She felt herself going over the edge and clung to him, her whimpering, gasping cries filling the silence as the wave hit her full on, tossing and tumbling her wildly, until she floated, thoroughly spent, back to the surface of reality.

With her body still quivering with aftershocks, she felt him come with a deep shudder against her, his large frame suddenly vulnerable in a way she had never imagined he would allow himself to be, especially not with her.

She stroked her hands along the length of his muscled back, her heart swelling with the need to tell him of her feelings.

'Jack?'

'Mmm?'

She waited a beat or two as she garnered her courage.

Jack raised himself up on his elbows and looked into her eyes. 'If you're going to say what I think you're going to say, then don't.'

'How do you know what I was going to say?' she asked, her tone instantly guarded.

'I've seen that look before,' he said. 'Just about every woman I've ever slept with gives me that look.'

'What look?'

'The how-many-bridesmaids-and-groomsmen-do-you-think-we-should-have look.'

She set her mouth, annoyed that he had spoilt one of the most precious moments of her life. What they had just shared had been beyond anything she'd ever experienced before. Her previous relationships had certainly been intimate but not completely satisfying, a fact which she had always blamed on herself. With Jack, every pulse in her body had come alive, the love she felt for him making the pleasure she'd felt all the more exquisite. And now he had trashed it, turning it sour.

'Well, you're wrong,' she said, pushing him off her roughly. She picked up his shirt off the floor and put it on to cover her nakedness, glaring back at him. 'I wasn't thinking of saying any such thing.'

He got off the bed, disposing of the condom before stepping into his trousers. 'What were you going to say, then? That you've suddenly discovered that you love me?' He gave a rough snort of cynicism and added, 'Of course that's the other predictable outcome of spontaneous sex. Most women, in spite of all the ground they've made up on sexual issues over the last few decades, still seem to need to rationalise their pleasure by confessing to emotions they don't really feel.'

'Right at this moment I don't feel anything for you but unmitigated dislike.'

'Good. Better keep it that way.'

Becky inwardly seethed as he bent down to straighten the bed, repositioning the squashed pillows as if he wanted to remove all trace of her from his room.

'Do you treat all your lovers with the same disdain or is this just a one-off speciality for me?' she asked.

'Look, Becky, we had a brief moment of madness but it's over. The itch has been scratched and hopefully now it will go away.'

'Is that how you see it?'

'You and I would never work.' His eyes shifted away from hers. 'We're not compatible.'

'Apart from sexually,' she pointed out wryly.

His eyes came back to hers for a moment. 'Yes…apart from sexually.' He turned away to give the bed covering one last twitch.

'Must you keep doing that?'

'What?'

'You're decontaminating your bed of my presence. Do you have any idea how offensive that is?'

'I'm doing no such thing. I'm simply remaking the bed.'

Becky took hold of one end of the cover and pulled it off the bed, throwing it on the floor to land in a crumpled heap. She gave the cover a kick with her foot, her flashing brown eyes sending him a challenge. 'Now you'll have to make it all over again.'

Jack knew what she was doing. He'd known her long enough to know she liked to press his buttons and wouldn't be happy until she made him lose control.

He was very close to it, probably much closer than she realised. Although he'd said the itch had been scratched, his was still burning for more of her touch, his body hardening even further as he watched her stomp towards the pillows and toss them one by one on the floor.

'You are being extremely childish,' he said through tight lips.

She snatched up the last pillow, but before she could turn around to throw it at him he removed it from her grasp and tossed it on the bed. His fingers were suddenly like steel around her wrist, his body jamming up against her, shocking her into immobility.

'I know what little game you're playing,' he growled down at her. 'It's called push-Jack-until-Jack-cracks. You do it all the time. You've been doing it for years, haven't you, Becky?'

She compressed her lips, refusing to answer him.

'You're playing a very dangerous game, sweetheart,' he warned her silkily. 'One day very soon you're going to get a whole lot more than you bargained for.'

'You think you can scare me, Jack?' she taunted him recklessly. The highly charged atmosphere between them was sending sparks of desire to her very toes but she couldn't control the urge to push him just a little further. 'If so, you're going to have to try a little harder.'

He held her defiant glare for a long moment before speaking, his voice low and husky, the gravel-against-silk sound sending a shiver of reaction right down her spine. 'Don't say I didn't warn you.'

One small gasp escaped from her lips before his mouth swooped down and covered hers, his hands going to her hips to lock her against him in an embrace that bordered on the thin edge of control. She could feel the simmering anger pulsing between their bodies, anger that was looking for an outlet.

He tore his shirt from her body as her fingers ripped at his trouser fastenings, their mouths locked in a battle of crash-and-burn need as they fell on the bed in a tangle of hungry, searching limbs.

Becky's heartbeat escalated as he left her mouth to move down her quivering body, his lips leaving a trail of fire wherever they touched her.

She drew in an almost painful breath when his warm breath caressed her intimately, his lips and tongue discovering her, tasting her, delighting her, bringing her to the brink before backing off again until she started to beg unashamedly.

'Please, Jack—oh, *please...*'

He came back up over her body and held her fevered gaze for endless heart-kicking seconds as the sensual silence throbbed between them.

'*Please!*' Her single word came out on the back of a broken breath as she writhed restlessly beneath him.

Becky felt her stomach give a flutter of something that hovered somewhere between excitement and fear of the unknown, when with one last burning look from his passion-fired eyes, his strong hands flipped her over so she was on her stomach.

She sucked in a deep scalding breath as he entered her in one deep stroke that nudged her womb, sending a riot of sensation from the very soles of her feet up to where each hair on her head had lifted in sensual reaction.

There was no way she could stop the tumult. Each deep determined movement of his body sent her closer to the precipitous edge until she was finally flung over, her body shaking with the shock waves of release which triggered his own free-fall into paradise.

She felt the expulsion of his life force, the great shudders of his body behind hers joining them in a way she had never experienced before, the sheer eroticism more than she had even imagined her body could cope with.

It had not only coped with it, it wanted more.

Jack had awakened needs in her twelve years ago that in spite of time and distance her body still recognised, the deep throb of need sending her blood with scalding heat through her system every single time his eyes came in contact with hers.

'Jack?'

He eased himself away and gently turned her back to face him, reaching out to brush a strand of wayward blonde hair off her face, his touch surprisingly gentle, his green eyes shadowed with something she couldn't quite identify...was it regret?

Please, don't let it be regret, Becky mentally chanted as the silence stretched endlessly, awkwardly—painfully.

CHAPTER TWELVE

'TELL me I didn't hurt you, Becky,' Jack's voice sounded rough around the edges. 'That was not my intention, no matter what I said.'

'You didn't hurt me.'

His eyes held hers for what seemed a very long time.

'You are the most exciting lover I've ever had,' he finally confessed, although, it seemed to Becky, a little reluctantly. 'I don't think I've ever felt that way before.'

'Neither have I,' she answered with complete honesty.

He traced a fingertip over the upper curve of her mouth, his chest rising and falling in time with hers.

'Jack?'

His thumb and index finger gently pinched her mouth closed.

She tried again, 'Jaffft.'

The corners of his mouth kicked up in a little smile. 'You know, I could get really used to this, having you quiet for once.'

The telephone jangled by his bedside and, without letting her gaze go, he reached out with his left hand and picked it up to answer it.

'Colcannon.'

'Jack?' Ben's low urgent whisper sounded in his ear.

'Yeah...hang on a sec.' Jack released his hold and got off the bed to put some distance between the phone and Becky. He mouthed 'Excuse me' to her as he moved to the other side of the room, out of her hearing. 'Sorry about that,' he said into the receiver, his voice low. 'I'm not alone.'

'Becky's with you now?' Ben asked in a hushed tone.

'Yes.'

'Thank God for that.' Jack heard Ben draw in a breath of relief. 'Don't let her out of your sight. Promise me, Jack. It's really important.'

Shouldn't be too hard, Jack thought as he glanced back at his bed where Becky was lying like a kitten that had overdosed on cream.

'Where are you?' he asked Ben.

'I can't tell you. Just keep my sister out of harm's way.' The phone clicked off as if someone had snatched it out of Ben's hand.

He stared at the receiver for a moment or two, his brow furrowed.

'Wrong number?' Becky asked, sitting up and tucking her hair behind one ear.

'Yeah.'

After a long silence she slipped out of the bed and, taking the sheet with her to cover herself, stood just in front of him, her eyes shadowed with worry as they met his.

'I thought I should tell you I'm not currently on the Pill.'

It took a full thirty seconds for his brain to register what she'd just said. He hadn't used a condom the second time. He had wanted her so badly he hadn't stopped, hadn't, in fact, been able to stop.

He stared at her in a shocked silence as the blood drained from his face, the extremities of his body suddenly feeling icy cold.

'Tell me you're joking.'

'I'm not joking.' She chewed on her lip. 'I was taking a break. I was changing brands and wanted to make sure I had a month or two off between.'

'You should have told me.' He dragged a hand through his hair. 'You should have stopped me.'

'I think I'm in a safe period.'

'You *think?*'

She gave him an uncertain little glance. 'I hope.'

He dragged in a deep breath and paced the floor.

'Don't get any ideas, Becky,' he said, turning back to face

her. 'I'm not interested in marriage. I've seen what a bad relationship can do and I want no part of it.'

'But you've seen good relationships as well,' she pointed out. 'What about my parents? They've been married thirty-five years and are as in love now as they ever were.'

She had a point, he had to admit. The Baxters were the most stable, loving couple he'd ever met, and if he could be assured he'd have that sort of relationship, nothing would stop him from going for it. But he wasn't the easygoing man Becky's father was, and Becky was certainly nothing like her quiet and somewhat shy mother.

'Your parents are great people and I admire them for lasting the distance, but I haven't got any plans for a long-term relationship, and certainly not with someone who irritates the hell out of me most of the time.'

'There's that inimitable Colcannon charm, smashing every female ego in sight again.' Becky sent him a caustic look. 'Hell, you really know how to make a girl feel great about herself.'

'Listen, Becky, we wouldn't even be in this situation if you weren't the most tempting woman I've ever been associated with. I've been fighting this for years as it is.'

Becky couldn't help feeling slightly mollified by his confession, grudging as it was. 'Thanks.'

'I mean it, Becky.' His hands came down to rest on the top of her shoulders, his eyes commanding hers to meet his. 'I don't know how I've kept my hands off you for so long. Tonight was...unbelievable.'

'But you don't want it to continue.'

His chest rose and fell on a sigh. 'If I thought we could have an affair without leaving any lasting damage after it's over, I would take you right back to bed here and now.'

'Don't you ever get lonely way up there in that ivory tower?' she asked.

He held her look for a long moment.

'What are you trying to say, Becky? That you want some sort of relationship with me?'

Becky lowered her gaze from the intense probe of his. 'I don't know what I want,' she lied, even as the words began to drum incessantly in her brain: *I want you! I want to have your children. I want you for ever.*

'As I said before, this is a very unsettling time for you,' he said. 'Your parents are out of the country and Ben's not around. You're looking for security, which is understandable given the circumstances. I can offer you a house to stay in for as long as you need it but as to long-term promises, I'm definitely not your man.'

Becky was glad he'd turned away so he didn't see the disappointment on her face. She felt totally crushed. She had loved him for so long and yet while he clearly desired her, he had no permanent place for her in his life. She was no more than a passing interest, an itch he'd had to scratch in order for it to disappear once and for all.

She knew it would be pointless trying to convince him of her love for him: her three broken engagements hardly helped prop up her credibility. But while he maintained his desire had been slaked once and for all, Becky couldn't help hoping it would return just as hers was doing, the tentacles of clawing need coiling their way through to where her heart lay beating behind her breast, where his mouth had so recently been.

The female change room was abuzz with excitement as soon as Becky walked through the door the next morning to get changed for Jack's list.

'Well, well, well, here she is now.' Gwen gave Becky a knowing wink as she nudged one of the other nurses on duty for theatre. 'Word has it this is the new woman in Jack Colcannon's life.'

Becky stared at the women in blank bewilderment, her cheeks firing up guiltily.

'You're surely not going to deny it, are you, Becky?' Gwen asked.

'I—I don't know what you're talking about.' Becky reached

for theatre overalls and began taking off her outer layer of clothing to put them on over her underwear.

'David Barker, the new orderly, told us,' Gwen said. 'Apparently David lives in the eastern suburbs and saw you at the beach on Sunday. He does the odd shift as a lifeguard. He lives around the corner from Jack and saw you and Jack leaving his house together this morning.'

'So?' Becky snapped up the buttons on her overalls.

Gwen put her hands on her hips, her eyes twinkling.

Becky reached for her pink bandana to cover her hair and tied it roughly, her movements agitated and jerky.

'I've been having some trouble at my flat lately.' She addressed the mirror in which she could see the interested faces behind her. 'Jack offered me his spare room till things get sorted out.'

'What sort of trouble?' Jenny, a nurse, asked, frowning. 'A break-in?'

'Among other things.'

'What other things?' Jenny and Gwen asked in unison.

Becky gave a despondent sigh. 'It seems I have some sort of stalker.'

'A stalker!'

Not only were the two nurses very good at unison, they had the wide-eyed look of shock down pat as well, Becky mused wryly.

'Have you called the police?' This was from a still wide-eyed Gwen.

'Yes, and they're doing all they can.'

'Wow.' Jenny exchanged glances with Gwen. 'Somehow I've never imagined Jack Colcannon as the bodyguard type. He's bad enough to work with at times, being so picky and all. What's he like to live with?'

'I'm not living with him,' Becky insisted. 'I just stayed with him a couple of nights. Anyway, I'm planning on getting another place as soon as I can. There was an advertisement on the staffroom noticeboard this morning—one of the new recovery staff is looking for a housemate. I'm looking at it this evening.' She dug out the piece of paper she'd written the name and number on. 'Lyndal Hanlon. Do either of you know her?'

Gwen shook her head. 'Don't think so. What about you, Jen?'

'Can't say the name rings a bell, but it can't hurt to have a look at what's on offer. Sharing an apartment is a whole lot more sensible than living alone, especially since you've been having a bit of trouble lately.'

'That's what I thought,' Becky said, tucking the paper in her locker with the rest of her things.

'Come on,' Gwen said, glancing at the clock. 'Jack will be bawling us out if we're late. You know how much he hates service lists as it is.'

Becky knew exactly what Jack thought about them. Service lists were initiated by the hospital administration to reduce the ever-lengthening public waiting lists. A service list meant that there was no training, just the consultant operating with the registrar assisting, and getting through as many of the longest backed-up cases on the waiting list.

Over the next eight hours the operating team was meant to get through five laparoscopic cholecystectomies, three laparoscopic hernias and a haemorrhoidectomy. On the end of the list there were three skin lesions called 'on call' cases. Those patients would be done only if there was time. They would wait at home, fasting, and would either be called to come into the hospital or be informed their operation had been cancelled due to lack of time.

While service lists had become a virtual necessity to bring some semblance of movement to public waiting lists, they robbed registrars of hands-on operating, and made operating seem like a production line, where there was pressure to perform a given operation in a specified time.

Becky knew the reason Jack was given these lists was that the administrators knew he could perform at that level. He was a competent surgeon with the sort of experience under his belt that made him work quickly and efficiently—they could virtually time a routine operation in his hands to within ten minutes.

She followed the women out of the change room and mentally prepared herself. Jack wasn't going to be in a good mood, and once she told him about the alternative accommodation she'd organised it would only get worse.

Jack did his initial scrub at the sink, recalling his short but disturbing conversation with Ben. Ben wasn't normally the panicking type but there had definitely been something in his tone that suggested things weren't going to plan.

He wondered how his friend dealt with the stress of it all. His own work-related stress was bad enough, but at least none of his patients ever threatened him, other than with a thankfully rare legal suit. He couldn't imagine what it would be like to wake up each day not sure if it was going to his last, as Ben did—as, he supposed, many police officers did.

He couldn't imagine his life without Ben in it, or indeed Veronica and William Baxter, who had been substitute parents for as long as he could remember. Those holidays at the farm had been his life raft in those difficult teenage years when outright rebellion had often tempted him. Steady, easygoing William had guided him, while Veronica had nurtured him in her quiet unassuming way.

And then there was Becky.

He'd been ignoring his feelings about her for so long, doing his best to keep away from the temptation of becoming involved with her, telling himself it would complicate his relationship with her family, when all the time it had had more to do with his need for control in his life.

Becky made him feel out of control. She always had. She threatened him at the most elemental level, but there was no point hiding away from it any longer. He'd hardly slept most of the night, agonising over it, his body burning with the scent of her on his skin, his flesh still aching for more of her touch.

He recalled his words to her with a mental cringe, how he'd

insisted on no long-term promises, when all the time he wanted permanency—with her.

He loved her.

He wanted to spend the rest of his life waking up next to her. He wanted to see that tousled blonde head and those sparkling-with-mischief brown eyes every single morning. He wanted to see her bring his children into the world, he wanted to live a long and happy life doing the things he'd missed out on as a child—picnics, holidays and the sort of family celebrations that gave structure and security, maybe even meaning, to one's life.

But while Becky was in love with the idea of settling down, she wasn't in love with him—or, if she was, it wasn't likely to last much longer than any of her other relationships. Her third engagement had set some sort of record by lasting more than two months. The other two hadn't made it past the first three or four weeks.

What hope would he have of getting her to commit to him for life? Wasn't that the whole reason he'd shied away from the whole notion of marriage in the first place? He hated failure. He didn't want to replicate the disaster of his parents' marriage and divorce, knowing firsthand the heartache it caused.

He'd seen the way his parents had destroyed each other's happiness and that of everyone around them. He had cousins he hadn't seen since he was ten, aunts and uncles who never contacted him in case it upset either his mother or father, who had insisted on their relatives taking sides.

Would he be able to convince Becky to marry him in spite of all he'd said to the contrary?

He *had* to convince her.

She might even now be carrying his child! The thought took hold, spreading an unfamiliar, tantalising sense of warmth right through his body. He could almost picture her soft curves swelling with the presence of his baby, her creamy skin glowing with the surge of hormones, her brown eyes luminous.

For years he'd thrown himself into a punishing work routine to avoid facing the truth of how he felt about her, how he'd always felt about her. But there was no escaping it now. His body had decided it for him, tying her to him in the most primal way possible.

If only he could fast-forward the day so he could get her alone and tell her how he felt.

He took a deep breath and shouldered open the theatre door to reach for a sterile towel before donning his gown and mask. His eyes went to where Becky was in position, with the patient anaesthetised. She lifted her gaze briefly to meet his, but her normally expressive face for once gave nothing away.

He shifted his gaze and encountered speculative looks being passed between the theatre staff, in particular Gwen, who was smiling her usual knowing smile.

'Let's get started,' he said with a mental grimace, and began issuing instructions to Jenny, the instrument nurse.

'Betadine prep, please,' Jack repeated for the fourth time on starting the fourth gall bladder.

'Steridrape,' he went on, 'diathermy on 30 coag, cutting off, zero degree telescope, please, turn on the stack, white-set—'

'Listen, Jack,' Becky said from behind the anaesthetic machine, 'this is the fourth gall bladder you've done today, right?'

'Yes. So?'

'Jenny's been a theatre sister for…let's see now, twelve years, right?'

'Thirteen,' said Jenny proudly.

'What's your point, Dr Baxter? Scalpel, please, Jenny.'

'That *is* my point. Jenny can see you want the scalpel. You don't need to tell her every time. It's so monotonous and doesn't recognise the professionalism of the theatre staff. Jenny's been scrubbing for laparoscopic cholecystectomies for years. She's done hundreds of them. She knows the routine. You don't have to go through the whole list of things time and time again. Women are not completely dumb, you know.'

'Did I say women were dumb?' Jack said, frowning at her behind his mask. 'Langenbach retractors.'

'They're in her hand—ready, see. Tell him what he'll want next, Jenny.'

'Next he'll want the scalpel again for the linea alba.'

'Scalpel, please, Jenny.'

Jenny rolled her eyes and handed it to him.

'Look, will you stop it?' Becky glared at Jack. 'Just let her give you what you need, and cut out the repetition. It's driving me nuts.'

Jenny held out the seven-inch artery forceps ready for Jack to take.

'Seven-inch artery forceps,' Jack said automatically.

'Why do you have to go through everything every time? What is it with you?' added Becky, hoping her insistence would counter the rumours that were circulating about them.

'Listen, Dr Baxter,' Jack said in the patronising tone she'd come to expect from him, 'when was the last time you flew to Melbourne? Diathermy hook, please.'

'Last year.' She caught the tail end of Gwen and Jenny's she's-trying-to-put-us-off-the-scent look, narrowed her eyes at them briefly, then turned back to Jack. 'What's that got to do with recognising nursing professionalism?'

'Gall-bladder grasper, please.' Jack said. 'What did you see the pilot doing as you went past the cockpit?'

'Hell, I don't know. Chatting up one of the cabin staff probably.'

'Clip applier, please. No, what you saw him doing was going through a checklist, checking all procedures. Endoscissors.'

'So?'

'Would you feel safe flying if the pilot ignored the procedures, just started up the plane and took off, ignoring the weather and disregarding the control-tower instructions?'

Becky compressed her lips without answering.

'Well, that's how I operate,' Jack said. 'Logical, sequential. One step at a time, check and talk through each step at a time. Gall-bladder extractor, then we'll close.'

'I give up, Mr Perfect step-by-step,' Becky said, as Jenny handed Jack the closure suture for the linea alba.

'Gentamicin for the wound, then subcuticular vicryl for skin, right?' Jenny said. 'And by the way, you used the airline pilot lecture three weeks ago when Di was scrubbed in. She told me in the tearoom.'

'You'd be amazed at what you hear in the tearoom,' Gwen said from behind the stack where she was changing a carbon-dioxide bottle, sending a wink in Becky's direction.

'I can just imagine,' Jack murmured darkly.

'Usually it's boring stuff like which Hollywood celebrity is sleeping with which starlet,' Jenny said, twinkling at Gwen.

'Humph.' Jack's grunt told the scrub nurse exactly what he thought about the trashy magazines that littered the tearoom.

Becky gave the nurses a warning glance but Gwen was clearly not responding to it.

'Word has it you have a new lady in your life, Jack,' Gwen said.

There was a short, hard silence, broken only by the sound of the anaesthetic machine doing its job. Jack's eyes collided with Becky's for a brief moment before returning to the patient on the table.

'You shouldn't believe everything you hear on the hospital grapevine,' he said as he closed the wound.

'No, but when a member of staff actually sees you together at the beach and then leaving your house this morning, one has to assume something's going on. Right?'

Jack was glad he'd put the last stitch in. He put the instruments in the dish Gwen was holding out for him and explained, 'Quite by coincidence we happened to be at the beach when a lady with diabetes had a fit. Dr Baxter and I stabilised things until the ambos arrived.'

Becky extubated the patient as the transport bed was wheeled in and positioned next to the operating table.

'Ever the hero, Jack.' Gwen grinned as the patient was slid over onto the bed. 'But what about the rest?'

He gave her an icy look. 'The rest?'

Gwen's eyes danced with middle-aged mischief as she met his chilly look. 'Was it also just a coincidence that Dr Baxter was seen leaving your premises with you this morning?'

Jack's mouth opened and closed, but before he could get anything out Becky spoke up on her way past with the patient.

'I told you, Gwen, in the change room. I'm using Jack's spare room until I find another flat, which I hope will be this evening after work. And as for coming to work in Jack's car, my car has been in the garage and is being delivered to the hospital this afternoon.' She pushed the trolley through the doors with the orderly's help and added over her shoulder, 'I can assure you there's nothing going on. Jack's not my type anyway.'

Jack stripped off his gown and stuffed it in the bin, his stomach turning over in panic. Becky was already hunting for another place to live. He had to stop her, and fast. As for her car, he'd told the mechanic to take his time repairing it. He didn't want her driving around in it until he was absolutely sure it was safe to do so. Shredded tyres were one thing, but the mechanic had mentioned something about the brakes being faulty. What if someone was tampering with her car?

He glanced at the clock once more and stifled a groan of despair. It could be hours before he could speak to Becky alone.

'What's next on the list?' he asked, as all eyes turned his way. 'Tell me it's not going to be the haemorrhoidectomy.'

Gwen looked at up from the list pasted on the wall and sent him a teasing wink as he shouldered open the scrub room doors. 'Bummer,' she said.

Jack caught up to Becky in the corridor outside the main tea-room once the list was over. Before she could offer a word of protest he ushered her into one of the equipment rooms and closed the door behind them.

'What are you doing?' she asked, brushing his hand off her arm.

'I need to talk to you.'

'Look, I didn't tell Gwen or Jenny a thing, if that's what you're going to accuse me of.'

'Who saw us?'

'David Barker, the new orderly. He does the occasional stint as a lifeguard at Bondi. He also apparently lives near you, too.'

'Damn.' He clenched and unclenched his fists. 'I didn't want anyone to know just yet.'

Becky threw him a caustic look. 'Look, Jack, I'm a little tired of these mixed messages I'm getting from you. If you're so embarrassed about having slept with me, why don't you just come out and say it? I can handle it.'

'It's not that,' he said. 'I wanted to sleep with you. I just didn't want the whole hospital speculating on our relationship before we had time to negotiate it.'

'Negotiate it?' She gave him a confused look. 'Does that mean you're thinking about having some sort of relationship with me? I thought you said last night—'

He took one of her hands in his and brought it, palm upward, to his mouth, pressing a soft kiss to it before closing her fingers one by one as if to lock the imprint of his lips there.

'W-why did you do that?' she asked, searching his face.

He held her gaze for endless seconds. 'I've been doing some thinking and I've decided I want to have a relationship with you.'

She gave one small swallow. 'W-what sort of relationship?'

'I don't know.' His mouth twisted as he fought with his emotions. 'Can we just try it on for size and see what happens?'

She pulled her hand out of his and stepped back from him. 'You know, if I didn't already know you were a Capricorn I would swear you were born under the sign of Gemini. Talk about a split personality.'

'I mean it, Becky,' he insisted. 'I want to have a relationship with you.'

'What sort of duration are we talking about here?' she asked after a small silence.

He gave a loose-shouldered shrug, hoping it would disguise his feelings of vulnerability. 'Who knows? What's your record?'

'I don't have a good record. Three months is the longest, but the last month of that was hell on wheels so it doesn't count. What's yours?'

'A month or so.'

'Not great odds, then, for either of us,' she commented.

'No, but at least the sex is great, so that should notch up a few more weeks or months.'

'I can't live with you,' she said. 'I'm getting a new place this evening. It's all organised.'

'But you have to live with me!' Jack blurted, his heart dropping to his stomach in panic.

Becky stared at him for a moment. 'Why?'

'Because…because I like having you around.'

'You *hate* having me around,' she said. 'I see the way you grit your teeth when I don't rinse my cup or straighten the cushions on the sofa.'

'That's just because I'm not used to sharing my space. I can change.'

'Jack, come on. Surely you don't expect me to buy that? You're a control freak through and through. Every little thing I do annoys you. We wouldn't last a week before you kicked me out on my butt.'

'I don't want you to live by yourself.'

'I'm not going to be living by myself,' she announced proudly. 'One of the new recovery staff posted an ad on the staff noticeboard this morning, looking for a person to share a cottage at Bronte. I'm going to check it out this evening. It sounds perfect.'

'Recovery staff? Which one?'

'A new one. What does it matter which one?' she asked. 'What are you, some sort of snob? The recovery staff are just as important to running the theatre as a surgeon is, probably more important when you come to think of it.'

'You know nothing about this person and yet you're committing to living with them?'

She rolled her eyes at him. 'I will not be *living* with them in the sense you mean. I will simply be sharing accommodation.'

'You shared accommodation with me, and look what happened,' he pointed out.

'That was different,' she said.

'How so?'

'Well…' She chewed her lip for a moment. 'We have a sort of chemistry.'

'Then move in with me and let's get on with it.'

'No.'

'Marry me, then.'

Becky's mouth dropped open, her eyes growing as wide as saucers. 'W-what did you say?'

'Marry me, Becky.'

She slapped the side of her head with her hand as if to dislodge some errant thought. 'I need to get my hearing tested. I thought I heard you ask me—no, not ask, *tell* me—to marry you.'

'I did.' His throat moved up and down in a swallow.

'Are you feeling all right, Jack?' She gave him a narrow-eyed, suspicious look.

'I mean it,' he said. 'I want you to marry me. Let's skip the engagement part. It obviously hasn't worked all that well with you, and I have no time for it. I want you in my bed and in my life without any unnecessary delays.'

Becky couldn't believe what she was hearing. A few hours ago Jack had been telling her she had no permanent place in his life. Now he was asking—*instructing*—her to marry him.

'So I'm assuming from this out-of-the-blue proposal that that itch of yours hasn't yet responded to treatment?' she said with an arch of one brow.

'It's driving me out of my mind,' he said, staring down at

her mouth. 'I want you, I've always wanted you. I was being a jerk last night. I didn't mean a word I said. You got under my skin and I didn't want you to know how much. Put it down to stupid male pride but believe me now, Becky. I couldn't sleep last night for thinking about how you make me feel.'

'Jack...' She couldn't help staring up at him in a combination of shock and growing wonder. 'Are you saying you—you care for me?'

His green eyes meshed with hers. 'I love you, Becky.'

Her mouth opened and closed and her heart seemed to trip over itself in her chest. 'You love me? As in *love* me?'

'Yeah,' he said, reaching for her. 'You got a problem with that?'

She nestled against him, her head settling against his chest where his heart was beating, her senses filling with the scent of his maleness.

'No,' she sighed. 'I don't have a problem with that at all. I just can't believe this is true.' She wanted to believe it, but...

He eased her away from him, looking down at her with earnestness. 'I think I probably started loving you when you scratched my car.'

She gave him a worried look and captured her lip between her teeth momentarily. 'I still haven't paid you for that. It totally slipped my mind. It must have cost a fortune.'

He smiled. 'I wasn't talking about the other day.'

'You weren't?'

He shook his head. 'I was talking about that time I tried to give you a parking lesson twelve years ago.'

'Oh.' She looked away in embarrassment. 'That.'

'Yes, that.'

'I was being petulant and childish—'

'You were beautiful and irresistible and I'd wanted to kiss you for ages,' he said. 'It gave me the perfect excuse to do so.'

She raised her eyes back to his, slowly. 'Really?'

'Really. Why else do you think I was out at your parents' property weekend after weekend?'

She gave this some thought, her brow furrowing slightly. 'Does Ben know how you feel?'

'I haven't told him but I think he's probably guessed.'

She eased herself out of his hold slightly so she could look up at him properly. This was all happening so fast she had to put the brakes on to get her head around it.

Jack loved her.

He wanted to marry her when just hours ago he had said exactly the opposite.

What in the world had changed his mind?

She wanted to believe it had been one of those bolt-of-lightning revelations where the truth had hit him the way it had her, but something about Jack's manner worried her. He seemed way too tense, his proposal hurried and out of character for someone who was renowned for his self-control.

She gave an inward frown as she considered what had happened over the last few days.

'Have you spoken to Ben lately?' she asked after a little silence.

Jack didn't answer immediately, which he knew made her even more suspicious. He could see the reflection of it in her brown eyes as they centred on his, her expression wary, the line of her mouth hard instead of soft and trusting.

'Ben? No,' he lied, hating himself. 'Have you?'

'No, but I'm afraid for him.' She stepped away from him, rubbing her hands up and down her upper arms as she paced the small room. 'I can't help thinking he's in some sort of trouble. It's been weeks since he called me. He never leaves it that long. I'm worried, Jack. Really worried.'

'He's an undercover cop, Becky,' he said in his best reassuring tone. 'You know he can't contact you or anyone when he's on a mission. It's the name of the game. He'll come out when he's good and ready.'

'If something doesn't happen to him first,' she said, her tone despondent.

Jack put his hands on her shoulders and turned her to face him, his eyes steady on hers. 'Stop worrying about him. He's a big boy, he can look after himself.'

She gave a little sigh and rested her head on his chest once more, her arms slipping around his waist and squeezing tight. 'I don't know what I would have done without you, Jack, these last few days.'

He stroked his fingers through the silk of her hair, breathing in the scent of her, his chin coming to rest on the top of her head. He couldn't believe it had taken him so long to recognise his feelings. It was like a whole facet of his personality had been locked away until now. The way she made him feel was a revelation. Each breath he drew in seemed to carry her on it until he felt as if she was taking up residence inside him, her softness soothing the rough edges of his embittered soul.

He simply couldn't imagine life without her now. She completed him in a way no one had ever done before. Why had it taken him so long to recognise it? Hell, what if he hadn't and she'd gone ahead and married someone else?

'Jack?' Becky nestled even closer, her soft body pressing against him in all the right places.

'Mmm?' His voice cracked on the sound, his throat feeling as if a walnut had lodged itself halfway down.

'I love you,' she said.

Jack wished he could believe her but she fell in and out of love like some people fell in and out of bed.

'Since when?' he asked after a small silence.

'Since always,' she said, and reaching up on tiptoe pressed a soft kiss to his neck.

'So, does this mean you're going to cancel the apartment you were going to look at?' he asked, running a fingertip down the length of her nose.

Becky was torn with indecision. On one hand she could think of nothing she wanted more than never again leaving Jack's side, but on the other she needed some time to get used to the knowledge of his love. It was all so new, so sudden and unexpected, and she wanted to be absolutely sure she didn't ruin things in the way she had in the past, by rushing headlong into a relationship that had only just started to grow.

'I don't want to rush into this.'

'But we don't have time to waste,' he said. 'You might be pregnant.'

She lifted her eyes back to his, her expression instantly clouding. 'Is that why you've changed your mind so abruptly?'

'No, of course not!' Jack insisted hurriedly. 'I love you, Becky. I want to marry you as soon as possible. I told you, I've finally come to my senses and I don't want to waste any more time than I already have. You're so good for me, surely you can see that?'

Becky was still thinking about how to answer him when both their pagers went off, signalling an emergency in A and E.

Jack read out the short message and instantly frowned. 'Gunshot wound. Come on, Becky, looks like our day hasn't quite finished. This doesn't sound good.'

CHAPTER THIRTEEN

'ARE you on call *again?*' Becky asked as they rushed down the stairs instead of waiting for the lift.

'No, but all the other theatres must be tied up.' He held the exit door for her and added, 'What about you?'

She shook her head as she brushed past. 'Not officially, but I said I'd cover for Graham Rogers for a couple of hours. He had an important appointment.' She checked her watch. 'He's due back in half an hour or so.'

'Let's see what we've got,' Jack suggested. 'You can always hand over when Graham gets here.'

When Jack pushed open the doors of A and E there were at least five police officers in full uniform pacing the department, two of them shouting into mobile phones, with the A and E nursing director shouting equally loudly at them to either turn off their phones or get out of her emergency room.

On the trolley of the resus bay was a blood-soaked male body, which had trailed a series of splatters right from the front door of A and E to the resus room. He had obviously not been brought in by ambulance through the ambulance bay, and, judging from the bloodstains on a couple of the police officers hanging around the emergency room door, Jack guessed that they had rushed him in.

'What have we got?' Jack asked John Hickson, the emergency physician in charge of Resus.

'Thirty-five-year-old male shot twice, Jack. In the left chest, entry wound left pectoral. We haven't log-rolled yet to check exit wounds. Haemopneumothorax clinically on the left, breathing spontaneously and sats OK, but hypovolaemic, pulse 150 and BP 80 systolic.' He glanced at Becky and asked,

'Becky, can you assume airway management while I get a left chest drain and a second IV line in.'

Becky stood completely frozen as she looked down at the patient. It was the plainclothes officer Matt Daniels had spoken to the other night. She'd thought then that he'd looked familiar and now she remembered why. He had come into A and E with a patient who had been under police guard a few weeks ago. She'd been called down to assess the prisoner prior to administering an anaesthetic, and the detective had introduced himself to her as Tony Dubrovnik. She'd remembered the name as it was the same as the Croatian city she'd visited on a European trip the year before.

'Dr Baxter? Are you with us on this or not?' John asked impatiently.

'Right,' Becky said as she moved to bag and mask the patient on high-flow oxygen prior to intubation. 'Sucker,' she ordered the assisting nurse, her heart thumping heavily in her chest as she forced herself to go onto autopilot.

Becky suctioned out the mouth of the now semi-conscious patient, then bagged and masked him. 'Give 100 milligrams sux now through that second line, John. He needs intubation now, he's hard to ventilate and his JVPs are up to his jaw. Trachea's midline.'

'I'm putting in the chest tube,' Jack said. 'That'll leave you to oversee the resus, John.'

'Good, thanks, Jack. Sux is in, Dr Baxter.'

The patient gave several brief twitches as the sux took effect, paralysing him so that Becky could intubate. Grasping the laryngoscope, Becky inserted an endotracheal tube and connected it to the insufflation bag, ventilating until the sats stabilised.

'I'm using 20 mls one per cent Xylocaine with adrenalin LA,' Jack said, so that John could keep tally of all the drugs used, even though the entire resuscitation was being recorded on video from the ceiling-mounted camera, as was routine in A and E.

'This might be the time to ask the audience to leave,' Jack said over his shoulder, referring to the milling police.

'They won't budge,' John informed him. 'This is one of their officers. Plainclothes. They're not saying much but they insist he be under police guard at all times.'

Jack grunted. He prepped the left chest, and made an incision over the lateral chest wall. He tracked over the top of the sixth rib and punctured the pleura with a popping sensation, then inserted a clamped intercostal drain towards the apex of the left lung, connected it to the underwater seal bottle and released the clamp. Immediately fresh blood poured out into the underwater bottle, the flow slowing over the next few minutes. Jack sewed in the drain with heavy black silk and taped the connectors to the tube and bottle. The drain continued to swing and bubble, but there was no further major bleeding.

'That's a total of less than 500 mls blood from the left chest, hardly enough to drop his BP to 80. Chest sounds clear. What's his pulse and BP now?' John asked.

'Pulse still 130, BP is now 70 systolic.'

'I don't get it,' said John. 'How come the BP is so low with only 500 mls loss?'

'I don't think there was a tension on the left with mediastinal shift,' Jack said. 'That would markedly drop his BP from mediastinal compression, but his trachea was midline wasn't it, Becky?'

'Yes, midline, but his jugular venous pressure is still up,' Becky said.

'Get the ECG dots on, Rachel,' John Hickson ordered the A and E nurse. 'And I want to listen to his chest again.'

John placed his stethoscope over the patient's praecordium while Becky secured the endotracheal tube with tape and Jack examined the abdomen and gave instructions to the radiologist, who had just arrived.

'Heart sounds are muffled, Jack, and look at the ECG— very low voltage,' John observed.

'You're thinking cardiac tamponade?'

'Got all the signs, and he's now had three litres of colloid and no response whatsoever.'

'That'll mean a cardiac injury if this is just a gunshot. His BP is desperate, John. It justifies the risk of a pericardial tap.'

'I agree. If we don't do something now he's going to expire. Jack, you're the trauma surgeon, I'd prefer you do it.'

'Yes of course. Get me a 12-gauge cardiac needle, Nurse, and skin prep. John, get straight onto Cardiac Theatre. A pericardial tap is only likely to give short-term improvement. See which cardiac surgeon is in the hospital and tell them to see if one of the cardiac anaesthetists can get a bypass machine on line quickly.'

Jack prepped the epigastric region with Betadine, and made a small nick in the skin. Keeping one eye on the ECG monitor, he inserted the cardiac needle at a 45-degree angle, aiming towards the tip of the left scapula. On the end of the cardiac needle was a three-way tap and syringe. Centimetre by centimetre Jack advanced the needle, each time aspirating on the syringe and checking the monitor for VEBs. When the needle reached about 15 centimetres, aspiration produced fresh blood.

'I've got fresh pericardial bleeding,' reported Jack. 'Sixty mls out and still coming. Any improvement in BP?'

'BP 80,' Rachel replied. 'No real change.'

'There's blood still coming out fast and fresh, John. This guy's got a cardiac injury that has got to be closed quickly. What's the cardiac theatre situation?'

'There's no hope there, Jack. They're in the middle of a triple bypass, which will tie up the cardiac theatre, their anaesthetist and the bypass machine for at least another hour and a half.'

'This guy's not going to last twenty minutes unless we crack his chest and repair that cardiac defect. Are there any other cardiac or thoracic surgeons around?' Jack asked.

'Not in the hospital, no, I already asked,' John said. 'You're it, I'm afraid. He's dying in front of us. If you can't crack the chest we may as well start calling his relatives with the bad news.'

'Get him up to my general theatre now,' Jack ordered. 'Becky, hand over ventilation to Rachel, get on the phone and tell Jenny to set up for an immediate thoracotomy plus the vascular extras. Get Robert and the Surg. B or C registrar in to help and I'll stay with him on the way up to control this pericardial tap and get O-negative blood started. Get patient transport now, John.'

Less than four minutes later, Jack, Rachel and John were in the patient lift, struggling to maintain some blood pressure, while two porters held the bed steady. The police were forced to use the normal lifts, but they weren't happy about it.

The lift seemed to take for ever to travel the four floors up to the operating theatre.

'Looks bad, Mr Colcannon,' David, the new orderly, commented as the lift hydraulics hissed beneath them.

'He's definitely not well,' Jack agreed.

'He's a cop, right?' David asked.

'Yeah,' Jack answered vaguely, mentally preparing himself for what was ahead.

'Should have been wearing a bulletproof vest,' David said. 'I guess that means the place will be crawling with cops.'

Jack didn't answer.

The lift doors wheezed open, and the trolley and its entourage headed up the corridor towards Jack's theatre, theatre overshoes and paper headgear ignored in the emergency.

Jack ordered the patient straight onto the operating table in the left lateral position, while he, Robert and the Surg. B registrar scrubbed.

Jenny already had the theatre set up, and Becky immediately connected the patient to the anaesthetic machine, administered propofol and more muscle relaxant, and gave orders to two anaesthetic registrars who had come in to assist her to maintain rapid IV infusion and get the cross-matched blood, which had just arrived, in the blood fridge.

Jack rapidly prepped and draped the left chest, including the existing chest drain, and made an incision, entering the pleura with a slight hiss.

'I'm in the chest, Becky. There's a peripheral lung injury from one gunshot but it's not bleeding. The pericardium is tense.'

'Jack, I've got virtually no BP. Do something now or he'll arrest,' Becky urged.

Jack incised the pericardium laterally, releasing a gush of arterial blood, which kept on coming at a furious rate.

'That's improved things. His BP's jumped to 100,' Becky reported.

'There's a cardiac defect from the second gunshot. His heart movement is making it difficult to control.'

'Blood loss is catching up with us, Jack. His BP is falling again,' Becky informed him.

'Jenny, give me a 2/0 prolene on a large needle and 2 centimetre square felt pledgets,' Jack ordered.

'Right here,' Jenny said, loading the needle at Jack's preferred angle in the needle holder.

Jack passed the needle through one felt pledget, took a big bite of myocardium through the slit-like defect caused by the passage of the bullet, passed the needle through another pledget, then reversed the process, making a U-shaped suture through the defect with a pledget on each side. He tied the suture, compressing the cardiac defect between the pledgets. Immediately the blood flow slowed to a trickle. Jack repeated the procedure with another pledget, stemming the bleeding completely.

'That was fantastic, Mr Colcannon. I've never seen anything like that, ever,' Robert said.

'I've never done it before,' Jack said. 'I learnt it at the last DSTC course. Damage control was the emphasis.'

'Amazing,' Robert said, shaking his head in awe.

Jack closed the chest, leaving the pericardium open and the existing chest drain in place, and left Robert and his companion registrar to resecure the drains and close the skin while he stripped off his gear. The police were waiting outside the operating theatre, peering in through the porthole-like windows.

He exchanged a short glance with Becky as she prepared to

accompany the patient out to ICU. 'You OK?' he asked, frowning at her unusually pale face.

'I'm fine,' she said. 'Robert's right. You did a great job.'

'So did you.' He gave her a small smile. 'I'll have a word with the police. Don't leave without me, we need to talk some more. I'll wait for you in my office.'

Becky had only just stepped into the lift on her way to Jack's office half an hour later when David, the orderly, called out to her.

'Hold that lift, Dr Baxter.' He raced up to block the doors with one arm and gave her a quick grin as they sprang back open. 'Phew! Thought you were going to leave without me. I hate taking the stairs unless I have to.'

'Me, too,' she said, reaching out to press the button for Jack's floor.

David stepped in front of the number pad, his eyes suddenly losing all trace of his previously easygoing friendliness. 'Let's not go to that floor. I have other plans for you.'

Becky's gaze flicked to the emergency button just out of her reach, her mouth suddenly drying out with fear.

'W-what are you talking about?' she asked, forcing her tone to remain calm.

He gave her a smile that sent a chill down her spine.

'We have an apartment to look at, remember?'

She frowned in confusion. 'I don't know what you're talking about. I have an appointment with one of the recovery staff...' She hunted her brain for the name. 'Lyndal Hanlon. We've arranged to meet later this evening at the property at Bronte.'

'Lyndal is my girlfriend,' he said. 'She does whatever I tell her to do.'

Becky stared at him, trying to make sense of what he was saying. 'You mean it's *your* apartment?'

He smiled that same chilling smile. 'What's wrong, Dr Baxter? Don't you fancy the idea of a threesome?'

'I think you've got the wrong person,' she said coldly. 'Now step aside and let me out of this lift.'

He took her arm in a vice-like grip while his other hand prodded her in the belly with a hard cold object. 'Don't make me pull the trigger,' he said. 'Haven't you seen enough blood for one day?'

Becky swallowed the solid lump of fear in her throat.

A gun.

He turned her so she was facing the front of the lift, the gun now prodding her in the back as he pressed the button for the first floor.

She forced herself to think clearly and calmly even though her heart was racing behind her chest wall, the deep throbs of the lift's acceleration making her feel sick and light-headed.

The first floor was the medical ward. There would be staff and patients and visitors within calling distance. She could alert them to the danger even if it meant taking the first shot herself.

The gun stabbed at her again as the lift came to a halt. 'Don't get any ideas,' David said. 'Just keep walking. We're going to the fire escape on the right. If you give off any signals or say a word to anyone, I'll shoot you first and them second.'

Becky did what he said, in some ways almost relieved when no one appeared. He escorted her roughly down the stairs to the locked door of the basement.

'Why are you doing this?' she asked.

He kept the gun trained on her as he took a key out of his top pocket and unlocked the door leading out to the hospital car park.

'Shut up and keep moving.' He shoved her through the door, walking by her side with one arm around her, the other pressing the gun to her side.

A hundred horrible scenarios raced through Becky's brain. She could almost imagine the pathway of the bullet as it tore through her flesh, the spurt of blood, the loss of consciousness as her blood pressure dropped and her life drained away.

'We'll take your car,' he announced, steering her towards where she'd parked it that morning.

'I haven't got my keys on me,' she said. 'My bag is in my locker.' She didn't tell him her keys were at front reception where she'd arranged for the mechanic to leave them. She couldn't risk him brandishing his gun among so many innocent people.

'Don't worry,' he said with a sly smile. 'I have my own set.' He took out a set of keys and aimed them at the car.

Becky swallowed convulsively as the central locking responded, her startled gaze swinging to the coldness of his.

'You're the one who broke into my flat! I didn't even think about my spare car keys—'

'Get in and drive.'

She got in the car with every limb shaking with reaction, her hand fumbling with the key in the ignition.

'Start the car.' His voice was devoid of all emotion. 'I'll give you ten seconds. One, two, three—'

In her panic she forgot to put her foot on the clutch. The car started with a jerk and bumped into Jack's car, parked in front of hers.

David swore viciously and gave her another prod with the gun. 'You think I don't mean it, don't you? Drive, bitch, or you'll regret it and so will your brother.'

Becky almost stalled the car as she stared at him. 'You know my brother?'

'Keep your eyes on the road,' he commanded. 'Yes, I know your brother.' He gave a throaty laugh that sickened Becky to her stomach. 'You could say we've had some *dealings* recently.'

Becky's brain tumbled over the possibilities. She knew Ben had been doing some time in the drug squad. Was David somehow involved in dealing with drugs? But how did he know Ben? Ben was a cop, not a dealer...but, then, if Ben was working under cover maybe he had to pretend...

'What sort of dealings?' she asked. 'Drugs?'

'Take the next left,' he said, looking back over his shoulder. 'Yeah, drugs.'

'What sort?' She checked her mirrors, hoping for a miracle, but none showed up. Where were the police when you needed them? 'Cocaine, heroin?'

'You ever heard of crystal meth?'

A wave of fear washed over her. She'd not only heard of crystal meth, she'd seen the effects of it during one of her terms at St Vincent's. They had a drug unit there with a padded room for people who had overdosed on crystal meth. It was a frightening drug. Perfectly normal people turned into vicious uncontrollable animals on it, became delusional and paranoid and incredibly dangerous, most never even remembering the things they'd said or done once the drug wore off. Some, she'd heard, never fully recovered from the personality changes or psychotic conditions the drug triggered.

'Yes, I've heard of it.'

He gave another one of his stomach-churning laughs. 'Your big brother thinks he's so smart. He thought he could infiltrate the company. But he seriously underestimated me.'

'Where are we going?' she asked as he indicated for her to take the next street.

'A meeting place,' he said. 'Ever gone fishing?'

'Yes...'

'Well, this time you're the bait,' he said. 'Your brother has something I want and now I have something he wants.'

Becky could feel the smugness of his smile even though she didn't look his way.

Never in her wildest dreams had she ever imagined Ben's work as a cop would throw her into the path of dangerous criminals. She didn't know how to deal with someone as maniacal as David Barker. He'd seemed such a normal sort of guy before today, working as an orderly as if he'd been doing it for years.

'Is that why you came to work at St Patrick's?' she asked. 'So you could kidnap me when you had the chance?'

'You're smart, you know that?' he grinned at her. 'I bet

you're smarter than your brother. Of course I got the job to get to you.'

Becky frowned in confusion. 'But if you wanted to kidnap me, why didn't you do it that first night?'

'What first night?'

'The night you broke into my flat and shone that torch in my face.'

'Wasn't me,' he said and indicated for her to take the next road. 'Turn here and park behind that silver Mercedes.'

Becky parked the car somewhat crookedly as her brain tried to grapple with what he'd just said.

'What do you mean, it wasn't you?' She turned to look at him.

'Get out of the car and no fancy moves,' he said, ignoring her question.

She got out and walked stiffly to where he pointed towards a neat cottage, the perfectly manicured lawn and the heady scent of gardenias in the tidy garden beds totally at odds with what she'd been expecting.

The door opened as they approached and a well-dressed man greeted her. 'Welcome, Dr Baxter. How nice that you could take time out of your busy schedule to visit us.'

She gave him a filthy look. 'Who are you and what do you want?'

'You can call me Carl. Come in and make yourself comfortable.'

David shoved her through to the lounge where a woman was sitting, smoking. Becky assumed from the way the woman got up to greet David that she was Lyndal, his girlfriend.

'Have we heard from our friend?' David asked Carl.

'The message has been circulated that we have his sister,' Carl said, glancing at his watch. 'Let's see how long it takes him to get here.'

'I need to use the bathroom,' Becky said, wishing it was indeed a lie.

The men exchanged glances and Carl turned to Lyndal,

handing her a small pistol. 'Take her. Don't let her out of your sight.'

The woman scowled as she dragged herself to her feet. 'Come on. It's out the back.'

On her way to the bathroom Becky did her best to get an idea of the layout of the cottage in case she got a chance to escape, but all of the doors along the hall were closed except for the bathroom at the end.

Lyndal shoved her into the bathroom and stood in the open doorway. 'Hurry up.'

Becky knew it would be pointless asking her to turn her back. She gritted her teeth and reminded herself that men did this all the time. It was a perfectly normal bodily function after all.

She flushed the toilet afterwards and washed her hands, shocked to see how pale her face was in the mirror.

She had to get out of this, but how?

'Why are you doing this?' she asked the woman as she turned back to face her. 'Can't you see what a creep David is?'

The woman sneered at her. 'He's going to be a very rich creep if things go according to plan.'

'You're throwing your life away,' Becky said. 'Drugs are not going to buy you the sort of riches that count.'

'Shut up and get back to the lounge room,' Lyndal said, poking the pistol at her. 'Your brother should be here any minute.'

Becky wished she had the courage to make a grab for the pistol. Lyndal was about the same height as her so she might be able to overpower her if she could take her by surprise.

She was still thinking about how she was going to do it when there was the sound of a knock at the door at the other end of the hall.

Lyndal ushered her back to the lounge room, shoving her into one of the seats as the well-dressed Carl went to answer the door.

Becky held her breath, wondering what Ben was going to say when he saw her sitting here with a gun trained on her.

But when Carl came back into the lounge room it wasn't her brother that accompanied him.

It was Matt Daniels.

CHAPTER FOURTEEN

'So, WE meet again, Dr Baxter,' Matt said, his coffee-brown eyes stripped of all warmth.

Becky stared at him, her fear-flooded brain having trouble connecting the cold hard tone to the man who had treated her so nicely—was it only yesterday?

The man called Carl addressed Matt. 'I heard you did a good job on Dubrovnik. He's not expected to live.'

Matt gave a grunt of satisfaction, his eyes still on Becky's.

'*You* shot that cop?' she gasped in shock.

Matt gave her a soulless smile. 'He'd served his purpose, right, Carl?'

'Right,' Carl said, 'Just as you will, Dr Baxter.' He turned to Matt. 'Any news from Baxter?'

'He's not responding,' Matt said and shifting his steady gaze back to Becky's, he added, 'I think we might have to up the stakes a bit to get his attention.'

Becky didn't like the sound of that, neither did she like the way Matt was looking at her as if she was going to be the means to do it. Her stomach gave a lurch of pure terror and she felt the urge to go the bathroom again.

Jack had been right. Matt Daniels was corrupt, drawn into some sort of drug network that played with people's lives like pieces on a chessboard.

'Why don't we send him a photo via your phone of his sister after you've roughed her up a bit?' Carl suggested.

'Can I watch?' David asked.

Matt gave him a dismissive look before turning back to look at Becky. 'No, I think I'd like to have the pleasure all to myself.'

'Take her out to the back room,' Carl directed. 'And keep

the noise down or we'll have the neighbours alerting the police.'

'On your feet,' Matt said to Becky.

Becky didn't move.

Matt's mouth tightened and he dragged her upright, his fingers biting into her flesh as he pushed her in front of him out of the room. 'Keep moving and if you scream you'll be sorry.'

Becky felt tears of disappointment, fear and anger sting her eyes. She could barely see for them as she stumbled in the direction Matt was pushing her, to a room on the right of the bathroom at the back of the house.

He closed the door once they were in the room and before he could speak she turned on him, her voice crackling with fury.

'If you think I'm going to give you the satisfaction of hearing me beg for my life, then think again. I'm not scared of you, Matthew Daniels. I'm ashamed of you. I feel sorry for your parents and your poor sister who deserve much better than a piece of scum like you. How could you do it? How could you betray your colleagues? How could you get mixed up with those creeps out there?'

Matt put his finger to his lips in a gesture of silence.

Becky opened her mouth to continue her tirade but he stepped closer and, leaning down, whispered into her ear.

'I can't talk too loudly, this place is probably wired. Just do as I say. I'm not going to hurt you. Ben would kill me if I let anything happen to you.'

Becky's eyes widened as she looked at him once he'd stepped back. 'You're not one of them?' she whispered.

He shook his head, his voice low. 'They think I am. Dubrovnik was working for them but he tried to skim some cream off the top. The police wanted him alive. The company wanted him dead. I took the middle ground.'

He took a small capsule out of his trouser leg pocket and handed it to her.

'What's this?' She turned it over in her hands.

'It's a capsule of fake blood. I want you to give a couple

of decent yelps as if I've hit you, then chew on that and I'll take a couple of photos to show Carl.'

'But what about Ben? What will he think when he sees the photos?'

He smiled. 'He'll know you're safe.'

'You've planned this?'

'I didn't plan for you to be brought here,' he said. 'David is a loose cannon, I'm afraid. I think you and Jack seriously annoyed him by saving Dubrovnik's life. Also, he has a score to settle with Ben.' He clenched and unclenched his fist. 'Ready?'

She nodded.

He swung a punch into the wall and she yelped, not because he'd told her to but because he'd genuinely scared her.

'Good,' he said. 'One more then chew the capsule.'

He thumped the cupboard this time. She gave another yelp and started chewing. Red liquid spilled from the sides of her mouth, dripping over her blouse and skirt.

'Lean against the wall there and look dazed,' he instructed, and aimed his phone at her.

'That'll be easy,' she mumbled, doing as he directed.

He checked the shots and showed them to her. 'What do you think?'

She peered at the small screen and gave a little shudder. 'Not my best angle but this hasn't been a great day for me.'

'It'll be over soon,' he said. Moving across the room, he reached behind the window-blind and opened the window.

'What are you doing?' she whispered.

'I'm letting some much-needed fresh air into this house,' he said with a conspiratorial smile. 'Come on, it's show time again. Just act bushed and do whatever you're told.'

Becky stumbled back towards the lounge room with him, wondering if Jack was angry with her for not showing up as arranged.

If only he knew!

*   *   *

Jack looked at his watch for the tenth time and frowned. He'd called ICU and the staff had informed him Becky had left over an hour ago. He'd been tied up talking to the police for longer than he'd expected. They'd insisted on a twenty-four-hour watch on the patient, who was still hovering between life and death, with no sure bets on either side as yet.

Jack had tried Becky's mobile but the message service indicated it was switched off. When he tried her pager it, too, signalled it was out of range.

He went to the window to look down at the car park and his frown deepened when he saw the space where Becky's car had been parked was now empty.

He had just reached for his keys when his pager rang and he unclipped it from his belt to answer it. 'Colcannon.'

'Jack, it's me, Ben.'

'Ben!'

'They've got her, Jack.'

Jack felt his stomach turn over. 'What?'

'The company has Becky,' Ben said. 'They planted a guy in the hospital. He's been working as an orderly. He's taken her as bait.'

'Oh, God!'

'Listen,' Ben said. 'I want you to drive to this address…' He read it out to him and Jack scribbled it down with trembling fingers.

'Don't park anywhere near the house. Keep well back. There's a room at the back of the house, a window has been left open.'

'What about the police?' Jack asked. 'Shouldn't we?'

'I'm acting independently until I know what the score is,' Ben told him. 'I'm probably going to be hauled over the coals for involving you as it is, but I don't want to put Becky in any more danger. Just get to the house and lie low in that room. Turn your phone to silent and I'll text you with any further directions.'

Jack drove to the house in the quiet unassuming street a few kilometres from the hospital and parked well away from the house. He could see Becky's car parked behind a silver

Mercedes and in spite of the stress and fear churning his stomach he couldn't help a tiny wry smile as he noticed the crooked angle of her car and a bright pink scratch along the side of the Mercedes.

He made his way to the rear of the building, finding the window Ben had told him would be open. He eased himself up over the sill and dropped into the room with a soft thud, his eyes going immediately to the bright splattering of what looked like blood on the carpet in the middle of the room.

Matt shoved Becky back into the chair she'd been sitting in earlier. 'Sit down and shut the hell up.'

'Go to hell,' she snapped back, wiping her hand across her blood-smeared mouth.

'Bitch.'

'Pig.'

'Cut it out,' Carl growled at them. 'You sent that photo?'

Matt gave a single nod. 'If that doesn't work, I have something else in mind.'

Carl's lip curled upwards in a cynical smile. 'You're one sick cookie, Daniels.'

'You'd better believe it.'

'David, check the street to see if any cops are about,' Carl said.

David left the room and came back a short time later. 'Nothing. It's all quiet.'

'I need to use the bathroom again,' Becky said.

Lyndal rolled her eyes and stubbed out her cigarette as she began to get to her feet.

'I'll take her,' Matt said, waving Lyndal back down in her chair. 'It'll be my pleasure.'

Carl laughed and fingered the cold steel of the gun he was holding. 'Why don't you take her into one of the back rooms and get it over with? It'll be one more thing to press Ben Baxter's buttons with, a photo of his sister being done by a colleague.'

Becky threw him a contemptuous glare that encompassed both David and Lyndal as well. 'I hope you all rot in hell.'

Matt took her arm and dragged her from the room. 'Come on, motormouth. Let's go.'

He waited until they were in the bathroom before asking, 'Do you really need to go?'

She nodded and shifted from foot to foot. 'Sorry, but my bladder is hopeless when I'm scared.'

'I can't turn my back in case Carl or David looks down this way but I'll shut my eyes, OK?'

'All right.'

After she was finished Becky flushed the toilet and moved across to wash her hands. 'You can open your eyes now.' She washed her face and rinsed out her mouth but she still looked as if she'd been given a punch. Her eyes were shadowed and her cheeks pale, her hair almost standing on end in fear.

'I look a total mess.' She turned from the mirror to see Matt listening to an earpiece he'd inserted in his ear.

He took it out and hid it again. 'Listen, Becky.' He leaned in to whisper to her. 'I'm going to take you to the room we were in before. There will be someone in there to help you escape. Just get away from the house as fast as you can.'

He moved her to the room he'd used before. Opening the door, Becky came face to face with Jack.

'Get her out of the house,' Matt instructed him in a low urgent tone. 'Ben is about to make his move.'

As he spoke there was the sound of a hard knock at the front door. Becky reached for Jack's outstretched hand and gripped it tightly.

'*Go on!*' Matt said, pushing them towards the window.

Jack hoisted Becky up over the window-sill and she dropped to the garden bed below. She watched as he came down to join her, taking her hand in his and pulling her towards the side of the house where the lounge room was situated.

'Are you all right?' Jack whispered, quickly running his eyes and hands over her.

'I'm fine,' she said somewhat breathlessly.

'You've got blood on your shirt.' His eyes went to her breasts.

'It's fake.'

'Fake?'

'Matt gave it to me. He's not corrupt, Jack. He's doing a double-agent thing. He's trying to help Ben. He shot the cop you operated on. He was an informer or something.'

Jack's hand tightened on hers. 'Listen, I think I can hear them. You stay here out of sight. I'm going back to the window we came out of to get back inside.'

'Jack! No!'

'Shh!' Jack held his finger to his mouth. 'Just stay out of sight in that hedge, there.'

Becky watched as he hoisted himself back over the window-sill, disappearing into the house. But instead of hiding where he'd instructed, she edged closer to the curtained French doors of the lounge room, her back pressed flat to the wall of the house as she listened to what was going on inside.

'Where's my sister?' Ben was asking, his tone rough and angry.

'She's tied up in the back room,' Matt said. 'She doesn't know when to keep her mouth shut so I shut it for her.'

'You bastard!'

'Where's the CM?' Carl asked. 'The shipment arrived two hours ago. My people haven't arrived with it yet and I want to know why.'

'It's coming.'

'So is Christmas, but I want that stuff in my hands before I hand over your sister,' Carl said.

'I'm afraid that won't be possible,' Matt said as he pulled a gun and pointed it at Carl's head. 'You're under arrest, Carlos Mandolos, for the illegal trafficking of drugs. You have the right to remain silent—'

David's gun boomed, but Ben had anticipated it. He shot him in the chest. David went down in a crumpled heap and Lyndal reached for her pistol, but Ben knocked it out of her hand and snapped a pair of handcuffs on her, securing her to the arm of the heavy recliner chair she'd been sitting in.

Carl made a grab for Matt's gun, and another shot put a hole in the ceiling, sending plaster dust all over them. Blood was pouring from a wound on Matt's shoulder from the first bullet David had fired, and Ben could see his hold on Carl was loosening.

Suddenly Carl had Matt's gun, and Matt was slipping to the floor unconscious.

'Drop it, Baxter, or I'll blow your head off,' Carl bit out.

Ben hated this part. This was what happened in the movies. It wasn't supposed to happen in real life. He dropped his gun on the floor.

'Kick it towards me,' Carl commanded.

Ben gave it a small kick.

'Further.'

'If you want it, come and get it.'

'You think you're so smart,' Carl said through clenched teeth. 'But you're not smart enough to get out of this. I'm going to shoot your guts out and then I'm going to do your sister. By the time I'm finished with her no one will recognise her.'

Ben laughed. 'My sister is miles away by now, you jackass. Why don't you leave this stuff to the professionals? You're an amateur, Mandolos, you don't even know who's for or against you in this operation. It's over. The haul was collected by the drug squad hours ago. Dubrovnik was too stupid to clear up after himself—he left a trail everywhere he went.'

Carl gestured for Ben to move away from the door. 'Stand over there. Now say goodbye, Baxter.'

Becky could stand no more. Without thinking of the consequences, she threw her whole weight against the French doors, the force of her entry pulling the heavy curtains off their tracks, wrapping her like a mummy as the shattered glass fell around her.

'Well, well, well,' Carl drawled as he dragged her to her

feet, the gun still trained on Ben. 'Looks like your sister can't bear to be away from you.'

Becky gave Ben an agonised look.

'Let her go,' Ben said, his voice raw. 'She has nothing to do with this.'

'No, I don't think I will let her go.' Carl smiled a hateful smile as he dragged Becky closer to his body, the click of his gun's safety catch being released making her flinch.

Becky watched as Ben's throat moved up and down in a swallow and her legs loosened with dread as she mentally prepared herself for the horror of seeing her brother executed in front of her.

'Let her go,' said a deep voice behind Carl.

Carl swung around to face Jack, firing off a bullet that missed him by mere millimetres. Ben moved like lightning, his swift punch to Carl's head dropping him like a bird from the sky. He picked up the still smoking gun.

'Say goodbye, Mandolos,' he said, snapping handcuffs on him. 'You're going away for a very long time.'

Becky suddenly found herself in Jack's arms but later couldn't quite recall how she'd got there. Surely her legs hadn't been stable enough to make the distance?

'You got your doctor's bag with you?' Ben asked Jack as he straightened from handcuffing the unconscious prisoner. 'Better have a look at Matt while I call in reinforcements.'

Jack quickly retrieved the EMST emergency kit from where he'd left it in the back room, but when he returned Becky had already removed Matt's shirt and applied pressure to halt the bleeding from the bullet path across his right deltoid muscle. He handed her a pressure dressing and after sufficient pressure the bleeding slowed and then stopped. With still shaking fingers Becky inserted a cannula and started the one bag of normal saline from Jack's kit. Matt was soon ready for transport to St Patrick's A and E for definitive care.

The ambulance had come and gone while the police were still taking everyone's statements and dealing with all the investigation formalities. Finally they were cleared to leave and Becky gratefully accepted a lift with Jack, not trusting herself to drive in her state of sheer exhaustion.

'I'll arrange for someone to pick up your car for you tomorrow,' he said as he helped her into his car.

'Thanks.'

He cupped her face in his warm hand and looked deep into her eyes. 'You were very brave, Becky.'

'No, I wasn't, I nearly wet my pants, twice.'

He laughed and leaned forward to kiss her softly.

Ben met them at Jack's house a few minutes later, throwing a casual arm around his sister's shoulders and giving her a squeeze. 'What in the world were you thinking, barging into the room like that?'

'I didn't want you to be killed.'

He ruffled her hair. 'You were one hell of a worry for me, Becky, right up until the very end. I had the devil's own job getting you out of your flat.'

Becky eased herself out of his embrace to look up at him. 'What are you talking about?'

Ben flicked his gaze towards Jack. 'Haven't you filled her in yet?'

Jack shook his head. 'She's tired. I thought it could wait till morning.'

'What's going on?' Becky looked at them both before turning to focus on Jack. 'Jack?'

'Ben called me a few days ago to warn me to get you out of your flat. He said you were in danger.'

Becky looked at her brother for verification. 'Is that true?'

'Yes. I was working undercover. I heard that someone suspected the company had been infiltrated and that various buttons were going to be pushed to see who jumped. It wasn't a problem for Matt, his family are overseas, like our parents. It was just you I had to protect.' He let out a deep breath of relief. 'It was touch and go there for a while. You weren't taking any of my hints.'

'Hints?' Becky looked at him blankly. 'What hints?'

Ben grinned. 'It took all my specialist training not to laugh out loud at you pointing that shoe at me.'

'You were the intruder?' She gaped at him in shock.

'Yes. I had to do what I could to scare you out of there. Carl had instructed me to rough you up a bit. He wanted to see if I was Ben Baxter, the mole. It was a test. Of course I couldn't hurt you so I just told him you pulled a gun on me.'

'What about the break-in?' she asked.

'That was David. He went after your car keys. I tried to put your car out of action but you kept getting it fixed.' He sent Jack a quick glance before turning back to her. 'Matt began to suspect something when he covered the break and enter. He was trying to work out who the police informant was. For a while he thought it was me but then Dubrovnik slipped up and the truth finally came out.'

'Matt told me he thought there were two people after me,' she said, recalling her conversation with him.

'Yeah, he wanted to check what you knew about my movements. We were playing cat and mouse there for a bit but I wanted to make sure *I* could trust *him*. He's a good cop, sharp as a tack. He eventually put two and two together over the messages.' Ben grinned again.

'Messages?' Becky asked, frowning.

'That message in lipstick I scrawled across your mirror. I came in after David had been.'

'"Get out or die bitch face"?' She gave his arm a hard slap. '*Bitch face?*'

Ben chuckled as he moved out of her reach. 'It worked, didn't it?'

'But I don't understand,' she said, trying to get her head around it all. 'What about the sunscreen?'

'Me again,' Ben confessed. 'I was tailing David Barker at the time. I wasn't sure what he was capable of so I thought I'd send another warning to keep you and Jack on your toes.'

'You knew about all this?' Becky stared at Jack.

'Not all of it,' Jack said.

'I didn't tell Jack much. I couldn't,' Ben said. 'I just told him to get you out of the flat and into his house. Of course, I know how stubborn you can be, it was a nightmare to make sure he convinced you to move in. Hey, mate, did you pretend to be in love with her like I said?'

Becky froze at Ben's words, her breath locking in her chest. She turned to look up at Jack, her fingertips turning icy cold as the slow crawl of sick realisation dawned.

'Is that true, Jack?' she asked, her voice catching on her growing anger. 'Did my brother ask you to pretend to be in love with me?'

Jack's throat moved up and down. 'Yes, but it's not quite how it—'

She raised her hand and slapped the side of his face, the sound of her palm connecting with his jaw like a gunshot.

'Whoa there, Becky.' Ben pulled her away before she took another swipe. 'What's the matter with you? Jack helped to save your life!'

She pushed Ben's hand off her arm and glared at him furiously. 'He didn't have to sleep with me, though—or were those your orders as well?'

'He slept with you?' Ben's eyes widened.

'Not only did he sleep with me...' she sent Jack a cutting look '...he also took the play-acting to a whole new level of farce by asking me to marry him.'

Ben's mouth opened and closed.

'Becky, you don't understand.' Jack stepped towards her. 'I was going to explain but—'

'*Explain?*' she choked. 'How could you possibly explain what you did? You made a complete fool out of me, talking of happy-ever-afters. You make me sick, do you hear me? I hate you. I never want to see you again.'

'Listen to me, Becky,' Jack said raggedly. 'None of this is how it seems.'

Becky stomped out of the room without another word, slamming the door behind her.

Jack stepped forward to follow her but Ben put out an arm to stop him. 'Leave her, mate. Let her sleep her anger off.

She's been through a lot. She'll have a good cry and it'll all
start to make sense in the morning.'

'Ben...' Jack raked a hand through his hair and faced him,
his expression a little sheepish. 'About that marriage proposal...'

Becky waited until she was sure Ben and Jack were asleep
before leaving the house. She caught a taxi to the hospital,
asking the driver to wait while she collected her bag out of
her locker and then directing him to take her to the city.

She didn't think it wise to book into The Principal On The
Park again, and because she was feeling so low she headed
for the more upmarket harbour end of town and checked into
the Harbour Edge Hotel.

She left a message at the hospital switchboard that she was
taking a few days' sick leave, turned off her phone, ran a deep
hot bath and soaked for an hour, trying not to give in to the
tears that were banking up behind her stinging eyes.

Jack's betrayal was so hard to believe. How could he have
sunk so low as to *pretend*?

Of course it was all so obvious now. She kicked at the
bubbles around her in frustration and anger. All those mixed
messages she'd thought he was sending were not the work of
her imagination after all. He'd been trying to act like a man
in love while gritting his teeth at having to play babysitter
until Ben could give him the all-clear.

She wished she hadn't been so gullible as to fall for it. Why
hadn't she realised what was going on? Then she could have
played along with it and had the last laugh, instead of having
her heart smashed to pieces.

She got out of the bath and dialled for room service. She
hadn't eaten in hours and diets had no place when it came to
healing a broken heart.

Once she placed her order she called St Patrick's to ask
how Matt Daniels was doing. Robert took the call and filled
her in. 'He's awake and doing really well. I'm standing right
next to his bed. Do you want to talk to him?'

'Sure,' Becky said.

'Becky?' Matt's voice sounded a bit thin around the edges. 'Are you OK?'

'Yes, thanks to you.'

'No, thanks to Jack,' he said. 'And you, of course. I heard you two did a good job on me before the ambulance arrived.'

'Just doing my job,' she said.

'Your brother saved my life and yours by getting you out of the line of fire,' he said. 'Carlos Mandolos is a ruthless killer. He wanted to kill you from the first day and would have done so if Ben hadn't involved Jack. He stuck to you like glue. Mandolos knew that if he took you out he'd have to take Jack out too, but shooting one of Sydney's best surgeons was going to attract too much attention. He couldn't risk it. That's why David Barker was sent in to see if he could get you alone.'

'He seemed like such a normal guy,' Becky said with a little shudder.

'Most criminals seem normal people on the surface,' Matt said. 'It's part of the whole profile of a criminal mind. They think and act normally when they need to but when it's time to party they slip into criminal mode with ease.' He gave a muffled yawn. 'Hell, what did that registrar put in this IV line?'

'I'd better let you get some sleep,' she said. 'You're dosed up on morphine for the pain. I'm glad you're doing OK.'

Becky put the phone back down and sighed. Matt was right. She did owe Jack her life, and not just for the way he'd stepped in tonight, distracting Mandolos. Jack had only done exactly what her brother had asked him to. She knew how strict the code was on contact with family members during an undercover operation. Ben would have called Jack in desperation to make sure she was kept safe, not wanting to compromise himself or his colleagues by revealing his true identity.

There was a discreet knock on the door and a male voice called out, 'Room service.'

Becky gathered her robe around her and padded across to

open the door, her eyes growing wide with shock to see Jack standing there, dressed in the hotel servicemen's uniform, a food trolley in front of him.

'Did someone call for a large fries, a double cheeseburger, a Coke and a chocolate and blueberry cheesecake?' he asked.

She pursed her lips at him and opened the door a little wider for him to bring in the trolley. 'I suppose there's no point asking how you found me.'

'Your brother gave me a few hints,' Jack said. 'I think I could make it as an undercover cop if ever I fancied a career change.'

'You'd totally suck at it. You're a terrible actor.'

'You think so?'

'I know so.' She folded her arms across her chest and gave him a cold hard glare. 'I hope you're not expecting a tip. I'm short of cash right now.'

'I'm not here for a tip.' His eyes locked with hers.

'Why are you here?'

'Can't you guess?'

She searched his face but she was at a loss to know what was going on behind his green gaze.

'Did Ben tell you to come here?' she asked, her eyes narrowing slightly.

'No.'

He stepped towards her and took one of her hands and gently unpeeled her locked fingers, one by one.

'W-what are you doing?'

He pressed a soft kiss into the middle of her palm and closed her fingers back over it, his eyes still holding hers.

'I'm telling you that I love you,' he said.

'I don't believe you.'

'Then I'll have to find another way to convince you,' he said, and took her other hand and did the same to it. 'Convinced yet?'

She shook her head, the line of her mouth still tight.

'Hmm.' He gave the side of his head a little scratch as if in deep thought. 'How about this?' he asked, and kissed her on the lips, his own gentle but firm, his tongue sweeping just once over the tight seam of her mouth.

Becky's lips tingled with the sensation and a wave of desire hit her from below, making her sway towards him, her eyes starting to shine as she looked up at him.

Jack smiled and kissed her again, this time a little more thoroughly, his tongue curling around hers until she was breathless and clinging to him.

He lifted his head and asked, 'Am I making any headway here or am I going to have to call in the big guns?'

'What sort of guns are we talking about?' she said, pressing herself to the hardness of his body, her arms going up around his neck.

'Shotguns,' he said. 'You know, the ones that make people get married in a hurry.'

'But I'm not pregnant,' she said, a little smile starting to kick up the edges of her mouth as she saw the leaping glint in his eyes. 'Or at least I don't think so.'

'Then let's get started on it,' he said, 'Right here and right now.' He backed her towards the bed, untying her bathrobe as he went, his burning gaze feasting on her already quivering flesh before his weight pinned her to the mattress.

'Jack!' She wriggled out from under him, torn between wanting to laugh and cry all at the same time. 'Are you really telling me the truth?'

'I told you the truth yesterday but you wouldn't believe me,' he said, reaching for her again. 'I know it seemed out of character and I did a lousy job of my proposal but I was desperate. I suddenly realised I loved you. I couldn't bear the thought of anything happening to you. I made a promise to Ben to look after you but I had no need to pretend to be in love with you. I guess that's why I've been pushing you away all these years—you threatened my neat plan of no emotional entanglements. When I kissed you twelve years ago it made me realise you were the one person who, if I allowed you to, could slip under my guard and disrupt my carefully planned life.' He gave her rueful little smile as his finger traced a soft pathway over the curve of her mouth. 'Do you have any idea of how totally irresistible you are?'

'Irresistible, huh?' Becky's eyes began to dance as she wriggled back under him, her arms going around him to hold him close. 'I thought you said I was the most annoying person you'd ever met?'

'Did I say that?' He pressed a soft kiss to the edge of her mouth.

'You sure did.'

'And you believed me?'

'Why wouldn't I believe you?' she said. 'All the evidence at hand seemed to suggest you couldn't bear to even look at me.'

'Then maybe you should re-examine the evidence at hand,' he suggested, capturing her hand and placing it where his body most ached and throbbed for her touch.

'Mmm,' Becky mused as her fingers moved over him. 'It seems the evidence at hand might be telling me the truth after all.'

'You'd better believe it, baby,' Jack growled as he pressed her backwards. 'This is one body that never lies.'

'Jack...' Becky said a few breathless minutes later. 'I could be wrong but I'm getting the distinct impression your body is seriously in love with mine.'

Jack eased himself up on one elbow, his passion-glazed eyes holding hers. 'So I've finally managed to convince you?'

She gave him a teasing little smile. 'I wouldn't go as far as saying that.'

'You mean I have to do it all over again?' he asked in mock-affront.

She grinned at him as she worked her way down his body with a pathway of hot breathy little kisses that threatened to boil his blood.

'Hey! What are you doing?' he asked, sucking in a breath as she finally found what she was looking for.

'What do you think I'm doing?' she asked, her eyes glinting up at him with mischief.

'I think you're making it absolutely impossible for me to resist you,' he said.

'*Touché*,' she said, and pressed him back down on the bed. 'Just for the record, this is one mouth that never lies.'

'I thought you said I wasn't your type?' Jack dragged some air into his lungs.

'Did I say that?' She lifted her head momentarily to give him a totally guileless look.

'You did.'

'And you believed me?'

'I guess I should have examined the evidence a little more closely.'

Becky gave him a twinkling little smile. 'You should definitely always examine the evidence, but right now I have other plans for you.'

'You do?' He sucked in another sharp little breath as she moved a little lower.

'Damn right I do,' she said, and with one last glinting look she bent her head and took his breath completely away.

THE ITALIAN SURGEON
CLAIMS HIS BRIDE

ALISON ROBERTS

Alison Roberts lives in Christchurch, New Zealand. She began her working career as a primary school teacher, but now juggles available working hours between writing and active duty as an ambulance officer. Throwing in a large dose of parenting, housework, gardening and pet-minding keeps life busy, and teenage daughter Becky is responsible for an increasing number of days spent on equestrian pursuits. Finding time for everything can be a challenge, but the rewards make the effort more than worthwhile.

CHAPTER ONE

WHAT the hell was going on here?

It was like a good-cop, bad-cop scenario. Hardly what Jenna Freeman had expected when fronting up to this fabulous old house in Hamilton Drive, one of the most exclusive parts of town, to attend a job interview.

A woman who looked to be in her seventies was beaming at Jenna approvingly. The other woman, twenty years her junior, had fixed Jenna with a steely glare. Both had formidably strong personalities.

'I'm not sure I understand,' Jenna said carefully. 'Is there something wrong with the little girl?'

'With Danielle? Good heavens, no! She's perfect.'

The gazes of all three women shifted automatically to focus on the subject of their conversation and Jenna found herself smiling.

Yes. Danielle did look perfect.

As babies went, this one was a stunner.

Jenna had met a lot of babies in her career as a paediatric nurse and could almost always find something appealing about them. Some looked like they should be advertising baby food in glossy magazines. Others had heart-melting smiles. Some were placid and cuddly and easy to care for, others noisy and fascinated by the world around them.

They were all different and yet this one—nine-month-old Danielle Romano—was in a class of her own.

She looked ready for a photographer's attention in the beautiful pink smocked dress, long white socks and pristine patent leather shoes. A band that matched her dress squashed some of the silky-looking black curls on her head and sported a bow on top as perfect as the similar decoration on the shiny white shoes.

Small fingers were playing with the bow on one shoe right now. Carefully. As though Danielle was confident she had all the time in the world to explore the shape and feel of the object. The wealth of bright toys surrounding her in the playpen couldn't compete for her interest.

She must have sensed the direction of the women's attention, however, because her fingers stilled and she looked up. Big, dark eyes regarded Jenna with no hint of alarm at the presence of a stranger. There was no hint of a smile either, but that was hardly unexpected, especially in a child serious enough to find the bow on her shoe so compelling.

Jenna's smile faded as she looked back at the women sitting opposite her.

Danielle's grandmothers.

'Your advertisement specified a qualified nurse. Someone experienced with children.'

'That's right.'

'But the position you're describing is looking after a perfectly healthy child. It's a job for a nanny, not a nurse.'

The older of the two women, Maria Romano, looked away quickly, giving an impression of discomfort. If it hadn't been a weird thought, Jenna would have described her as being nervous.

The younger woman, Louise Gibbs, looked almost smug as she nodded less than subtle agreement.

'I said that, Maria,' Louise murmured. 'She's not suitable for the position.'

Not suitable? Jenna bristled. Surely the decision should be hers, given that she was over-qualified for the work being offered. If she took it, she wouldn't be using more than a fraction of the knowledge and skill she had worked hard to attain so far in her career.

'Jenna's more qualified than anyone with just a diploma from a nanny school, Louise. We want the best for Ella, don't we?'

'Danielle.' The correction seemed to be automatic. Louise dropped her gaze to Jenna's CV, now lying on the coffee-table between them. 'You're a little younger than I had in mind.'

'I'm thirty-one.' Getting rapidly older, in Jenna's opinion. All her friends seemed to be married and starting families by now. Only Jenna remained single and childless. Destined to silence the ticking of her own biological clock by caring for the children of other people?

Awful thought. Maybe she'd made a mistake even fronting up for this interview. The idea of being a private nurse in a new city had been appealing, however. An easy job. Time to come to terms with the difficult changes life had presented recently and reset herself. A chance to meet new people in a place that wasn't haunted by too many memories.

An old friend she had kept in touch with since they had trained together had applauded the notion.

'*Do* come to Christchurch,' Anne had urged Jenna. 'It would be so good to spend some time together again.'

'And you're single.' Louise made it sound like some kind of disease.

'Yes.' Jenna straightened her back. The last man in her life had done his best to leave her feeling she hadn't made the grade. She wasn't about to let someone's grandmother dent the fragile self-esteem she had managed to restore. 'I wouldn't be applying for a live-in position if I wasn't single.'

'Of course you wouldn't,' Maria agreed. 'And you're quite old enough to be very experienced. How long have you been a paediatric nurse?'

'Six years. And before that I worked in the emergency department.'

'There you go, Louise. Wouldn't it be wonderful to have someone who could cope with any emergency or illness that Ell—Danielle might have?'

Maria's smile was warm. An Italian woman, her English seemed almost flawless, though quite heavily accented, and she used her hands a lot when speaking. She was a little on the plump side and her clothes, while of the best quality, appeared to have been chosen for comfort rather than style. With her lovely smile and hair a natural silver, she reminded Jenna quite strongly of her own mother and so she smiled back with a genuine response to that warmth.

'Hmm.' Louise's gaze was still blatantly assessing and cold enough to provide a startling contrast to the eye contact Jenna had just broken with Maria.

Not that she had to try and hold this gaze. Louise dropped hers deliberately to take in the plain black skirt and blouse Jenna had deemed suitable for this interview and the way her long hair was neatly tied back in a ponytail. It even seemed to take particular note of her lack of jewellery and her short, neatly trimmed, unpainted fingernails.

And then it suggested comprehension of her single

status. Annoyingly, Jenna felt a stain of colour touching her cheeks. OK, maybe she wasn't model material like this woman's beautiful grandchild or the gorgeous blonde woman that featured in numerous photographs dotting the mantelpiece of this room, but she wasn't *un*attractive.

Involuntarily, her gaze flicked to one of the larger images. A wedding photograph, which looked too perfect to be real. The man was gorgeous. Tall, dark and in command, with his hand possessively covering the one linked through his arm that belonged to the blonde princess in the cloud of silk and tulle.

There was a resemblance there to the younger of the two women opposite Jenna. More than simply the wealthy, over-groomed look. There was a sharpness to the features that didn't exactly scream warmth. Jenna wasn't at all sure she liked Louise Gibbs and she was rapidly coming to the conclusion that this job wasn't what she was looking for.

She shifted in the chair. 'I feel I may be wasting your time.'

'No, no!' Maria reached out a hand, a gesture designed to pre-empt any further movement on Jenna's part. 'Please, stay.'

For an instant, Jenna saw something new in Maria's face. This was more like fear than nervousness. It was gone too quickly to identify reliably but it resurrected that undeniable curiosity. There was something rather strange about this interview and it would be unsatisfying to leave without discovering what it was.

Jenna stayed put.

'Danielle's father is Paul Romano,' Louise said into the silence. She was watching Jenna carefully. 'A paediatric surgeon here in Christchurch. You will have heard of him, I expect?'

The Paul Romano? Jenna couldn't help looking impressed. He was well known as a specialist in dealing with the removal of childhood tumours. In conjunction with the paediatric oncologists, the reputation was enough to have children sent long distances to receive treatment here.

'Of course. We often referred our more complicated cases here. He's well respected.'

'Yes.' The simple word spoken simultaneously by both women carried a weight of pride.

'Paolo's my son,' Maria added. 'My only child. My only family in this country. Sadly, his father passed away three years ago. We—'

'Paul was married to *my* only child,' Louise interrupted. 'My daughter Gwendolyn. Tragically, she experienced massive complications from an embolism following the Caesarean needed for Danielle's birth and...and she died when Danielle was only three hours old.'

Louise looked away, struggling for control, and Maria tutted sympathetically, murmuring something soothing in Italian as she reached out again, this time to pat her companion's arm. Jenna couldn't help warming to them both.

'I'm very sorry,' she said quietly. 'It must have been a dreadful time for you.'

Louise rallied. 'Paul was devastated, of course. He still hasn't come to terms with losing Gwen, and having Danielle doesn't help.'

'Oh?' This was puzzling. Surely having a child, a living part of someone you had loved, would be the greatest comfort possible? A man with the intelligence necessary to become such a renowned surgeon couldn't blame the infant for her mother's death or had his love for his wife been such that any reminder could only keep the grief alive?

'Paolo moved home so that I could help with raising Ella,' Maria said.

So this house belonged to the Romano family. Maybe Louise was not a key player after all.

'And I moved to Christchurch.' Louise made it sound as though she was sacrificing more on behalf of her granddaughter. 'Although I would have been—still am—more than happy to take on the full responsibility of raising Danielle.'

The full responsibility? Did the father not have anything to do with his daughter? Were these two grandparents fighting over custody? No wonder there was an odd feel to this household. Doubts about the advisability of working here resurfaced and must have shown on her face.

'It's not that he doesn't love Ella,' Maria said hurriedly. 'It's just that it's been difficult for him. He's always being terribly conscientious about his work and it became an escape for him to put more and more into his career in terms of hours. He's not at home very much.'

'It would be a demanding job.' Jenna looked back at Danielle, who was now busy removing her shoes. 'It's lucky that you are both able to help.'

'As if I'd do anything else.' Louise sounded faintly outraged. 'Danielle is all I have left of my precious daughter. My only child.'

'Paolo was an only child, too,' Maria reminded her. She waved her hand apologetically at Jenna. 'Louise and I are both widows,' she added, as though that explained everything.

Which it did to some extent. This baby was very important to them both as the sole member of the next generation of their families. Jenna was aware of how close Italian families were so Louise must be very determined to keep her stake in Danielle's upbringing.

They were both determined and, for some reason, in competition with each other.

Interpersonal politics could detract from any job. Condensed into an intimate domestic situation that encompassed inevitable cultural differences and included an outsider such as herself could make a working environment intolerable. The warning bells were ringing loud and clear for Jenna.

So did the cry from Danielle. Maria stood up immediately and went to the playpen. The baby held up her arms and Jenna could see it wasn't easy for the older woman to pick her up.

'Oh, dear, you're very wet, aren't you?' Maria cuddled the baby. 'You need a clean nappy, *cara*.'

'I'll do it.' With smooth grace, Louise rose and took the baby, allowing no time for protest. 'You may as well show Jennifer the flat.'

May as well? Was she going to be allowed to view living quarters she wasn't going to be using just to fill in time while Danielle was having her nappy changed?

'Yes, of course!' Maria seemed eager to comply. 'Come with me, Jenna.'

Reluctantly, Jenna followed Maria. The self-contained flat was attached to the vast old house through a short passageway that was accessed through a large, gleaming kitchen. Yet another older woman was busy near the sink. She glanced up curiously as Maria led Jenna across the tiled floor.

'This is Jenna,' Maria said. 'I'm going to show her the flat. I hope she might be joining us to help look after Ella. Jenna, this is Shirley. She helps me in the house. You wouldn't be expected to take on cleaning duties, which I know are expected of some nannies. Or cooking. I love to cook. I teach Italian cookery at the evening classes.'

Shirley gave Jenna an up-and-down glance and clearly liked what she saw. 'You'll like the flat,' she said matter-of-factly. 'Would you like a cup of coffee when you're done?'

'Maybe later,' Maria said. 'When Paolo gets home.' She seemed keen to usher Jenna through the door of what must have originally been servants' quarters.

It had clearly been upgraded considerably. The sitting room was tiny but tastefully decorated and it contained a television, music system and well-stocked bookshelf. The bedroom looked comfortable and there was a sparkling bathroom and a small kitchen area with a microwave and facilities for making tea and coffee.

'You would have complete access to the kitchen, of course. And the laundry,' Maria said. 'There's a—what do you call them? The baby-radio thing?'

'A baby monitor?'

'Yes, thank you. Ella can sometimes be hard to get to sleep but when she is sleeping, she doesn't wake often at night.' Maria raised her eyebrows. 'What do you think?'

Shirley hadn't been mistaken. 'It's a lovely flat,' Jenna said sincerely.

'Do you think you might like to take the position?'

'Ah…' Jenna let her doubts show. 'Can I ask how you've been managing up till now?'

'We had a nanny. She left two days ago. Louise didn't…ah…find her suitable. There was an argument and…' The shrug was eloquent. It suggested that falling out with Louise was a terminal condition.

'Mrs Gibbs obviously doesn't think I'm particularly suitable either.'

'It is not just her decision. It is Paolo who has the final say.' But Maria sighed. She cast a glance over her shoulder at the door she had closed behind them. 'Louise is very protective of Ella,' she said. 'And of Gwendolyn's memory. I'm embarrassed to admit it, but she thinks that any woman who comes into the household is going to…um…'

'Make a play for Danielle's father?' Jenna supplied helpfully. Hardly a suggestion from left field, given the attractions obvious in that wedding photo. Judging by this house, he had a very wealthy background. His fame as a surgeon was another hefty drawcard and his Mediterranean background would be the icing on the cake for some women.

Maria was nodding unhappily. 'Ridiculous, I know. Of course, I hope that Paolo does find someone eventually and that Ella will have brothers and sisters but I suspect Louise is determined that no one is going to try and step into her Gwendolyn's shoes.'

Jenna almost smiled. Talk about offputting. Louise Gibbs would be the mother-in-law from hell, irrespective of whether she was related to her granddaughter's stepmother. 'I can assure you I have absolutely no interest in forming a relationship with any man at this point in my life. I'm very happily single for the moment.'

Which was absolutely true. Jenna wasn't about to complicate her life with the potential for more unhappiness and even if she *was* open to meeting someone, there were a lot of qualities far more important than looks or the state of bank accounts. Intelligence for one. And compassion. And a sense of humour. Tolerance and warmth and…

'So you might consider taking this position?'

Jenna focussed again with a blink. 'I still don't understand quite why you want someone with my qualifications.'

Maria was silent for a moment. And then she gave another small, resigned sigh. 'You've probably noticed that Louise is a lot younger than I am. I was nearly forty when I had Paolo and Gwen was ten years younger than him. Louise is only forty-two. I'm seventy-four and things are not as good as they used to be,' Maria continued quietly. '*Artrite*. Arth-aritis. Another bone thing I can't pronounce.'

'Osteoporosis?'

'Yes.' Maria nodded approvingly. 'I think so. And I have the blood… Oh, what is it? *La pressione alta.*'

Translation seemed surprisingly easy. 'High blood pressure? Hypertension?'

Maria nodded again. '*Si.*' As she relaxed into her confidences, her accent became stronger—her English less perfect. 'And now I have been told I have the diabetes. The bad one.'

'Type one? You need insulin injections?'

'Yes. *Iniezione*. The needles. I have to start them soon. Tomorrow, maybe. I have an appointment with the doctor. It's difficult. Sometimes my English is not as good as it should be for being here in *Nuova Zelanda* for more than twenty years. Shirley has been helping me but she knows no more than I do. We are like—how do you say it? The blind leading the blind.'

At last, Jenna understood at least part of what had made this interview so puzzling. It wasn't the baby who was the potential patient. It was Maria. The older woman touched her arm. It was almost a plea.

'Paolo needs time to get used to being a father by himself. I don't wish him to know that it is difficult for me to help. If we were still in Italy, it would be no problem, of course, but Paolo will not consider leaving his job and families are not the same here, are they? If Ella was taken to Auckland by Louise, she would be lost to us and that would be…a *tragedia.*'

Dark brown eyes that had not faded with age were swimming with tears. 'It's not for me,' Maria said. 'And it's not just that Louise doesn't share the same things of importance in raising a *bambino*. It's because Ella needs her papa. And he needs her. He just hasn't realised it yet.'

In other words, Jenna would be stepping into an emotional minefield. The passions of an Italian family on the one side and a cold and determined woman, possibly obsessed with the memory of her daughter, on the other. Hardly the easy job she had anticipated but it wasn't going to be pleasant to disappoint someone who clearly cared so much about the best interests of others. Especially when one of those 'others' was a baby girl who had no idea of the undercurrents in the world around her.

That concern for others made the reminder of her own mother stronger than ever. Jenna had wanted to help her mum so badly but had been unable to do any more than make her last few months as comfortable as possible.

She *could* help Maria, though.

'I'll have to think about it,' she said slowly.

'Of course.' But Maria's shoulders slumped a little and she muttered something inaudible in Italian. Then she blinked away the remainder of her tears. 'Come back to the lounge for a moment. Paolo promised he would try and get home in time to meet you so you would not have to come back for another interview.'

Perhaps Paul Romano was a man of his word.

Due either to good management or luck, the surgeon was entering the front door of the house just as Maria and Jenna emerged from the kitchen and Louise was arriving at the foot of the sweeping staircase with Danielle in her arms.

For a moment nobody moved.

An eloquent snatch of time in which the situation and everybody's reactions to it were registered. The atmosphere was suddenly electric and Jenna had to take a deep breath as the swirl of undercurrents threatened to suck her under.

Louise's hold on Danielle struck a discordant note and her determination to advertise her right to be there was almost palpable. 'Look, Danielle,' she said brightly. 'Daddy's home.'

Maria's smile of welcome faded as her gaze travelled from her son to the woman holding her granddaughter. Jenna could sense the anxiety all too clearly.

But what made the air really crackle was the fact that Jenna realised instantly that Louise had no show of being the one in control. The man in that photograph had been a single dimension. The reality was overpowering.

Too good-looking, in a dark suit reminiscent of that wedding attire. The only incongruous note in the immaculate appearance came from the large, stuffed toy giraffe he was holding by one leg in the same hand as a sleek leather briefcase.

He was also charming. But the smile was well practised and did not disguise the keen assessment coming from eyes even darker than those of his daughter. His head dipped in a single nod. The kind of nod, Jenna thought with amusement, that one of his new theatre nurses might receive. She was there and, of course, she wanted the job, but she would have to prove her capability. The benefit of any doubt was not about to be bestowed.

The awkward tension broke as the briefcase was deposited beside an antique umbrella stand and Paul Romano flicked one of Danielle's silky curls with his forefinger.

'*Ciao, cara.*' He held out the giraffe, which Louise took, shaking her head.

'You spoil her, Paul. She already has an entire zoo of animals.'

Danielle took no notice of the toy. She beamed, twisting in Louise's grip to hold out her arms. 'Pa-pa!'

But her father was already turning away as his mother spoke.

'Paolo, this is Jenna Freeman.'

'Yes.' This time he held out his hand. 'Pleased to meet you, Ms Freeman.'

His English was perfect. Just enough trace of an accent in that deep voice to give it an edge that made you want to hear more. And his grip was strong. Sure. This time the eye contact was more personal. Penetrating, even. If Jenna had found the physical presence of this man overpowering, the effect of this physical contact was extremely disconcerting.

Intimidating?

Yes, but Jenna wasn't about to be intimidated. The subtle put-down of treating her as no more than a prospective employee didn't matter because Jenna had no intention of working for this man.

Not after the way he had just ignored his daughter's plea for contact. How cold a person would you have to be to resist those little arms held out like that, begging for a cuddle? And was 'Pa-pa' the only word that Ella had learned so far? Out of desperation, perhaps?

However 'difficult' Paul might find it, being left as a single father, the baby should always come first.

Yet Jenna wasn't getting the impression of a cold man from this contact. Quite the opposite, which only added to her curiosity about the dynamics of this household.

Too late, Jenna became aware that she had been staring at Paul Romano for a shade too long.

That Maria was beaming approvingly.

And that Louise had a gaze that felt like it was being filtered through the sights of a high-powered rifle.

Jenna hurriedly pulled her hand clear of Paul's touch.

That he resisted her intention to pull her hand away was hardly surprising. This was a man who was very used to being in charge. It was only for a fraction of time. A single heartbeat. Just long enough for Jenna to be startled by a flash of what could have been annoyance. Or maybe resignation.

Something that she instinctively knew was not directed at her but was a result of him being just as aware as she was of the undercurrents swirling around them.

'Come this way, Ms Freeman. I won't keep you long.'

He led her back into the room in which she had been interviewed by the grandmothers. He ignored the pages of her CV still lying on the coffee-table, but Jenna had the impression he was already familiar with its contents.

'So…Jennifer, is it?'

'I prefer Jenna.'

The smile was definitely charming. 'So do I,' Paul said. 'It sounds almost Italian.'

Then the smile faded and the gaze fixed on Jenna focussed sharply.

'You're a highly qualified nurse. Why are you applying for a job that will use virtually none of your skills?'

'I…wanted a change.'

'Why?'

Jenna took a deep breath. Talk about getting straight to the point. Fair enough, too. She'd want to know the motivation of someone she was going to employ to care for *her* child. There was no point in being less than honest.

'Six months ago I applied for a year's leave in order to

care for my mother. She was terminally ill with cancer and I wanted to nurse her myself, rather than use a hospice.' Jenna did her best to keep her tone calm and professional but she couldn't help a small wobble. 'Sadly, the end came a little sooner than expected.'

The face of the man facing her softened as she spoke and when he spoke, his voice was also softer. Deeper.

'I'm *so* sorry, Jenna. I had no idea.'

Sympathy enveloped Jenna like a soft blanket. Unexpected and apparently so genuine she found, to her horror, that tears were not far away. She blinked hard. It shouldn't be a surprise that Ella's father could be this caring. After all, this was a man who had clearly loved his wife so passionately he was finding it impossible to bond with their child.

'It was the right thing to do,' he said approvingly. 'Nothing is more important than family, is it?'

'No.' Especially when it was the last of any family Jenna had.

'And you didn't want to return to your hospital position immediately?'

'I couldn't. And it also seemed like a good opportunity to make sure it *is* what I want to do. Where I want to be.'

'You have doubts?'

Doubts?

Of course Jenna had doubts about returning. Having to work in the same hospital as Simon, who would now be parading his new fiancée on his arm at every opportunity.

Paul would have understood, Jenna thought suddenly. Irrelevantly. He knew how important family was. He wouldn't have ended a relationship because a beloved, sick mother was demanding all her attention. He wouldn't have issued an ultimatum of using a hospice or losing him.

Her mother had given her a last, unintentional gift in a way. Saved her from staying in a relationship that could never have been good enough.

'I need a fresh start,' she found herself confessing. 'And I've been thinking of relocating to Christchurch. I thought I'd get more of a feel for what it would be like to live here if I took a job outside a hospital.'

Paul nodded but then frowned. 'I am a little concerned that there are time constraints on your availability,' he said, 'but, then, poor Danielle has had several changes already.' He hesitated for a moment, as though undecided whether to expand on his comment, but then his gaze dropped to the papers on the coffee-table. 'It would certainly be to our advantage to have someone with skills such as yours, even temporarily.' His nod was decisive as he looked up again. 'I want the best for Danielle. The job is yours if you want it.'

Jenna opened her mouth to say that she would have to think about it. That she had a few major reservations about a working environment that included the influence of someone like his mother-in-law. But it would hardly be politic to criticise his child's grandmother and, in any case, Jenna's momentary hesitation cost her the opportunity to say anything at all.

Paul was on his feet and the interview was over. A pager on his belt sounded as he opened the door for Jenna and he moved swiftly past Maria and Louise, who were still in the foyer, towards a phone on a small table.

Within seconds he was clearly in communication with a paediatric intensive care unit,

'What was the CBC differential?' Jenna heard him query. 'Electrolytes? Ultrasound results?'

He listened for a longer time, seemingly oblivious to everyone else standing in the foyer.

'OK. Sounds like it's only a partial obstruction but I don't want a three-day-old baby deteriorating any further. Get a consent form for Theatre signed. I'm on my way.'

With concise, well-practised movements, Paul was on the move again. He collected his briefcase, gave his mother an apologetic smile and made perfunctory farewells.

And then he was gone, as suddenly as he had arrived.

'I'm sorry,' Maria said. 'It was obviously an emergency.'

'I should probably go now as well,' Jenna said.

A grandfather clock chimed.

'Goodness, is that the time?' Louise moved towards Maria, preparing to hand over the baby. 'I have a dinner date tonight.'

Danielle and the toy giraffe were passed into Maria's arms as Jenna turned to make her farewell, and at the sight of the small girl's face, her heart lurched. Danielle was staring at the door through which her father had just disappeared. Her eyes were swimming with tears that had just started to overflow but she was making no sound.

What kind of baby cried silently?

Lifting her gaze, Jenna had the feeling that Maria was reading her mind and a snatch of their private conversation replayed itself.

Ella needs her papa. He needs her. He just hasn't realised it yet.

And maybe he didn't realise that a cuddle was a far more precious gift than a soft toy could ever be. Ella apparently had a whole zoo of stuffed animals but how much physical contact did she get with her only remaining parent? Not much, if any, Jenna suspected. How sad was that?

Louise was putting on her coat. 'Same time tomorrow?'

An answer wasn't expected. 'Goodbye, Jennifer. It was a pleasure to meet you. I hope you find the kind of job you're looking for in Christchurch.'

Jenna waited until Louise was on the other side of the door. A flash of anger at the blatant dismissal from this very unpleasant woman had been enough to put her back up.

To make her want to protect someone as innocent as a baby from such a person. It was a feeling strong enough to shunt aside the considerable misgivings she had about taking this job.

Jenna reached out and stroked a tear from Danielle's pink cheek and then she smiled at Maria.

'How soon would you like me to start?'

CHAPTER TWO

'YOU'RE up very early today, Jenna.'

'Only because someone else decided to get up so early.' Jenna smiled at Paul but quickly dipped her head to drop a kiss among the silky black curls resting on her shoulder. To hide any expression that might reveal embarrassment.

This was the first occasion since that initial interview that she had been in Paul's company without one—or both—of the grandmothers being present. She had only been half-awake as she'd responded to the cry over the baby monitor but why hadn't she taken the time to brush her hair? And why had she just pulled on the clothes lying on the end of her bed in her haste? Her oldest jeans and a faded, racer-back T-shirt were hardly likely to impress her employer.

Ella was still in her pink, fuzzy sleepsuit. The busy conversation of unintelligible but happy sounds she had been entertaining Jenna with on the way downstairs stopped suddenly. The baby had her thumb in her mouth as she watched her father's movements at the kitchen bench. A pot of coffee was waiting for the plunger to be depressed. Paul was busy buttering a piece of toast.

'Would you like coffee, Jenna?'

'I'll get one later, thank you. I just came down to find some more formula for Ella. We've run out in the nursery.'

'How is she today?'

'She seems much better. Her nose is still a bit runny and it was her coughing that woke me, but she's certainly a lot happier than she's been in the last couple of days. I'll keep up the paracetamol and hope her temperature stays down today.'

'Good.' Paul was slicing the toast into soldiers, one of which he offered to Ella. She accepted the gift with a coo of surprise that made both Paul and Jenna smile.

'It seems my mother was right,' Paul said. 'It *is* very reassuring to have a trained nurse caring for Danielle.'

'It's only been a mild virus.'

But the praise was warming. Or was it the unexpected bonus of Paul's company that was creating that warmth? Maybe Jenna should encourage Ella to wake early more often to try and increase the time Paul spent in the company of his daughter. So far, they very rarely saw him in the mornings and only for an hour at the most before Ella's bedtime in the evenings. A period that could easily be missed or curtailed thanks to an existing or emergency case that required the surgeon's professional expertise.

They needed more time together. A lot more.

Ella and Paul, that was. Not Paul and Jenna. Her own inclusion was desirable simply because it was necessary as a facilitator. She may have only had time to gather impressions and set an agenda so far, but her goal was crystal clear. In the space of only a week, ever since she had seen those silent tears, Ella had won her heart to the extent that the challenge now ahead of Jenna was paramount. She had six months to try and foster the bonding of a father and daughter, and success had never seemed so important.

'She likes that toast.' Smears of butter and Marmite were spread across fat pink cheeks. Any thoughts of offering to let Paul hold Ella were squashed. Imagine if he had to go and change that pristine white shirt?

Paul offered Ella another thin slice of toast, which she accepted but didn't eat. This time she held it back out, as though trying to return the gift. Paul didn't notice because he was glancing at his watch.

'It's nearly six. I'll have to run.'

'Yes. It's Wednesday.' Jenna nodded. 'It's one of your heavy theatre days, isn't it?'

An eyebrow rose. 'You know my schedule so well already?'

'Let's see.' Jenna ducked as the piece of buttery toast was waved too close to her hair. 'You operate on Mondays and Fridays as well, have outpatient clinics on Tuesday and Thursdays and you do ward rounds at least once every day. You also have umpteen departmental duties, teaching slots and, of course, way too many emergencies.'

Both of Paul's eyebrows had risen to meet the flop of dark, wavy hair on his forehead.

Jenna tried not to blush. Instead, she took advantage of the opportunity provided.

'Ella doesn't get to see that much of you,' she explained, 'and your mother always looks forward to any time you have at home.'

Maria probably didn't get that weird sensation of having swallowed a whole tribe of butterflies on anticipating Paul's company, though, did she?

A sneaking sympathy for Louise had been inevitable. It was no surprise that Danielle's other grandmother was convinced that any woman coming within an inch of Paul would want to throw herself at the man. He was, without doubt, the most physically attractive man Jenna had ever met.

Tall and dark. Lean and lithe—with the kind of dark, brooding aura that so many women found irresistible. And there was the voice. Like rich chocolate with that barely discernible but intriguing foreign inflection, not to mention the ability to switch to fluent Italian as he sometimes did with his mother. You wouldn't be a heterosexual female if you didn't respond to that attractiveness at some level.

It would wear off.

It might wear off a lot faster if she had enough time to get used to it. To file it where it belonged as simply a physical reaction to a very attractive male. Even if Jenna had been interested in Paul on a personal level—which she *wasn't*—she was focussed enough on her new goal to know that getting distracted would be a hindrance. A disaster, in fact, if Paul actually became more interested in her company than that of his daughter.

It couldn't be allowed to happen.

It *wouldn't* happen.

Things needed to be kept professional. She shouldn't have made such a personal comment. Not yet, anyway, when there were still too many large, missing pieces of the puzzle this family represented.

Jenna tried to open Ella's little fist to remove the mashed piece of toast. She also tried to sound as though Paul's timetable was purely of professional interest.

'Anything interesting on your list today?'

'Yes.' Paul drained the last of his coffee from the mug, highly relieved at the change of topic. He heard more than enough from his mother concerning the number of hours he spent at work. He certainly didn't need Danielle's nanny joining the chorus. 'A three-year-old boy, Darren Symes. He's got a Wilms' tumour.'

'Unilateral involvement?'

The surprise of having an intelligent medical question being asked in his own home was rather pleasant. There was more than one benefit in having a trained nurse as the new nanny. Paul put his coffee-mug into the sink and turned on the tap to rinse his hands.

'I'm hoping so. We haven't found any metastases but there's a question mark hanging over the state of the un-affected kidney. And, of course, I'll have to be very careful to avoid any tumour spillage.'

'How did he present?'

'Abdominal mass. GP found his blood pressure raised and a urine dipstick test detected blood. Ultrasound con-firmed the nephroblastoma.' Paul dried his hands on a towel. 'I must go.'

'Good luck.'

Jenna was smiling at him. There was an understanding of the importance of what he was facing in that smile. There was also confidence that he would succeed in her tone—the wishing of luck was just a verbal token that he was unlikely to need.

He liked that.

Even more, he liked the fact that, for the first time in nearly a year, he could go to work and concentrate on what needed to be done, without having to deliberately switch off any background anxiety about what might be happening at home.

Thanks to Jenna.

An unlikely nanny. It was just as well Louise couldn't see her right now, looking like she had so recently tumbled out of bed. That cloud of dark curls falling over her shoulders, old clothes that hugged a figure far more attractive than those straight skirts and classic shirts had ever advertised and a face that obviously needed no make-up to stand out from a crowd.

Not that it would have mattered what Jenna looked like. Anyone who could have altered the atmosphere in this house to such a degree in the space of only a week would have been welcome. Paul had not seen his mother this happy in a very long time.

Curious that he was taking longer than he needed to dry his hands. That he wasn't in his usual rush to leave for work. It was this new phenomenon that was developing— the notion that dealing with the demands of his family could transcend duty and perhaps even provide a degree of pleasure.

Yes. Everybody had been happier since Jenna had arrived.

Except for Louise, of course, but if Paul was honest, the fact that his mother-in-law was not pleased only added to his current level of satisfaction. Maybe she would just give up now.

And go home.

Not that he would deny her rights as part of the extended Romano clan. Family was everything, was it not?

Yes. Paul smiled as he reached out to touch Danielle's curls.

'*Verdere piu tardi, cara*. See you later.'

He was careful to give Jenna no more than a casual glance of farewell.

Not that he should have trouble keeping the lid on any hormonal stirring he might be experiencing. He'd had more than enough practice in the last eighteen months and the lessons of treading that particular path had been learned exceptionally well. It was Danielle and his mother who would reap the benefits of that sparkle of real intelligence, the ready smile, the soothing voice and what would, undoubtedly, be a soft touch.

He let himself out of the house and strode towards the garage. Being outside was good. Sometimes it was disconcertingly difficult to keep matters of importance in perspective when he was in the company of Danielle's new nanny.

Things may be looking brighter but he needed to tread carefully. To remember the lessons learned. But he could never have difficulty remembering, could he? Danielle was living evidence of the fallout possible from making a mistake. A mistake he would never repeat.

'What is it?'

'Twelve point three. See?' Jenna held the small blood-glucose monitor so that Maria could see the display.

'That's high, is it not?'

'We're aiming to get it stable in single figures but it's better than yesterday and you're due for your insulin anyway.' Jenna stooped to tickle Danielle, who was now crawling on the floor of Maria's bedroom. The baby giggled and held up her arms. 'Just a tick, sweetheart,' Jenna responded. 'I'm going to give Nonna her injection and take her blood pressure and then we'll all go and have proper breakfast. Are you hungry or are you still full of toast?'

Danielle flapped her arms and Maria laughed.

'It's so good having you here, Jenna.' Maria discarded the tissue she had been holding on her fingertip since the prick required for the blood-sugar test. She grimaced at the sight of the approaching syringe. 'I hate needles.'

'You know you barely feel this.'

'It's the waiting for it. The...what is the word?'

'Anticipation?'

'*Si*. The anticipation. It magnifies things.'

'Mmm.' Jenna's agreement was heartfelt. She was already thinking ahead herself. Wondering how to make best use of the time when Paul returned from work that evening.

Wishing they could see a little more of him than they did.

Be careful what you wish for!

Jenna shook off the mental warning. She could handle whatever it was going to take on this new mission of hers.

'I'll never be able to do that by myself.'

Jenna rubbed the spot, having injected the insulin, and smiled. 'I have the feeling you could manage anything you set your mind to, Maria. It can't have been easy, coming to a strange country, away from all your friends and family, to raise your son.'

Maria shrugged. 'His father wanted it so that's what we did. *His* brother went to Australia and became a big success. Roberto wanted to be the one to be successful in *Nuova Zelanda*.' The older woman pushed up her sleeve and watched Jenna wrap the blood-pressure cuff around her upper arm. 'I could not manage this.'

'You won't need to. Once we know your blood pressure is stable on the new dose of medication, you'll only need it checked when you go to see Dr Barry.'

'Wasn't it nice of him to lend us this…what is that impossible word?'

'Sphygmomanometer,' Jenna supplied. She put the disc of the stethoscope on the crook of Maria's elbow. 'Yes, he's a lovely man. And a very good doctor, from what I could see.'

'He was very impressed that you came to the appointment with me.'

Jenna grinned. 'I think he was more impressed at your initiative in hiring a private nurse.'

Maria shook her head. 'I saw him watching you with Danielle, too. When we were leaving he said, "You've got a treasure there, Maria," and I said, "Don't I know it?"'

Jenna concentrated on the mercury level as she released the valve to hide the flush of pleasure at Maria's praise. 'Good. One-fifty on ninety. That's the same as yesterday.' She noted the pressure in a notebook along with the blood-glucose level and the dose of insulin given. 'Now, we'd better get some breakfast into you. I don't want you getting hypoglycaemic and shaky again.'

'I feel like it's taking over my life,' Maria sighed. 'The blood prick. The injection. The right food. Tests and more tests! Watching the clock all the time to make sure that nothing is missed.'

'It'll take a while to get used to.' Jenna scooped up Danielle, who was already making a beeline for the door. Still wearing her cute pink sleepsuit and with her curls still tousled, she was irresistibly cuddly. Jenna gave her a quick kiss before turning her head to smile at Maria. 'You'll be amazed at how it becomes part of the routine in a while. Like cleaning your teeth. Once we get to know how your body reacts to the insulin and what effect things like exercise have, you should be able to get down to only two injections a day. You might even be a candidate for having a pump system that sits under your skin and administers insulin automatically.'

They were halfway along the wide, upstairs hallway now. The door to a bathroom was on the left and Jenna knew the closed door on the right belonged to Paul's bedroom. She adjusted her hold on the baby whose fuzzy sleepsuit made her feel like a living teddy bear.

What did Paul wear to sleep in?

'I do not like that idea,' Maria announced.

'Sorry?' Jenna had been dealing with an idea that was disconcertingly attractive. More than one idea, in fact. Old pyjama pants tied up with a string? Boxers? Nothing at all…?

'A pump. The needle would be there in my skin? All the time?'

'No. Actually, the whole pump system is placed under the skin. Like a pacemaker. You wouldn't feel it.' Jenna's steps slowed. 'I should get Ella dressed before we go downstairs.'

'Why bother?' Maria ruffled Ella's curls and kissed her. 'What's so wrong with having breakfast in your pyjamas?'

'Absolutely nothing.' Laughing, they moved on together towards the stairs. 'And are you sure you don't mind me wearing jeans?'

'You must wear whatever makes you happy, Jenna. I'm going to get into old clothes soon. It's such a lovely day and I wish to do some gardening.'

'But it's Wednesday.'

Maria sighed. '*Si*. So it is.'

Wednesdays weren't just one of Paul's heavy days for the operating theatre. It was also one of the weekdays that Louise chose to pay an extended visit to Hamilton Drive.

She arrived while they were still in the kitchen and the laughter Ella had generated with her own attempts to get porridge and stewed apples anywhere but into her mouth faded abruptly.

Louise bent to kiss Ella but drew back. 'What *is* that in her hair?'

'Porridge.' Jenna grinned. 'I'll go and get her cleaned up. It's time to get dressed anyway.'

'Yes.' Louise eyed the jeans Jenna was wearing as she stood up to lift Ella from the high chair. The housekeeper, Shirley, distracted her from making any comment.

'Coffee, Mrs Gibbs?'

'Yes. Black. No sugar.'

Shirley caught Jenna's gaze as she went past the back of Louise's chair. The subtle roll of the housekeeper's eyes was eloquent. As if she didn't know by now how Louise took her coffee. It was also intended to be encouraging, Jenna realised. They were all in for a long day.

One that didn't start very well.

'I'll take Danielle out for her walk,' Louise announced when Jenna brought her back downstairs.

Weather permitting, the walk was part of the routine on the days Louise visited—at least three times a week.

'She likes to show her off,' Shirley had confided to Jenna on Monday evening. 'That's why she likes to have her all dolled up in those clothes she keeps buying.'

Like the smocked dress and shiny shoes Jenna had dressed her in that morning.

'I'll bet that where she picked up her bug,' Shirley had added in a mutter.

A bug she wasn't completely over.

'I'm not sure it's a terribly good idea today,' Jenna said to Louise. 'She's been running a temperature and was coughing in the night.'

'She looks fine to me.' Louise took Ella from Jenna's arms. 'And it's a glorious day.'

Jenna couldn't contradict either statement. Ella *did* look much better, even though very little of that breakfast had made it anywhere near being swallowed. And it was a gorgeous day. One of those autumn gems that was still enough to leave the warmth of the sunshine undiminished.

If they stayed at home, she would have encouraged Danielle to spend time playing outside. Was there any real difference in being taken for a walk in her stroller?

She caught Maria's gaze and the hint of alarm that Jenna, the expert, thought that her precious Ella might still be unwell. If Paul was here, Jenna thought, he would make the decision in an instant and nobody would dare argue. But if Jenna put her foot down, Louise would be very unlikely to comply. Maria would oppose her fiercely and Jenna might find herself caught in the middle of a small domestic war.

'Maybe just for a little while,' she heard herself suggesting. 'It *is* a lovely day.'

'I'll take a complete change of clothes for her.' Louise had already assumed victory. 'And a warm jacket. Get them ready, would you, please, Jennifer?'

Jenna climbed the stairs, annoyed with herself. If she had been on the familiar territory of a paediatric ward and wearing a uniform, instead of faded denim jeans, there was no way she would have hesitated to wield authority of behalf of someone as vulnerable as a baby.

But she had no authority here. Or not enough. Louise would be a formidable adversary and quite apart from the stress a disagreement with Maria could cause, her discontent had seen the last nanny sent packing. Jenna couldn't understand why Louise was accorded the power she seemed to have—it was a piece of the puzzle she had yet to find. And it was a power bestowed purely by default. Paul could remove it with a click of those long surgeon's fingers any time he chose.

So why didn't he?

Whatever the reason, if Jenna wanted to keep this job and succeed in the challenge she had set herself, she would have to choose any battles with care, and the evidence that Ella needed to be kept within the confines of her own home today was not strong enough. Even Paul had seemed happy enough that morning with the improvement in Ella's condition.

The phone call at 11.30 a.m. to pass on the information that Louise had met a friend and would be lunching at a café was no surprise but it was a worry. The easterly breeze that had sprung up was cool enough to bring Maria in from tending her basil and tomato plants.

Jenna passed on the message, adding that she hoped Louise would not have Ella sitting outside.

'Surely not!' But Maria cast an anxious glance at the clock. 'She will need to have her back in time for her sleep.'

'There's a man involved,' Shirley warned. 'You mark my words.'

Jenna had lunch in the kitchen with Maria and Shirley and Shirley's husband, John, who helped in the garden. She couldn't help casting frequent glances through the windows at scudding clouds that were now blocking the sunshine at regular intervals. By 1.30 p.m. the temperature had dropped significantly and there was still no sign of Ella's return.

'Maybe I should go and collect them in my car,' Jenna said finally. 'Even if they had lunch inside, it's a good fifteen-minute walk home and I'm really not happy about Ella being outside. It looks like it could start raining at any minute.'

'We could ring her cellphone,' Shirley suggested, 'and find out what café they're in.'

But there was no need, because they heard the sound of the front door and a moment later Louise pushed the stroller into the kitchen. A stroller that contained a wailing baby.

'She's just a bit tired,' Louise said defensively, as Maria rushed to pick up and comfort her grandaughter.

'*Dio mio!* She's cooking!'

'It got cold. She needed her jacket on.'

'Jenna?' The plea from Maria was almost desperate but Jenna was already in action, her instincts sounding a loud alarm.

She took Ella from Maria, quickly removing her outer clothing, but it did little to cool her and she was too distressed to swallow the liquid paracetamol Shirley fetched under Jenna's direction. What worried Jenna more, however, was the rate and depth at which the child was breathing.

Trying to calm her down had to be the first priority. Jenna cradled Ella in her arms, letting the small head snuggle into her shoulder. She rocked her and made soothing sounds.

'It's OK, sweetie… Everything's OK…'

Maria stood nearby, twisting her hands, her forehead creased with worry. Shirley stared at Louise between helping Jenna by fetching the medication and supplying a damp facecloth, but Louise was ignoring everybody. She helped herself to coffee and then sat down at the table.

Ella's exhausted sobbing finally ebbed and it was then that Jenna could assess what she had instinctively feared. The baby was in quite severe respiratory distress. Tiny nostrils were flaring and the muscles around her ribs retracting with the effort to breath. It was taking longer for her to breathe out than in and Jenna could now hear a faint wheeze. And the rate was high. Far too high.

'We need to take Ella to hospital,' she announced.

Maria went pale and crossed herself. Louise lifted her head sharply.

'Don't be ridiculous! She's just got a bit of a sniffle and she's tired. I'm sorry we didn't get back earlier but I met…Gerald, the man I had dinner with last week and he asked me to have lunch and…well, I could hardly refuse, could I?'

Shirley gave a soft I-told-you-so sort of snort but nobody bothered answering Louise.

'Could someone bring a car around?' Jenna asked. 'I don't want to put Ella down until I have to. Getting upset again is only going to aggravate the trouble she's having with her breathing.'

'She can't breathe? *Oh…*' Maria was hovering like a mother hen.

'What's wrong with her?' Louise demanded.

'I think she may have bronchiolitis.'

'But she seemed so much better this morning,' Maria almost wailed. 'I don't understand!'

'It often presents as a mild viral illness and the symptoms were well controlled with the paracetamol. If it had just been a cold, she wouldn't have deteriorated like this.'

'You should have known it was more than a cold. You're a nurse, aren't you?' Louise was getting to her feet. 'I hope you're not suggesting this is *my* fault.'

'What's important right now is that we get Ella to hospital so she can be monitored properly and treated if this gets any worse.'

'I'll get the car,' John offered.

'I'm coming, too,' Maria said firmly.

'So am I,' Louise snapped.

Maria paused with dramatic suddenness in her route to the door. She waved her arms in the air. '*Wait!* I must ring Paolo and let him know we're coming.'

Jenna blinked. Of course Paul should know his daughter

was about to turn up in the emergency department, but what would he think if he received an alarmed call from his mother—probably in voluble Italian? Keeping everybody calm was part of her job in order to prevent the atmosphere around Ella becoming overly tense.

'Maybe Shirley could do that,' she suggested. 'That way we won't be held up.' She caught the housekeeper's gaze. 'Just let him know I'm a bit worried so we're coming in to get Ella properly checked.'

'Sure.' Shirley nodded. 'I guess they'll let me leave a message if he's busy in the operating theatre or something.'

This wasn't the way Jenna would have wanted any of them to see more of Paul Romano. She *should* have been more careful what she wished for.

Both grandmothers had been asked to wait in the relatives' waiting area and Ella was sitting on Jenna's knee in an emergency department cubicle. This was due solely to the fact that if anyone tried to remove her from Jenna's arms she immediately began to cry. With her nanny, she was calm enough to allow oxygen tubing to be held in the vicinity of her face in an attempt to bring up the level of oxygen circulating in Ella's blood.

'What's the saturation now?'

'Ninety per cent.' The paediatric registrar summoned to examine Ella flinched visibly at the unexpected, crisp query coming from behind his back. Paul had finally appeared, still dressed in his theatre scrubs and clearly impatient to find out what was going on.

Jenna was thankful she had her arms full of Ella and something she could at least pretend to be completely focussed on. She was also thankful for the conversation now going on between the consultant and the registrar, however, because it gave her a legitimate excuse to steal frequent glances at Paul.

She had never seen him looking like that.

She had never seen *anyone* looking like that.

The suggestion of weariness and, undoubtedly, anxiety for his daughter had given the surgeon an even more sombre professionalism. Or was it because they were now on his working turf?

Jenna was struck anew by this man's apparent aloofness to his child. He was acting like any other doctor might in discussing a patient. Apart from his customary flick of Ella's curls in greeting, Paul had made no attempt to comfort his sick daughter. No cuddles. No soothing words.

Was Jenna dreaming in thinking she could establish a loving connection if there was so little to build on?

The aloof, professional demeanour was at complete odds with his appearance. Too many hours under a theatre cap would have flattened those black curls. Had Paul run distracted fingers through his hair to make it look so tousled and unruly?

And the scrub suit was baggy. A deep V-neck revealed dark curls on his chest and his bare arms also had a covering of fine, very dark hair.

Jenna felt almost embarrassed. It felt like catching her employer on the way out of the shower with just a towel wrapped around his waist. Much worse than a casual chat in the kitchen of his own home. Worse even than idle curiosity about what he might wear to bed. She could feel herself flushing, as though at any moment Paul would look over to see her thoughts in a bubble over her head.

How ridiculous! As if she hadn't seen surgeons around hospitals or in wards, still wearing theatre clothing.

But she had never been involved in their private lives, had she? Jenna felt uncomfortable. Like she was stepping over a boundary of some kind. Only she didn't know what the boundaries were.

'You'll have to admit her, then,' Paul was saying.

'Yes.'

'Provisional diagnosis?'

'Bronchiolitis. Probably RSV. We'll try a viral nasal wash to identify the causative pathogen but it won't make any difference to treatment at this stage.'

'Which is?'

'We'll give oxygen to keep the sats above ninety-two per cent. IV or nasogastric fluids at seventy five per cent maintenance and we'll keep a careful watch on her and transfer her to the paediatric ICU if she deteriorates.'

'Chest X-ray?'

'Not indicated, given that she has typical clinical features.'

Those typical clinical features that were listed in any paediatric textbook were feeling far more personal to Jenna. This was Ella in her arms. Feeling too hot, her nose rubbing against Jenna's shoulder as her head twisted in discomfort. Feeling heavy and exhausted but forced to continue the laboured breathing.

Poor little thing. Jenna had never experienced empathy with her patients to quite this degree—even the ones that had stolen her heart. She rocked Ella gently and shifted the end of the oxygen tubing a little closer to the baby's flushed features.

Paul's attention, with startling suddenness, was transferred to Jenna. 'Why did you leave it so long to bring her in?'

The scrub suit and the body it revealed were forgotten instantly. So was any embarrassment. The unfairness of apportioning blame for Ella's condition got her back up just as instantly.

'We came as soon as I saw she was in respiratory distress.'

His gaze didn't leave hers but Jenna wasn't going to be the first to look away. To imply guilt. It wasn't easy. The weight of Ella in her arms and her concern for the child was making her feel bad enough already. Guilt was only a heartbeat away, even if it was unjustified.

'You're a paediatric nurse. I would have expected you to pick this up well before it required urgent hospital admission.' The approval of her care of Ella that he had expressed only that morning seemed long forgotten.

He was a paediatric surgeon, for heaven's sake. He had seen how well Ella had looked at 6 a.m., stuffing a piece of toast into her mouth, and he must know just how quickly the condition of young children could deteriorate.

Then again, maybe Ella hadn't gone downhill so suddenly. There had been a period of several hours when she had been away from the observation of trained eyes.

'Mrs Gibbs had taken Ella out for a walk.'

'And you allowed this?' Paul looked astonished. And then disappointed. Jenna felt a wave of shame. He had every right to be disappointed in her. The fact that she had let herself down in a professional capacity was bad enough to make Jenna feel that disappointment like a physical blow.

She hated that Paul thought less of her. There was no point trying to defend herself or, worse, suggest that he had been in a position to make the judgement call himself.

Or to explain that there had been no clinical grounds on which to forbid the outing later in the morning and that she had been trying to act as a professional and keep her own emotions out of an already volatile mix. That she had been trying to act as a nanny and not a substitute mother.

She may have nothing to feel guilty about but from Paul's point of view, she had failed in her duty to his child. Bad enough for a nanny to be negligent but for someone who was supposed to be a senior paediatric nurse, it was inexcusable.

The bright flush in her cheeks might have gone unnoticed except that Paul paused, having flicked back the cubicle curtain. He turned once again.

'My mother tells me that Ella prefers your care to anyone else's at present.'

Jenna lifted her chin but said nothing. Did he really have to sound as though the idea that she could still do any part of her job well enough was surprising?

'She will need someone to stay in hospital with her during this admission. Day *and* night.'

Jenna nodded her agreement. She had no argument with his statement. She approved of the fact that Paul recognised its importance. Maybe he did care, just a little. Many babies were left to the care of nursing staff overnight because family circumstances made it necessary. Some even had to be separated from their family members during the day as well, but the co-operation and recovery of children who had a familiar, loving presence with them at all times was measurably better.

'I would prefer that person to be you.' The words were uttered with a certain caution. As though Paul had been persuaded—against his better judgement—that it was preferable.

Had Louise complained that she couldn't manage such a commitment, perhaps?

Was Paul concerned that the prospect of long days with a miserable baby and potentially sleepless nights might be too much for his own mother?

Or had it been necessary to curtail the competition between the two grandmothers?

Somehow, Jenna didn't think any of these explanations sufficed. Paul Romano was not someone who would be easily swayed from his better judgement and it would have been quite possible to arrange a roster system that allowed both Louise and Maria to share the care.

Was she being given a second chance here?

If so, she'd better make damned sure she came out with a better report card than she had just been issued with for her care of Ella. For the sake of her own self-esteem, if nothing else. Besides, she *wanted* to be the one to care for Ella.

'Of course,' Jenna said. 'I hadn't considered otherwise.'

'Good.'

His expression softened with the same fluid ease that Jenna had been startled by in that first interview. It wasn't that he was blaming her for this situation. It was more that he was understandably anxious about his daughter and perhaps he realised that he was taking it out on her. It could almost be a kind of apology.

But even if it was, why did it have the curious effect of disturbing that nest of butterflies? Of creating tension rather than relief?

'I'll see you on the ward, then.' With a nod at both Jenna and the registrar, Paul left. Presumably to start his afternoon theatre list.

The registrar eyed Jenna curiously. 'So you're a paediatric nurse?'

'Yes.'

'Working as a nanny?'

'Temporarily. I took a year's leave of absence from my job to care for my terminally ill mother. The...end came a lot sooner than we expected.'

'I'm sorry to hear that.' The registrar's glance shifted to the cubicle's curtain. The direction in which Paul had vanished. 'Must be a challenging job for you?'

'I expect it will be. I've only just started, really.' Jenna pulled a rueful face, pressing her cheek gently to the top of Ella's drowsy head. 'This isn't the best way to impress one's new boss, is it?'

'At least you'll know your way around a paediatric ward.' The registrar smiled as he saw Jenna give her charge a soft kiss. 'And you are obviously fond of wee Ella here. You're the perfect person to special this case. She's a lucky little button.'

'I just hope she gets through this without any further complications.'

'We'll make sure we keep you in long enough to be certain. Come on, I'll take you up to the ward.'

'You just have the one?'

'There's a paediatric intensive care unit, of course, but hopefully you won't need to get acquainted with that. There's also a smaller ward for acute assessment. More of an intensive observation unit.'

'So you have both medical and surgical cases on the same general ward?'

'Yes. Did you have them separated?'

'No. There's such a big overlap, isn't there? With the number of specialists that get called in from all fields, it's easier to have them all heading for the same place.'

'Exactly. We'll keep you in a private room, though. Wouldn't want RSV to spread.'

Jenna followed the registrar. They would collect the grandmothers on their way to the ward.

A ward that would have all Paul's inpatients. He would be doing rounds there probably twice a day and would be called in to assess new admissions or deal with complications at all sorts of other times.

Potentially, Ella would see much more of her father in the next day or two than she did at home.

Jenna's heart skipped a beat.

So would she.

CHAPTER THREE

ELLA still had a bottle of warm milk last thing at night to settle her for sleep and it was a time of day Jenna had already come to love.

In the past, the opportunity to sit comfortably in an armchair, cradling an infant to feed it, had always been a moment of peace in a hectic work routine. With Ella, always reluctant to surrender to sleep, it was something really special.

Jenna would find herself under the scrutiny of those serious, dark eyes that always seemed to be asking a question. One tiny, starfish hand would be on the bottle. The other would be grasping Jenna's arm and squeezing rhythmically, like a kitten kneading its mother's stomach.

Tonight, with feeling unwell and all the stress of a long and frightening day, feeding time was a blessing. Ella could come out from beneath the oxygen tent overhanging her cot and be held properly.

Comforted and fed.

The hand that normally stayed in touch with the bottle was encumbered with a bulky splint and bandage, keeping the IV line protected, but the other hand held onto Jenna's arm with a new, fiercely determined grip, and the questions in the baby's eyes had an urgent quality.

'I'm here, sweetheart,' Jenna whispered. 'I'm not going anywhere.'

Ella accepted the teat of the bottle but sucked only once or twice, half-heartedly, and her little hand retained its firm grip with no release to begin the customary squeezing.

When Jenna went to remove the teat from her mouth, however, Ella's face crinkled miserably and her chest heaved with the effort of preparing to cry. She might not be hungry—probably thanks to the IV fluids she was receiving—but she needed the cuddle that went along with the routine of the feed. Jenna slipped the teat back into her mouth before the first audible squeak emerged and, at the same moment, a nurse poked her head through the doorway to their private room.

'Everything OK, Jenna?'

'Fine, thanks.'

'Is she still wheezy?'

'A bit. I think it's improved a little.'

'You'll put her back in the tent when you've finished feeding her? Her sats are probably dropping again.'

'Sure. I'll put the monitor back on as well and increase the flow if necessary.'

The nurse smiled. 'It's not often we get a trained nurse to help care for our babies.' The faint sound of a fractious child filtered in from the main ward and the nurse sighed. 'Looks like everybody wants to wake up tonight. Call me if you need anything.'

'I will.'

'And try to get some sleep yourself. That's what the bed's for, you know.'

Jenna nodded again. She should get up, she thought, and close the door properly, but she didn't want to disturb the bundle in her arms and their isolation was only semi-formal. The important issue was that Ella didn't come into close contact with any of the other inpatients.

Her gaze was already refocussed on Ella. Keeping the eye contact and trying to answer those unformed questions with reassurance.

Alone again, she rocked the baby and sang a soft song.

Surely she would fall asleep soon. It was so far past her normal bedtime and she had to be totally exhausted.

Jenna certainly was.

It had been one of the longest afternoons she had ever experienced. Even after the drawn-out trauma of the admission process and insertion of the intravenous line in Ella's hand, there had been no chance to rest. Jenna had had to liaise with the medical staff and try to keep both the grandmothers calm.

Especially Maria.

'But how will I manage without you?' Maria had been forced to wait until Louise had finally decided she would go home before she'd been able to speak to Jenna on the private matter that had clearly been weighing almost as heavily on her mind as Ella's condition. 'I can't do it! Not by myself.'

'You don't have to.' Pressing another handful of tissues into Maria's hands hadn't seemed to be sufficient, so Jenna had given her a hug. 'We'll manage together, you'll see.'

'But *how*?'

'The house is very close to the hospital. It's perfectly reasonable for you to be coming back and forth often—like you did when you fetched Ella's sleepsuit and toys. You remembered to bring everything so we'll just keep your blood-glucose kit here. I'll hide it in the drawer, see? I'll keep the insulin in the fridge and if anybody notices, I'll just say it's mine.'

'But the *pressione*. Do I need to bring the…the…?'

Jenna had shaken her head confidently. 'We won't worry about taking your blood pressure. It's only for a day or two.'

Maria had gone away looking hopeful. 'Our *segreto*,' she had murmured quite comprehensibly. 'You are an *angelo*, Jenna.'

So far it had worked. Bringing items Ella needed had been the cover for the late afternoon treatment and she had stayed long enough to deal with the evening dose. She would be back first thing in the morning.

Which wasn't far away. It had to be well after midnight as Jenna sat singing to Ella and, at last, the dark eyes were heavily lidded. The little body was getting heavier as it relaxed.

There were no signs of increasing respiratory distress so Jenna didn't rush to put Ella back in the cot. She wanted to make absolutely sure she was not going to be roused by movement and the more deeply asleep Ella was, the better the chances.

And it was comforting. For both of them.

Jenna's song dropped to a hum. She carefully took the teat of the bottle from Ella's slack lips and put it to one side. Then she simply cuddled the baby close. Every so often, she pressed a very gentle kiss to the silky, black curls.

That was how Paul found her, a little after 1 a.m., when he paid his first visit to the room since Ella had been admitted.

It wasn't that he hadn't tried. Maria had spoken to him on the ward much earlier but he'd been paged to the paediatric ICU to see the patient he'd operated on that morning. The registrar had informed Jenna that he'd rung for an update on his daughter's condition in the evening but he was on call and about to go into Theatre again to deal with a toddler's internal injuries after being struck by a car.

Jenna had not expected to see him until the next day. In fact, she was beginning to wonder if she would see him at all on the ward. It should have been something of a relief that she might not, given his disapproval of her care of Ella earlier but curiously a sense of disappointment was building.

She certainly hadn't expected a visit at this time of night.

Or the expression on his face that lacked even a smile of courtesy as he stood there, still wearing a very crumpled set of theatre scrubs, staring at her as she held Ella in her arms.

The hum died on her lips. She should have had Ella back in her cot by now. Under the clear, plastic tent that was keeping the oxygen levels well up in the air she breathed. How far would her saturation levels have dropped? Was Jenna about to face further—justified—disapproval of her nursing skills?

She held his gaze.

Or was he holding hers? Jenna doubted that she *could* have dragged hers away no matter how hard she tried. Paul closed the door softly behind him without breaking the eye contact and by then it had gone on a fraction too long.

Long enough for those damned butterflies to start beating a tattoo against Jenna's ribs.

Weird that she could hold the gaze of the miniature version of those eyes and respond to the unformed questions so willingly. In the subdued lighting of this quiet hospital room, Paul's eyes were black. Assessing. Asking questions that made Jenna feel the need to put herself on guard. To raise some kind of emotional sword and be ready to parry and defend herself.

And then—at the same moment he broke the eye contact—he slipped beneath that guard with an ease that took her breath away.

'I owe you an apology, Jenna,' he said.

He knew to keep his voice down but the rumble was familiar enough in any case to cause little more than a contented stretch from Ella and then a slump into a deeper unconsciousness. The tiny rasp of the baby's breathing and the faint hiss of oxygen escaping from the valve on the wall were the only sounds to fill the room.

How did Paul move so silently? Or with such grace for such a large man? With the controlled stealth of a hunting cat, he crossed the room, moved a chair to face the one Jenna was sitting on and then folded his long body to perch on its edge.

He reached out to touch Ella's curls, the way he always did in greeting.

Only this time it felt as though he was touching Jenna herself. A prickle of sensation seemed to be conducted through the baby to ripple through Jenna's entire body.

Suddenly, she was all too aware of how she must look. Probably a lot worse than she had so early that morning. Washed out. Her make-up would have worn off long since and she always went a little pale when overtired. Her clothes were grubby. Her hair a tangle of curls that hadn't seen a brush for too long. But what did it matter when it was Ella Paul had come to see?

'How is she?'

'A little better, I think,' Jenna whispered. 'This is the first real rest she's getting.' She could feel her cheeks flushing as Paul's gaze lifted to catch hers again. 'I…I should put her back in the tent.'

'I'll do it.'

His eyelids looked heavy—rather like Ella's had looked just before she'd succumbed to sleep. The lines around his eyes were deeper than normal and his chin heavily shadowed with stubble. Paul had to be even more tired than she was. She hadn't been on her feet since before 6 a.m., dealing with major surgery and emergencies. But he wasn't going to sit back and watch what needed to be done now. His hands slid beneath Ella to lift her gently.

A task that necessitated a physical contact that was astonishingly disturbing.

He's just a parent, Jenna reminded herself with a touch of panic. You've handed sleeping infants to their parents a thousand times. Times when she hadn't even been conscious of the brush of a hand against the skin of her arms.

Or fingertips that reached her breast.

Right now she was conscious of nothing else, but fortunately Paul seemed unaware of the small, shocked intake of her breath. He took his daughter with all the care he might extend to a particularly intricate surgical technique, managed to transfer her to the cot without getting the IV line tangled and then laid her on the soft mattress and slipped his hands free so slowly Jenna had to keep holding her breath.

She could feel the slow slide of those hands on her own back.

She *wanted* to feel them.

A delicious dragging sensation that would leave an aching want in its wake.

Jenna had to move. Reaching for the oxygen saturation probe that clipped to Ella's foot was the ideal way to shake this appalling reaction she was experiencing.

One that surely was only there because she was so tired.

And because of the odd intimacy of this dim room, shut away from the rest of the ward, where conversation was taking place in whispers. Or was it more because of the way Paul had destroyed her ready defences by saying he owed her an apology?

Had he been referring to the blame he had bestowed in the emergency department? And was that hushed statement the extent of the apology?

Maybe not.

Paul sat down again on the upright spare chair and this time he sat on it properly, as though he intended to stay there. Jenna returned to the armchair. She pulled her feet up and curled into its soft cushion, wrapping her arms around her legs. A physical defence, perhaps? Was it simply exhaustion making her feel oddly vulnerable?

She also kept her gaze on the small screen that was showing the percentage level of oxygen circulating in Ella's blood as the figures climbed slowly to an acceptable range.

Eighty-four…eighty-six…ninety-two…ninety-five…

Jenna could breathe again.

Almost.

Keeping his voice down gave Paul's words a seductive edge that made it difficult to concentrate on what he was saying.

'My mother tells me you tried to stop Louise taking Danielle out today.'

'I…' She hadn't tried hard enough, had she?

Paul misinterpreted her hesitation. 'She is not always the easiest person to negotiate with. I know this.'

He lifted a hand—a casual but eloquent gesture that suggested Louise's faults might be a trial but they were something they all had to accept.

'Thank you for bringing Danielle into the hospital. It was where she needed to be.'

'Not for long, I hope.'

'No.' Paul cast a glance at the nearby cot. 'I shouldn't imagine so.' He rose to his feet and then stooped to pick up a toy that had fallen from the cot. A grey, beany rabbit with overly long limbs and fluffy white feet and ears.

'Poor Letto,' Paul murmured. 'Getting all dusty.'

'That's her favourite toy,' Jenna said. For some reason she wanted to try and draw out the conversation. 'Is Letto an Italian name?'

Paul's nod was absent-minded. 'Short for *coniglietto*. Means rabbit. Or bunny.' He dropped the toy near Ella's feet. 'I will be back in the morning. I will bring my mother and you will be able to have a break.'

'I'm happy to stay with Ella.' Mind you, a long, hot shower might be very welcome by then.

She was getting that assessing look again but this time it didn't seem threatening.

'My mother has become very fond of you already, Jenna,' Paul said evenly. 'So has Danielle, by all accounts. You are doing well.'

The praise was sincere. Just as she had known the first time he'd looked at her that she would have to earn a good impression, she knew now that praise was not bestowed prematurely.

The smile that touched his lips was weary but it was also sincere. Not part of that automatic charm that was as much a part of Paul Romano as his dark eyes and olive skin. It made the corners of his eyes crinkle and softened the hard line of that determined jaw.

Jenna couldn't help smiling back.

A smile that returned, unconsciously, a little while later as Jenna finally dozed in her chair.

* * *

Any lack of seeing Ella's father on the day of her admission was shaping up to be made up for on the following day when Paul arrived in the room at 7.30 a.m.

The visit was perfectly timed as far as Jenna and Maria were concerned. Maria's blood test and insulin dose had been long since dealt with and Jenna was now seated in the armchair again, this time with Ella showing far more enthusiasm for her bottle of milk.

Maria was bustling about. Supplies from home had been emptied onto the bed from the cavernous black bag she liked to carry and she was now sorting baby clothes and putting the ones that needed washing back into the bag. The task was abandoned the instant her son walked through the door.

'Paolo!' she cried with delight. Her outstretched hands commanded a response but Jenna couldn't detect any hesitation on Paul's part to walk into them. You would have thought these two hadn't seen each other for a week, given the affectionate greeting, as Paul bent his head to kiss Maria on both cheeks. His own cheeks were then patted firmly enough to raise their colour but Paul was smiling.

'You are well, Maria? You look well.'

'I am fine, Paolo. You were so late last night—I was worried about you!'

'I came to visit Danielle. And then I had another call. It was so late by then, I decided to sleep here.'

He can't have had more than a couple of hours' sleep, Jenna realised. Why didn't he look as jaded and dishevelled as she was feeling? He was wearing the dark suit she remembered from her first meeting with him. With a crisp, white shirt and a carefully knotted tie. Consultant's clothes. Funny that she had been far more impressed when he had been wearing those crumpled scrubs.

'Danielle is looking so much better, yes?' Maria was

turning her son towards the armchair, but his first glance was towards Jenna rather than his daughter. A glance that lingered just long enough to reflect the smile of greeting.

A smile that was just as warm as the one she had received so late last night. The kind that had haunted those half-dreams in her attempts to catch some sleep during the night.

Some neural circuit had been reinforced through repetition and its effect was instantaneous. Jenna could feel her heart rate increase and the extra blood flow that chased away fatigue made every cell in her body come a little bit more alive.

Jenna had time to come to the conclusion that the sensation was very pleasant after Paul's gaze dropped to watch Ella sucking on her bottle. Matching dark eyes were watching the surgeon's every move as he stepped closer to touch her curls, and she released the teat of the bottle with a noisy gurgle to smile at her father. Ella let go of the bottle to wave a hand and Jenna shifted the weight of the baby as she smiled at Paul.

'Would you like to hold her?'

He didn't visibly flinch or step back but Jenna could sense the sudden wariness as clearly as if he had. Her suggestion was being bounced back at her, like a kind of shock wave.

Paul avoided her gaze and Jenna felt suddenly weary again.

You idiot, she told herself. *Don't push it!*

'I can't stop,' Paul said smoothly. ' We had a lot of admissions yesterday and I'm late for a huge ward round. I'll be back later.' He flicked one of Ella's curls again. 'Finish your breakfast, *cara.*'

His fingertips brushed Jenna's bare arm but the touch felt like a warning. The boundaries were becoming clearer and Jenna was forced to step back. She turned to Maria.

'Would you like to hold her, Nonna?'

'Yes, yes—of course!'

The day-shift nurse, Beth, appeared in the doorway as Jenna handed Ella to Maria.

'Dr Romano? They're bringing Darren down from ICU now. You said you wanted to know.'

'Yes, thank you. I'll go and meet them.'

'And, Jenna? The bathroom's free if you'd like a shower. I can come and look after Ella.'

'*I* am looking after Ella,' Maria announced.

'OK.' Beth smiled. 'Just ring the bell if you need anything. Come with me, Jenna. I'll find you a towel and show you where everything is.'

When Jenna emerged from the bathroom fifteen minutes later, refreshed and dressed in the clean clothes Maria had brought from the flat, she felt ready for anything.

Except for what she saw in the private room next to Ella's.

There was quite a crowd of people around the bed. Nursing staff and junior doctors were arranging personal belongings and enough monitoring equipment to suggest that this patient required a high level of care. The parents of the patient were looking rather lost, standing back and watching the activity, but the small boy on the bed was looking surprisingly happy. He had a huge grin on his face, in fact, clearly due to the toy that was being waggled above his head and apparently making funny noises.

What brought Jenna to a startled halt and made her jaw drop was that the person holding the fluffy toy and making the noises was the patient's consultant surgeon.

None other than Paul Romano.

The man who, for some unidentified reason, couldn't even play with his own daughter!

Beth was back in Ella's room, changing the sheets on the cot.

'Who's next door?' Jenna asked. 'The patient from ICU?'

'Yes. That's Darren.' Jenna was already accepted as an honorary staff member by these fellow paediatric nurses and the normal rules of confidentiality were ignored. 'Dr Romano did a nephrectomy on him yesterday morning for a Wilms' tumour. They thought the remaining kidney was going to fail, but he's bouncing back.'

'Cute kid.' Jenna was still trying to assimilate the sight of Paul entertaining the child. It was so out of character for the man she'd thought she was getting to know. And it was disturbing. Compared to how he was with a child who was a comparative stranger, he was cold with his own child. Jenna didn't like that.

She hadn't needed to see him interacting with one of his patients to know he was capable of affection. He clearly loved his mother. Why on earth couldn't he love his daughter? It obviously wasn't that he didn't know how so it had to be a deliberate choice not to interact with Ella so closely.

Maybe she was wrong in accepting those boundaries. Maybe she should have pushed harder, in fact. Just shoved his daughter into his arms, instead of asking for acquiescence.

'He does look like a cutie.' Beth bundled up the used linen from the cot. 'We'll special him for a day or two but I don't expect he'll be any problem.' She smiled at Ella who was being bounced gently on Maria's knee. 'He's a lucky boy, having your daddy to look after him. Now, are you ready for a clean nappy, chicken?'

'I can do that,' Jenna offered.

'That would be great. The team will be in to see you

soon on their rounds, which I'd better get ready for. With Ella feeding as well as she did this morning, they'll probably take that IV line out. Her breathing sounds a bit better, too.'

'Maybe they'll let us go home today.'

Beth chuckled. 'Don't bet on it. They'll want a completely clean slate before they discharge Dr Romano's child. I'd put money on you having at least one more night here.'

The medical consultant confirmed Beth's opinion when he came to do his rounds.

'I'm happy for us to go to oral hydration but I want her temperature right down and her chest clear before we let you go. Maybe tomorrow for discharge.'

Jenna was happy with the decision, not just because the responsibility for Ella was being shared with experts. Being back on such familiar territory was a reminder of how much she missed the job she was trained to do.

It didn't matter that it was a strange hospital. What went on inside it was the same and she was a part of this world. The ready acceptance by staff she had encountered made her feel completely at home. It was even easy to find the staff cafeteria at lunchtime when Louise was taking her turn to look after Ella and Maria had gone home for a break.

Jenna's friend, Anne, was waiting for her outside the cafeteria door.

'Are you sure you've got time for lunch?' Jenna queried. 'It sounded like you were being run off your feet in ED when I rang.'

'We are. It was a mistake to start day shifts. I think I'll go back to nights.'

'How are Dave and the kids coping?'

'I'm only doing two shifts a week so far. Let's grab some food and then we'll have time to talk. It's so good to see you.'

'I'm sorry I haven't been to visit. You were working on the only nights I've had off so far.'

'Well, I've got half an hour now and I'm hanging out to hear about you and Dr Romantico.'

'Dr *who*?'

'No, no!' Anne laughed. 'Not Dr Who! Good grief, Dave's even got the kids watching his DVD collection now. No, I'm talking about your new boss. Paulo Romantico.'

Both women leaned over the counter to choose from the triangular plastic packages containing a variety of sandwiches.

'You're the envy of every nurse in ED, you know,' Anne continued. '*Living* with him!'

'That's not what you've been telling people, is it?' Jenna widened her eyes in mock horror but the thought that even light-hearted gossip could get back to Paul was a worry.

If he was still so much in love with his dead wife that he couldn't bond with his daughter, he wouldn't appreciate the idea that anyone thought he might have chosen a replacement as a live-in companion. And if Louise heard, Jenna would be gone from her position in a flash.

'I'm not living *with* him, as you well know, Anne. I have a self-contained flat, which is really nice. You should come and see it. I've got a separate entrance so it shouldn't be a problem to have visitors, and I'm sure Maria wouldn't mind.' Jenna chose a bottle of water and a banana to complete her meal. 'Maria's lovely. She'd probably insist on making you a lasagne or spaghetti Alfredo or something. She teaches Italian cooking, did you know that?'

'No.' And Anne clearly wasn't going to be distracted by

Jenna's babbling. 'He is gorgeous, though, isn't he? I couldn't believe it when you told me who you were going to be working for.'

Jenna thought about that smile. That look of total focus that eyes as dark as sin were capable of bestowing.

'Oh, yes,' she murmured. 'He's gorgeous, all right.'

'Aha!' Anne led the way to a corner table. 'So you do fancy him, then? Hooray! It's about time something good happened in your love life.'

'*Nothing* is happening!' Jenna cast a quick glance at the nearby tables, hoping no one would be overhearing this conversation. Hospital grapevines were more lush than any jungle plants.

'But it *could*,' Anne said encouragingly. 'And why not? You're young, single and gorgeous. He's…not so young but gorgeous enough to make up for it.'

'His last nanny was sacked because she fancied him.'

'Really?'

Jenna shrugged. 'The official reason is that she had a row with Louise but that was the reason for the row as far as I know.'

'Who's Louise?'

'Paul's mother-in-law. Hey, did you know his wife? Gwendolyn?'

'I met her once at a barbecue. That was enough.' Anne made a face as she opened her sandwich package. 'She worked in Theatre.'

'I know.' Jenna peeled the seal from her water bottle. 'Louise told me. A *theatre* nurse, she said, as though it was the pinnacle of any nurse's career aspirations. Far superior to being a paediatric or ED nurse, that's for sure.'

'She used to supply her own hats, apparently. Cute ones

with pictures on them like puppies or ducks. She probably had designer scrub suits as well.'

Jenna could believe it. 'She could have been a model, according to Louise. Or a concert pianist. Or an Olympic horserider. She only chose to be a nurse because she was such a caring person.'

Anne almost choked on her mouthful of food. Having swallowed hastily, she snorted. 'She cared about herself. Not that I'm going to speak ill of the dead or anything, but I have to say she wasn't very popular around here.' Anne grinned. 'Took after her mother, by the sound of it. Is she driving you nuts, telling you how perfect Gwennie was?'

'Paul adored her.'

'Let me guess—Louise told you this?'

'I think it's true. Maria thinks that's why he can't bring himself to love Ella.'

'He doesn't love Ella?'

'He avoids having anything much to do with her.'

'But he loves kids. It's one of the things that makes him so gorgeous. I've seen him in ED once or twice and he's great with children.'

Jenna nodded. She had seen that for herself, that very morning.

'Is Ella a difficult kid?'

'No way. She's adorable. I can't understand it.'

'Neither can I.' Anne was looking fascinated. 'He's Italian. They're supposed to be totally into family stuff.'

'He loves his mother. Maybe the grandmothers are right. He misses the perfect Gwendolyn too much to be able to bear the company of her child.'

'No.' Anne was staring thoughtfully at her friend. 'I don't buy that. I mean, I adore Dave in spite of the Dr Who

DVDs and if he dropped dead, I'd be hanging onto every memory. Especially the living ones. His kids…*our* kids.'

'That's what I thought, too. It's a mystery.'

'Maybe not.' Anne reached for her second sandwich. 'Maybe he didn't want to have children. Maybe their marriage wasn't so perfect and she got pregnant to try and solder it together and now he's left with a kid to raise and a mother-in-law who won't go home and he can't enjoy being single again.'

Jenna didn't want to believe that Paul could be that distant. Uncaring. But, in a way, it had a ring of truth. He had such a strong sense of duty. It was caring, but without the most important factor. The emotional involvement. And no matter what the marriage had been like, Ella was his child.

'I think he's just buried his grief in his work so success-fully he doesn't want to rock the boat.' If she could persuade Anne, maybe she could hang onto the belief herself. 'He just needs time and enough contact with Ella. Nobody could resist her if they spent enough time with her.'

'Time!' Anne shot a glance at her watch and groaned. 'How did that half-hour go so fast? I've got to go.'

'Me, too.' Jenna collected the wrappers. 'I'll come and see you on my next night off. You'll be home if you're still on days, anyway.'

'Yes. Come for dinner. You'll have to put up with Dave and boys but we can shoo them off to watch TV or some-thing after dinner.'

'I'll look forward to it. A dose of "normal" family would be great.'

Anne frowned as they reached the corridor. 'Are you not enjoying this job, then? You could always resign, you know. ED is *so* short-staffed. Paeds probably is as well. You'd get a job like a shot.'

'No.' Jenna shook her head as their paths separated. 'I couldn't do that.'

Jenna found herself quickening her pace on her way back to the ward, surprised at how the thought of abandoning Ella could have struck such a nerve.

Lost in her thoughts, she veered into Ella's room a few minutes later without looking and walked straight into the figure that was coming out.

She didn't need to look up to know that the hands gripping her arms to steady her belonged to Paul. Her body told her that instantly, with a curious tingling that only intensified when she looked up.

'Sorry,' she muttered. 'I wasn't looking.'

Another fault a good nurse would not have, but Paul sounded almost amused.

'My fault entirely,' he said. 'I was in too much of a hurry. You are all right?'

Jenna nodded. She didn't need his hands to steady her now but he was blocking the doorway. He would need to let go so that she could step backwards.

'Is that you, Jennifer?' Louise's voice came from behind Paul. 'Good. I've been waiting for you to get back. I'm going to be late for my appointment with my hairdresser if I don't leave now.'

Paul had kept eye contact with Jenna as Louise had been speaking and there was a message there. We have to put up with this difficult woman, it suggested, for Ella's sake. She *is* her grandmother.

And more. The hint of a smile said that they might have to put up with it but they didn't have to *like* it.

It was a moment of real connection. Just a split second, but it was enough for something fundamental to change. And then Paul let go of Jenna and they both stepped back simultaneously and the connection was broken.

Well broken. Jenna could see Ella staring at her father. She was holding her treasured grey bunny by its ear but even as Jenna caught sight of her, she let the toy drop to the floor.

Poor Letto.

No. Poor Ella. Anyone could see she wanted her father. Would it have been such a big ask for him to have spent a few minutes alone with his daughter so Louise could have gone to her appointment without waiting for Jenna's return?

Jenna couldn't help staring at Paul as he moved to pass her.

'Excuse me.' His tone was clipped now. Dismissive. 'I've got a patient I have to visit.'

Which was probably true, but it didn't excuse all the other opportunities Paul had had—even in the short period of time Jenna had been involved in this family.

Maybe that was what was so strange. As far as Jenna was aware, Paul never spent time alone with Ella. Or held her. Or played with her by waggling fluffy toys to make her laugh. He only saw her when she was in the care of others because she was *always* in the care of others.

A kind of indignation on Ella's behalf surfaced that Paul could treat his patients with more warmth than his own child.

It was more than unjust. It was wrong.

Jenna stared thoughtfully at Paul's back for a moment as he headed further into the ward.

Time wasn't all that was needed, was it? Ten months should have more than long enough. The shock of having his daughter sick enough to be admitted to hospital should have been enough to make him realise what he stood to lose.

Forcing the issue wasn't going to be the way forward. Too easy for Paul to take shelter behind the demands of his career. But stepping obediently back from the barriers she sensed wasn't the way to go either.

There had to be another way to bridge the gap. And Jenna had to be the perfect person to build that bridge. On the one hand, she understood and respected Paul's devotion to his work. On the other, she already loved his daughter.

And the material for building that bridge might have just made itself apparent in that moment in the doorway.

That flash of connection.

Would she be playing with fire to even consider getting closer to Paul Romano on a personal basis?

Of course she would.

Would it be worth it, for Ella's sake?

The forlorn cry as Louise put the baby back into her cot and turned to collect her handbag was like an answer in itself.

Of course it would.

CHAPTER FOUR

THE child collapsed without warning.

One moment the ten-year-old girl was walking down the ward corridor, passing Ella's room, and the next she had crumpled gracefully to the floor.

Paul was at the nurses' station at the other end of the corridor, and for just a split second he was stunned—his brain trying to register the significance of what he was seeing.

Jenna reacted faster. By the time Paul's body was gathering the momentum to run, she was crouched over the child, shaking her gently and calling for a response.

There didn't appear to be any.

Paul turned his head swiftly to see who was available but the station was empty. The nursing staff were busy on their last round of the evening, dispensing medication and trying to settle children for the night. Junior medical staff were either occupied elsewhere or had gone home.

Jenna had tilted the child's head back now and lifted her chin to open the airway. He could see the automatic position she adopted, leaning down with her cheek close to the girl's face, with a hand resting lightly on her abdomen to check for respirations.

She knew what she was doing.

Was it just a syncopal episode? A faint that would resolve itself within seconds? He had seen the girl earlier, spoken to her even, when she'd been in the playroom with her mother and younger brother who had been playing with one of Paul's patients. What was her name?

Jessica. She'd been limping badly. Rheumatic fever, that's what she'd been admitted for—a complication from an untreated streptococcal infection of her throat. She had migratory polyarthritis, giving her painful joints. And hadn't her mother said something else?

Carditis.

Paul didn't need to see how Jenna's head dipped, her mouth covering the child's to deliver a breath, to know how serious this was. He'd already reached that conclusion from the knowledge that the infection Jessica had was affecting her heart and could cause an arrhythmia.

Neither did he need to hear Jenna's clear call.

'Help! I need some help here!'

He veered into the treatment room at a run, grabbing the crash cart. It hit the doorframe with a metallic clang as he swivelled to jab a finger at the cardiac arrest button on the wall.

Jenna had started chest compressions by the time he got to them, which had to be only thirty seconds since the collapse. He threw her a bag mask, which Jenna picked up and held securely over the girl's face, squeezing the bag to deliver another breath.

'Oxygen?' she queried.

'Not on the cart. We'll send someone for a portable in a tick. Carry on—you're doing a great job.'

Paul plugged the cable for the leads into the defibrillator and unzipped the side pouch to pull out the package containing the pads. No paddles now, with the new CPR protocols in place. Aware of what Jenna was doing, he could tell she was also up with the play.

Thirty compressions to two breaths. For all age groups. Carefully timed and delivered breaths to avoid hyperventilation, which could cause poor cerebral perfusion and blood flow.

She looked calm. The tension was there because she knew exactly how serious this situation was but she was perfectly confident that she was doing what she should be doing. Paul liked that. It was precisely the way he operated himself.

Pounding feet along the corridor advertised the arrival of more nursing staff.

'Shall I take over compressions?' one asked.

'No.' Paul was attaching the sticky pads to Jessica's chest. 'Jenna knows what she's doing.'

'It was a sudden collapse,' Jenna said. 'No evidence of prior symptoms. She'd just said hello to me as she went past the door.'

'I know. I saw it.'

'What's she in for? Does she have a heart condition?'

'Rheumatic fever. Myocarditis.'

'So this is probably arrhythmic?"

'Yes.' The pattern on the screen was settling. A wild squiggle incompatible with a functioning heart.

'VF,' Jenna breathed.

'Clear!' Paul ordered. He was adjusting the joule setting on the life pack. A ten-year-old child, approximately thirty kilograms. No, this girl was slight for her age. More like twenty-five. Five joules per kilo. First and subsequent shocks at one hundred and twenty-five joules, then.

'Stay clear,' he instructed after delivery of the first shock, already recharging.

Jenna's recommencement of CPR was so instant and so

smooth, following delivery of the third shock, it was like an extension of the protocol rolling through Paul's mind.

She was good. Very good.

Where was the arrest team? He needed expert help to intubate and gain intravenous access for drug therapy. He didn't know the level of skill available among the night staff gathering around them.

'Kendra?' Paul caught the gaze of the most senior nurse present. 'How are you on IVs?'

The nurse's jaw dropped. 'I haven't done one for ages!'

'Jenna?' The word was a snap.

'Confident,' she replied with equal succinctness.

'Right. Kendra, take over compressions, please. Someone get a portable oxygen cylinder. Someone else can see where that arrest team is. Jenna? See if you can get IV access, please. I'm going to intubate.'

A further, single shock was delivered after two more minutes of CPR. For just a few seconds a normal rhythm appeared on the screen and then it degenerated again into the fatal squiggle.

'Jenna?'

'I'm in.'

And she was. The IV cannula was in the crook of Jessica's elbow, the luer plug already screwed on. Jenna was taping it down, a syringe and ampoule of saline ready on the floor beside her to check and flush the line.

'Forget the flush,' Paul instructed. 'Draw me up 1.2 mils of adrenaline.'

Paul inserted the endotracheal tube while Jenna was drawing up the first dose of medication. She held the ampoule for him to check and was following directions to inject the medication when the cardiac arrest team arrived.

A doctor stared at Jenna. 'Who the hell is that?'

'She's a paediatric nurse.' Paul's tone made it clear that he took responsibility for any irregularity and he was not going to waste time right now defending himself. 'A very good one.'

Nevertheless, Jenna was rightly shunted aside as the more qualified medics took over. Amiodarone, another anti-arrhythmic drug, was given. More CPR. Another shock. And then, finally, a normal sinus rhythm appeared. And held.

'We need a stretcher,' someone said. 'Or a bed. Let's get this girl up to Intensive Care.'

Paul went with them—a small, travelling circus of personnel and equipment. Still tense but triumphant. The resuscitation had been successful.

Paul couldn't wait to get back to the ward and let Jenna know just how successful. An hour after her collapse Jessica was sitting up in bed in the paediatric intensive care unit, surrounded by monitoring equipment and consultants, wondering what all the fuss was about.

Her parents had been summoned but hadn't arrived until after their daughter had regained consciousness. They, too, had been bewildered but happy to accept that the danger was over for the moment and with careful watching, there was every chance that this frightening episode had been a one-off complication of an illness that was being appropriately treated.

Disappointingly, Jenna was not in Danielle's room.

Maria sat by the cot, knitting needles clicking in time with the hum of a lullaby that didn't appear necessary because Danielle was sound asleep.

No IV line or oxygen tent now. Keeping her in tonight was merely a formality. She would be checked on the paediatricians' round in the morning and Paul fully expected her to be discharged.

'Maria? Where's Jenna?'

Maria answered him in the language he'd automatically used—the native Italian that had always been spoken at home until his father had died.

'I sent her to make herself a cup of tea. She looked tired, poor angel.'

Hardly surprising. The aftermath of the kind of adrenaline rush an arrest scenario could generate was often a sharp downward trajectory. Especially when you didn't get the chance to talk it over with someone. To debrief. He'd had an hour of interacting with his colleagues as they'd instituted new management for Jessica's case and he still felt drained himself.

'She'll be back soon. Sit, Paolo. Talk to your mother for once.'

Paul received a keen glance when he didn't respond immediately but then Maria clucked her tongue and her mouth twitched. 'I expect she's in the kitchen.'

A moment of very uncharacteristic indecision assailed Paul. His mother was reading too much into his desire to see Jenna. When it came to his reaction to any new woman that swam into his orbit, her antennae were as sharply tuned as Louise's.

The difference was, Maria wanted happiness for her loved ones. She was not on a mission to ensure he worshipped a ghost for the rest of his life. A mission that was so focussed he didn't even have to show interest himself. The last poor girl that had been employed to help care for Danielle had made the mistake of making *her* interest obvious, and Louise had swooped like an eagle onto an unsuspecting *coniglietto*.

It was just as well he had learned to keep his own feelings so well hidden. There was no need for Louise to know that Gwendolyn's ghost was one that Paul would have difficulty respecting, let alone anything implying more reverence.

And life at home was much more pleasant. Paul wasn't about to risk the new status quo by allowing Jenna to become anything other than the nanny.

Except…that there was a new respect in that quarter. Was it because of the way she had taken on board with such dignity that unfair accusation that she had failed in her duty of care to Danielle? That she had been able to accept an apology without making him pay in some way?

Or was it a professional respect due to the manner in which she had handled Jessica's sudden collapse? He would certainly trust her from now on. He would be happy to have her on his team in the hospital. He was lucky that she had chosen to care for Danielle. Another good reason to make sure he didn't give Louise any ammunition.

Yes. His mother might have it wrong but it would make him happy at this moment to see Jenna.

To pass on the news about Jessica and see those hazel eyes light up with pleasure. Her lips curve into one of those delicious smiles usually reserved for others—like his mother or Danielle.

'Go!' Maria commanded, pointing a knitting needle towards the door. 'Tell Jenna I am happy. She doesn't need to hurry back.'

So Paul went, amusement vying with a slight annoyance. He was thirty-six, for heaven's sake! He had long since given up calling his mother 'Mama' but his affection for her could still persuade him to obey her commands a little too readily at times.

Sure enough, Jenna was alone in the staff kitchen.

She stood at the bench, lifting a teabag from a steaming

mug. She turned at the sound of Paul's entrance and her reaction was startling, to say the least.

The teabag fell from the spoon to land on the stainless-steel bench with a splat, but Jenna didn't notice. Her eyes were fixed on Paul and there was just enough light from the fluorescent ceiling strip to see the way her pupils widened.

Why would someone as calm and collected in a life-and-death situation involving a child be so disturbed by his, albeit unexpected, entrance?

A question that was no less intriguing because Paul had a perfectly good idea of the reason.

He was experiencing a similar kick in his own gut.

He'd noticed it earlier today—during that little mix-up at the doorway to Danielle's room. After she had bumped into him with enough force to flatten her breasts against his chest. He'd held her arms, both to curtail the contact before Louise could get the wrong idea and to steady her. Inevitable that they should both share the same distaste for the tone of voice Louise had chosen to issue orders to Danielle's nanny.

But it had been more than a simple recognition of another's viewpoint.

It had been an understanding.

The kind that needed a chemical pathway to travel along.

The kind of chemistry that only came when attraction was mutual.

No! Don't go there!

The whisper was superfluous. Paul had no intention of exploring that pathway. It was, however, rather pleasant to know that it was there. It added considerably to the pleasure he was already experiencing.

'I just wanted to let you know that Jessica is fine,' he told Jenna. 'Quite stable. She's conscious.'

'Oh!' Jenna's face flushed and her eyes positively lit up, the joy accentuating tiny gold flecks in her irises that Paul hadn't previously noticed. But, then, he hadn't been this close to her before, had he? Not since his opinion of this woman had undergone a new definition anyway. Why *had* he stepped quite this close?

'That's fabulous,' Jenna was saying. 'I was so worried.'

'Her parents wanted me to pass on their thanks. I told them that your admirably prompt response was a major factor in averting a much more serious situation.'

Jenna ducked her head. 'Hardly!' She noticed the teabag lying on the bench and reached to pick it up. 'You were only a couple of seconds behind me and I didn't even know where the crash cart was kept.'

So she was modest about her talents. Paul liked that.

'But it was several minutes before the arrest team arrived. The staff on tonight were obviously all less experienced than you.' His gaze tore themselves away from the sight of her fingers squeezing the remaining moisture from the teabag before dropping it into the rubbish bin.

The tilt of her head as she leaned towards the bin revealed the faint movement of her carotid pulse. It was beating just a little faster than normal but you would expect an increase in heart rate to go with those dilated pupils. Disconcertingly, Paul could feel his own heart rate speeding up to match.

Even more disconcerting was the urge he had to sweep the tendrils of her long, dark hair aside properly so that he could feel the beat of that pulse with his lips. His tongue...

His line of vision was as palpable as any touch. Jenna could *feel* him staring at her neck.

Dear lord, was he thinking of *kissing* her?

It wouldn't be the first time a kiss had been stolen in a deserted ward kitchen late in an evening. Always illicit, thanks to the setting, but some were far more illicit than others.

The heat from the teabag was still intense enough to scald her fingers but Jenna held onto it as a means of buying just a brief flash of time.

She could *not* kiss Paul Romano, despite the affirmative messages now pulsing from every nerve ending in her body.

He was her employer.

No. Strictly speaking, Maria was Jenna's official employer but Paul was Ella's father.

Ella.

The name was enough to bring Jenna to her senses. That little girl needed her. So did Maria. So did Paul, although he might not realise it. How stupid—selfish— would it be to jeopardise what she stood to achieve for the sake of a few seconds of physical pleasure.

And Jenna needed the success of this mission herself. For the satisfaction of feeling she might have contributed to sorting out a small, troubled corner of the world. A kind of catharsis to cancel out the sadness of the last few months of her life. A stepping stone to a new and more positive future.

The teabag landed amidst a few empty yoghurt cartons and some snack-bar wrappers. Jenna kept her gaze carefully away from Paul's. It would be a fatal mistake to get locked into eye contact right now.

'Would…would you like a cup of tea?'

'*Grazie.*' Paul stepped back as Jenna straightened and turned. The lapse into Italian and his faintly startled blink made Jenna wonder if he'd even realised how close he had been standing to her. Or how intense his stare had been.

She filled another mug with boiling water and dropped a fresh teabag into it.

'Milk? Sugar?' The mundane could be a blessing, she decided. Nerve endings were settling now. She had only imagined his intention to kiss her. Why on earth would Paul be attracted at all? His adored wife had been a willowy blonde with strikingly defined features and an air of sophistication Jenna wouldn't even want to emulate. She couldn't be more different.

'No sugar. Just milk.'

Jenna handed over the hot drink and debated whether to cross the room to sit at the small, Formica-topped table. No. That would be inviting Paul to sit with her and might suggest that she wanted to encourage his attentions.

And she didn't.

Well, she did to some extent but it was going to be a fine line to travel, trying to create a relationship that would allow enough trust to further her mission without tipping over into intimacy.

It couldn't be rushed. Better to try and stay professional. Jenna leaned back against the bench. She held her mug with both hands and hopefully gave every impression that she was enjoying a drink that was, in fact, tastelessly burning her mouth.

Paul copied her stance, one hip resting against the edge of the bench and a relaxed line to his body that was at odds with the way he was looking at her over the rim of his mug.

Oh, help!

Keep it professional, she reminded herself.

'How's Darren?' Jenna heard herself asking with a touch of desperation. 'The little boy next door to Ella,' she added hurriedly. 'With the Wilms' tumour?'

Paul inclined his head. 'Yes. I know who Darren is.' His

lips curved just enough to suggest a smile being repressed. He *knew* what she was trying to do, dammit! Was he *teasing* her?

'He's doing very well. Renal function is picking up nicely for the remaining kidney. He'll probably be discharged by the weekend.'

'He's a cute kid.'

'He is.' Paul smiled properly now and once again Jenna couldn't control her response. Smiling back at this man was as natural as breathing. She could feel the knot of tension unravelling inside her. Paul was actually a very *nice* man. Why on earth was she afraid of him?

'I saw you,' she confessed, 'playing with that toy. Making the animal noises…making Darren laugh.'

The subtle hint of embarrassment in the shrug was charming. Truly arrogant people were never embarrassed, were they?

'Not many surgeons play with their patients,' Jenna continued warmly.

'I love these children,' Paul said simply. 'Their welfare is my life.'

'But…' Jenna hesitated, her heart skipping a beat. No. She *couldn't* say that. Not yet.

'But what?' Paul raised an eyebrow. He leaned a little closer, inviting a response. Demanding one.

'I just wondered…' Jenna gulped in a breath, caution flying to the wind thanks to the warmth in that encouragement. 'You don't…play with Ella much, do you?'

'Scusi?'

That dark gaze was instantly and completely shuttered. Jenna had misjudged the opportunity. Again. But it was too late to back out now.

'Look, I know how much you loved your wife,' Jenna

said quietly, 'and I know that being with Ella can't help but remind you of what you've lost, but…' she caught her bottom lip, biting it, forced to look away from the spark of what looked horribly like real anger in Paul's eyes '…she's just a little girl, Paul. A baby. Your *daughter*.'

'And?'

'And…you seem to care more about your patients than you do about *her*.'

'Is that so?' The tone was pure ice. The mug of tea Paul was holding was placed on the bench. With care. Not a drop was spilt despite the amount of fluid still in the vessel. Paul's intake of breath was equally measured. Controlled. 'You are employed as Danielle's nanny,' he said without expression. 'Not as a family counsellor. I suggest you try and remember that.'

To Jenna's utter dismay, she could feel the prickle of tears behind her eyes. She should be feeling angry at this put down but, no, she felt like she'd put her foot in things well and truly.

One step forward.

Three steps back.

Paul's back was very straight. His shoulders square. Jenna was staring at that back now as Paul abandoned his drink and left the kitchen. His words were so quiet she almost didn't hear them, especially as he was facing in the opposite direction.

'What's more,' she thought she heard, 'you're wrong. You have absolutely no idea how wrong you are.'

How dared she?

In his household for all of five minutes and Jenna Freeman thought she'd earned the right to comment on his relationship with Danielle?

To *criticise* him?

Dio!

She was just a woman like every other. She had manipulated him. Pretended attraction and drawn him towards the noose and then used the power his involuntary—and mistaken—steps had granted.

He should fire her.

He *would* fire her.

And then what?

Paul's purposeful stride slowed as he neared the room at the end of the darkened, quiet corridor.

Maria would have to start searching again. She would try to care for Danielle herself and begin to look as tired and unwell as she had been far too often in the last months.

Maria would never agree to allow Danielle to be taken to Auckland and raised by Louise. And why should she? She adored the baby. The new generation.

Famiglia.

Family.

He couldn't take that away from her.

Paul sighed heavily. He was outside Darren's room now and he couldn't help his sideways glance. The little boy was sound asleep—as he should be—but his mother was awake. Sitting beside the bed with one hand in gentle contact with her son. She looked up and smiled at Paul.

The kind of grateful smile he was accustomed to receiving from his patients' mothers. Paul returned the smile and then his gaze travelled back to the serene face of the sleeping child.

They *were* his life, these children. The unguarded comment that had initiated the criticism from Jenna may have been unwise but it had been perfectly true.

Had her accusations had an element of truth as well?

Would he feel differently about Danielle if she had appeared in his life as one of his patients?

Of course he would. There would have been no need to guard his heart. No reason to employ deliberate avoidance tactics to try and close off a space he had no desire to revisit.

As his anger drained away, something else Jenna had said also rang true.

Danielle was just a little girl. A baby.

None of it was *her* fault.

Not that he needed to feel overly guilty. He was providing all that the child could need. The best of everything money could buy. A nursery fit for royalty. Toys galore. Clothes. The best nanny. And it wasn't that the child wasn't loved. Maria adored her. Louise loved her with an intensity bordering on obsession—a reincarnation of her precious daughter. And now Jenna loved Danielle. Enough to stand up to him and say something she must have known perfectly well he didn't want to hear.

A brave thing to do.

Paul entered Ella's room. His mother had dozed off in the armchair and the baby was also still asleep. On her back, with her arms flung over her head. Dark lashes lay like butterfly wings above plump cheeks, and rosy lips had a natural curve that was almost a permanent smile.

She was a beautiful child.

For the first time since her birth, Paul looked at Danielle. Really looked at her.

Taking the perspective of seeing her as a patient instead of his daughter changed everything, really.

She was an *ingenua*. An innocent.

And she was—for better or worse—a part of *his* family.

She deserved more than he had given her thus far in her short life.

Maybe things should change.

Not that he was going to give Jenna the satisfaction of knowing just how much of a nerve she had struck. He was still angry that he had made himself somehow—unintentionally—vulnerable, but he *could* try a little harder, couldn't he?

Make more of an effort to be a father?

For Danielle's sake?

CHAPTER FIVE

HE HATED her.

It took an infinitesimal amount of time—which was all the eye contact afforded when Paul arrived in the nursery the next evening—to know that he was still angry with her.

'How is she?'

The words were clipped and the tone as cool as that brief glance had been.

On the positive side, however, Ella's silky curls got more of a ruffle than the usual flick. She was clearly the focus of attention here.

'Bouncing back.' It was a struggle to sound professional. To ignore the hammering of her heart. Jenna had been dreading this encounter all day, knowing how difficult it would be to see Paul after that little confrontation in the ward kitchen last night. 'Bit of a cough still, but no wheeze or signs of any respiratory distress.'

'Temperature?'

'Been normal since yesterday.' Jenna had Ella perched on one hip as she tidied up after the nappy change. Her charge was eyeing her father with wide and very unsleepy eyes. A damp thumb was removed from her mouth with a popping sound.

'Pa-pa!' Ella announced.

'*Si.*' Paul tilted his head and smiled. 'That's me, *cara.* You are feeling better, yes?'

Good grief! Was Paul actually making an attempt to *converse* with his daughter? Ella seemed as surprised as Jenna. Her hand gripped the arm beneath it more tightly and the spare thumb went back into her mouth. Sucking sounds filled the slightly tense silence.

'You're hungry, aren't you, darling?' Jenna moved towards the microwave that rested on top of a bar fridge in one corner of the spacious nursery. 'Your milk should be ready.'

Surprisingly, Paul seemed in no hurry to go and get his own meal, even though it was 7 p.m. and he'd only just arrived home. He must have left his briefcase and suit jacket by the front door before coming upstairs, and right now he was loosening his tie and undoing the top button of his shirt.

Jenna closed her eyes briefly as she took the warmed bottle from the microwave. She wished she hadn't seen him doing that. It was bound to haunt her in the early hours. Jenna thought the knowledge that she had ruined any chance she might have had to build a more personal relationship with Paul had effectively squashed the desire that she had been all too aware of in the kitchen last night.

Almost effectively, anyway. It had sneaked back some time during the night. Taken on a life of its own, in fact. Amazing how easy it had been to conjure up that awareness…

And how hard to control it. Her mind hadn't stopped with just the memory, had it? Oh, no! Instead of remembering how she'd taken control by offering a cup of tea, Jenna's wakeful brain had invented a journey of its own. One in which she had just waited. Knowing that she would feel the press of his lips against that vulnerable flesh on her neck and his fingers burying themselves in her hair.

One where she turned her head a little and tipped it back to have her throat kissed, and then he cupped her chin and pressed it down so that he could stare at her mouth with the same intensity he had at her neck, and she knew that the next kiss could claim her lips…

Jenna stifled an inward groan. Now she could weave in the sight of those long fingers loosening that tie. Undoing the top button and parting the neck of his shirt.

'She's feeding well?'

Oh, *Lord*! Hadn't Paul left the nursery yet? Jenna pushed the door of the microwave shut, using the loud click as a means of closing off thoughts she shouldn't be encouraging, even in the wakeful, private moments of the night. *Especially* in those moments!

'She's fine.' Paul was standing in front of the chair where Jenna usually sat to give Ella her supper. It could have been an awkward moment but it was saved by Maria bustling into the room.

'Pillows!' she declared. 'And blankets. Paolo! You're home!'

'Yes, Maria.' Paul eyed the armful of bedding his mother was carrying. 'What are you doing?'

'Making a bed for Jenna. She's staying with Ella tonight in case she wakes up.'

'Oh?'

Jenna knew Paul was staring at her. She carefully didn't look back. Was he uncomfortable with the knowledge that his bedroom was beside the nursery? That Jenna would be sleeping just a wall away from him?

'She may be unsettled after her hospital stay,' Jenna said calmly. 'It's just for a night or two.'

Ella gave a small whimper and reached for her bottle. Jenna had to move.

'Excuse me,' she murmured as she brushed past Paul. 'I need to sit down to feed Ella.'

'Of course. Sorry.' But Paul seemed slightly bemused and stepped in the same direction as Jenna. His body bumped her arm. If the effect of seeing him unbutton his shirt collar was going to be in her memory bank for involuntary perusal, the reminder of what actual physical contact was like would be an equally hefty deposit.

This was getting ridiculous.

He hates you, Jenna reminded herself. You told him he sucked at being a dad. That he had a better relationship with his patients than his daughter. And to top it off, you reminded him how much he had loved his wife.

If she'd wanted to write a manual on how to kill even the possibility of a man fancying you, she couldn't have opened with a better ploy.

Not that she wanted a relationship. Or not an intimate one. Jenna had to refocus on her original goal and it was a good thing that they had stepped away from the minefield of physical attraction that had just appeared from nowhere to surround them. The sooner she put all thoughts of Paul as a man out of her head the better.

She'd think of him as Dr Romano, Jenna decided. Famous surgeon. Or, better yet, just as Ella's father.

That was good. No chance of forgetting her mission that way.

It became easier to think of Paul simply as Ella's father because he seemed to be embarked on a campaign to spend more time with his daughter. Had something of what she'd said sunk in?

If so, it was worth the personal sacrifice of driving Paul away from the distracting possibility of exploring that chemical attraction. Jenna could find satisfaction in being a martyr to a higher cause.

She could also be pleased with having the presence of mind to get dressed *and* brush her hair the moment she heard movements in the adjacent room that morning, because Paul poked his head around the door before he even went downstairs for breakfast.

'She's still asleep, then?' Was he relieved or disappointed? The tone was too neutral to analyse.

'She had an unsettled night.'

'Yes. I heard her crying.'

Had Paul been as aware of her through the wall as she had been of him? 'I hope it didn't disturb you too much.'

'I'm quite used to being disturbed at night.' But Paul was looking uncomfortable now. He cleared his throat. 'It's good that you stayed with her. My mother is getting too old to be up and down all night to Danielle.'

Not that Jenna would dare say it aloud but the thought that Paul might consider getting up to comfort his daughter himself couldn't be repressed. And maybe it showed on her face because, when Jenna risked the tiniest glance, she was met by a distinctly stony stare.

But something *had* changed.

Despite most probably hating her, Paul was still drawn back to the nursery as soon as he returned home that evening. He looked very tired.

'Maria said to say goodnight. She's off at her cooking class.'

Jenna nodded her acknowledgement. She was busy changing Ella's nappy. Chubby legs kicked up at her from the padded table and it was impossible to fasten the sticky tapes so Jenna caught both feet with one hand.

'You're full of beans tonight, aren't you, chicken? There. All done.' Jenna stuck the second tab down. Without thinking, she did what she always did on completing this particular task, ducking her head to blow a raspberry on Ella's bare tummy.

The baby shrieked with delight—a sound that subsided into her delicious, drainpipe gurgle, and it wasn't until Jenna turned to pick up the clean sleepsuit that she realised what Paul had just witnessed.

He didn't look angry, though. If anything, he had that faintly bemused air she had noticed when Maria had been moving her into the nursery for the night. As though he was in unfamiliar territory and unsure of the protocol. A woman's domain, perhaps, which could explain why he had made no protest at the idea of Jenna sleeping next door.

Then, as Ella's giggle continued, Paul smiled.

A smile that started slowly with crinkles at the corners of his eyes just before his lips moved. An unconscious response to the joyful noise Ella was creating. And then it grew until it stretched into a grin.

Jenna smiled, too.

And the tension that had been between them ever since that exchange in the ward kitchen suddenly evaporated.

'She's a happy little thing, isn't she?' Paul sounded as though this was a new discovery.

'She's gorgeous,' Jenna responded firmly. 'She's the most wonderful baby in the world. Aren't you?' She tickled Ella just to make her laugh again and then got on with the serious business of stuffing those fat little arms and legs into the soft, terry-towelling suit.

'I'll have to put you down for a minute,' she warned

Ella, 'while I make up your milk.' She wasn't about to risk destroying this new ambience by suggesting that Paul hold his daughter.

When she put Ella down on the carpet, the baby went into a fast crawl, making a beeline for her father. Reaching shiny, black shoes, Ella crowed with delight and tugged at the laces. Then she grabbed a fistful of pinstripe trousers.

Jenna watched from the corner of her eye as she spooned formula into the bottle and added distilled water. Sure enough, Ella wriggled her little bottom, planted her feet and used her grip on the trousers to lever herself up.

'Hey!' Paul was watching, dumbfounded.

'It's her new trick,' Jenna said proudly. 'She did it for the first time this afternoon. I'll bet she'll be walking in no time.'

Poor Paul. He clearly didn't know what to do. Ella was attached to his trousers like a large leech and beaming triumphantly up at him but swaying precariously. Any movement from her anchor and she would topple.

Which she did, anyway, just as Jenna pushed the start button on the microwave to heat the milk.

'Oops!' She swooped to pick Ella up before a second attempt could be made, but Paul had backed away.

'I'd better go and find my dinner,' he said uncomfortably.

'Sure.' Jenna settled Ella on her hip and pointed to the microwave. 'How many seconds, Ella? See? Ten…nine…eight…'

'Um…' Paul had paused by the door. 'Have you eaten, Jenna?'

'No. I'll get Ella settled first.'

'I'll save some of Maria's lasagne for you, then.'

The offer was startling but maybe it was a kind of peace offering. To underline the exit of that tension. It would be rude to say that she had been planning some instant noodles in front of television in her flat. So Jenna smiled.

'That would be great, thank you.'

Why had he said that?

And why on earth was he still pottering around the kitchen three quarters of an hour later, filling a basket with slices of a crusty French bread stick and debating which of the two very good red wines he had pulled from the cellar was the one he should open?

Anyone would think this was some kind of a *date*.

He just wanted a chance to talk to Jenna, that was all. Not that he was intending to apologise for a second time, but he wanted Jenna to know that he wasn't the monster she clearly thought he was. He wanted to ask questions. To show an interest in Danielle.

And maybe he also wanted someone to talk to at the end of a long and difficult day.

Someone who might understand.

'They're not very common, are they? Choledochal cysts?' Jenna finally appeared to have recovered from her astonishment at finding a place set for her at a kitchen table laden with bread, salad, wine and a deep dish of lasagne that gave off the most mouth watering aroma of meat and cheese.

'No. Only about one in one hundred thousand live births in Western Europe.' Paul was watching Jenna's hands as she took a round slice of bread and then tore it into two pieces. She had astonishingly beautiful hands. Delicate but strong at the same time. He had seen those hands busy snapping drug ampoules, finding a difficult vein and then slipping in a needle. Clever hands. Competent.

Suddenly realising he had been staring a little too long, Paul cleared his throat. 'They're a lot more common in Japan. They get one in a thousand.'

'And it's more common in females, isn't it?'

'Yes. A ratio of one to four.'

'The opposite of hypertrophic pyloric stenosis, then.'

'Exactly opposite.' The pleasant surprise was the same as he'd feel if one of his students had shown themselves to be unexpectedly knowledgeable. Wasn't it? 'That's four to one in favour of males. Far more common, too. About three per one thousand births.'

'So it was a difficult operation for the cyst?'

'This kid was pretty sick. The cyst wasn't diagnosed early enough and she presented with billary fibrosis, cirrhosis and liver failure.'

'She presented with abdo pain, I guess? And jaundice?'

'And vomiting. She'd been complaining of tummyaches off and on for the last eighteen months. The GP had diagnosed childhood migraine.'

Jenna's eyebrows had risen. It made her eyes wider than usual. Those little gold flecks more obvious. 'She's not a neonate, then?'

Paul blinked, deliberately shutting off the fascination of the gold flecks. 'No. She's nearly six. Would you believe a phobia of starting school was offered as the initial diagnosis?'

'Family problems?'

'Yes. Big family. Big, poor family.'

'Poor wee thing.'

Why was he surprised that Jenna could see straight to the heart of the matter? She must have been a damned good nurse. Bit of a waste to have her shut away caring for a single, healthy baby.

'Has it made a lot of difference to her prognosis? The delay?'

'Hell, yes! Possibly the difference between regression of the liver fibrosis and return of normal hepatic function and needing a liver transplant.'

'Oh…' Jenna's sigh captured everything Paul had been feeling about the case. 'How did the surgery go?'

'I wasn't happy. Only the mucosa of the cyst was removable with jejunal anastomosis to the proximal bile duct. Better than nothing but with the evidence of atresia…' Paul echoed Jenna's sigh. Then he made a deliberate effort to smile. 'Enough shop talk, anyway. Hardly what you want over dinner.'

'Actually…' Jenna smiled back '…it's exactly what I like over dinner. I miss it.'

'The nursing?' He had been right. Jenna was wasted in this position as a nanny and she knew it. Funny how the thought of her going back to where she belonged created such a sinking feeling in his gut.

'Medicine in general,' Jenna nodded. 'It's my world. Always had been. My father was a doctor, my mother was a nurse. That's how they met, of course.'

'Of course.' But Paul didn't want to go there.

'Dad died six years ago with an MI and Mum…I think she gave up on life after Dad died. I never got the feeling she fought too hard against the cancer.'

'So you're an orphan? Poor you!'

Jenna shook her head. Just enough to make the soft curls bounce against her shoulders. 'Being an orphan suggests dependency, doesn't it? Thirty-one is getting a bit old to expect sympathy for losing both parents.'

'Sympathy is always called for given the loss of family. I will never forget the trauma of losing my father and I'm nowhere near ready to contemplate not having my mother around.'

Dio, but Jenna's eyes looked huge at the moment. Shining with something that looked curiously like gratitude, mixed with unshed tears, perhaps. It made him feel as though he had given her something precious rather than simply an understanding of what she'd been through. It made him feel benevolent. Generous. Powerful, even.

The sensation was pleasant enough to make him want to give her more.

A lot more.

With an effort, Paul dragged his gaze away yet again.

'Eat,' he commanded. ' Maria will be offended if there are leftovers.'

Jenna ate.

Fast enough to risk indigestion.

Why had Paul done this? Set a table and then waited so that he could share his meal with her? It made her feel like he'd wanted her company.

That he didn't hate her after all.

The roadblock to the path she knew she shouldn't even contemplate stepping onto had been unexpectedly removed. And the temptation was wicked!

Jenna could only think of one way to avoid succumbing to that temptation and that was to remove herself from Paul's company as quickly as possible. So she ate fast and answered his questions as succinctly as she could between bites without appearing rude.

Yes, she loved nursing—especially children.

No, she had never wanted to be a doctor like her father. She liked the more personal involvement with her patients that nursing afforded.

Yes, she was enjoying Christchurch. She could see why it was called 'The Garden City'.

Yes, Ella seemed almost fully recovered now. Happy, despite some new teeth that were starting to emerge.

No, she didn't need any new toys or equipment to help her learn to walk. She would get there quite fast enough on her own.

And, no, she couldn't possibly eat another mouthful of food.

Or sit there a moment longer when every minute of listening to the sound of Paul's voice or seeing him tear a piece of bread or fork food into his mouth threatened to undermine any resolve she had made to think of him purely as Ella's father.

It was becoming way too difficult.

It became even harder over the course of the weekend.

Paul had done a ward round in the morning but he was at home for lunch and the day was so nice Maria had deemed they should have the meal outside in the cobbled courtyard beneath a pergola that was densely covered by a mature grapevine. Ella and Jenna had been included in the leisurely feast of bread and cheese and ham with all sorts of olives and other morsels of finger food.

'You should go, Jenna,' Maria said finally. 'This is your afternoon off.'

'I'll wait until Ella goes down for her nap.' Jenna caught Maria's gaze. She wanted to check Maria's blood-glucose level before she left the house for the shopping trip and then the dinner she had arranged to have with Anne. Having established control more easily than expected, Dr Barry was allowing Maria to try only two insulin injections a day, but the glucose levels still needed frequent evaluation.

'She doesn't look very sleepy,' Paul observed from over the rim of his glass of red wine. 'In spite of all that bread she's stuffed into herself.'

'No.' Jenna lifted Ella from the high chair. 'I'll let her crawl on the grass for a bit. She loves being outside.'

But Ella wasn't content to crawl. She wanted to stand.

It was unfortunate that Louise chose to let herself into the Romano household unannounced and then go to find the family outside in the garden. The distraction she produced was enough for attention to be off Ella for just a second or two.

Long enough for small hands to grasp the edge of the tablecloth hanging at just the right height. An anchor that probably looked as secure as Paul's trousers had but which proved thoroughly unreliable as Ella pulled on it to heave herself upright.

The crash of the first plate onto the cobblestones was more than enough to alert them all to impending disaster. Ella's small, trusting face was turned upwards, oblivious to the heavy platter of cold meats now sliding rapidly towards the edge of the table.

'Dio!' Paul moved so swiftly he was blur in Jenna's peripheral vision. He snatched Ella up and away as several more items crashed around her.

Startled, and then frustrated, Ella let out a bellow, but Paul simply lifted her higher.

'Flying baby,' he pronounced, proceeding to swoop Ella in a huge arc.

Her threatened wail of distress turned into a surprised squeak as she reached the top of the arc and then became a cry of delight as she fell backwards, cocooned in the safety of two large, strong hands cradling her body. Paul then swung her in a circle around him and she started laughing.

The three women stood among the shards of china and spilt food on the cobblestones, oblivious to the destruction around their feet.

Or even the near miss of Ella badly injuring herself.

And then Jenna began to smile.

Paul was *playing* with his daughter.

She looked at Maria and wasn't surprised to see the older woman catching a tear as it escaped her eye.

When she heard the sound of Paul actually laughing aloud for the first time, Jenna felt the prickle of tears of her own.

Paul was not only playing with Ella.

He was *loving* it.

He stopped whirling the baby before she could become giddy and then, there he was, with Ella in his arms, standing still and staring at Jenna, who was grinning like an idiot.

Paul was also grinning and the connection it created between them was so powerful Jenna felt like she standing on the edge of a precipice.

About to fall.

And she was.

At that moment Jenna was in terrible danger of falling…in love.

With a man who was not only stunningly attractive but perfectly capable of loving his own child.

He did already. Like Maria had said, maybe he just hadn't realised it.

But why not?

The answer came as Paul's grin faded and his gaze slid sideways.

'Oh. My. God,' Louise said with deliberate emphasis. 'What in heaven's name is going on?'

Jenna stepped towards Paul. She needed to hold Ella.

To justify her presence in this group. To have an excuse to escape before Louise's gimlet gaze could detect body language that might reflect thoughts that even Jenna wasn't ready to deal with.

Paul seemed more than happy to relinquish Ella. He seemed to have collected himself and had that vaguely bewildered air again. Perhaps he was as astounded at his own behaviour as everyone else had been.

'Thanks, Jenna,' he said crisply. 'I'll find a broom and clear this mess up.'

'But what happened?' Louise demanded.

'Ella has learned to stand up in the last couple of days,' Jenna said. 'Trouble is, she needs something to hang onto and doesn't know about tablecloths.'

'You weren't *watching* her?' Louise was outraged. 'She could have been badly hurt! What if one of those dishes had landed on—?'

'It's not Jenna's fault,' Paul interrupted smoothly. 'We were all here with Ella.'

'Yes.' The word carried a wealth of innuendo. Too much. Jenna could feel herself flushing. It had been a family scene. A picnic lunch in the garden. Why *had* Maria insisted she join them? And thank God Louise hadn't seen her having dinner with Paul last night.

'I must go,' she said aloud. It was time to ease the tension by reminding everyone of her status as an employee. Including herself. 'It *is* my afternoon off after all.'

'I'll come in, too,' Maria said hastily. 'To find the broom.'

'I'll take Danielle, then, shall I?' Louise made it sound as though she had arrived in the nick of time. 'Perhaps you could find me a coffee-cup while you're inside, Maria.'

* * *

The spell away from the Romano family was well timed. It gave Jenna breathing space and, in time-honoured fashion, a chance to determine how she was feeling by having an intimate discussion with a close female friend.

'I should probably resign right now. Maybe I'm not needed. Paul is starting to act like a *real* father.'

'Since when?' Anne countered. She didn't wait for a response from Jenna. 'Since you told him he cared more about his patients than his own child, that's when. This is your doing, Jenna, and it's only just begun. Disappear now and I guarantee things will revert to exactly how they were before you arrived.'

'But how can I stay? It's impossible!'

'Why, because you think you might be love with Paul? Why don't you stay long enough to find out how he feels about you?' Anne's grin was wicked. 'You might succeed where many have tried and failed.'

'No.' Jenna's head shake was virtually a shudder. 'You should have seen the way Louise was looking at me. I'd be dead meat if she knew. I might be already because I'm sure she's suspicious.'

'Nothing's happened,' Anne soothed. 'And nothing will…unless you want it to.'

'I *don't*!'

'Really?'

'Yes…no…oh, I don't know, Anne. I'm confused.'

'I'm thinking that Paul probably is as well. What *was* with that romantic dinner the other night?'

'I have no idea.'

'You do want him to bond with Ella, though, don't you?'

'Of course.'

'So see it through. Make sure that bond is as strong as it can be. Then you can decide what you want to do about Doctor Romantico.'

CHAPTER SIX

As IF the decision was ever going to be hers!

Jenna realised just how wrong Anne had been in making that assumption at precisely 3 a.m. the next morning.

She hadn't heard a telephone ring but maybe that was what had woken Ella. By the time Jenna had stumbled over to the cot the baby was asleep again. Jenna was still half-asleep herself, otherwise she might have thought to grab a robe before heading out of the nursery towards the bathroom.

She woke up fast enough on the return journey when a dark figure seemed to materialise in front of her. Paul was fully dressed. Not in a suit, of course, but the faded jeans and black jersey were perfectly respectable.

Unlike Jenna's silk boxer shorts or the singlet top with a scrap of lace at the bottom of its deep V neck and a hemline that failed to cover her belly button thanks to how much it had shrunk in the wash.

Instinctively, she stepped aside, although the upstairs hallway was more than wide enough for a whole group of people to pass. She put a hand out to touch the wall as though hoping, by some magic, it would pull her in and make her invisible.

It felt, horribly, as though she was standing stark naked in front of Paul Romero.

'I…um…had to use the bathroom,' she faltered.

'Are you unwell?'

'No!' Was that why he was staring at her with an intensity even the dimmest light couldn't disguise? Physical awareness hummed between them and it took an incredible effort of will for Jenna to break that eye contact. 'Not at all. I only woke because Ella did. She's fine. She's asleep again.'

She was babbling. Too uncomfortable to do anything but look desperately past Paul, hunting for an escape route. He was a large man, certainly, but he wasn't exactly blocking her way. Why wouldn't her feet obey the simple command to move?

'I imagine the phone woke her. I have to go in to the hospital. That little girl I told you about seems to be running into trouble. Liver failure.'

'Oh…I'm sorry. I'd better not hold you up.'

'No. Sleep well, Jenna.'

As if! But it wasn't as if Paul had been staring at her body. The intense gaze Jenna had been sucked into before managing to avert her eyes so determinedly had been directed at her face.

So why did her body feel…scorched? Why was she still tossing and turning and awake enough to hear Paul's return two hours later? Jenna had to give up any possibility of sleep at that point as she imagined him peeling off those jeans and climbing wearily into his own bed to snatch another hour or two of rest if he was lucky.

It was high time she moved back into the flat. Ella didn't need her nanny sharing the nursery any longer and Jenna *had* to create some distance for her own peace of mind.

* * *

A week later, Jenna was congratulating herself on how well the strategy was working.

Louise didn't appear to be suspicious any longer. She had stopped watching Jenna's every move and trying to analyse her facial expressions if Paul was at home. She seemed, instead, to be sharing Maria's fascination with the way he was interacting with Ella.

And interacting he was. Virtually every day. He played with his daughter. One day he sprawled, still in his pinstripe suit, on the lounge floor within minutes of arriving home.

He built towers of bright plastic cups, discussing the colours as though they were as intellectually stimulating as a peer-reviewed article in one of his surgical journals.

'This one is *giallo*. Yellow. A very bright yellow. You get sunflowers this colour and maybe a very ripe lemon.' The yellow cup was balanced carefully on top of the blue one. 'And this one is *rosso*. Red. *Scarlotto*. If it was darker, it would be *color cremisi*. Crimson. It's smaller than the yellow cup, see? It fits on top. And right up here we're going to put the little pink one. What happens now, Ella?'

Ella knew. Her face changed from the dreamy contentment of listening to the deep rumble of her father's voice and her eyes crinkled in pure mischief just a fraction of a second before her lips curled into a wide smile.

Just the way her father's did.

Ella raised her hand, leaned forward and shoved hard enough to topple the rainbow tower.

'Yes! Shall we build it again, *cara*?'

Ella clapped her hands—another new skill—and Maria sighed happily and then sniffed and reached for a tissue. Louise, present on that occasion, simply watched with a carefully benign smile.

* * *

Neither of the grandmothers were present on the Thursday of the following week, a day when Paul often managed to get home a little earlier after one of his clinics.

Jenna was sitting, cross-legged, on the floor, thinking it was time to start tidying up the scattered toys.

Paul was bent over so far he had to be hurting his back. Ella had been standing beside a couch as he'd entered the lounge and he had responded to the commanding little hand that waved at him. Now he was holding both Ella's hands as she stood in front of him, beaming and swaying.

And then it happened. Instead of the usual plonk onto her well-padded bottom, Ella lifted a bare foot and lurched forward. Paul instinctively adjusted the space between them and it happened again. The other tiny foot lifted and stepped forward. And Ella was still on her feet, grinning up at her father.

But he was looking at Jenna.

'Did you see that, Jenna? Did you see it?' His face shone with pride and the words tumbled out excitedly. 'She took her first step! Her *first* step!'

'Yes.' The pride was contagious. A spark ignited somewhere deep and Jenna could feel the glow radiating through her body.

'It was the first, wasn't it?' An anxious frown creased Paul's forehead. 'She hasn't been doing this when I'm not around, has she?'

'No.' Jenna had to smile but there was a poignancy in the mix of emotions as she watched Paul lift Ella for a congratulatory cuddle.

She loved the pride she saw. The satisfaction in having been there to witness a new milestone. The relief in knowing that the bond between father and daughter was growing stronger every day.

But most of all she loved it that they were sharing this moment. Like…

Like any proud parents.

She was too involved.

Travelling too far down a path that could only lead to heartbreak.

It didn't help that Maria was determined to make her a part of the family. Like when she insisted that Jenna join them to celebrate her birthday a couple of weeks later.

'But you must come, *cara*. You and Ella. I am making my special risotto. It is a *celebrazione*. For *famiglia*. It could not be complete without you, Jenna.'

And Jenna agreed readily because she loved Maria. Loved feeling like part of this small family. Mothered, even. Every day, Maria would ask how well she had slept. Would comment if she thought Jenna looked tired or pale and asked, so often, if she was happy. She would insist that Jenna taste any recipe she was practising for her cooking classes and frequently made special treats for a meal or snack just because she wanted to. Jenna felt as cared for and petted as Ella sometimes and she couldn't deny that it was healing the very raw patch on her soul that her own mother's death had left.

It wasn't a one-way street by any means. Jenna was proud of the way Paul's mother was getting both braver and more competent with the management of her diabetes. Maria could measure her own blood-glucose level now but she still depended on Jenna to administer the insulin injections.

And she still refused to let Paul know about the change

in her medical condition. Jenna had tried hard to persuade her. Increasingly, she didn't like Paul not knowing. It was like lying by omission. A wedge that separated her from being a real part of the family.

'He has to know,' she had said more than once. 'It's important, Maria. You should be wearing a medic-alert bracelet and someone other than myself and Shirley and Dr Barry needs to know.'

'Why?'

'Just in case something goes wrong. Not that it's likely to,' she added reassuringly as a fearful expression appeared on Maria's face. 'It's just…important.'

'Not yet,' Maria had said decisively. 'Not until I can manage—all by myself. I do not want Paolo to think I am *vigliacca*…a… What is the word for someone who is silly by being scared?'

Jenna had grinned. 'A wimp?'

'*Si*. I do not want to be a wimp.'

But Jenna knew there was more to it than that and it worried her, becoming another aspect to why the thought of leaving to return to her nursing position was becoming harder every day.

Yes, she felt like part of the family, but she also felt distanced. Was that how Louise felt? Jenna still didn't understand some of the bonds but they were there and strengthening. A strength that became suddenly a lot more obvious on a day the following week.

A Wednesday, when Louise was there. She arrived, as usual, before breakfast was complete and while she had coffee, they were planning Ella's first birthday party, which was only a few weeks away.

Or rather, Louise was planning it. Maria wanted just a family occasion. Louise was determined to have the house filled with balloons and flowers. To hire a magician and possibly a pony as well.

'She's a baby, Louise,' Maria protested. 'She won't remember. All she needs is love.'

'She'll see the photographs when she's older.' Louise had made a note. 'I must book a photographer. Danielle will look back in years to come and she will know how much her grandmother loved her.'

Maria scowled. Louise glared. Ella was oblivious to the tension, however, and banged her spoon on her plate.

'Nen -nah!' she declared.

Louise gasped. 'She said *Nana*! She knows who I am!'

Maria shook her head. 'I think it was *Nonna*. Paul is teaching her Italian. *Nonna* is Italian for grandmother.'

Jenna said nothing, so close to tears it wasn't funny. Paul had certainly taught Ella the new word but it was as close as the little girl had been able to get…to *Jenna*.

The bonds were tightening.

It was going to be very hard for Jenna to leave the Romano household.

But not impossible.

The idea that it could, in fact, become unbearable was born just a day later. On Thursday, when Paul had been held up after his clinic by a departmental meeting and didn't arrive home until 6.30 p.m.

When Ella was having her bath.

He'd never ventured into the bathroom to include himself in this part of the daily routine so it was something to be celebrated that he only seemed a little hesitant to do so. Jenna's smile of welcome was sincerely delighted but she felt obliged to issue a warning.

'You might not want to get that suit wet. Ella can get a

bit excited in the bath.' Too late now to worry about how wet her own clothing might be. Whether her T-shirt was clinging a little too closely in places that might not be appropriate.

'It's only a suit.' Paul smiled back. That delicious, *real* smile, so like his daughter's, where the corners of his eyes crinkled just before his lips curved. He sat on the closed lid of the toilet, watching as Jenna rinsed shampoo from Ella's dark curls, which were almost long enough to hold a ribbon now.

Ella played with a flotilla of plastic ducks, once clutched firmly in each hand as she stirred the shampoo suds collecting on the surface of the water. Jenna concentrated on soaping her charge's chubby body, which wasn't easy because Ella wriggled and giggled and waved the ducks in the air. The task usually kept a smile on Jenna's face all on its own. That Paul was also there should have made the time far more joyous but Jenna couldn't help the poignancy that stole through her.

The bond between father and daughter was so much stronger now. It would still be there when Jenna was gone.

She should be happy that she was succeeding in her mission. Ridiculous to feel bereft imagining total success. That she wouldn't be needed any longer. Wouldn't be missed...

Ella smacked her ducks onto the water hard enough to splash soapy water onto both Jenna and Paul. He didn't seem to mind. He wasn't even annoyed when Ella threw a duck at him. Laughing, he slid down to kneel on the bathmat beside Jenna to return the toy. Close enough to touch his daughter's cheek.

Close enough for his hip to be touching Jenna's. For her to feel the warmth of his whole body. The warmth of her *own* body, which seemed to be increasing at an alarming rate.

Ella thanked her father by scooping up handfuls of bubbles. Her offering was enthusiastic enough to leave her hands at speed. Her aim was off, however, and the soapy suds missed him and landed on Jenna's face. She shook her head, laughing, but then glanced up at Paul to see if he was sharing her amusement.

And that was a huge mistake.

He wasn't laughing. He wasn't even smiling, and the look Jenna was receiving seemed to turn her to stone.

No, not stone.

A stone could never feel this...*alive*.

She was just still. Waiting. Because time had stopped.

Like that moment in the ward kitchen. Or the one in the upstairs hallway. Only this time Paul wasn't going to distract himself by attending to his duty. And Jenna was not going to distract either of them by offering a cup of tea. Or attending to her own duty other than keeping hold of a slippery baby. She couldn't do anything else.

Jenna was incapable of doing anything other than waiting.

Even Ella seemed to be waiting. Jenna could feel the baby's stillness, although she couldn't see it because her gaze was locked on Paul's. The incomprehensible babble of contented sounds from the bath had also ceased. Or maybe Jenna just couldn't hear them any more because her awareness was so totally focussed on the man beside her.

As his was. On her.

He lifted his hand, using his middle finger to smooth a blob of soap suds from just below her eye. The touch was so light, so intense, it could be nothing less than a caress.

Then he stroked another away from her cheek. Only this time his finger didn't leave her skin. It traced a line from her cheek to the corner of her mouth and Jenna's lips parted involuntarily as the finger kept moving.

It wasn't a conscious decision to touch the tip of that finger with her tongue. She would have done it instinctively to catch the taste of him on her lips and it was simply that Paul's movements were so slow and deliberate that she hadn't been able to wait.

The connection unleashed something almost frightening. Jenna wouldn't have believed that Paul's eyes could darken that much. Or that she would ever hear him utter a sound that was pure, raw desire.

'You,' he said very softly, 'are beautiful. *Bella.*'

And then, with Jenna completely helpless as she held Ella safely upright in her bath, Paul tipped his head and kissed her.

Softly.

Slowly.

With the same deliberate touch his finger had made.

It wasn't enough. Not nearly enough, and Jenna knew Paul was thinking exactly the same because her gaze was still locked onto his—as it had been from the first moment he had touched her face.

There was no question of whether or not they would make love. It was simply a matter of when.

Which was most definitely not going to be now!

'I…I need to dry Ella and get her to bed.' Jenna almost groaned aloud. How stupid was that, to utter the word 'bed' when sexual tension heavy enough to be practically flattening them both had not even begun to dissipate?

The quirk of Paul's eyebrow revealed absolute comprehension. The lopsided curve to his mouth suggested both resignation and amusement.

'Of course you do. And I need to help Maria in the kitchen. Louise is coming to dinner tonight.' The flash of distaste in his expression eased a significant part of the tension. 'Apparently she wishes her new boyfriend to meet her granddaughter.'

Jenna nodded, lifting Ella from the bath and ignoring her squeak of protest as she wrapped her in a soft, fluffy towel. 'Yes. I'm to bring her down for a few minutes before her bedtime.'

'You'll come back, won't you? When Ella is asleep?'

Jenna stared. Did Paul realise that this was the first time he had ever used the diminutive of his daughter's name?

He misunderstood her hesitation.

'Please, come,' he said softly. 'As Maria said on her birthday, you are one of the family now.'

His gaze dropped to her mouth and Jenna watched, mesmerised, as he slowly licked his lips.

'You belong,' he added simply, 'with *me*.'

CHAPTER SEVEN

'SHE's a princess, Lulu. An absolute princess!'

Ella was sitting on Gerald Bagshaw's lap. A rather slippery lap because the pants were a very tight fit, but Ella didn't seem to mind. She was staring with open-mouthed fascination at the heavy gold chain resting on a thick patch of dark hair the open-necked shirt was revealing. Jenna watched with some concern as small pink fingers started their journey towards the chain but her lips twitched.

Lulu?

The cough that came from Paul's direction could well have been a disguised snort of amusement. Jenna risked a quick glance as Maria screened Louise by offering an anti-pasto platter laden with pâté spread on crostini, pickles and cold meats.

Sure enough, there was a look of unholy glee in his dark eyes that had to be because of learning the pet name Gerald had for Louise.

'Try one of these stuffed olives, Jenna. My own recipe. You'll love them.'

Jenna thanked Maria and chose one of the fat green olives, but it wasn't enough of a distraction. Surely the tension generated by that kiss should have evaporated by now—nearly an hour after Ella's bathtime? But it hadn't. She had discovered that the moment she set'd foot in the formal lounge.

There it was all over again.

That kiss.

Just hanging in the air between them, like a ticking clock. Or maybe an unexploded bomb.

Nervously, Jenna flicked another glance in Paul's direction at the precise moment she was opening her mouth to eat her olive. No hint of amusement on Paul's face now. He actually closed his eyes as he shifted uncomfortably on the overstuffed wing chair. Jenna knew exactly what he was thinking. She was thinking the same thing the instant the tip of her tongue touched the olive.

Oh, *help*! This was going to be a lot harder than she had anticipated.

Jenna would have to find an excuse not to join the Romano family for dinner. At least they weren't planning to eat in the kitchen as they usually did, but the formal dining room wasn't that far away. And the kitchen was only a few steps away from Jenna's apartment. Who would know if Paul chose to visit her there late at night?

Tonight, even?

The olive was proving difficult to swallow, until Jenna's glance slid sideways to find Louise staring at her. Then it went down painfully fast. How long had she been watching? Had she seen the way Paul had almost visibly winced as he'd watched her putting the olive in her mouth?

Gerald let out a timely squeak as a small fist tugged on his chest hair.

'Lu?'

Louise had to move to rescue Gerald. She tried to prise

Ella's fingers clear. 'It's your chain she likes, Gerry. She's not really trying to torture you.'

'She's a princess,' Gerald repeated with a sigh of relief as Louise lifted Ella from his lap. 'Good taste 'n' all. Twenty-four-carat gold this chain is. Cost a bomb! I bought it to celebrate my first million, y'know.'

'What is it that you do, Gerald?' Paul's question was courteous.

'Septic tanks,' Gerald told him proudly. 'There's a lot of money in sh—'

'Gerry!' Louise's reprimand was coquettish.

'Sorry, pumpkin.' Gerald licked his lips as he watched Louise walk back to her chair, getting a rear view of the way her black dress clung to slim hips. 'Hard to believe she's a grandmother, eh? I said I *wouldn't* believe it. Show me the evidence, I said.'

The evidence was now scowling at him over Louise's shoulder. Jenna could feel Paul's gaze but refused to look in his direction. She couldn't lighten the atmosphere by shared amusement at how awful this visitor was. Did Louise really see him as a potential life partner? Was it just the blatant show of available spending power or did he have hidden qualities like…like being a totally amazing lover?

As Jenna knew with absolute certainty Paul was going to be. She mimicked his earlier gesture, closing her eyes for a second to try and regain control. It seemed to help. She was able to focus on someone other than Paul when she opened them again.

Maybe Gerald wouldn't appear so brash in another setting, she decided. Like a beach barbecue, perhaps. It could be that the discreet and tasteful wealth of the Romano family was highlighting a very different set of values. Whatever the reason, nobody was feeling comfortable.

'Would you like to try an olive, Gerald?' Maria, typically, was trying to fix whatever was wrong by offering food. 'Or some prosciutto?'

'Proshy what?'

'Ham,' Paul supplied.

Gerald eyed the platter with deep suspicion. 'I'm a steak and potatoes man myself,' he declared. 'Always have been. Still, it'd be rude not to, eh?' He fumbled for an olive. 'Might need a drop more bourbon to wash it down with, mind.'

'Allow me.' Paul's lips seemed thinner than usual as he moved to refill Gerald's glass but Jenna couldn't tell whether he was trying to suppress amusement or understandable irritation.

Ella's lips were also compressed but her expression was far easier to interpret. She had twisted in Louise's arms to try and catch sight of the glittering treasure around Gerald's neck. The prize she had been denied.

'It's getting past Ella's bedtime,' Jenna said hurriedly in an attempt to avoid disaster. 'Should I take her upstairs?'

'You're the nanny, right?' Gerald stopped watching the rising level of spirits in his glass to leer at Jenna. Then he frowned at Paul before returning his gaze to Jenna. 'You a relative?'

'No!' Jenna was horrified. Was the electricity between herself and Paul detectable even to a complete stranger?

'You just look kinda Italian,' Gerald pronounced. He took another long appreciative look as he nodded.

Louise's eyes narrowed. 'I think it would be a very good idea if you took Danielle upstairs now, Jennifer.'

Jenna rose swiftly, but not before Ella opened her mouth to let everyone know just how tired and frustrated she was.

Louise raised her voice over the bellow but still managed to sound casual.

'While you're in the nursery, Jennifer, could you keep an eye out for my gold watch? I'm wondering if I might have left it beside the change table somewhere.'

'Oh?' Jenna couldn't remember when Louise had last offered to change a nappy. Or set foot in the nursery even. She usually waited downstairs, sipping her black coffee, while Jenna got Ella ready for her outings.

Gerald's glass paused in mid-air. 'Not the watch *I* gave you, was it, pumpkin?'

Louise favoured him with a very apologetic look. 'I'm afraid so, Gerry. Ella took a fancy to playing with it, just like she did with your chain.'

'Good taste.' Gerald nodded. 'Told you so.'

'I took it off,' Louise continued smoothly, 'because I didn't want it to get dirty.'

'Or broken!' Gerald eyed the now howling Ella and nodded approvingly. 'She's got a grip like a gorilla, the little monkey!'

The 'little monkey' rubbed her nose on Jenna's shoulder and hiccuped sadly. Jenna kissed her and made for the door, noticing a rather odd expression on Paul's face as she paused to let him say goodnight to his daughter. He stood up and leaned close.

'I'll come up, too, shall I?' he murmured, quietly enough not to be overheard. 'And help tuck Ella in?'

Jenna's eyes widened in alarm. That would really set Louise off. Then she caught the ghost of a wink from Paul.

'Take no notice,' he said. Then he kissed Ella gently on each cheek, ruffled her hair and raised his voice. *'Buona notte, cara. A presto domani.'*

It did weird things to Jenna's knees when she heard Paul speak in Italian but luckily it didn't show as she walked through the door he was now holding open for her.

Maria followed. 'I must check on dinner,' she excused herself.

Jenna waited until the door closed behind them. 'Are you feeling all right, Maria? Have you checked your blood sugar?'

'I'm fine.'

'Are you sure? You look a little pale.'

'I am *arrabbiata*. Angry! It starts all over again!'

Jenna rocked Ella who was almost asleep in her arms. She would be able to take her upstairs and simply slip her into bed in a minute. She should do it right now but there was something in Maria's tone that was a warning. 'What starts, Maria?'

'This is how she makes the trouble,' Maria said fiercely. 'She said that Susan stole one of her rings. Paolo offered to buy her another but, no, that was not good enough. She would go to the police if it wasn't returned. Poor Susan could not return it, could she, because she had not taken it in the first place. She did not want a bad…what do you call it? Recommendation?'

'Reference?'

Maria nodded distractedly. '*Si*. So she left. Louise had her way. And now it starts again.' There were tears in Maria's eyes. 'Take no notice, Jenna. *Per favore*. I do not want to lose you.'

Paul had advised her to take no notice as well. Surely Louise's preferences couldn't override them all? Jenna held Maria's gaze and tried to offer reassurance.

'I'm not going to let Louise drive me away with false accusations, don't worry.'

'I can't understand why she does this now,' Maria continued unhappily. 'It's not as if you and Paolo...' She paused, searching Jenna's gaze and then her eyes widened. 'Oh...' she murmured. 'Oh...*Dio mio!*'

But then she pinched Jenna's cheek. 'Take Ella to bed,' she advised calmly. 'I will see to dinner.'

Maria turned swiftly but not before Jenna caught the beginnings of what looked like a pleased smile.

She was not going to get away with it.

Not this time.

No way was Paul going to allow Louise to drive Jenna from his home.

His life.

No surprise that Louise suspected something might be brewing. Paul had never felt this kind of physical desire for any woman other than Jenna, and Louise was far from being stupid.

He had known that all along. He had been so confident he could ignore what his body was telling him—way back, that night in the paediatric ward's kitchen when he'd felt that insane desire to kiss Jenna's neck. He'd known what a mistake it would be to give in to that desire. It would have pre-empted another fiasco like the one that had surrounded the departure of Ella's last nanny. The needs of his family had to come first and Jenna being forced to leave would upset both Ella and his mother.

Of course, it had become rather more difficult after that night he'd met Jenna in the upstairs hallway wearing nothing but those short silky pants and a top that revealed far more than it covered, but even then he had been confident of controlling any hormonal urges.

What had happened this evening, in the bathroom?

Seeing Jenna kneeling there, flushed and damp and laughing, with soap bubbles all over her face. Something had snapped. Quite painlessly. In fact, the rush of something warm and tender that was pure pleasure even before he'd tasted Jenna's lips had been a new experience.

The first step on a journey he knew he *had* to take. A voyage of discovery that Paul suspected would lead him somewhere he'd never been before. A curious mix of excitement and wariness bubbled within him so, no, it wasn't surprising that Louise had detected something different about him.

It also wasn't that surprising that Jenna had not made an excuse to escape the dinner and Louise's barely concealed fury. He had already witnessed Jenna's courage, hadn't he, when she had stood up to him and told him what she thought of his relationship with Danielle?

How things had changed since then!

A door Paul had never thought to try had swung open and he had fallen in love.

With a baby.

With Ella.

With having a family. His mother, Ella, Jenna and himself. To lose Jenna would change what had become a delight. As important in his life as his career.

Something to look forward to being a part of, every day.

Something that deserved all the protection he was capable of bestowing. Paul knew what the biggest threat was to this family unit. He forced himself to smile at Louise.

'More Chianti?' he offered.

'No.'

'Oh, go on, Lulu!' Gerald drained his wineglass and held it towards the bottle Paul had picked up. 'Do you good. You need to loosen up a bit, pumpkin.'

Jenna followed Maria in from the kitchen. She had been quick to help collect the empty scallop shell dishes and tiny silver forks after their entrée and had earned an almost approving nod from Louise as she escaped the dining room.

Paul would have liked to escape as well. He hated formal rooms. The kitchen was where he should be eating. In the heart of the household. With his family.

'Ossobuco,' Maria announced as Jenna carefully placed a large, lidded earthenware dish on the table. 'One of my specialities.'

'Smells great,' Gerald enthused. 'Steak, huh?'

'Slow-stewed veal shanks,' Maria told him.

'It's like steak,' Paul murmured. 'You'll love it, Gerry.'

'No pasta for me.' Louise eyed a steaming bowl of ribbon pasta and sniffed the rich aroma of cheese. 'Just salad.'

'You'll fade away,' Gerald warned. 'And where would that leave me, gorgeous?' He blew a noisy kiss towards Louise and then grinned at Maria. 'Love of my life, this woman is,' he said firmly. 'Love of my life.' He leaned sideways to squeeze Louise's knee and she jumped visibly.

'*Gerald!* Not at the table, *please*!'

Paul tried to keep the sympathy out of his smile. If Gerald really did love Louise to such an extent, he was in for heartbreak.

Like mother, like daughter.

Although he was beginning to wonder if he had ever actually been really in love with Gwendolyn.

The thought distracted him enough to let the rest of this awkward meal pass without undue stress.

Was the degree to which you fell in love dependent, at least initially, on the level of physical attraction you felt for someone?

No. He couldn't allow that because if he did, he would

have to acknowledge that he was in real trouble right now. Physical attraction equated purely to lust.

The kind of lust he was feeling for Jenna.

It was almost unbearable to watch as she ate the delicious tiramisu Maria had made for dessert. The way she put the spoon in her mouth and then turned it upside down, obviously using her tongue to remove the chocolaty morsel…the dreamy look of pleasure that clouded her eyes…

A kind that far surpassed anything he'd ever felt in his life.

Yes. Any good intentions of staying well away from Ella's nanny had been blown completely out of the water. As though they had never even existed.

He would find a way to deal with Louise's displeasure.

He would *have* to.

The shared relief of seeing the front door close behind Louise and Gerald was not enough to justify the unusual serenity Maria was displaying.

Jenna eyed the older woman cautiously. Where was the concealed anxiety that would only dissipate when she had supervised the nightly blood-glucose test and dispensed reassurance?

'I might just pop upstairs and check on Ella,' she said casually. 'And then I'll help with the washing-up.'

'No, no!' Maria waved a hand airily. 'I can do that. By myself.'

The words were as casual as Jenna's but the significance of the hidden meaning was anything but.

'Are you sure?'

'*Si.*' Maria beamed at Jenna. 'If I need help, I'll call you.'

Jenna had to smile back. This was all part of her mission, wasn't it? For Maria to become independent and confident as far as managing her diabetes went?

'I'll get on with clearing up, then. It was a wonderful dinner, Maria.'

'Molte grazie, cara.' Maria stood on tiptoe to kiss Paul. 'You will help Jenna, yes?'

'Of course.'

It wasn't until Jenna's third trip from the dining room to the kitchen that she realised what Maria was up to. It wasn't that she had suddenly decided she was ready to manage her own testing and medications. She had taken this brave step because something was more important than her own nervousness. And that something was to encourage whatever she believed was happening between her son and Jenna.

She was forcing them to spend time together.

Alone.

And it was working. Clearing the table wasn't difficult because they were moving, and loading the dishwasher was a breeze because Paul did it while Jenna took the linen to the laundry and wiped down the table, but the scallop shells and wineglasses needed to be washed by hand. They found themselves standing side by side in front of the huge old ceramic double sinks.

Paul rolled up his sleeves and watched as Jenna filled one of the sinks with hot water and added detergent. The moment she saw the soap bubbles begin to form she knew that washing these dishes was going to be an exercise in exquisite torture.

Jenna bent her head, allowing her loose hair to screen her face as she tried to concentrate on the task at hand. Maybe Paul wasn't feeling the same irresistible magnetic pull. Maybe that kiss in the bathroom had been a spur-of-the-moment thing and him saying that she belonged with him was just an example of the kind of Italian passion that had to be taken with a grain, or two, of salt.

Then again, maybe not.

Staring at the soap bubbles, Jenna could feel Paul staring at *her*.

Just like he had that night in the ward kitchen.

Like the start of that first fantasy she had had about him.

Only this was no fantasy. This was so real that every one of Jenna's senses were heightened. She could hear Paul's breathing as she hastily twisted the tap to close off the flow of water. She could feel the warmth from the nearness of his body and even smell the faintly musky aroma that reminded her exactly of what the taste of him on her lips had been.

When he lifted his hand to brush the hair screening the side of her face back, Jenna could feel each individual hair drag across her skin and the coolness as her neck was uncovered.

And then the warmth and sheer thrill of the touch of Paul's lips on her neck as his hand cradled the back of her head. The dishcloth fell from Jenna's hand and a tiny sound of longing escaped her lips.

Did her head tilt back of her own volition or had it been due to the subtle pressure of the hand and lips that were blotting out anything other than a physical response?

It mirrored her fantasy so well it was confusing. As though she had stepped into a dream. Her throat was being kissed. She could feel the beat of her pulse against the tip of Paul's tongue, then his hands moving from her hair and coming to rest against her cheeks. He held her face gently, staring not at her mouth but into her eyes. A look that was not shuttered by him closing his eyes until the moment his lips claimed Jenna's.

This was nothing like that soft, questioning kiss in the bathroom.

That stepping over a boundary and discovering the taste of each other was over.

This was about an appetite unleashed. Passion that demanded satisfaction.

It was so smooth. The thrust of Paul's tongue exploring her mouth, the stroke of his hands as they travelled down her back to cup her bottom and pull her closer. So smooth, it felt like flying.

Jenna was weightless. A leaf buffeted by the winds of desire. Her fingers were anchored in the waves of dark hair on Paul's head that felt almost as silky as Ella's. One of her breasts, the nipple painfully sensitised, pressed against the buttons of his shirt.

Until he broke the kiss and murmured something in Italian. Jenna couldn't understand the words but the tone was an invitation and Jenna would have agreed to anything Paul suggested at that moment. Her shaky smile became a gasp as Paul touched first one breast, and then the other, his fingers dragging slowly enough to send ripples of sensation that tugged sharply at something deep within Jenna.

She had to close her eyes and simply hang on then. Paul's hands slid beneath her top and the clasp of her bra sprang open. Jenna was hardly aware of leaning into his hands as they brushed a bare nipple. Of almost hanging from his neck as his leg nudged between hers, the rhythm of his rocking matched by the sweep and curl of his tongue against hers.

Paul broke the kiss and said something she couldn't catch. 'You're wet,' he said again.

Jenna started to blush. Who wouldn't be, with the magic Paul had been creating with his hands and mouth? But at the same moment she became aware of another sensation and it *was* a very wet one.

Warm water was trickling down her back. With the distraction she'd had when she'd turned off the tap, the fact that the movement had not been complete must have gone unnoticed. Water had continued to trickle into the sink Jenna was leaning back against and enough time had passed for the sink to fill and now overflow onto the tiled floor.

'Oh, no!'

'*Non importa,*' Paul soothed. He leaned behind Jenna to give the tap a firm twist. 'It doesn't matter.' He pulled her close again. 'Now, where were we, *cara*?'

His lips covered hers again but it wasn't the same.

It *did* matter. Jenna could feel the puddle of water beneath her feet. Maria would not be happy when she came downstairs.

Or maybe she would share Paul's view that it didn't matter. Had she already come down to check on the clean-up operation and then stolen away because she had not wanted to interrupt what she had seen?

That idea bothered Jenna. The closeness of an Italian family was one thing but to have a relationship fostered because of maternal approval was something else.

And what if Maria had not come down yet?

Why not?

Had she run into problems with her blood-glucose monitor?

Was she alone in her bedroom, fretting but unwilling to interrupt what she *hoped* might be going on in her kitchen?

Paul pushed Jenna back far enough to see her face. 'What is it, *cara*? What's wrong?'

'Maria…'

'She has gone to bed. Don't worry.'

He pulled her into his arms again but Jenna was tense. Paul sighed and then frowned.

'Something *is* wrong, isn't it? Is Maria unwell?'

She should tell him. Jenna *wanted* to tell him but this just wasn't the right moment. It would drive him away because his family came first, and rightly so. But right now Jenna wanted him for herself, so badly.

Just for herself.

The battle in her head must be showing on her face. Paul was looking concerned now. She had to say something.

'I…don't think so but…but I should check. On Ella, anyway.'

Paul's frown deepened. He gave Jenna a searching look and then straightened, dropping his hands from her body. The mood was broken and Jenna was unhappily aware of her damp skirt and unfastened bra.

'We will both check,' Paul decided. 'On Maria and Ella.' With another frown—this time of concentration—he applied himself to the task of refastening the bra clasp but then he smiled wickedly. 'And then we will come back and finish what we have begun, yes?'

Jenna had to smile back. She knew he wasn't talking about doing the dishes and when she was reassured about both Maria and Ella, there would be nothing to stop her surrendering completely to what she wanted more than she had ever wanted anything in her life.

With her hand firmly clasped in Paul's, she went with him from the kitchen and up the stairs. A light shone from beneath the door to Maria's bedroom but only silence greeted Paul's knock.

'She is asleep,' he predicted. 'I shall turn off her light.'

He opened the door and it took only a split second for Jenna to realise her fears had not been unfounded.

Maria lay slumped on the floor, fully dressed and apparently unconscious.

'*Dio!*' Paul was by her side in a moment, shaking his

mother's shoulder. 'Maria? Can you hear me? What's wrong?'

Jenna knelt on the other side of Maria, feeling for her pulse. 'She's tachycardic,' she said a moment later. 'And clammy. I think she's hypoglycaemic.'

'Unlikely,' Paul snapped. 'She has type ll diabetes. It's a struggle keeping her levels down.'

'Not since she started insulin.'

Paul had tilted Maria's head back to protect her airway but his movements suddenly froze.

'What?'

'She…didn't want you to know. I've been helping her since I arrived but tonight she wanted to do her blood-glucose level by herself. She wasn't due for more insulin but if she took it by mistake…'

The look Paul was giving her was the coldest Jenna had ever seen. Much worse than when she had appeared in the emergency department with his daughter and had been blamed for at least contributing to the situation.

This time a member of his family was clearly in real danger and Jenna's responsibility was in no doubt.

Paul's order was terse. Just as cold as that look had been.

'Call an ambulance.'

CHAPTER EIGHT

THE calm efficiency of the paramedics was like balm in the face of Paul's ill-concealed level of tension.

They worked swiftly, gathering a case history while they started to assess and treat their patient, placing an oral airway, putting oxygen on, attaching ECG electrodes and taking baseline vital-sign measurements.

'How old is Maria?'

'Seventy-five,' Paul supplied. He was watching closely and Jenna knew he would be finding it difficult not to take charge of this assessment. He might be a doctor, but in this case he was also a relative and he needed to let the paramedics do their job.

'Pupils equal and reactive,' the female paramedic noted.

Jenna let her breath out consciously. At least this wasn't likely to be a stroke and no evidence of head injury had been found.

'And she's an insulin-dependent diabetic?'

'Apparently so.' Jenna could feel Paul's wrath in the clipped words like a physical blow.

'For how long?'

'About two months,' Jenna told the male paramedic.

'She's tachy at 120,' his partner said as she watched the screen of the life pack. 'Sinus rhythm.'

'When did she have her last dose of insulin?' The question was directed at Jenna rather than Paul, and she could actually feel the way he was trying to contain his frustration at not having the knowledge himself.

'Six p.m.'

'And she's eaten since then?'

'Yes,' Paul snapped.

'I'm not sure how much she ate,' Jenna said cautiously. 'It was a dinner party. I think Maria might have been more concerned about how much other people were eating.'

'Other medical conditions?'

'Hypertension,' Paul told him. 'She's on a beta-blocker. And osteo-arthritis. She takes high-dose aspirin.'

There was a moment's silence, in which the hiss of a deflating blood-pressure cuff could be heard, as the significance of Paul's statement sank in. Aspirin could trigger hypoglycaemia.

'She's not on aspirin any more,' Jenna said, almost reluctantly. No doctor would enjoy relaying inaccurate details but Paul would find this even more appalling. He hadn't known, had he? And this was his own mother. He must be cringing every time Jenna opened her mouth. 'Her GP changed her to another non-steroidal anti-inflammatory when she started the insulin.'

Jenna didn't dare risk looking at Paul.

'And she administers that herself?' The male paramedic was watching his partner insert an IV line. He took the cannula case from her and used the small amount of blood it contained to coat the tip of the test strip. The small blood-glucose monitor beeped as he slotted in the plastic strip.

'She's been doing her own blood-glucose levels,' Jenna replied, 'but she still relies on me to do the insulin injections.'

'What was the last blood-glucose level?'

'I don't know,' Jenna admitted unhappily. She looked at Maria's dressing-table but the monitor was nowhere to be seen. How long had she and Paul been in the kitchen? Half an hour? She walked closer to the dresser.

The paramedics' monitor beeped. 'Low,' one of them noted. 'Shall I repeat it?''

'Yeah. I'll set up the giving set and dextrose.'

'Where's Maria's monitor?' Paul loomed behind Jenna. 'The last result will be in its memory.'

'She keeps it in here.' Jenna opened a small bottom drawer and moved a pile of neatly folded underwear.

'She keeps it *hidden*?'

Jenna swallowed. 'She didn't want you to know.'

'And the insulin?' Paul sounded dangerously calm. 'Where do you hide *that*?'

'In the nursery fridge.' Jenna had taken the small black case from the drawer. It clearly hadn't been used since dinner so Maria had had no warning that her levels had been dropping. If Jenna had tested her earlier she might have been able to prevent this situation by giving oral glucose. The jar of jelly beans in the nursery were not there for Ella's benefit.

Paul snatched the case from Jenna's grasp and she kept her gaze down, looking at the top of the dresser as she heard the zip open. Even that sounded angry.

'Oh.' The exclamation was involuntary.

'What?' Paul demanded.

'There.' Jenna picked something up from among a collection of small perfume bottles. Crumpled silver foil.

Aspirin packaging.

'You said she wasn't taking aspirin any longer.'

'She's not supposed to.' Jenna steeled herself to look up and meet the fury in Paul's eyes. This was getting worse by the minute.

Or maybe not. The paramedics had been busy behind them and a cheerful female voice broke the tense silence hanging between Paul and Jenna.

'Maria? That's it, love. Open your eyes. Do you know where you are?'

As often happened, the administration of intravenous glucose had produced a miraculous result and Maria was going from being in a coma to full consciousness extremely rapidly.

'Who are you?' she demanded in a tone that reminded Jenna very much of her son. 'And what are you doing in my bedroom?'

'Maria!' Jenna's importance was dismissed as Paul swiftly knelt by his mother's side. *'Come sta?'*

A rapid-fire conversation in Italian followed. The paramedics exchanged a glance that conveyed both amusement at this unexpected development and satisfaction in a job well done. They began tidying up used packaging and equipment.

Jenna stayed where she was, beside the dresser, the little ball of crumpled foil in her clenched fist. Jenna recognised the word for aspirin in the conversation Paul was having with his mother and Maria looked both guilty and defiant. Then the tone changed and it was clear that they were arguing about something. Maria kept shaking her head and Jenna heard her name more than once. Paul was adamant in negating whatever Maria was so determined about. Was she refusing transport to hospital?

The paramedics seemed to share Jenna's interpretation.

'Do you want us to take your mother to hospital?' one asked Paul.

'Of course,' he responded.

'No,' Maria said firmly. 'I want to stay here. Jenna will look after me.'

'*No,*' said Paul, even more firmly.

'It might be a good idea to go to the hospital for just a little while,' a paramedic suggested. 'Your blood-sugar levels will need careful watching for a bit.'

'Jenna can do that,' Maria insisted. She looked up. '*Scusi*, Jenna. I did not do the test. My hips were sore and I couldn't find my new pills and so I took the aspirin. I forgot I was not supposed to. *E colpa mia*…it is *my* fault.'

'No,' Paul said. 'It's not.'

'Of course it is, Paolo. I will not allow you to blame Jenna.'

The senior paramedic snapped the catches on his kit shut and looked at his watch.

'I will not be happy unless you go to the hospital, Maria. I want to make sure you are properly monitored.'

Maria looked from Paul to Jenna and back again. She had to be aware of how angry her son was and Jenna could almost hear the wheels turning as she tried to think of a way to defuse the situation.

'Very well,' she said finally. Almost regally. 'I will go to the hospital. For just a little while.'

The female paramedic came in with a carry chair to get Maria down the stairs and into the ambulance.

'I'm coming with you,' Paul announced. 'Jenna will stay with Danielle, of course.'

'Of course.' The weight of misery settled more heavily over Jenna thanks to the way Paul hadn't even bothered to make eye contact as they left.

And it continued to grow as she found herself in a house that was empty apart from herself and a soundly sleeping baby. Carrying the receiver for the baby monitor, Jenna paced, far too wound up to consider anything else.

How could things have changed so radically in such a

short time? Less than an hour ago she and Paul had been in a passionate embrace. On the point of making love.

Now he was not only absent physically, he had to be a million miles away from her emotionally, in the wake of discovering she had as good as deceived him about his mother's medical condition. And, worse, she had failed to live up to the responsibility she had taken on board by agreeing to keep it secret.

Sadly, he seemed to be automatically distancing himself from his daughter once more. Back to calling her Danielle instead of Ella.

Jenna finally stopped pacing and sat down. Just where she happened to be, which was at the foot of the staircase. She buried her face in her hands, too miserable to even cry.

From being at the point of virtually stepping through the finish flags on the mission Jenna had set herself by taking on this position, she felt like she had been picked up and rudely dropped right back at square one.

The chance of success had never seemed more remote.

Jenna was the picture of misery sitting there on the stairs.

She must have actually had her head in her hands but it was being lifted as Paul opened the front door and stepped back into his home.

Even from this distance, he could see how pale Jenna was. How huge and distressed her eyes were. It was suddenly much harder than he'd expected to stay angry with her.

'Is Maria all right?'

Paul nodded curtly. *No thanks to you,* the gesture said.

Jenna was getting to her feet and Paul noted with satisfaction her picking up the monitor on the stair beside her. At least she was attending to the responsibility of caring for Danielle. Then his gaze flicked back to the woman moving towards him. She seemed stiff, as though she had been sitting there for a long time. Waiting for him to come home? Surely not for the whole two hours he had been with Maria in the emergency department before they'd transferred her to an observation ward for the rest of the night.

'I'm sorry, Paul,' Jenna said. 'This shouldn't have happened.'

'You're damned right it shouldn't.' The door closed behind Paul with a bang.

Never mind that the ED consultant had reminded him how easy it was for an insulin-dependent diabetic to get hypoglycaemic. That sometimes the triggers couldn't even be identified and that it could happen when a dose of insulin precipitating the event might be identical to the previously normal dose. The fact that his mother had suffered this crisis was not what Paul was so angry about.

Not at all.

'You had *no* right,' he informed Jenna, 'to withhold this information from me. Maria is my *mother*. *I* am the one who should be supervising her medical care.'

A flash of something like understanding showed in Jenna's eyes. Possibly regret. But then her face tightened.

'I withheld nothing,' she responded. 'It was not my information to hand out and your mother asked me not to…repeatedly.'

Yes. His mother had said something along the lines of Jenna wanting him to know. Saying how important it was. It was no excuse.

'And this was acceptable to you? To someone who has medical training and knows how serious any complications could be?'

'I… We seemed to be managing.'

'*Seemed?*' Paul sucked in his breath with a hiss. 'What

does that mean? Has my mother run into problems like this before?'

Maria had denied it. Had said that Jenna was the perfect nurse.

An *angelo*. Paul was not to blame her.

'She's never lost consciousness.' Jenna was standing straighter, as though preparing to defend herself against whatever he chose to throw at her. 'Or even come close. She got a bit light-headed and wobbly once or twice when we first started. A bit diaphoretic on another occasion. Nothing that oral glucose couldn't reverse. I've kept a very careful watch on levels.'

'Not tonight, you didn't.'

'Your mother's starting to try and manage things herself. She knows I'm only going to be here to help her on a temporary basis.'

The reminder that Jenna intended to go back to her nursing position should have been a relief. Life would get back to normal.

Except that Paul didn't want the normality that had been his life before Jenna had come.

He didn't want her to leave.

'Maria insisted on doing her BGL by herself tonight. I thought she was being brave...that I should encourage her.'

They stared at each other. Paul was trying to remember. Maria had been insistent but it had been about something else. About checking on Ella.

Part of the subterfuge? Secret verbal signals? A loop that involved the safety of his family that he had been excluded from. By Jenna. A pact that had seen him lured into spending time alone with Jenna. In the kitchen.

Seducing the nanny.

Even now, the thought of that seduction and where it had inevitably been leading gave him a shaft of desire that cut through every other turbulent emotion Paul was dealing with. He pushed his reaction away with a vicious mental shove, but the effort was draining.

'I don't understand,' he said more quietly, 'why Maria didn't want me to know.'

'She…' Jenna took a deep breath. Sincerity was in every line of her face and there could be no doubting the truth of what she was about to say. 'She thought she would lose Ella. That you would think she wasn't physically capable of looking after her and that you would let Louise take her back to Auckland and raise her.'

Paul opened his mouth but no words came out. He was stunned. Did his mother really believe that he could have allowed her grandchild to be taken from her? To have her future removed? The reason the sun had truly begun to shine in her life again?

Just how much did Maria know?

Louise was being well paid to keep the secret. She wouldn't have told his mother.

Was it possible that he had been too late? That he had shut the stable door after the horse had bolted?

Did his mother believe that *she*, in fact, was protecting *him*?

This was disturbing. Easier to try and rewind the conversation and focus on the anger he had brought home with him from the hospital where his mother still lay.

'This could have happened at any time,' he said coldly. 'What if you'd been out visiting that friend of yours? Anne, isn't it? What if you'd gone out and I hadn't known? Hadn't been able to check on Maria's glucose level? Hadn't been able to check on her before I went to bed?'

He was distracting himself perfectly from any deeper issues now and the words were flooding out like machine-gun fire. 'I would have found her tomorrow morning, would I not? *Dead!*' he finished aghast.

There. Let her try and defend herself now. He was more than ready for a good fight. Perhaps he needed one.

But to his dismay all Jenna's defence mechanisms clearly deserted her at that point. Hazel eyes filled with tears.

He was a brute, wasn't he? Why had he felt the attack so justified?

Oh, yes. He had wanted to blame someone because it had been so hurtful that his mother had kept her condition a secret from him. Had trusted Jenna more than her own son. She was family. *His* family. His to cherish and protect, and he'd been denied the opportunity.

And, yes, Jenna could have told him but she would have broken his mother's trust in her and the bond between these two women was of great importance to Maria. She adored Jenna. Since the arrival of Ella's new nanny, his mother had been happier and healthier than he had seen her in many, many years. He should be grateful to Jenna.

Instead, he had upset her with his harsh words. By his insinuation that her actions could have led to a fatal outcome. He had been too hard on her. She didn't deserve it.

Anger fled and Paul gave a soft groan.

'Ti prego, non piangere,' he said. 'Please, don't cry.'

He stepped closer, a hand outstretched instinctively to catch the tear that had just begun to roll down her pale cheek.

The moment he touched her, something else fled besides the anger. Any trace of barriers were simply swept away.

The frustration of having been interrupted in the kitchen.

The fear for his mother's safety.

The tension of the paramedics treating her.

The unexpected hours in the emergency department.

The anger and the hurt all coalesced into a surge of energy that demanded release.

Release that only this woman could give him.

Jenna closed her eyes at the touch of Paul's fingers on her cheek.

It wasn't soap bubbles he was stroking away this time but the evidence of sheer misery.

He had been so angry with her and yet now he was being so incredibly gentle.

Jenna had known, with absolute surety during that awful period of sitting on the stairs tonight, that she had come as close as she was ever going to come to making love with Paul Romano. A woman that had endangered a member of his family would never be acceptable in his bed. It was over, at least on his part.

Was it knowing that it would never happen that made her want it even more?

Or was this feeling of having the rug pulled from under her feet? To face Paul's wrath and now feel this gentle, *caring* gesture as he brushed away her tears?

Whatever.

Jenna had been transported from knowing that making love with this man was what she wanted more than she had ever wanted anything in her life to the sudden feeling that she might actually *die* if she didn't.

It was overwhelming. Confusing.

Frightening.

She snapped her eyes open, knowing that she would find the answer in the face that was now so close to her own.

An apology probably.

Or regret, perhaps.

Closure of some sort, anyway.

The answer was there, all right, in those eyes as dark as sin, but it wasn't an answer Jenna had been prepared for.

Opening her eyes had established a contact that had flicked a switch and opened a connection as powerful as a lightning bolt.

Jenna was staring into a desire just as fierce as her own. No words were needed to confirm what they both wanted. What they *had* to have.

And as though they both knew the steps to this particular dance, Jenna's hands slipped around Paul's neck and he swept her into his arms and off her feet.

Jenna felt weightless in his arms as he took the stairs two at a time, not pausing until he was inside his own bedroom. A room Jenna had never seen before. She took in a momentary impression of a vast antique sleigh bed as Paul set her onto her feet and she placed the baby monitor on the beside table. She saw a blur of dark wood and rich burgundy drapes and sensed an aura that was purely masculine.

Somehow Jenna knew that she was the first woman to share this room with Paul and that knowledge increased a desire she wouldn't have believed could have become any stronger.

Jenna surrendered herself to that desire. She reached out, ready to be swept off her feet again and thrown onto the expanse of the bed beside them. To have her clothes ripped away and…

And it was nothing like that.

Slowly, carefully…almost reverently, Paul undressed her, caressing and kissing each new piece of her skin that was exposed.

Jenna tried to reciprocate, undoing the buttons of Paul's shirt and slipping her hands over his skin. Feeling the tight buds of his nipples and the iron-hard muscles beneath the satin surface of his body. But each of his new kisses made her pause, unable to do anything but revel in the touch of his hands and lips.

On her shoulders, her breasts, her waist… By the time Jenna was wearing only her knickers and Paul's fingers slipped beneath the elastic band, she was trembling all over, her fingers fumbling with his belt buckle.

'Please…' she whispered incoherently as her hands brushed the hardness below his belt.

Paul said something in Italian. A husky growl Jenna didn't understand, but it didn't matter.

The unbearable tension was broken as Paul took over the task she couldn't complete. He shed the rest of his clothes with startling swiftness and then Jenna was swept off her feet again and thrown onto the bed.

They were a tangle of limbs. Skin sliding on skin. Desperate to feed a hunger that only seemed to grow.

Until finally Paul was poised above Jenna. Between her legs. Her hands locked in his and held on either side of her pillow.

She was helpless. Totally vulnerable. Pinned by his gaze as much as by his body.

And she had never felt safer.

He entered her heart as completely as he did her body. Deeper with every thrust, and even as Jenna gave herself up to the ultimate physical satisfaction, a part of her knew she could never love any man as totally as she loved Paul Romano.

Heaven help her but her trust and her love had been won—probably at the moment he had touched her to brush away her tears.

And won absolutely.

CHAPTER NINE

THE alarm was set for 5.30 a.m.

Early enough for Paul to leave Jenna's apartment and creep upstairs to prepare for work in his own room as though nothing had changed in the Romano household.

'Do you think Maria knows what's going on?' Jenna turned back from checking the clock to find herself drawn very close to the man sharing her bed yet again.

'I don't think so.' Paul smoothed back Jenna's tousled hair and kissed her forehead. 'She is too excited about this new project of hers.'

'She is, isn't she? I think it's wonderful. She's managing so well now, isn't she? I think that night in the hospital and the extra tests and new management plan have given her a whole new lease on life. Did I tell you that her medic-alert bracelet finally arrived today?'

'I hope she is going to wear it. She's still being stubborn about telling Louise.'

'She's wearing it already. Didn't you notice at dinner?'

'No.'

'Maybe Louise won't notice either.'

'She'll notice.'

'Mmm.' Bed wasn't the place to be thinking about

Louise Gibbs or the unpleasantness she would undoubt-edly create when she learned that Paul and Jenna had embarked on a passionate affair that showed no signs of burning out. 'Anyway, I think this new idea of Maria's is fantastic. I'm sure her recipe book will be a huge success.'

'I'm not so sure.'

'But her cooking's fabulous!'

'That's the problem.' Paul kissed Jenna's nose. 'I think we might all get very fat, tasting all this new food she keeps creating.'

'Mmm.' Jenna smiled as Paul's lips covered hers. A lingering kiss that spoke of familiarity and sheer pleasure. A moment later her tone was mischievous. 'So, you think I'm getting fat, then?'

'Let me see!'

Jenna giggled as Paul threw back the covers but then she stilled as she felt Paul's gaze roam her body.

'You are *fantastica*,' he murmured. *'Perfetta!'*

His hand traced the route his gaze had taken, lightly stroking Jenna's breast, trailing over her belly and then sliding over the curve of her hip. He drew her even closer and Jenna felt desire spiral again, as so often happened when they should have been lulled into satiated sleep in the wake of passion.

It seemed that neither of them could get enough of the other. That each time they made love it was just another taste of something much bigger. Part of a feast that could still not begin to assuage a mutual appetite. Whenever Jenna thought their physical relationship couldn't possibly get any better, Paul would discover some new place she loved to be touched. Or a new location—like the shower. Or he would change the pace.

Or just hold her and she would fall asleep in his arms

aware of nothing other than the sheer bliss of his presence and warmth and the astonishing capacity she was discovering that he had to be both fierce and gentle at the same time.

He was holding her now. Neither of them were ready to sleep but Paul's outward breath sounded like a sigh. Jenna touched his cheek.

'You're tired.'

'It's been a long day.'

'How did the meeting with Louise go?'

'As well as could be expected. She cried a lot but Gerry was there to hold her hand.'

'It's a shame that there will always be a cloud over celebrating Ella's birthday. That…it's the day her mother died.' Jenna's words were tentative. By tacit consent, until now, they had never really discussed Gwendolyn.

Had they created a bubble? An unreal kind of space that was floating among the stuff of real life—still unnoticed thanks to their discretion?

If so, it was quite a tough bubble because it had lasted nearly a month already and seemed to get stronger every day. And, like a bubble, it seemed to spread a little magic into real life.

Things other than the bed Paul chose to sleep in when he was not on call were changing. He left for the hospital a little later in the mornings and he was managing to get home a little earlier some days. When he had time off at the weekends, he surprised his small family by suggesting outings. To the beach and the wildlife park and even an open-air opera in the city's huge central park, which had his mother sighing happily for days afterwards.

It was not just their physical relationship that was going from strength to strength. Paul and Jenna were sharing the joy of watching Ella develop. A bond that made them… almost…a real family. Jenna suspected Maria must have a very good idea of what was going on under her roof but she had also chosen discretion. To maintain a new—and wonderful—status quo, perhaps?

Had Jenna risked pricking the bubble by mentioning Ella's real mother?

Apparently not.

'It's only this first anniversary of Gwen's death that needs to be commemorated,' Paul said. 'It will be enough. It's time to put the past behind us.'

Jenna took a deep breath, encouraged enough to ask something that had begun to taunt her.

'Do you miss her very much?'

'Gwen?' Paul was silent for a moment. 'I think of her often,' he admitted finally. Heavily. 'How can I not, with Ella here to remind me?'

Jenna was silent, too. Of course he would remember. Every day. How could she ever hope to compete with such a ghost?

Paul seemed to sense her doubt. His hold on her tightened. 'Does it bother you, *tesoro*?'

'I am a little jealous.' Jenna tried to keep her tone light-hearted. Paul could just laugh at her if he wished. But he didn't.

'There's no need to be,' he said. 'You are as different from Gwendolyn as…as chalk and cheese. How I feel about you is nothing like how I felt about Ella's mother.'

His tone and touch were reassuring. And surely no one could kiss like this if they weren't in love? But Jenna needed more. She wanted to hear the words.

'But you were in love with Gwendolyn, weren't you?' she asked quietly.

'Totally,' Paul agreed. 'And she was clever. She refused to sleep with me before marriage. I was obsessed. I had no choice.'

Jenna's heart sank. He had a choice now. She had given herself—completely—without asking for even a hint of commitment. Had she made a terrible mistake?

'It didn't last, of course,' Paul continued evenly. 'The infatuation wore off and there was little else there. If it hadn't been for the baby I'm quite sure the marriage would not have lasted. It *couldn't* have lasted.'

'Oh…' Jenna absorbed the surprising information that the marriage had not been so perfect after all.

And Paul had said she was nothing like Gwendolyn.

Chalk and cheese.

That was a *good* thing, then. She cuddled closer, extending sympathy in her touch but also a promise. They had far more than a physical infatuation. They had something that *could* last. For ever. She didn't need to rush anything. Ask for anything Paul wasn't ready to give. He had been manipulated by a woman once before and Jenna was certainly not going to make the same mistake.

'We have arranged a short church service on the actual day of the anniversary,' Paul said then. 'It's best that we have Ella's party on a Saturday, anyway, because that way I can be here to enjoy it all.'

'It will be fun.' It was a relief to turn to a subject they both loved. 'I think Ella's excited.'

'She is always excited. Every day is a new adventure for that little one.'

'She's doing so well, isn't she? Almost walking properly and I'm sure she learns a new word every day.'

Paul chuckled. 'I hear "No!" more than anything else. And I'm not sure I approve of this foot-stamping.'

Jenna grinned. 'She takes after her father.'

Oddly, her words created an instant tension in Paul's body.

'What do you mean by that?'

'Just that she knows what she wants and how to get it.' Jenna twisted in Paul's arms. 'Are you offended?'

She felt him relax. 'No. Of course not. But I told you her mother was an expert in getting what she wanted.'

And Jenna had reminded him. Stupid. It seemed to have changed something in the intimate atmosphere of their private time. Paul seemed withdrawn. Lost in his own thoughts. Jenna propped herself up on one elbow and bend down to drop a brief, gentle kiss on his lips.

'You're not getting sick of this, are you?'

'Of being here? With you? What a ridiculous notion!' Paul buried his fingers in the tousled waves of Jenna's hair, holding her head as he kissed her properly, but he sighed again when they broke apart to draw breath.

'It is getting a little tiresome,' he admitted, 'sneaking around my own house in the dark like some kind of burglar. I think it's time we stopped trying to be so discreet.'

Jenna caught her breath. 'You want to tell people? *Louise?*' If he was prepared to weather that storm, it could only be taken as a kind of commitment to a future, couldn't it?

'Not yet,' Paul said cautiously. 'Not until this memorial service is over with. When we can all put the past behind us and start again. We will remember and then we will celebrate Ella's birthday and then…' He kissed Jenna once more. 'Then there will be no need to tiptoe around the feelings of others. We will enjoy our time together without hiding from anyone.'

Our time together.

How long would it be?

There was a letter sitting near the clock on Jenna's

bedside table. A query from her old hospital in Dunedin asking her to confirm whether she intended to return to her position because the woman currently filling it was keen to continue on a permanent basis.

The halfway point of Jenna's intended stay with the Romano family as their nanny had come and gone. Her time with Paul could be running out and it was difficult not to think about it when the need to respond to the letter was gaining urgency.

She couldn't broach the subject yet, however. Not this week, in the run-up to the memorial service and then the party. As Paul had said, the anniversary marked the end of a period most would consider appropriate for mourning. With a new start and especially with the plan to bring their relationship into the open, the opportunity to discuss the future would naturally present itself.

Their future.

Jenna wasn't going to rush anything. It was far too precious to risk.

Danielle Romano's first birthday party might have been toned down enough to acknowledge the more sombre aspects of the date, but it was still enough of a production to be a blaze of colour.

The house was a rainbow of helium balloons. The dining-room table was covered with bite-sized treats and a gorgeous birthday cake Maria had created that looked exactly like Ella's favourite toy, Letto the rabbit. Brightly wrapped parcels dominated the lounge and Ella was a princess, wearing a gorgeous white smocked dress and with silver ribbons adorning the ends of two miniature black pigtails. She had knee-high white socks with a ruffle of lace on the top, but she was flatly refusing to keep shoes on her feet.

'No!' she pronounced yet again, hurling one shoe and then the other back at Louise while the photographer waited patiently to try and get a family shot.

'Give it a rest, Lulu,' Gerald advised. 'Nobody'll notice.' He grinned at Paul. 'Not too early for a spot of bourbon, is it, mate?'

'But the photo!' Louise protested. 'I want it to be special.'

As special as the one of Gwendolyn, perhaps, that Louise had insisted be placed beside the cake on the dining table. They had all trooped in to admire the feast earlier and Ella had been awestruck by her cake.

'Letto!' she had said joyously. The grandmothers had smiled proudly at yet another addition to an expanding vocabulary.

Louise had picked up the photograph beside the cake. 'It's your mummy,' she had reminded Ella. 'Can you say "Mummy", darling?'

And Ella had almost obliged. *'Mum*—ma!'

She wasn't being so obliging now, however and for once Maria was in agreement with Louise. 'Wear the shoes, *cara*,' she begged. 'Just for one photo.'

'No!' Ella said. And grinned.

Jenna watched as both grandmothers tried to buckle a small shoe onto each of Ella's feet.

'What is that?' Louise suddenly asked. 'What *are* you wearing, Maria?'

'Just an alert bracelet.' Maria's tone was deliberately offhand but not very successful. The undertone of signifi-cance was unmistakable and she seemed unable to prevent the anxious glance she cast at Paul, who was pouring a drink for Gerald.

'What's it for?'

'My diabetes, that's all.'

'But why wear a bracelet?'

'It's in case someone finds you unconscious in the street,' Gerald said helpfully. 'You've seen the one I've got one for my dodgy ticker.' He leered and Jenna and lowered his voice to a stage whisper. 'It's the only thing I *never* take off, y'know.'

Jenna didn't want to know. She caught Paul's gaze and they exchanged a look of complete understanding.

'I didn't think your diabetes was that serious.' Louise seemed to have forgotten her mission with Ella's shoes. 'I mean, you don't have to have injections for it or anything, do you?'

'I do now,' Maria said reluctantly. 'There. Shoes on!' The distraction was clearly welcome. 'Let's get a picture quickly before they come off again.'

The family was positioned on a couch. Gerald and Jenna watched from behind the photographer who had a squeaky, rubber toy to catch Ella's attention and make her smile. Paul held his daughter who was holding Letto and had a grandmother sitting on either side. Three generations of Romanos, with the same dark hair and eyes. The same smile. Louise looked like an outsider, with the blue eyes and blonde hair she had passed on to her own daughter, but she wasn't, was she? She was as much a part of this unusual family portrait as anyone else. It was herself and Gerald who were the outsiders.

Paul was smiling at Jenna as the shutter clicked and then clicked again but, strangely, it made her feel more excluded. She was reminded of that very first time she had been in the same space as this group—when Paul had arrived home in time to conduct the interview for the position as Ella's nanny. It seemed such a long time ago.

Had anything really changed?

Maria still had an anxious air and Louise still emanated determination to stake her claim and an almost smug appreciation of her power.

And Jenna felt no closer to understanding the missing link but there could be no doubt that something fundamental *had* changed. Ella was looking up at her father. She stretched out a small hand and touched his face and he was smiling back at her. He murmured something in Italian that made Ella smile and then he bent his head and pressed a kiss to the smooth hair at the top of one pigtail.

'Yes!' the photographer enthused. 'That's lovely!'

And it was. If nothing else, Jenna had succeeded in what she'd set out to do with this interim period in her life. She had helped create and then cement a bond between a father and a daughter. Paul was not going to stop loving Ella, whether or not Jenna was part of their lives in the future.

'We need a photograph with Jenna as well,' Maria decreed. 'Come and sit, Jenna!'

The brilliant smile Louise had turned on repeatedly for the photographer vanished. 'These are *family* photographs,' she said with deliberate clarity.

'*Sì*.' Maria nodded her agreement. 'And Jenna is part of the family.'

Louise turned her head with even more deliberation. 'There's hardly room on the couch, is there?'

'Mmm.' Paul was also in agreement. 'You could swap places with Jenna for this one, Louise.'

The photographer and Gerald were the only people slow to catch on to the subtle way Louise froze. The ice in the atmosphere. The stare Jenna was subjected to was calculating. Louise was weighing her options. Quite unexpectedly, the boundary Jenna had known would have to be approached was visible. Were Paul and Maria ready to step over it or were they missing the significance of what they were suggesting?

Louise was missing nothing and she looked as though she would simply refuse. Create a scene that could well ruin the celebration of Ella's birthday. But she was undecided. Confused, perhaps, over the significance of the desire to include Jenna? Was she just a much-appreciated employee? Or something more dangerous?

Jenna felt a moment of panic. This wasn't the time. She wasn't ready. She opened her mouth to demur but instinctively she caught Paul's gaze for an instant.

Was he choosing this moment to make a statement about the future?

If so, Jenna had to feel sorry for Louise because, while it was Ella's birthday and a chance to celebrate life and the possibility of happiness in the future, it was also very close to the anniversary of the death of this woman's daughter.

Of Paul's wife.

The undercurrents swirled more strongly than they ever had. Maybe Paul was simply asking for Jenna's support to get through a difficult time and his needs had to take priority over those of his mother-in-law.

So did Maria's. Her gaze was pleading. Was she ready and willing to support anything her son wished to do in the name of his future happiness but didn't want to rush Jenna?

Whatever the motivations, both Maria and Paul wanted her there beside them. They wanted a record of Jenna's presence. On this occasion and as part of their family.

Out of nowhere, the words that Paul had spoken once before echoed in Jenna's mind.

'You belong,' he'd said. *'With me.'*

And she did. Jenna returned her gaze to meet that of Louise and she took a deep breath and straightened her spine.

And after what seemed an interminable pause, Gerald saved the day.

'Come on, Lulu. Let me pour you a glass of bubbly.'

Louise conceded. She rose and walked with dignity to where Gerald had taken charge of the drinks on the sideboard. She accepted the flute of champagne and drank it with her back turned to the group on the couch as the photographer squeaked the toy again and took another volley of shots.

Then Maria stood up. 'I would like champagne, too,' she announced. 'This is a *compleanno*, is it not? A birthday!'

'Gotcha.' Gerald winked. 'Coming right up!'

So Paul and Jenna and Ella were left on the couch and the session seemed to be over. Ella was getting bored. She pulled off her detested shoes and then climbed to her feet on Paul's lap. Paul held her securely around her waist as she leaned toward Jenna.

'*Mum*-ma!' Ella crowed happily.

Jenna caught Paul's gaze, horrified, but he simply smiled with only a hint of resignation.

'*Nice,*' the photographer murmured, the shutter clicking again.

'Oh…my…God,' Louise breathed. She drained her glass and set it down soundlessly on the sideboard. Then she turned and walked through the open French doors and into the garden.

'Lu?' Gerald watched in bewilderment. 'You all right, babe?' He hurriedly refilled the flute and topped up his own glass then followed Louise outside.

The photographer was scrolling through his shots. 'These are great,' he said. ' You want a break before we start on the presents or do you want to do the cake next?'

'Let's have a break,' Maria said. 'Come with me to the kitchen and I'll get you some coffee. You must try my *biscotti*.'

'Sounds good.'

'My cooking is always good,' Maria said serenely. 'Come! I wish to discuss the photographs with you. Tell me, have you ever taken pictures of food? For a recipe book?'

'Oh, dear,' Jenna said into the new silence. She gazed sadly at Ella's small face. 'You have no idea what you've done, have you, sweetheart?'

'*Mum*-ma,' Ella said again. She bounced on Paul's knee and then climbed into Jenna's arms to hug her.

'I'm sorry,' Jenna said to Paul over Ella's shoulder. 'I don't know what to say. This must be upsetting for you as well as Louise.'

'Why?' Paul sounded unperturbed. 'Ella has never known her birth mother. You are the closest thing to a mother she's ever had.'

And maybe that wasn't a good thing. She was too involved. With everybody here. It was a recipe for heart break.

'But I'm not…I'm not even going to be here for much longer.' She hadn't wanted to be the one to initiate a discussion about their future but it was going to happen whether she liked it or not.

'You have another three months before you can even think about returning to your nursing position,' Paul pointed out. 'A lot can happen in three months, *bella*.'

'I may not last the three months,' Jenna said ruefully,

giving Ella another cuddle. 'I suspect Louise is really on the warpath now.'

'This has nothing to do with Louise. She will just have to accept things the way they are. I'll deal with it.' Paul smiled and tweaked the end of Ella's pigtail. 'We can't let you leave, you know. You're far too important to all of us.'

Jenna's smile was as wobbly as the pulse she could feel beating in her throat. They had started so they might as well finish this.

'I can't stay for ever.'

'Why not?'

That pulse skipped a beat. 'I'm not really a nanny,' Jenna said carefully. 'I never intended leaving my nursing career for good. You know that.' Ella wriggled in her arms impatiently and Jenna let her slide down to the floor.

'Who said you had to?' Paul watched Ella's fast crawl towards the pile of gifts. 'We could work something out. If you took a nursing position here, we could all work around your shifts. Maria is so much better now and she would be delighted to help. If you did night shifts, *I* could help.' He caught Jenna's hand. 'We could employ a nanny.'

Jenna had to laugh. 'What? Employ a nanny? *For* a nanny? That would be crazy.'

Paul was silent for a moment. *'Si,'* he agreed then. 'It would not work, would it?'

Jenna's heart sank even as she felt Paul's fingers curl around her own with a more intense grip.

'But…' Paul seemed to be waiting to catch Jenna's gaze and his tone gave no clue as to the words he was about to utter. 'What if I was employing a nanny to help my *wife*?'

'I…don't understand,' Jenna said hesitantly. But that wasn't entirely true, was it? Jenna could practically feel the blood fizzing in her veins as the implication of Paul's words sank in.

'Ella loves you,' Paul said softly. 'You are her "*Mumma*".'

Jenna held her breath. Was he finally going to say it? But the suspense was too much and she had to break the short silence herself.

'You're proposing to me? Because you want to keep Ella's nanny?'

'No.' Paul's grip tightened on her hand to the extent it was almost painful. 'I am proposing to you because I love you, Jenna. I want you to be my wife. To stay in my life. To be a part of my family...for ever.'

'But...what about Louise?'

Paul raised an eyebrow. 'This is between you and me, *cara*. Louise will have to accept it.'

Jenna swallowed hard. 'Maybe it's too soon. It's only been a year since...'

'It's not too soon. This is a new start. And, like I told you, the way I feel about you is nothing like how I felt about Gwendolyn. Chalk and cheese, remember?'

Jenna nodded. Of course she remembered. Paul's smile was as reassuring as his kisses had been in bed the other night. *Loving*. His eyes begged for understanding.

'I want to start living again. I want *you*, Jenna, and if you are my wife, Louise will have no choice but to accept it. Say yes, *carissima*. Say you'll marry me.'

Did the undercurrents matter? That he wasn't in love with her the same way he had been with Gwendolyn? That Jenna's relationship with Ella might be the precipitating factor? He'd said it, hadn't he?

He loved her.

The kiss Paul pressed to her lips was so tender. So sincere. So full of promise that Jenna had no difficulty allowing joy to smother any doubts.

'I…love you, too, Paul,' she whispered as they broke the kiss. 'More than I thought I could ever love anyone.'

'So you'll marry me?'

'Of course I will.'

He kissed her again but Jenna was too conscious of those open French doors and the couple that could walk back into the room at any moment.

'Is now the time?' she wondered aloud.

'We are celebrating today. We have remembered and agreed to put sadness behind us. What better time to make a new start?'

Jenna couldn't help a fearful glance towards the doors. Gerald's voice was becoming louder.

'Time for a top-up,' they heard him say. 'Come on, Lulu. Chin up, babe!'

Paul chuckled. 'Gerald might be a godsend when it comes to dealing with Louise,' he said thoughtfully. 'I will speak to her later today. When the party is over.' He stood up and drew Jenna to her feet. 'For now, let me get us both some champagne. We will toast our future.' His smile said everything Jenna could have wished to hear. 'Our love.'

CHAPTER TEN

THE presents had been opened and nobody minded that Ella had been more interested in the bows and wrapping paper.

Paul had been the one to hold Ella up and help blow out the candle on the 'Letto' cake and the photographer left the gathering as they did their best to taste every special food Maria had created for the occasion.

It was one very tired baby that Jenna finally took upstairs to bathe and get ready for bed.

The nod from Paul when he had given Ella a goodnight kiss had been accompanied by what seemed a significant glance.

The party is over, it said. *I haven't forgotten that I'm going to talk to Louise.*

Jenna could think of little else as she quickly bathed Ella and dried her and dusted her with sweet-smelling talcum powder. She prepared the formula and while it warming she tidied a few things around the nursery. Humming a song for Ella, Jenna dimmed the lights and switched on the baby monitor so she wouldn't forget and have to come upstairs again. The unit she kept with her in the evenings was downstairs somewhere. Paul would know where it was. He'd taken it with him that morning in case Ella woke up while Jenna was in the shower.

The microwave beeped and it wasn't until Jenna sat down in the armchair with Ella and the bottle of milk and stopped singing that she became aware of the voices.

'Don't you dare walk out on me, Louise.'

It was Paul's voice and the controlled fury she could hear made Jenna's jaw drop. She looked down but Ella seemed unperturbed. She insisted on hanging onto her bottle with both hands for this supper drink now. Jenna could put her into her cot to drink it but she was loath to give up this last cuddle of the day.

She would have to disturb Ella to get up and switch the channel on the monitor so it wasn't broadcasting two ways but the baby's eyes were drooping already. She'd be asleep in a very short space of time and Jenna could attend to the channel as soon as she'd put Ella into her cot.

'We're going to settle this,' she heard Paul say. 'For good.'

'It's already settled. You can't break your promise, Paul.'

'You made a promise, too, Louise. Remember? Or am I not paying you enough to keep remembering?'

Jenna's eyes widened. She shouldn't be listening to this. She *shouldn't*.

'You promised you wouldn't marry. That you wouldn't repl—'

'Actually, I said I had no intention of marrying again,' Paul cut in. 'And I didn't at the time. Things change.'

'I can't believe you've fallen for the nanny, Paul. Can't you see what a cliché it is?'

'I haven't *fallen* for Jenna. I might have made that mistake with your daughter, Louise, but that's never going to happen again. That's one promise I'll have no trouble keeping. Maria adores Jenna. So does Danielle. She has become a part of the family and my family matters to me above all else. I will do whatever is within my power to make them happy, and that includes marriage to Jenna. It is *not* negotiable.'

Jenna had to press a hand against her mouth.

To cover the soft sound of distress that would have been impossible to repress.

A cry of pain. Jenna knew it was a physical impossibility but she could swear she actually felt her heart break. A kind of tearing sensation that left a dreadful ache behind it.

Paul might want her but he didn't really love her, did he? Not the way she loved him. He hadn't fallen in love with her at all. How could she have missed that realisation? He had told her as much himself, hadn't he? When he'd said that how he felt about her was completely different to how he'd felt about Gwendolyn.

Chalk and cheese.

To be in love. And to *not* be in love.

It was so true that eavesdroppers never heard anything about themselves that they might want to hear. Jenna had no desire to hear any more of this conversation. What she wanted to do was run. To run and hide somewhere like a wild animal. To find a private place to lick her wounds. But the blow she had just received felt mortal and any strength had deserted her.

Paul wasn't in love with her. He was doing this for his mother. And his daughter.

It was not negotiable. And it could never be enough. Not for Jenna.

Ella had fallen asleep in her arms. She should take her over to her cot but she couldn't move. Jenna was totally numb. Reeling with the shock of what she had just overheard.

She might not want to hear any more of the dreadful conversation taking place downstairs somewhere—presumably in the library that doubled as Paul's office.

But she had no choice.

Jenna sat there, holding Ella, with tears streaming down her face. She found herself rocking gently, not for the baby's benefit but for her own.

It seemed the only way to try and deal with the pain.

She was only half-aware of the voices she could still hear. Carefully controlled fury in both of them. They did not want to be overheard. Paul would have no idea at all that he'd left the monitor in there. Had he gone in early to check his emails perhaps? He had far more important things on his mind than anything that might be lying around his office.

It didn't matter any more that Jenna was eavesdropping because she couldn't possibly hear anything more shocking than she already had.

'You can't just replace Danielle's mother,' Louise said.

'She never *had* a mother. Not until Jenna came.'

A sound of outrage came from Louise. 'You did make a promise, Paul. You said that you would bring Danielle up to know how special her mother was. How is she going to know that if she thinks some gold-digging *nanny* is her mother?'

'I'm sure you'll remind her.'

'Oh…I *will*,' Louise said viciously. 'I'll do more than that. I'll get custody and she'll grow up with me. She'll grow up knowing exactly how special her *real* mother was.'

'Special? Oh, come on, Louise. She was just like you. Only interested in the prestige that money can buy.'

'How dare you?' Louise snarled.

'Oh, I dare.' The words were pure ice. 'And don't even think about trying for custody, Louise.'

'You know I'd get it. I'm the only blood relative Danielle has.'

It took a few seconds for the words to penetrate the mist of misery Jenna was in. She blinked, clearing the tears from her eyes. With a huge effort she pushed through the wall of pain surrounding her. She shook her head. If she listened more carefully she would realise she had not heard what she thought she'd just heard.

'And not as far as my mother is concerned. Ella is her granddaughter and I will simply not allow you to suggest otherwise.'

'*Suggest*! It's fact and you and I both know it. I think it's time Maria knew the truth.'

The truth? Jenna's jaw had dropped. This was incomprehensible. It was blatantly obvious that Ella was Paul's daughter. Did he really believe she wasn't?

It fitted, though, didn't it? It was the missing piece of the puzzle. The explanation of why Paul had failed to bond with a motherless baby. The cause of the marriage being less than perfect. The reason Louise had had an aura of power in this household. But if Paul wasn't Ella's father, why had he allowed everyone to think he was? Simply for the sake of his mother? Was family *that* important?

Maybe he knew at a subconscious level what Jenna had known from the first moment she had seen them together. The same hair and eyes. That same smile that began with a crinkle around their eyes. There was no way Ella could be anyone else's child. Jenna knew because she could see the similarities.

Because she loved them. Both of them.

The overpowering strength of that love was enough to

send a new wave of pain through her body. Paul didn't feel the same way. And if he was capable of pretending a child was his own when he didn't believe that was true, for the sake of his mother, then it was far less a leap of the imagination that he could marry someone for a similar purpose.

Had it all been a calculated act? Even the way he had made love to her?

She had missed something being said below. It was hard to refocus.

'Go home, Louise,' Paul was saying wearily. 'Before you say something you'll really regret. One word from you and I'll ruin you. Do you really think I'd let you take Danielle back to the kind of lifestyle you raised your own daughter in? You're a lot older now, Louise. How many men do you think are going to be happy to keep paying for your services?'

'I hate you,' Louise spat.

'*Non importa.* It makes no difference to me. I will not, however, allow you to harm my family.'

'I don't need you. I don't need your money. I have Gerald now. He'll look after me.' Louise sounded almost desperate. 'He'd pay any legal expenses if I decide to go for custody.'

'You think he'll still be happy to pay when he learns that the "love of his life" is after nothing more than his money?'

'Don't you *dare* say that about me!'

'It's the truth. You have no real morality. I think Gerald would be very upset to learn the truth. I can assure you that my marriage to your daughter would never have taken place if I'd known how like you she really was.'

Paul seemed to be pacing in the library because his voice was getting fainter. Or did he have his hand over his face, Jenna wondered, in a gesture of utter weariness?

His words became clearer. 'Sitting there at that farce of a service the other night made me almost ill, do you know that? The tributes to the excited mother-to-be. The loving *wife*.'

Jenna remembered that conversation she'd had with Anne. Gwendolyn hadn't been popular, had she? Her friend had been very perceptive. The idea of how perfect Ella's mother had been had only come through Louise.

Louise was obviously a master in using attack as a form of defence. Jenna actually gasped aloud at her next words.

'If Gwen had to go elsewhere to find satisfaction, whose fault is that, Paul?'

'Get out of my house, Louise.'

'You can't stop me seeing my granddaughter. *My* granddaughter. She's no relative of yours.'

'My mother is, however, and I will not allow you to damage her life. I will claim Ella as my child. She *is* my child now, thanks to Jenna.'

'You won't get away with this. I will not allow you to marry Jennifer.'

'You have no choice, Louise. None at all.'

Louise might not have a choice but Jenna did.

While it would break her heart to leave this house, that was exactly what she was going to have to do.

The very thought of leaving was so awful that Jenna couldn't allow herself time to think about it. It was a cut that would have to be made swiftly—before she could change her mind.

Tears were already threatening as she gently laid the sleeping Ella in her cot. What if she never saw this child that she loved so much again?

Or Maria?

Leaving Maria would be almost like losing another mother, and there was no way she could explain the real reason for leaving, was there? Not without telling Maria what she had accidentally overheard.

What if she was wrong? What if the similarities to Paul were simply coincidence because Ella's *real* father happened to have the kind of genes that could bestow that dark colouring?

She could understand Paul's determination not to destroy his mother's happiness. There was no way she could do it herself.

Did Maria have any idea of how much her son loved her? The lengths he was prepared to go to in order to make her happy? Jenna already knew he was a man capable of great passion but she'd had no idea of the scope that could encompass. He could live a lie perfectly convincingly if he felt the need. Even if he didn't know he *was* living one.

Jenna couldn't do that.

There was no way she could give herself in marriage to a man she loved and then pretend that everything was perfect. That he loved her as much as she loved him.

Not when she knew he didn't. When she knew the real reason he was prepared to do it.

Every second that passed, every new thought and emotion that assailed Jenna was going to make this harder. With a final touch of Ella's silky curls Jenna fled the nursery and ran downstairs.

The door to the library was open now and there was no sound of any voices. The door to the lounge was closed and Jenna slipped past. Through the kitchen and into her apartment.

An overnight bag was all she needed for the moment.

Anne would be happy to give her a bed for a night or two until she could decide what to do next. It took only minutes to fill and it wasn't heavy.

Nothing would ever feel as heavy as the emotional weight Jenna was carrying as she made her way back through the kitchen and into the hallway. It would have been much easier to let herself out through the separate entrance to the apartment but Jenna knew she would have to find Paul and explain why she was leaving.

At least she was finally too numb to feel any new pain.

And then she stepped from the kitchen into the hallway just as Paul stepped through the door to the lounge, and she knew she had been wrong.

She *could* feel new pain.

That smile. That look in his eyes as he caught her gaze.

'I was just coming to look for you,' he said. 'I've talked to Louise.'

Jenna's mouth was dry. 'I know. I heard you. You must have left the baby monitor in your office, Paul. It wasn't intentional but I overheard part of what you said.'

Paul's smile faded but he didn't seem to be listening to what Jenna was saying. He was too eager to speak again himself.

'All's well, *carissima*. It's all sorted.'

'No, Paul.' Jenna tried to swallow but couldn't. 'It's not.'

He frowned, his gaze sliding downwards. 'What is that? Why do you have a bag?'

'I'm leaving,' Jenna said simply. 'I can't stay, Paul. I can't…marry you.'

'What do you mean, you *can't* marry me? I don't understand.'

'You didn't tell me the truth.'

Paul's frown deepened. He cast a glance over his

shoulder to check that he'd closed the door to the lounge. 'How much did you overhear?'

'Enough. I know that you think Ella is not your daughter.'

'She isn't! But—'

Jenna gave an incredulous huff. 'You're wrong, Paul. Try looking in a mirror. Ella *is* your daughter. I don't know what Gwendolyn told you but maybe she had her reasons for lying. Or maybe she didn't know. Get a DNA test if you really want the truth, but I don't think you need to worry about Louise getting custody. It won't happen.'

Paul was staring at her with an intensity that would have been frightening if Jenna didn't still feel so numb.

'And don't stop loving her,' Jenna added. 'She's never going to betray you. You're her papa. Her *father*. She loves you.'

Like she herself did. With absolute trust. So sad that, in Jenna's case, that trust was broken.

'She loves you, too,' Paul said in bewilderment. 'I don't understand any of this, Jenna. What difference does it make? You can't leave! I'm going to marry you.'

'So you can have a mother for Ella? A nurse and companion for your mother? I heard you say you'd do anything for your family, Paul. You have already, haven't you, claiming Ella as your child when you don't really believe she is? You don't love me. Not the way you loved your first wife. You said so yourself. Chalk and cheese.'

'Of course it's not the same!' Paul ran stiff fingers through his hair, with a growling sound of frustration. 'It's—'

'It's not good enough,' Jenna interrupted. 'It could never *be* good enough. I can't marry someone who's not in love with me, Paul, no matter how I feel about you.'

'So you're *leaving*? You're *walking out* on me?'

He didn't like that. He hadn't allowed Louise to walk

out on him in the library, had he? Bewilderment was giving way to anger.

'*Women!*' Paul turned back towards the lounge, walked a couple of steps but then swung back to face Jenna. 'You cannot walk out on me, Jenna,' he declared. 'I will not allow it.'

'You can't stop me.'

They stared at each other in silence.

A painful silence that seemed to grow heavier with each thump of Jenna's heart.

And then it was broken.

Not by Jenna. Or by Paul.

The sound that broke the silence was a shrill feminine scream that came from behind the lounge door.

CHAPTER ELEVEN

THE scream had come from Louise.

She was standing near the sideboard that had a bottle of bourbon lying on its side, spinning slowly as its contents dribbled onto the polished wood. She had her arms around the not insubstantial figure of Gerald and she was valiantly struggling to keep him upright.

Gerald was slumped against Louise. His face was a terrible shade of grey and he was mumbling incoherently. Maria was rushing to assist Louise as Paul threw the door open and strode into the room, with Jenna only a step behind him.

'Sit him down!' Maria ordered. 'He's fainting!'

'No...' Gerald lurched as Maria grabbed one of his arms. 'I'm... Ah-h-h! It *hurts*!'

Paul stepped in behind the trio and slipped his arms under Gerald's. 'You can let him go,' he told Maria and Louise calmly. 'I've got him.' He began to step backwards, carefully easing Gerald to the carpeted floor.

Jenna grabbed some cushions from a couch. If Gerald wasn't actually unconscious, it would make it easier for him to breathe if he was propped up a little, rather than lying flat on the floor.

'Thanks.' Paul's acknowledgement was automatic. He expected Jenna to be there helping, didn't he? Just as *she* expected to be there. It was where she belonged. 'See what his pulse is like, would you, Jenna?'

'Oh, my God,' Louise sobbed. 'He's having another heart attack, isn't he?'

'It's possible,' Paul agreed.

'*Do* something, then!' Louise cried. 'You can't let him die!'

'Not…going…to…die…' Gerald groaned.

'Maria?' Paul looked up at his mother, who was wringing her hands in frustration at not being able to help. 'Could you find some aspirin, please? And a little water?'

Maria rushed out eagerly as Jenna knelt opposite Paul on the other side of Gerald and felt for a pulse in his wrist.

'No radial,' she had to report.

'Blood pressure must be well down. That's hardly surprising.' Paul put his fingers on Gerald's neck. 'Carotid's faint…too fast to count.'

'VT?' Jenna's heart sank. Ventricular tachycardia was only a step away from something much worse. Something with the real potential to be fatal.

'That'd be my pick, too,' Paul agreed. He pulled a slim mobile phone from his pocket and dialled a three-digit number. 'Ambulance,' he said tersely a moment later. 'Hamilton Avenue, number 438. We've got a cardiac patient here who needs urgent transport.'

'*Oh…*' Louise was pushing against Jenna as she dropped to the floor and grasped Gerald's hand. '*Gerry!*'

Maria came back and Jenna helped him take the aspirin tablet. 'Chew it up,' she instructed. 'I'll give you a sip of water to help it go down.'

It wasn't easy and Gerald gagged at one point, which

drew another distressed sound from Louise. Then he swallowed some water and his head dropped back onto the cushions.

''S all right…babe…' he said. 'Not…gonna…die…'

'Don't even say that,' Louise begged. 'I…love you, Gerry.'

'Love you…too, babe…' Gerald's chest heaved the effort he was making to breathe. He forced his eyes open again. 'Don't forget…we're…gonna take that…world cruise… for…our honeymoon…'

'*Oh-h-h!*' Louise's face twisted into desolate lines and she had to hide behind her hands as she began to weep uncontrollably.

Maria tutted in shared distress and folded her arms around Louise, drawing her back to her feet. 'Don't cry,' she said. 'It will be all right. Paolo is looking after him. Paolo and Jenna. He's tough, this *amore* of yours, he's got through this before. He's still alive and where there's life, there's always hope. You'll see…it will be all right…'

Jenna bit her lip. Maybe it was because Maria was also upset and her grasp on appropriate words of encouragement might be slipping, but she was making things sound very dire. Mind you, surviving a previous heart attack was hardly the best reference either. It meant there was already damage to the heart muscle and another blow—especially a large one—could well be the final straw. Gerald was gasping for breath now and perspiration glistened on his face, but Paul stayed perfectly calm.

'Hang in there, Gerry,' he said. 'We'll get you to hospital in no time and they'll sort you out.'

'Yeah…' Gerald had to make even more of an effort to open his eyes as he slipped further towards unconsciousness. 'Thanks…mate.' He rolled his head from side to side with a groan of agony. 'Lu…?'

'I'm here, darling.' Louise broke free of Maria's hold and threw herself down to kneel beside Gerald again.

'Stay…with…me…babe…'

'Always, Gerry.' Louise sniffed inelegantly and blinked hard. 'I'm here. I'm not going anywhere. We belong together, you and me, don't we? You're going to be all right, do you hear me? Everything's going to be all right…'

The passionate and reassuring patter continued behind Jenna as she ran to the door at the sound of the approaching emergency vehicle.

The sight of her overnight bag in the hallway came as a surprise and it took a moment to realise that the current crisis had made her own misery insignificant enough to be totally forgotten. It had seemed like such a matter of life and death when she'd stood there, ready to say goodbye to Paul for ever.

How ridiculous! Jenna pulled the heavy front door open. *This* was a matter of life and death. Louise had to be feeling a lot worse than Jenna had when she'd stood here, holding that bag. Death was the ultimate separation, wasn't it? No hope of going back.

Did she have hope that somehow things would come right for herself and Paul?

Of course she did. Maria's comfort might not have been the best thing for Louise to hear but she'd been right. Where there was life there was always hope, wasn't there?

She'd hang onto that thought. Pull it out again later, perhaps, when she had the time and inclination to think about something personal. That certainly wasn't going to be any time in the immediate future.

By coincidence, it was the same paramedic team that had arrived to treat Maria's hypoglycaemic coma.

'It's not Maria, is it?' one asked as they pushed a

stretcher laden with gear through the door. 'I don't remember her having a cardiac history.'

'No. This is a male patient,' Jenna told them. 'Gerry. He's a friend of...' Goodness, how could she begin to describe the complicated interconnections among this group of people she had become so involved with? 'Of...the family,' she concluded.

Not that Gerald's credentials mattered. The team went into action with commendable speed on entering the lounge.

'This is Gerald,' Paul informed them. 'He's fifty-two years old and has a prior history of MI. He collapsed ten minutes ago and was pale and diaphoretic. No radial pulse but carotid was present. Tachycardic but regular.'

'Not tachy now.' The female paramedic had already attached the electrode pads and they all stared at the screen as she took the oxygen mask from her partner and slipped it over Gerald's head.

'ST elevation,' Paul noted. 'And wide complex. Looks like complete heart block.'

'Yeah. I'll get an IV line in.'

Gerald groaned as the needle slid into a vein on his arm.

'Sorry, mate,' the paramedic said, snapping the tourniquet open. 'I'm going to give you something for that pain in just a sec.'

'He's already had aspirin,' Paul told them. 'Three hundred milligrams.'

'That's great. The sooner that's on board the better.'

Morphine was then administered. And an anti-emetic.

'Rate's down to forty-five,' one of the paramedics observed moments later. 'Gerry? Can you hear me? Open your eyes!'

Gerald's eyes remained closed. The painful stimulus

of knuckles rubbing on his collar-bone failed to elicit any response.

'Draw up some atropine,' the senior paramedic ordered.

The drug was effective in bringing up the heart rate. Too effective. The rate kept increasing and then became irregular with a few odd, ectopic beats. Then it became wildly irregular. Just a frantic squiggle on the screen.

'VF,' Paul warned.

The female paramedic had her fingers on Gerald's neck. 'No pulse.'

'Right. Stand clear,' her partner ordered. 'I'm going to shock him.'

'*Oh-h-h!*' Louise shrieked. '*No-o-o!*'

Jenna scrambled to her feet and went to stand on one side of the distraught woman. Maria was on the other side. They both held onto Louise as she sagged at the knees— a horrified response to the jerk that Gerald's body displayed on receiving the shock.

'Look at that! We're back to sinus rhythm.' The paramedic sounded delighted.

'Let's get rolling. We need to get this guy into ED.'

Jenna left Louise with Maria to help in the whirl of activity as they gathered equipment and loaded Gerald into the ambulance.

'I'll come with you,' Paul said.

'I'm coming, too,' Louise sobbed.

The paramedics nodded appreciatively at Paul's announcement but looked a little concerned by Louise's.

'Someone going to come with her?' one asked. 'We've got room for one more.'

'You go,' Maria said firmly to Jenna. 'I will stay with Ella.'

But Jenna hesitated. What would Paul want? She had

already declared her intention to leave. Would he prefer to keep his small, unusual family together in a crisis, without an outsider like her involved?

She couldn't ask, even with a questioning glance. Paul had already climbed into the back of the ambulance and was helping to untangle IV lines and electrode wires and put the oxygen tubing onto the main cylinders on full flow.

'Go,' Maria repeated. She gave Jenna a gentle shove in the direction of the door. 'You should stay with Paolo.'

Jenna responded to the shove without any further hesitation. It was where *she* wanted to be, after all.

'Ring me,' Maria called after her, 'as soon as you know anything.'

To begin with, Jenna sat alone in the emergency department's room for waiting relatives. Paul stayed with Louise in the resuscitation area as they treated Gerald. He came back, periodically, to let Jenna know what was happening and then she would ring Maria and pass on any news.

'He's conscious again but showing some major ST elevation in his inferior leads,' Paul told Jenna.

'It looks like he *is* having another heart attack,' Jenna told Maria.

'He's getting runs of VT,' Paul reported later. 'They've started him on an IV beta-blocker.'

'He's getting drugs to control his heart rhythm,' Jenna reported to Maria.

'Big rise in cardiac enzymes,' was Paul's next information. 'We're moving him up to the lab in a few minutes.'

'They're taking him up to the cardiac catheter laboratory,' Jenna explained to Maria. 'He's going to have angioplasty, which should clear the blocked artery and stop the heart attack before it can do too much damage.'

'*Dio mio,*' Maria tutted. 'Poor Louise! You'll stay with her, won't you? While Gerry has this operation?'

'Of course. I have no idea how long it will take but I'll ring you as soon as we know how it's gone. Are you OK?'

'*Si.* I have done my finger prick and my injection and another finger prick just to check. I am fine, *cara*. You look after Louise. And Paolo. And yourself.'

They were shown another area where they could wait. A tiny room with a row of upright chairs off the corridor that led to the day-surgery wing. It was well after normal working hours now and this area of the hospital felt deserted. So quiet they could hear the ticking of the clock on the wall of the small space. One of the chairs had some well-out-of-date magazines covering its seat but nobody took any notice.

They sat there, the three of them, in a rather strained silence. Jenna sat in the middle. Her offer to go searching for coffee or food had been declined. Another minute ticked by. And another. She took a glance to her right.

Louise looked dreadful. She had a box of tissues on her lap that had probably come from the emergency department. It was a square island in a sea of crumpled, used tissues now. Her normally immaculate hair was a mess and mascara streaks showed up vividly on her pale cheeks. No hint of lipstick remained on her lips and even the once matching nail polish was vanishing as she chewed one nail after another.

Jenna thought about offering to hold Louise's hand to comfort her. Then she thought about trying to hold Paul's hand...to comfort herself. She stole a glance to her left but Paul was sitting with his head resting on the wall behind them, his eyes closed.

Jenna followed his example with a sigh.

They needed to talk but it wasn't a conversation they could have here. Paul would hardly thank her for broaching such a private subject in front of Louise, would he? And it was hardly the time to cause Louise any further upset by reopening the topic she had overheard in the library.

It was a time of waiting. For all of them.

So they sat in this uncomfortable silence. Together and yet completely separate.

The wait seemed interminable.

Paul kept his eyes shut and gritted his teeth. He had to be there because, whether he liked it or not, Louise was a part of his family and was therefore entitled to his assistance and protection.

The frustration was unbearable. He desperately needed to talk to Jenna and convince her that she had taken an incorrect interpretation from what she had heard, but he couldn't desert Louise yet. Not until Gerald came out of the lab, hopefully with a good result.

And he certainly couldn't say anything that might invite Louise to threaten Jenna in any way. Not that she looked like much of a threat at this moment, but Paul knew Jenna would do a great deal to protect both Maria and Ella. If she thought that agreeing to marry him would cause grief to people she cared about so much, it could be enough to tip what was now a precarious balance.

Louise didn't know that their conversation in the library had been overheard and so she couldn't know how close she was to getting what she wanted—the cancellation of any marriage plans between himself and Jenna.

Paul couldn't get rid of the mental image of that bag in the hallway of his house. The symbol of Jenna's intention to walk out of his life. Maybe the balance had already tipped too far. Maybe he had already lost Jenna.

He couldn't understand it.

What better time to replay in his head that unpleasant conversation in the library? Again and again. Trying to find the interpretation Jenna had taken from his words.

Yes, he'd said that Maria and Ella both adored Jenna. It was true. And she loved them, didn't she? So how could that be a problem?

Yes, he'd said she had become a part of the family and he'd said that his family mattered to him above all else.

Also true. How could he say with any more conviction just how important Jenna was to him?

Family was *everything*.

He'd never felt like that about Gwendolyn. She'd been a very beautiful woman and he'd been overwhelmingly attracted to her, but she'd never *belonged* with him.

Not the way Jenna did.

For the first time Paul could understand what had gone wrong before and why he felt the way he did about Jenna. It went so much deeper than merely being 'in love'. It was about trust. Genuine commitment. A need to protect but, more than that, the trust that you could be protected yourself.

You could be vulnerable but safe at the same time.

Would Jenna understand that feeling? Would it help if he told her?

He *had* to tell her.

Paul opened his eyes and turned his head. Perhaps he could communicate something of what he was thinking through eye contact. A willingness to explain, perhaps. Appreciation that she was still here beside him, at least.

But Jenna's eyes were closed and her head drifting

slowly sideways. Paul shifted his body weight so that her shoulder touched his arm. So that there was something solid for her head to rest against while she dozed.

Jenna slowly became aware of the voices.

She knew it was Louise and that she was talking to Paul, but the conversation had a dreamlike quality to it. This was no argument. Louise sounded husky. Totally sincere. Almost broken.

She shouldn't be listening but, once again, Jenna appeared to be inadvertently part of a private conversation.

'You don't have to say it, Paul. I know how little you think of me.'

'You've never made it easy, Louise. I *did* try, you know, at first…'

'I had to take Gwen's side. She was my daughter.'

'I know.'

'I hate to say it but…she didn't deserve you…'

'Scusi?'

Jenna felt the sudden tension in Paul's body. She pressed her cheek against his shoulder, as though stirring in her sleep, and then she felt a different touch as he tilted his head to rest against hers. As though he was curling around her. To protect *her*, even when it seemed that Louise might be about to launch a new verbal offensive against *him*.

Except she wasn't.

'You're a good man, Paul.' Louise sniffed and then blew her nose. 'Thank you for helping with Gerry and for…for being here with me like this.'

'You're very welcome.'

'I really do love him, you know.' Louise sounded like

she was struggling not to cry again. 'I know what you think of me and it's true that I've used men in the past, but this is *so* different.'

'Is it?'

'I know he's not perfect but neither am I—as you pointed out yourself today—but you know what? Gerry *loves* me. He really loves me and it makes me feel like I'm *worth* loving. It's taken more than forty years but for the first time in my life I've discovered what love really is, can you believe that?'

'Oh, yes,' Paul murmured. 'I can believe it.'

'He can't die.' Louise sniffed again and Jenna heard the sound of another tissue being ripped from the box. 'I want to spend the rest of my life with him. I want it so much.'

Louise unsuccessfully tried to stifle a sob and Jenna felt her heart squeeze. She knew exactly how Louise was feeling. It was how she felt about Paul, wasn't it?

'I'm sorry,' Louise croaked. 'I shouldn't be telling you all this. I mean, why should you even care?'

'I care,' Paul said quietly. 'And I do understand, Louise.'

'You do?'

'Of course I do. It's precisely the way I feel about Jenna.'

Jenna's eyes flew open quite involuntarily. And her hand moved. Or had Paul's moved first? Their fingers touched and then intertwined, their hands joining like two bubbles of mercury finding each other. A completely fluid action that would have been impossible to resist.

'Well, why didn't you say so?' Louise sounded puzzled. 'I did.'

'No, you didn't. You said you hadn't fallen for her…not like you did for Gwen.'

'I did say that,' Paul agreed. 'And it's true. I fell for

Gwen, Louise. So hard I hit my head and couldn't think straight. It was accidental and…sadly it turned out to be superficial. For both of us.'

He shifted his head to look down at Jenna and seemed unsurprised to find her staring back at him. Of course, he must have known she was awake as soon as their hands touched.

'This time,' Paul said softly, holding her gaze, 'I knew exactly what I was doing. I knew the potholes that kind of road could have and I thought long and hard before I stepped onto it. This was no accident.'

He looked up, presumably straight at Louise. 'I'm not going to forget Gwen,' he said sombrely. 'How could I when she was responsible for bringing Ella into the world? Even if I'm not her genetic father, it makes no difference because I have come to love her…very much.'

'She could have been wrong,' Louise said. 'She was never very good with her dates about things.'

'*Non importa*. She is family now. And you, Louise, you will always have a place in my family as well. As Ella's other *nonna*. But Jenna's place is the most important because she holds the heart of the family. She holds *my* heart and we belong together. Just the way you and Gerry belong together.' His gaze locked with Jenna's again.

'*Ti amo, dolcissima. Amore mio*. I love you. Now and for ever.'

Jenna's eyes blurred with tears. Joyous tears. 'I love you, too,' she whispered.

'You forgive me, then? For saying whatever it was I said that upset you so much?'

'I didn't understand properly, that's all.'

'Maybe I didn't either.' Paul smiled. That delicious slow smile that started with a crinkle of his eyes and finished with a warmth that chased away any dark patches in

Jenna's soul. 'I'm still learning. You taught me a lesson, Jenna. I *never* want to see a bag in my hallway again.'

Jenna smiled back. 'You won't,' she promised.

'*Oh!*' Louise sucked in a nervous breath. 'Someone's coming!'

'They'll be just down here!' The cheerful voice of a nurse could be heard coming from the dimly lit corridor. 'There's a little waiting room. See?'

'*Grazie, grazie!*' A small, plump figure appeared through the doorway.

'Maria!' Jenna scrambled to her feet and Paul stood up beside her, still holding her hand. 'Is Ella all right? Are *you* all right?'

'We are fine. You didn't call, *cara*, and I was worried so I called a taxi and, *poof*! Here we are! A family needs to be together at a time like this, does it not, Paolo?'

'Indeed it does,' Paul agreed solemnly.

'Take your daughter,' Maria instructed. 'She is getting heavy.'

Paul took the bundle that was Ella wrapped in a blanket from Maria's arms and Jenna took the basket the nurse had been carrying.

'I brought food,' Maria said unnecessarily. A very appetising smell was coming from the basket. 'Lasagne. And bread. Enough for us all.'

Louise was on her feet now as well. She caught the arm of the nurse. 'Could you possibly go in there?' She waved through the doorway to the double doors excluding them from the day surgery area. 'Could you find out what's happening with Gerry? How much longer it might be before we hear anything?'

'Sure.' The nurse hurried off.

Jenna rearranged the blanket so it didn't cover Ella's

face. Letto's legs were poking out at an awkward angle but when she tried to straighten the toy, Ella's face scrunched ominously and she made a soft growling sound.

'So grumpy!' Maria smiled fondly. 'You were just the same, Paolo, when *you* were a *bambino*.' She sat down on one of the chairs and fanned her face with her hand. 'So hot, these hospitals,' she complained. 'Why is that?'

But nobody answered because they had heard the swish of the double doors opening again. The nurse they had sent as a messenger reappeared—with company.

'Good news,' the cardiologist told them all. 'Perfect procedure. He's got a bit of extra plumbing in there now but all signs of the infarct have resolved.'

'What does that mean?' Louise had a hand to her throat. 'Is he…going to be all right?'

'Probably in better nick now than he's been for years,' the cardiologist said. 'Are you his partner?' His mouth twitched only a little. 'Lulu?'

Louise nodded, clearly unable to say anything.

'He's asking for you.' The cardiologist grinned. 'In fact, he's *been* asking for you at about sixty-second intervals ever since he went in.' The doctor paused and sniffed appreciatively. 'Something smells awfully good in here.'

'It's my lasagne,' Maria said proudly. 'You want some?'

'No!' Louise clutched at his arm. '*Please*! Take me to see Gerry.'

Maria watched as Louise disappeared through the door. Then she looked up to where Paul and Jenna were standing so close together, with the sleeping baby between them, staring into each other's eyes. Their love was as obvious as the aroma of the hot food wafting from her basket.

Maria nodded with enormous satisfaction. All was well in her world.

Very well. There had been no need to fret so much about that bag in the hallway.

'Come,' she ordered her family. 'Eat!'

CITY SURGEON, OUTBACK BRIDE

LUCY CLARK

Lucy Clark is actually a husband-and-wife writing team. They enjoy taking holidays with their children, during which they discuss and develop new ideas for their books using the fantastic Australian scenery. They use their daily walks to talk over characterisation and fine details of the wonderful stories they produce, and are avid movie buffs. They live on the edge of a popular wine district in South Australia, with their two children, and enjoy spending family time together at weekends.

To Bill—
Thanks for letting us know about Deni
Pr 13:1

CHAPTER ONE

HENRY HARCOURT changed the radio station once more, shaking his head as he picked up yet another country and western tune. 'Well, what do you expect when you come out to the middle of nowhere?'

He glanced up at the road, long and straight before him, paddocks and farms on either side, the ground a yellowish brown due to the drought plaguing Australia. Thankfully, the deciduous trees and the evergreen gums stood tall and true, bringing more colour to the surroundings. He pressed the button on his car stereo to try and find a different channel but, apart from the few he'd found, all he got now was static.

Switching it off, he shook his head. Then he adjusted his sunglasses as he passed a side road, which was really nothing more than a dirt track. Henry did a double take and immediately slowed his vehicle down, craning his neck to look behind him.

There was a car at an odd angle, the driver's door flung wide-open, and someone appeared to be hanging half out of it. Doing a quick U-turn, glad there was no traffic around on the deserted road, Henry drove towards the stationary vehicle. As he came closer, he could see the tracks on the dirt road where the car had swerved several times before coming to a stop, black bits of car tyre littered here and there.

Stopping his car and switching off the engine, his hand automatically reached for the medical kit which he kept in the back seat, then he was out and striding purposefully towards the occupant, his brain clicking instantly into medical mode.

The person was a woman and she had somehow managed to get herself out of the car so she was sitting on the ground with her feet still in the car. She was also heavily pregnant and her skirt was wet.

'Hi. I'm Henry,' he said, crouching down beside her.

'Donna,' she panted, as she lay down on the hot ground.

'I'm a doctor, Donna.' Henry pulled a stethoscope out of his medical kit as though to prove his point.

'I've just called her. My doctor, that is.'

Henry looked at the flat surroundings as he hooked the stethoscope into his ears. 'Might be a bit of a wait.' He first checked Donna's heartbeat before listening to the baby's. 'Sounding strong and healthy,' he announced.

'A-ah-h. And impatient, too,' Donna muttered as she was gripped by a contraction.

Henry smiled as he pressed two fingers to her pulse. Apart from being slightly elevated, which he had fully expected, it seemed as though Donna actually had things under control. 'I take it this isn't your first?'

'No. Fourth.'

'Were the others born by the side of the road or did you actually manage to make it to a medical facility?' While Henry spoke, he pulled on a pair of gloves.

'A funny doctor,' Donna replied drolly. 'Just what this town needs. A-ah-h.' Another contraction gripped her and Henry looked at her stomach.

'That was closer.'

'You're telling me.'

'Listen, Donna. Mind if I take a look?'

'Be my guest. Outback hospitality and all that!' She chuckled to herself.

Henry started to shift around when he was assailed by a cloud of dust and looked up in time to see another vehicle pulling up, a utility truck. He closed his eyes and held his breath while the dust passed quickly over them, then nodded. Good. He could use another pair of hands. He watched as a slim woman, wearing blue jeans, cotton checked shirt and bush hat, climbed from the ute, well-worn boots on her feet. She carried a medical kit which was very similar to his own and that was the first clue that this wasn't just any well-meaning neighbour stopping to help.

'Donna?'

'Rayne?'

'You do pick the oddest places to give birth. G'day.' The last was directed to Henry, who'd just crouched down, medical gloves on his hands. 'I'm Rayne Hudson. GP for Deniliquin.'

'Henry Harcourt. Medic just passing by.'

'Good to meet you, Henry. I've called for an ambulance and told Janic to get his butt down here pronto.'

'How did he take that?' Donna asked, breathing heavily.

'Your husband? How do you think? He flew straight into panic mode. He's over in the far paddock and had no idea you were in labour.'

'I didn't want to bother him. Just called him and told him the tyre had blown out but that I was OK. Actually, when I spoke to him, I didn't realise I was in labour. It wasn't until I found I couldn't get out of the car without having a contraction that I sort of guessed— Oh, and when my waters broke.' Donna chuckled. 'Well, we are in the middle of a drought. At least I'm doing my bit to help.'

Rayne laughed. 'That's Donna to a T,' she told Henry. 'As practical as ever. Anyway, let's see how you're progressing, Donna, and then we can—' Her words were cut off as Donna's abdomen contracted again and this time it was accompanied by a push, the woman on the ground grunting in pain. 'I guess that answers my question. How about we start by getting your feet out of the car?' Rayne swatted away a few flies, glad at least that this wasn't happening at the height of summer. It was the first week in September—officially spring—and the weather was at least being nice to them today in that it wasn't too hot and wasn't too cold.

'Delivered a lot of babies?' she asked Henry. 'I mean, is it too much to hope that you're an obstetrician just passing by?'

'Sorry. General surgeon.' He said the words automatically even though he'd left Sydney three weeks ago on an indefinite sabbatical.

'Well, beggars can't be choosers, although I'm sure Donna and the newest addition to her brood aren't going to give us any trouble. The last birth was straightforward. Happened during the New Year celebrations at the beginning of last year but, still, straightforward.'

'Loud bangs seem to set my babies off,' Donna muttered, panting. She had her eyes closed to conserve energy and after Rayne had performed the internal examination, she sighed. 'Everything all right?'

'Perfect. You're about seven centimetres dilated. Henry, could you keep an eye on the baby's heartbeat, given that you've already got your stethoscope ready? I'll just get a few extra things from the car.'

Henry watched the woman walk away and asked himself if she was really old enough to be qualified.

'She's thirty,' Donna said, and he was surprised that she could read his mind until he realised he'd asked the question out loud. 'I know. I hate her, too. I'm younger than her yet I look far more hagg—' The word was cut off as another contraction hit.

Henry kept an eye on both mother and unborn child, glancing up to see what Rayne was doing. He also found it hard to believe he was actually here, in the middle of nowhere helping to deliver a baby. For the past two years he'd locked himself away in a small little bubble of people and he'd been fine…fine until three weeks ago when the need to get away from everyone, including that small bubble, had overwhelmed him.

'How long until we might expect the ambulance?' Henry asked when Rayne returned, carrying a portable sphygmomanometer, as well as a bag containing blankets and towels.

'Not for another twenty minutes at least.'

'You made good time, though.'

'I was at Donna's neighbour's house when she called me. She was next on my house-call list but apparently the baby wanted the attention immediately.'

'I told Henry the baby was impatient.'

'I never doubted you.' Henry smiled at Donna, and Rayne watched how the action changed the structure of his face. She'd looked at him several times, noting the firm squareness of his face, his three-day growth obscuring his jawline but giving him that rugged outdoorsy look a lot of city men liked to sport. Thankfully, it worked for him.

He looked up then, and caught her staring. For a moment, neither one moved. It was an extremely odd sensation and one Rayne had never felt before in her life. She swallowed, unable to look away, unable to get her mind to focus on what she'd previously been doing. His chocolaty-brown eyes were making her breathing increase and she was beginning to feel a little light-headed.

Ridiculous. She wasn't the type of woman to be attracted to a man at first sight. In fact, she wasn't the type of woman who allowed herself to be attracted to men at second or third sight. She was more than happy with her life at the moment—an outback GP in the town of Deniliquin in New South Wales's south-west—and she had no room for the sort of look she'd just shared with this handsome stranger.

When the next contraction came, along with a very long and hard push on Donna's part, Rayne was ready. She'd set up blankets and towels beneath their patient to at least make her a bit more comfortable. 'Fully dilated. Gee. I hope Janic gets here in time.'

'Well, I'm not holding on for him,' Donna protested.

Rayne laughed and Henry felt it wash over him like the warmth of the sun. 'I don't think this little one's going to let you. It's ready and it's impatient.'

They set to work, the three of them working hard—
Donna most of all—to bring this new little life into the
world. Janic arrived only moments before the ambulance.

'Do you want to cut the cord, Janic?'

'No. You do it,' he said, focusing on his wife. He'd
glanced at the baby Rayne held in a sterile towel before
looking at his wife again. 'You know I'm not good with
the blood, mate.'

Rayne smiled and looked down at a very healthy little
girl with a good set of lungs, making herself known. 'All
right. Henry? As I'm holding this gorgeous squirming little
girl, do you want to do the honours?'

Henry was surprised for a moment but didn't hesitate to
pick up the clamps and put them in place before using the
scissors to cut through the tough umbilical cord which had
helped to keep the baby alive these past nine months. It was
an odd sensation and one he hadn't actually experienced
before. Of course, he'd delivered a few babies during his
medical training but once he'd entered the general surgical
programme, delivering babies had become a thing of the past.

Another memory flashed into his mind, that of a dream
he'd once had…the dream of cutting the umbilical cord of
his own child. But that dream had disappeared years ago.
He blinked and refocused his mind.

'What are you going to call her?' Rayne was asking as
she handed the baby over to Donna to cradle.

'Davina Tanneth,' Donna announced proudly, kissing
her daughter's head. Janic looked at the little girl—his
youngest, his newest—and touched her cheek.

Rayne nodded. 'Original—like the others. You're not
going to refer to her by her initials, too, are you?'

'Why not?' Donna asked. 'That's how Janic calls all of them.'

'What are the names of your other children?' Henry asked, intrigued. He helped Rayne get ready to deliver the afterbirth.

'We have JJ, he's four and a half. CC, she's three, and then JR is twenty-one months and now DT—the newest addition to our family,' Janic supplied as Donna tensed with another milder contraction. 'What's happening, Rayne? Is she all right?'

'She's fine. Just getting ready for the next stage of labour.' Rayne smiled at him and then glanced at Henry. 'This is the closest Janic has been for the birth of any of his children. DT should be quite flattered.'

They continued to do their job and while he worked, Henry felt completely at ease. It seemed quite natural that this little life be born against such a peaceful and beautiful backdrop, the exact opposite of a sterile and impersonal hospital atmosphere.

'Are we ready to move me to the hospital now?' Donna asked, exhaustion starting to take its toll.

'Absolutely.' Rayne took little Davina Tanneth from her mother and after a very quick cuddle handed her to one of the paramedics who had a baby capsule ready and waiting for the newborn to be transferred alongside her mother.

Once they were organised, Rayne shut the back door of the ambulance and gave two sharp raps, indicating it was ready to go. 'You're not going to the hospital?' she asked Janic, who stood there with his hands on his hips, nodding proudly as the ambulance made its way off the dirt road and back onto the main road, heading towards Deniliquin.

'No. I'll get these cars organised.' He indicated both his and Donna's vehicles. 'And let people know the news. My other babies need their papa and then we will all go and see their brave mama.'

'Sounds like a plan.' Rayne nodded as she started clearing away all her equipment. The area did look a little like a used-car lot with vehicles parked at odd angles here and there. She turned to find Henry pulling off his gloves and locking his medical kit. 'Here.' She held out the bag used for rubbish.

'Thanks.' Henry ditched his gloves. 'I have to say, Rayne, that you're well organised.'

Rayne smiled. 'Let's just say I've learned to be. Out here, it's best to be prepared for any contingency.' She finished rolling up the blanket and towels before stowing them in the tray of her ute. Henry followed her over, bringing her medical kit as well. 'Thanks.' She took it from him and put it away, then she turned and held out her hand. 'We haven't been properly introduced. I'm Rayne Hudson.'

'GP and midwife all rolled into one.' Henry nodded and slid his hand into hers.

Rayne shook his hand, expecting the handshake to be light, quick and polite, but Henry's entire hand seemed to engulf hers in its warmth. The sensation of his skin brought a slight tingling awareness that flooded through her, and she quickly glanced down at their connected hands, half expecting to see them catch fire, the heat was that intense. Thankfully, that wasn't the case and when she returned to look at his eyes, she got lost again in the deep, rich brown. She watched as they widened imperceptibly and she noted he seemed just as surprised at the effect of their brief touch as she was.

Both let go instantly, Henry shoving his hand into his jeans pocket. Rayne cleared her throat and looked away, hoping she wasn't blushing.

'So…Henry. Uh…are you just passing through? Er… Deniliquin, I mean.' Rayne laughed nervously and indicated their surroundings. 'Of course you'd just be passing through *here* because *here* is just a few open fields but, uh…Deni. Are you planning to, um…stay?'

Henry couldn't help but smile at the way she was tripping over her words. When had been the last time a woman had made him smile like that? Or perhaps the question was, when had he had the time to notice? He couldn't remember. He also realised Rayne was waiting for an answer.

'Actually, yes. I heard there was a festival starting soon and was told it was something everyone should experience at least once in their lives, so here I am.' He spread his arms wide for a moment.

'Well, that's great.' Rayne tilted her head to the side. 'You do know the festival doesn't officially start for another two weeks?'

'Yes. I haven't booked any accommodation so thought if I got here early enough, something might be available.'

'There's bound to be something available now but you may be out of luck during the actual festival. Most people book a year in advance.'

'A year?'

Rayne nodded at his bewildered expression. 'Yes. You see, some people like to see the festival *more* than once.'

'Ah. Of course. I see.'

'I'm not sure if you do.' Rayne took her hat off her head for a moment and put it inside the tailgate so she could fix her hair. Quite a few strands had been blown loose and she hated it when her hair flicked around her face. 'Deniliquin is a sleepy little town all year around, boasting almost eight thousand residents in the district, but during festival time numbers swell to in excess of twenty thousand.'

Henry's eyebrows raised in surprise. 'Sounds like a bit more than a festival.'

'Which is why everyone *should* experience it. There's something for everyone. Craft and photography exhibitions, cake-making and decorating competitions. Schoolchildren take part and perform little plays as well as the school band concerts...' Rayne dropped her tone a little and said in a stage whisper, 'Where it's advisable to perhaps stuff a little bit of cotton wool in your ears.' She pulled the band out, tucked stray wisps back into place, then retied the band.

Henry was momentarily mesmerised at the way the sun glinted off her brown hair, giving it a coppery, bronze look and one which was highly appealing. 'Thanks for the tip.'

'There are jugglers, fire-eaters, all sorts of street performers. You name it, Deni has it.'

'Quite a claim to fame.'

'Yep, and the world record ute muster at the end,' Rayne added. 'That's the "blokey" bit, although a lot of women love it, too. Big concerts. Lots of larking about. It's all good fun and it's good for the town's economy.'

'And what about the health-care professionals? Do you all go a bit barmy during the busiest week in Deniliquin's year?'

Rayne laughed and Henry instantly wished she hadn't. Her bright eyes were turned in his direction, sparkling brightly. They were a deep green, almost the colour of a well-cut emerald, and when she looked at him like that...

Henry shook his head to clear it and watched as she stretched out a slim arm to reposition her hat on her head.

'You could say that. Why? Offering to lend a hand?'

'Uh…' He hadn't actually thought that far. 'Well…I guess if you wanted some help…'

Rayne blinked, her teasing smile in place. 'I was sort of kidding. It would end up being a sort of busman's holiday for you if you had to work on your vacation. Anyway, as you're heading into town…' Rayne opened the door of her car and pulled a set of car keys from the pocket of her jeans '…why don't you follow me? Perhaps once you're settled at a hotel, we could…I don't know…meet up for dinner?'

'Dinner?'

'Sure. Country hospitality and all that. It's the least I can do to say thanks for helping me to deliver little DT.'

Henry paused for a moment, as though considering what she was saying. 'OK. Sure. Would it also be all right if I visited Donna just to, er…?'

'See that she's all right?' Rayne nodded. 'Occupational hazard, isn't it? I was in Melbourne about six months ago…' She stopped for a second and Henry thought he saw the light go out of her eyes, but it was gone as quickly as it had come and he wondered whether he'd imagined it. 'And I helped out in an emergency. Woman choking on a chicken nugget in the shopping mall,' she went on. 'I followed the ambulance to the hospital, waited while she was checked, even visited her the next day just to make sure she was OK.'

'We seem to have a lot in common.' The words were out of his mouth before he realised it.

'What? Over-achievers? Or people who just can't switch off when they're supposed to be taking a break?'

'How about all of the above?'

Her phone rang at that moment and she rolled her eyes. 'Never off duty, it seems.'

'I know the feeling.'

Rayne checked the cellphone display. 'Hello, darling. What's up?'

Henry tried not to listen in, instead deciding to pack his own medical kit back into his car to give Rayne the privacy she needed. As he walked away, he idly wondered who 'darling' was. Rayne didn't wear any rings but that wasn't uncommon with medicos. Anyway, it was none of his business. She'd invited him to dinner to say thanks for helping and that was all there was to it. And, quite frankly, for the first time in an exceedingly long time, he was actually looking forward to it. After that, he might bump into the Deniliquin GP here and there during his stay but that would be about it. A polite 'hello' or even a little conversation about little DT's progress and then they'd move on. She had her life. He had his. They'd intersected for a very short time and that was all there was to it.

Henry followed Rayne's ute the short distance into Deniliquin and was surprised when she pulled into the hospital car park. He parked his car and climbed out, walking over to her.

'I thought you were going to take me to a hotel?'

'I was. I mean, I am but I called ahead to Sylvia's hotel—which is the best in Deni, by the way—and she said she'd get a room organised for you. I didn't have your number so I couldn't call and tell you and thought, well, why not go to the hospital first?' She shrugged a few times as she spoke, wondering for a moment whether she'd been too impertinent. 'I hope that's all OK. I tend to sort of take over.'

'You appear to be good at organising.'

'My life needs to be organised or I don't cope. Miss Hospital Corners. That's me.'

'Don't you mean, Dr Hospital Corners?'

Rayne laughed. 'I guess I do. Anyway, if there's anything I've arranged which you don't like, let me know because I can always undo it.'

'Undo a confirmed reservation at the best hotel in Deniliquin? Perish the thought.' He indicated the hospital. 'Shall we?'

Rayne nodded. 'We shall.'

They headed inside the hospital, which was newer than Henry had expected. For some reason, because Deniliquin was an outback town, he'd expected nothing but the basics, but this appeared to be quite up to date and almost state-of-the-art…for a population of eight thousand.

He watched as Rayne conversed easily with all the staff members, introducing him along the way to everyone she bumped into, including the cleaners. It wasn't that Henry was a snob but at the Sydney hospital where he worked, medical staff certainly didn't fraternise much with the domestics. Again, it was as though new doors were being opened to him and inside was a different world—a world which he liked much better than the one he inhabited on a regular basis.

When they found Donna and DT, she was sitting up in bed, nursing the newborn.

'How are things going?' Rayne asked as she walked in.

'Good. I've been checked out. DT's been weighed and measured and all that jazz and pronounced completely beautiful by everyone she's met.'

Rayne smiled and stroked the downy head. 'She is, Donna. Beautiful and perfect.'

'And you've brought the handsome stranger to visit me.' Donna held out her free hand to Henry and gave it a quick squeeze. 'I never did thank you for stopping to help, so thank you.'

He beamed, liking the way the simple words made him feel. He'd helped patients in difficult situations before and he'd been sent cards and fruit baskets and the like, but for some reason, this 'thank you' was more…personal.

'It was my pleasure, and thank *you* for allowing me to be a part of ushering your impatient daughter into the world.'

Rayne watched Henry as he interacted with Donna and the baby, noticing how he seemed to have a different light in his eyes. She had no idea why but for some reason she got the feeling he was almost rediscovering his love of medicine. She shrugged. Perhaps that was the reason he was on holiday? Anyway, it was no business of hers. He was simply someone who'd stopped to help out and who she was thanking by taking him to dinner. Period.

Rayne drove the short distance to Sylvia's hotel, checking her rear-view mirror to ensure Henry was following her in his flash car. Her ute, unfortunately, kept spluttering, as though gasping for air, and she hoped Godfrey would be able to fit the ute in for a service before the hordes of tourists came into town.

'Here you are. At last.' She stood outside Reception and

waited for him to join her. 'You're probably exhausted after driving for the better part of the day and then delivering a baby on the side of the road.'

'Actually, I've only come from Wagga Wagga today, which isn't all that far.'

'Oh. Just a couple of hours. Sorry. I thought you'd come from Sydney today.' She shook her head. 'Don't know why. Anyway, you're still probably eager to get settled in so I'll leave you to it.'

'OK.'

Neither of them moved. Both just stood there like statues, not blinking but somehow communicating. It was definitely something Rayne hadn't experienced before and while it probably looked quite strange—the two of them standing there, just staring at each other—it felt so right. She also knew, however, that she needed to snap out of it.

'Right, then. I'll leave you to it and meet you at the San Zucker Lane Hotel and Bistro. Sylvia will be able to give you directions.'

'Good.' He nodded and Rayne forced her legs to move.

'See you, then.' She turned and tried not to rush to the driver's side. She'd opened the door and was about to climb in when Henry called her name. She looked over at him expectantly.

'Uh…what time?'

'Oh.' She smiled, feeling slightly embarrassed. 'Uh… how's six-thirty?'

'For dinner?' His eyebrows shot up at the early time. 'Is there a dinner rush in the town as well? Have to eat before seven or something bad happens?'

'No.' She laughed. 'Nothing like that. If that's too early…'

'No. It's fine. San Zucker Lane Hotel and Bistro at six-thirty.'

'Yes.'

He grinned. 'I'm looking forward to it.'

Rayne smiled back at him. 'Me, too.'

Two hours later, after Henry had unpacked and studied the map of Deniliquin, circling the San Zucker Lane Hotel and Bistro, which was only a block away from where he was staying, the phone by the bed rang and he picked it up.

'Dr Har—' He stopped for a split second. He wasn't here as a doctor. He wasn't here in an official capacity at all and to that end he simply said, 'Hello?' just like a normal person.

'Henry? It's Rayne.'

She sounded younger on the phone but he liked the way her lilting tones washed over him. 'Hi, there. Need help with another delivery?'

She chuckled. 'No, but I'm afraid I do have bad news.'

'You need to cancel,' he stated.

'I do. I'm so sorry. Something's come up.'

'Anything I can help with?'

'No. No you're on holidays, remember? Besides, it's nothing out of the ordinary. Rain-check on the dinner?'

'Of course.'

'How about Wednesday?'

'For dinner?'

'Yes. It's just that for the next few nights I'm going to be held up with school stuff.'

'School?'

'Yes, and Wednesday is my first free night. Same time and place?'

'Sounds good.'

'Excellent and again I'm really sorry I need to canc—'

'There's no need to explain, Rayne. I completely understand. In fact, if you just wanted to forget it, that's OK, too. I promise to still believe in country hospitality.'

'I don't want to cancel.'

'Oh. All right, then. We'll make it Wednesday.'

'See you then—if not before. Bye.'

Henry rang off, then sat down on the bed and slowly let out the breath he hadn't realised he'd been holding. Disappointment swamped him at the thought of not meeting Rayne tonight and until that moment he hadn't realised how much he'd been looking forward to it.

The question was—why?

CHAPTER TWO

FOR the next two days, he took in the sights of the small outback town, realising it wasn't as small as he'd initially thought. Sure, it was nothing compared with Sydney or Melbourne but, then, it didn't profess to be. In the city life was all hustle and bustle and he realised that the pace of life here in Deniliquin was much slower, more leisurely. And he liked it.

As he walked around, being greeted by almost everyone he passed with a nod or a 'G'day' or 'How ya doin'?', Henry found himself taking deep cleansing breaths. Something he only belatedly realised he hadn't done for a very long time.

The last six months had been so full on, so high pressured, and the pressure had come from no one else but himself. He'd felt as though all eyes had been on him, had been watching him, waiting to see how he coped with the death of his wife, and he'd wanted to prove to all of those prying eyes that he was fine.

Now he was beginning to wonder if he hadn't overdone it. Getting away like this, simply taking leave and getting in the car and driving away from everything he'd ever known, was…liberating.

'OK. Thanks. See you later.'

The sound of a woman's voice, a voice he recognised, stopped him in his tracks and he turned to see Rayne coming out of the bakery carrying a box. She was across the street and before he knew what he was doing, he'd stepped off the deep, wide kerb and was heading in her direction.

'Hi. Rayne!' He called her name and she stopped, looking in his direction, her smile automatically brightening.

'Henry. This is a nice surprise. How are you enjoying Deni?'

'It's a great town.'

'No arguments from me.'

'Where are you headed?' he asked, pointing to the box. 'Back to your clinic?'

'No. I somehow got roped into helping at the hall today. The cupcakes are to bribe the builders.'

'Why?'

'Because I need them to build me another special table and they're not going to want to do it.'

'And cakes will help?'

'Oh, yes. These cupcakes, my friend, are the best in the state— No! Best in the country. In fact, I'd go as far as to say the best in the world.'

'Wow. They must be like magic.'

'They taste like it, too. Darren—he's the baker—is the judge of the cake competitions for the festival.'

'Glad to hear it. It would be hardly fair to have the man who bakes the best cupcakes in the world to be a contestant.'

They both stood there, looking at each other, grinning like silly Cheshire cats. Rayne couldn't believe how happy she was to have bumped into him, her thoughts having constantly turned to their dinner the next night.

For some reason, this handsome stranger had infiltrated her subconscious and several times in the past few days she'd found herself daydreaming and sometimes not when she was alone. At work, at home, while she was helping out at Jasmine's school. This man, this man she knew next to nothing about, had piqued her curiosity and she found herself wanting to know more. That in itself was a frightening prospect because Rayne had made a vow years ago to simply be friends with men, to keep them at arm's length and to protect herself.

'Well…I'd better let you get to where you're going,' Henry eventually said.

'Huh? Oh, right. Hey, if you're not busy, would you like to come along? If you have any skill at swinging a hammer, I'm sure you'd be more than welcome.'

'And if I can't?'

'Then you'll be given one job or another. There's always too much to do and not enough people to do it.'

'And if I help, that makes me eligible for one of the world's best cupcakes?'

Rayne's smile increased. 'It most certainly does.'

'Then count me in.' They headed off, Henry a little surprised when it didn't appear as though she was heading to her ute. 'We're walking?'

'Yes. Is that a problem? The hall's not too far.'

'I know that. I've done quite a bit of walking around the town, familiarising myself with the layout.'

'And?'

'And it's really nice. I particularly like the heritage walk and the wildlife reserve, and then there's the Edward River which always seems to have people either walking along the banks or enjoying watersports.'

'It's a good time of year for it and at least we have a river to water-ski on. Some towns up north, their rivers have almost dried up.'

'It's a harsh time for our country.'

'Yes.'

'But we *do* have the best cupcakes available to us.'

Rayne grinned, surprised to find his sense of humour seemed to work on the same wavelength as her own. 'An added advantage to the drought.'

As they walked across the hall's car park, Henry looked around for Rayne's ute but it wasn't there either. 'Where's your car?'

Rayne groaned and rolled her eyes. 'In the shop. Godfrey has promised me he'll fix it before the festival begins. I hope he does. The last time he had my ute, it took him five weeks to fix it.'

'Really? Perhaps you should take it to a different mechanic.'

'*What* different mechanic? Godfrey's it for the town.'

'One mechanic?'

'Well, one mechanic and a few apprentices. He gets by. Hopefully this time the ute won't need an extra part. That's why it took so long before. He had to send away to Sydney for the part and, well, it would have been much faster for me to drive to Sydney, find the autoshop, buy the part and drive it back only I, uh…didn't have a vehicle to do it.'

'How on earth did you get around for five weeks without transport? Don't you have house calls and things like that?'

'Yes, but we're a close-knit community and I had people scheduling themselves on to give me lifts or let me borrow their cars. It all worked out in the end and I got to meet a lot of people.'

'Sounds as though it didn't bother you all that much.'

'It wasn't long after I'd moved to Deniliquin so it was a really good way to introduce myself to the masses.'

'What? "Hi, there, I'm the new doctor in town. Can I get lift to Timbuktu?"'

Rayne laughed again, opening the door of the hall. 'That's it. Exactly.'

Henry liked her laugh. It was bright, uplifting and made him feel glad to be alive. It was a strange sensation but it wasn't the first time Rayne Hudson had evoked a different emotion in him since they'd met. The woman seemed to have a love of life and that was something else he hadn't come across all that often.

'Hi!' she called, addressing the room in general.

'Oi, Doc. Good timing,' one man said as he fitted his hammer into his belt and wiped the sweat from his brow.

Henry watched in fascination as six burly blokes dressed in workboots, shorts and navy-blue singlets—all of them wearing tool belts—carefully chose a pretty, iced cupcake from the box Rayne was holding open.

'Mmm. Delicious,' one mumbled, mouth half-full, pink frosting on his nose. Henry couldn't help but chuckle to himself.

Rayne looked up at him. 'I know. They look like attack dogs but they're really puppies at heart.' The rest of the hall was filled with women sorting out tables of jumble-sale items and various craft things and pinning up photographs onto a specially made cork-board. They took their time in finishing up what they were doing before joining in the cupcake devouring.

'Help yourself,' Rayne offered, as someone brought her a cup of tea.

'Oh, is this the new doctor?' one of the women asked. 'I haven't met you yet but Sylvia's told me you're very neat and tidy. Always a good thing to discover about a man,' she said, giving Rayne a nudge. 'Need to know whether or not he can pick his socks up and put them in the wash basket.'

'My Willard doesn't,' another lady complained. 'Drives me mad.'

'Why do you think I do it?' a man, whom Henry deduced was obviously Willard, replied.

Everyone chatted on, enjoying the break and pumping Henry with questions. Rayne simply sat back and listened as she sipped her tea, interested to hear his answers. He was single and, of course, at this piece of information, a few of the ladies looked pointedly her way. And a general surgeon at a Sydney hospital. He had no children, liked all sorts of animals but preferred dogs to cats, and his favourite colour was blue.

'So why haven't you ever married?' came the question, along with a lot of agreeing from the rest of the women gathered around him. The men had gone back to work, their hammering and sawing not deterring the ladies, only making them talk louder.

'It's not right that a good-looking bloke like you should be single. Don't you think, Rayne?'

'Oh, indubitably,' she answered with a grin.

'Rayne's not married either,' Joyce offered. Her name was the only one Henry could remember at the moment. 'She's a career-woman and while there's nothing wrong with that, there comes a time when every woman should settle down.'

'So why haven't you ever married?' The question persisted and Henry glanced across at Rayne, almost as though he was begging for help.

She shrugged. 'You agreed to come.'

'Yes, but I didn't realise I'd be facing the Spanish Inquisition.'

'True.' She stood up from the table she'd been sitting on, swinging her legs. 'All right, ladies. Enough of grilling poor Henry. He's here on holidays, remember? So let's leave him be and let him have a proper holiday.'

'Ooh, well, you know, a proper holiday must always include a little holiday romance.' Joyce gave him a suggestive wink, which Rayne was delighted to note shocked him a little.

'That's right,' another woman agreed, and quite a few of them giggled as they made their way back to what they'd been doing before the cupcake break.

'How many of them aren't attached?'

'Three, but just to keep you on your toes, I won't tell you which ones.'

'Rayne, that's not nice.'

'Hey. I just rescued you, didn't I?'

'Hmm. I suppose.'

'Anyway, let's see if Willard's got something you can do to help. *If* you're still willing to help, that is.'

'I volunteered and I'll face the consequences.'

'That's the spirit. Like a lamb to the slaughter.' Rayne led him over to where the men were working and while she was there, Henry watched as she sweet-talked and charmed all of them to agree to make her two extra tables for the festival, one for the hospital and the other for the school. And the interesting part was that she'd made Willard, who seemed to be the leader of the motley crew, think it was all his idea.

They all worked on for a few hours before Rayne looked at her watch. 'Oops. Gotta go. School's almost out.' Henry was in the middle of cutting a piece of wood and watched as she said goodbye to everyone and made for the door. He wanted to go to her, to offer to walk with her to the school, to spend more time with her, but he knew that wouldn't be a good idea.

Before she left, though, she turned and looked directly at him. 'Thanks for your help, Henry. I'll see you tomorrow night.'

'What's tomorrow night?' Willard asked once she'd gone.

Henry started sawing again. 'We're having dinner.'

'Ooh. Really?' Joyce had heard.

'It's just a sort of "thank you" for helping her deliver Donna's baby the other day.'

'Of course.' Joyce nodded and touched the side of her nose, indicating she didn't really believe him. Henry opened his mouth to explain further but Willard clapped him on the back.

'Don't bother, son. Once they get an idea in their heads, it's impossible to get it out.'

Henry decided to listen and returned his attention to manual labour, which he hadn't done or enjoyed so much since high school.

* * *

'Oh, and don't you look dashing,' Sylvia said as Henry came out of his room the following evening. It was a quarter past six and he wanted to make sure he left enough time to walk to the San Zucker Lane Hotel and Bistro where he was meeting Rayne.

'Thank you.'

'Now, you take it easy with our Rayne. She's a very special girl.'

'So I've been told.' And on more than one occasion. It appeared the town of Deniliquin was more than protective of their GP.

'Got a lot of heart in her, she has, and she's not afraid to give to others, but she finds it very difficult to take for herself.'

Henry nodded. That much he'd worked out for himself. It was also what people said about him so it appeared he and Rayne had more in common than they'd initially thought.

'Anyway, Sylvia, I'd best be going. Don't want to be late.'

'No. Of course not. Off you go. Have a wonderful time.'

Henry made his way to the San Zucker Lane Hotel and when he walked in he was surprised to find Rayne already there, chatting with the bartender. She was dressed in a pair of three-quarter-length trousers and a green top that highlighted the amazing colour of her eyes. He also noticed she kept looking out the side door, watching intently but listening to what the young man was saying. As Henry came a little closer, he followed her gaze and saw that outside was a small children's area consisting of a long chalkboard and small sandpit. A little blonde girl was busily drawing, her tongue between her teeth as she concentrated.

'Henry. Hi.'

He returned his attention to Rayne, who had spotted

him. She beckoned him over and introduced him to the bartender. 'Henry, this is Damian Simmons, otherwise known as Simmo.'

The two men shook hands.

'How are you enjoying Deni?'

'It's great.' Henry nodded for emphasis. 'Everyone's so friendly.'

Rayne smiled at the small hint of surprise she could hear in Henry's voice but didn't make mention of it.

'I thought it might be nicer to sit outside. Suit you?'

'Uh…sure.' They placed their orders and headed outside into the garden, sitting at one of the tables. Henry kept glancing at the child, who was still drawing on the board—a beautiful picture of an emu. Who did the child belong to? Was she supposed to be out here? She wasn't bothering anyone and seemed quite content to keep on drawing. Rayne didn't call her over or say hello or anything and Henry wasn't sure what to do, so he did nothing.

'How did things go at the hall yesterday after I left?'

'Good. In fact, I was back there today, helping out. Everything's starting to come together and Willard said he can even find me something to do tomorrow.'

'Some holiday.'

'Actually, it's really nice.'

'What? Being told what to do by a retired headmaster?'

'Yes.'

Rayne looked at him, a slow smile appearing on her face. 'You really mean that, don't you? I guess, working at the hospital, you have everyone jumping to attention the instant you snap your fingers.'

'Something like that.'

'Are you fairly high up the ladder? Head of department or something like that?'

'Something like that.'

'And they were able to spare you for a few weeks' holiday?'

'Apparently.'

'Am I being too inquisitive?'

He raised an eyebrow at that. 'After Joyce and her friends?'

'Good point. I guess I'm quite tame in comparison.' She looked up at the sky and then marvelled at the vibrant oranges and reds mingling together and signifying that tomorrow would be another fantastic spring day. She mentioned this to Henry but when he didn't reply, she returned her eyes to meet his. 'What?' she asked, when he didn't say anything.

'I didn't mean to cut you off just now. You can ask me questions, Rayne.'

'It's fine. You're on holiday. The last thing you need while you're relaxing is to be constantly answering probing questions from nosy locals.'

'True, but I confess I do have an ulterior motive.'

'Really?' Rayne rubbed her hands together. 'This is getting interesting. What is it?'

'Well, if you ask me a question of a personal nature, then I can ask you one.'

'You're curious about me?'

'You seem surprised.'

'Well, yes, but I just thought everyone in the town would have already told you my story so you'd definitely know more about me than I know about you.'

'Actually, people have only told me that you're very special and it seemed to come more in the way of a warning.'

Rayne smiled at that. 'I guess they're a little protective of me.'

'Because they're worried about losing you to some big city?'

'No, actually. It's not that at all.' Rayne thought, trying to figure out the right way to phrase what she was about to say. 'I had a…disjointed upbringing. I guess that's the best way to put it. Anyway, when I came here to Deniliquin I found…I don't know, a sort of sanctuary. It's almost as though this town is a place of healing.'

'I can believe that and I've only been here for three days.'

'The people are friendly. They're genuine. They know how to smile. It's a great place.' Rayne gestured to where the little girl had almost finished drawing her picture on the chalk-board. 'Jasmine's certainly enjoying it and, goodness knows, she needs it most.'

'Jasmine.'

'Yes. She's my…' Rayne paused and Henry watched as sadness came into her eyes. 'You know, I've never had to introduce her before. I guess Jasmine's my daughter.'

'You guess?' Henry was gobsmacked. 'You mean, you don't know?'

'I'm sorry. Again, I sort of thought the town gossiping tongues would take care of the explanations.'

'Perhaps they're all too busy getting ready for the festival.'

'Perhaps. Anyway, I…um…inherited Jazzy. Her parents died about six months ago in a car crash. Jazzy's mother was my best friend—well, we were blood-sisters.' Rayne smiled sadly. 'You know. Like blood-brothers. We pricked our fingers together when we were about twelve and smeared our blood together so we could really be sisters.'

Henry looked at the child and his heart went out to her. 'She's about five?'

'Yes.'

'And how's she taking everything?'

Rayne shrugged. 'Kids are resilient. I think she's doing quite well, given the circumstances. Better than me some days.'

Henry reached over, placing his hand on hers. 'I do understand, Rayne.'

She looked up at him, realising he, too, had known great personal loss and suffering. She was about to ask him what had happened when their meals were brought out. Henry withdrew and Rayne called Jasmine over.

'Jasmine, this is Henry. He's a doctor, like me, but he's in Deni for a holiday.'

The little girl gave a shy smile. 'You'll like Deni for holidays. I me-member coming here with Mummy and Daddy to see Rayne. We liked having holidays here and now I get to live here and I even go to school here.'

'That sounds great.'

They ate their meals, Jasmine doing more than her fair share of keeping the conversation flowing. Rayne was content to sit back and watch how Henry interacted with Jazzy. He'd obviously had some experience in dealing with children yet she was sure he'd said he didn't have any.

'I like your name,' Jasmine said, after watching him intently for a few minutes. 'Henry.' She repeated it and then nodded approvingly.

Henry's lips twitched at the grown-up way Jasmine spoke. 'Thank you. I like your name, too.'

'You can call me Jazzy if you like. Heaps of people do. Nobody called me that before I came to Deni but now I'm here I like it. I like it a lot.'

'Jazzy. That's very pretty.'

'I'm five, you know, and soon I'll be five and a half. I live with Rayne. She's my godmother and my mummy and daddy decided that she was the best person to look after me when they died so when they died and went to heaven, I came here.'

Henry glanced up at Rayne and could see the pain in her eyes but he was also pleased she was letting Jasmine speak freely about her parents. Talking about those who had died was supposed to help with the grieving process. He knew that all too well but when it came to the topic of his wife, he was strictly a doctor who didn't practise what he preached.

Rayne stroked Jasmine's blonde hair.

'But first I had to go and stay with some other people,' Jasmine continued. 'They were OK but not as great as Rayne, and the woman told me off for crying so much because I missed my mummy and daddy. Then Rayne came and picked me up and we went and spent some time with Granny and Grandpa. They were really sad, too, but they love Rayne and so do I. Granny and Grandpa are coming to Deni soon for the school holidays and it will be so much fun to have them here. It's always good fun because Granny likes to bake cakes and she's going to bake some cakes and put them in the festival and she said I could help!'

The excitement was almost glowing from Jasmine as

she spoke and Henry brightened at the beauty that shone from the five-year-old.

'We did craft things at school today and I'm going to put my craft material in the festival, too, so I'll have two things in it. First we had to tie a piece of material up with rubber bands and then we dunked it in special purple paint which doesn't come off the material and then we took the bands off and there was a really pretty pattern, but I got some paint on my hands and we can't get it off, can we, Rayne?' Jasmine held up her hands to prove her point.

'No, we did try scrubbing a bit when we got you home from school but I think it'll just have to wear off.'

'Purple hands.' Henry seemed impressed. 'Groovy.' He smiled at them both. It was clear Rayne was doing her best to provide love and care during such a terrible time—that much was clearly reflected in the way Jasmine's voice warmed whenever she mentioned her guardian's name.

Jasmine giggled. 'You're funny.'

They finished their meals and Rayne and Jasmine quickly visited the ladies' before coming out to find Henry with his back to them, staring up at the sky. Stars had begun to appear in the almost cloudless sky.

'Found the Southern Cross?' she asked, and he quickly turned to look at them.

'Ready to go?'

'No. We can stargaze for a bit if you'd like.'

'I know where the Southern Cross is,' Jasmine offered, and pointed her little hand up in the correct direction. 'The bottom star always points to the south,' she announced proudly.

'Very good,' Henry murmured.

'Rayne taught me that. When I came here to live, the

stars were so bright. They're not bright in the city but you can still see them.' Jasmine still spoke with authority, even though her sentence structure was a little garbled.

'You're right, Jasmine. You can certainly see more stars here than in the city.'

'How about we go for a walk?' Rayne suggested. 'You'll be able to see even more from the park.'

'Sure.' Henry turned to look at her but hadn't realised just how close she was standing to him. Rayne found she couldn't move, didn't want to move, and so stayed where she was, looking into his eyes and liking what she saw.

For the first time she found herself *wanting* to know about someone else and this someone else was the man standing next to her. He intrigued her and no man had ever done that. Usually, she was able to figure them out quite quickly, what they wanted out of life, what they wanted from her, and with all of them she just hadn't been interested. Her heart was locked away safe and sound and she knew that even if she got to know Henry better, she would still be safe because he was only here on holiday.

'Something wrong?'

'Huh? No. Nothing. Just thinking.' Rayne managed to break her gaze away at last, desperate to try and get herself under control. The trembling, which had spread throughout her, started to settle down. His eyes had been so powerful, so strong and protective, and yet for some reason she hadn't been surprised to see it there. It was almost as though she'd expected it, expected Henry to protect her for now and for ever.

CHAPTER THREE

THE sound of a loud crash coming from inside startled them, breaking the spell. Rayne took Jasmine's hand and they quickly went to investigate.

'Rayne?' The urgent call coming from the direction of the kitchen had them rushing through the swing door that led to the kitchen. There they found Damian's wife leaning over her husband, who was lying on the floor, writhing in pain.

Shattered glasses and amber liquid surrounded him and Rayne immediately told Jasmine to stay back. Rayne snapped her phone off her waistband and called the hospital, requesting an ambulance, while Henry ordered Damian's wife to bring him their first-aid kit. He grabbed a few kitchen towels from the racks and placed them on the floor over the glass and liquid. Then he picked his way carefully towards the injured man.

'It's all right, Damian. It's OK. Try to stop moving if you can so I can get closer to take a look.'

'There's blood,' Rayne called as she came round the other side, glad she'd worn flat-heeled shoes. Cynthia came back with the first-aid kit and Rayne took it from the frightened woman. 'He'll be all right.'

Cynthia was wringing her hands together. 'It all happened so quickly. He was carrying glasses and bottles and I don't know, I think he just slipped or lost his footing or— Oh, my…' Her eyes went wide as she saw the blood on the floor. 'He's bleeding! Rayne!'

'Cyn, it's OK. Henry is a general surgeon. He not only sees this sort of thing all the time but he's also the man who can fix it. Why don't you take Jazzy out and keep her company? You can both go and flag down the ambulance. How about that?'

Jasmine took Cynthia's hand, apparently not at all squeamish about what was happening right in front of her. A few people who'd been dining in the bistro came in to help and while Henry and Rayne attended to Damian, they were able to clear up some of the mess surrounding them.

'You have a very nasty gash to your abdomen,' Henry told Damian. 'But don't worry about it, I can fix it.'

'Good.'

When the ambulance arrived, they made sure Damian was secure on the stretcher. Henry rode in the back with the patient to keep him stable. Rayne and Jasmine sat up front with the paramedics.

'Why aren't the sirens on?' Jasmine wanted to know.

'Because there's no traffic on the road to block our way to the hospital.'

'But this is an ambulance. The sirens are s'posed to be on,' she said.

'You're absolutely right. Sorry, Jaz.' The paramedic dutifully switched the siren on and Jasmine clapped.

'Much better.'

When they arrived at the hospital, Rayne left Henry to deal with getting the patient into the treatment room and took Jasmine to the ward where her friend Tanya was on duty.

'Emergency?' Tanya asked as Jasmine ran to her and gave her a big hug.

'Yes. You'll take care of Jazzy?'

'Do you even need to ask? Go.' Tanya shooed her away and Rayne returned to A and E, pulling on a protective gown as she entered the emergency treatment room. Henry had just finished washing his hands as the nursing staff cut away Damian's clothes and the makeshift bandage Henry had fashioned.

'Are you happy for me to take the lead on this?' he asked as he pulled on a pair of gloves.

Rayne followed suit. 'Absolutely. You're the general surgeon.'

'The anaesthetist has been called?'

'I'm presuming so.' She checked with the triage nurse and had it confirmed. 'Stuie Rhodes should be here soon. He doesn't live far.'

'Good.' Then he turned his attention to the room. 'My name is Henry. I'm a general surgeon from Sydney. Patient status, please?'

'BP is 100 over 50.'

'Plasma intravenous, saline intravenous. Laceration measuring approximately seven inches across.'

'Blood alcohol level is zero.'

Rayne had hooked on her stethoscope and was checking Damian's heart and lungs before continuing with the rest of her neurological observations. Henry carefully began assessing the abdominal laceration, a frown on his face. When he was finished, he replaced the dressing and looked at the nurse closest to him.

'Cross-type and match. I'll need to see the anaesthetist the instant he arrives. Rayne, take me to Theatres so I can familiarise myself with the set-up.'

With that, Henry headed from the room, Rayne hard on his heels. 'You'll be assisting me.'

Rayne only nodded at this information, not about to look a gift horse in the mouth.

'Is that all right?'

'It's fine.'

'Really? A lot of GPs don't like Theatre.'

'So why do you want me to assist?' She pointed to the right and pressed the keypad to unlock the door that led to the theatre prep and scrub area.

Henry took quick stock of his surroundings before looking at her. 'I don't know. I'd just like you to be in Theatre with me.'

'Consider it done.'

'Now, are there any forms I need to sign? I'm not registered to work at this hospital.'

Rayne waved his words away. 'We can take care of that afterwards. This isn't a big, bustling hospital, remember. Anyway, changing rooms are this way.'

Once they were both dressed in blue theatre garb, they came out to start scrubbing, Henry talking through some of his thoughts about how he planned to fix Damian's injury. He noticed that Rayne didn't seem at all fazed by the prospect of assisting him.

Before Henry could ask any more questions, Stuie

Rhodes came in and the two doctors started to discuss the case, Rayne listening.

All too soon they were in Theatre. Rayne was standing opposite Henry, the X-rays of Damian's abdomen were up on the viewing box, a unit of blood was being transfused into their patient, along with a unit of saline, and they'd almost finished debriding the wound.

She held the retractors, passed Henry the suction and had the sutures ready when he needed them. Henry performed the procedure in a methodical way, taking each organ in turn and making sure everything was perfect before moving on to the next.

'You're very apt at surgery,' Henry commented after the first hour. 'Have you done training?'

'Two years.'

'What happened?'

'My mother became ill.'

'Oh?'

'She passed away two years ago.'

Henry processed this information. Two years ago Rayne had moved to Deniliquin. Had it been to escape bad memories? He knew all about those. Two years ago his wife had been in a terrible accident and his life had changed overnight.

'Do you have any plans to continue with surgery?'

'Not directly.' She wished he'd change the topic to either what he was doing with the operation or something else…*anything* else, rather than putting her under the spotlight.

'Suction,' was the next thing he said, and Rayne was thankful he wasn't going to persist with his present line of questioning. Once they'd installed a wound drain and checked its position with an X-ray, Henry was satisfied and began to close the wound in layers.

Finally, after two hours, Damian was wheeled to Recovery and Rayne began to degown. 'You were brilliant,' she told Henry.

'Thank you.'

'You saved his life.'

'It's my job.' He didn't seem all that excited about it. She guessed that for him this had been just like another day at the office.

'I'm not sure you understand, Henry. Out here, we're pretty remote. If you hadn't been here, Damian would have been airlifted to Wagga Wagga, and with the rate he was bleeding, he might not have made it,' she felt compelled to point out. They'd removed their theatre garb and were on their way back to the nurses' station to write up the paperwork.

He processed this information, seeing the bright light in her eyes, seeing the love of what she did radiating out from her. How he wished he felt as good about his job as she did now. 'Well, he did make it and that's what really counts.'

Rayne was a little concerned with how he was brushing this aside. It was as though he didn't really enjoy what he did any more, and for a surgeon that would be quite disheartening. 'Sorry. I didn't mean to go over the top. I just want you to know I am grateful for you being here.'

'You're welcome. Now, how about we get the red tape taken care of and then figure out how to get home tonight?'

'No sweat. There are several people here who can give us a lift or let us borrow their car.'

'Really?'

Rayne laughed. 'This isn't Sydney, Henry.'

'I think I'm finally starting to get the message.'

Rayne sighed, unable to believe the way she felt when she was with him. He was handsome, brilliant and quite funny. A winning combination and a very dangerous one as well. He would only be in town for a short time before heading back to wherever he lived to continue working as a general surgeon, no doubt with a gaggle of pretty colleagues chasing after him.

That thought didn't appeal to her at all and she pushed it out of her mind. Henry was a new friend and that was all there was to it. The fact that she was attracted to him meant nothing. She was in control of her life and she intended to remain so.

At the nurses' station, Henry started writing up Damian's operation notes while Rayne found the forms he needed to complete to ensure the red tape was stuck firmly in place. She called the ward to check on Jasmine and was told by Tanya that the child was currently asleep in a spare bed.

'Jasmine's all right?' Henry asked when she'd finished on the phone.

'Yes. She's sleeping, which is good because she has school tomorrow.'

'And how are you coping with instant motherhood?'

Rayne thought on his question for a moment. 'Getting better, or at least I like to think I am.'

'I'm sure you're doing just fine.' Henry had finished writing up Damian's notes and had picked up a piece of paper, which he folded, his fingers moving with sure, firm strokes.

'You don't have any children?' She was sure he'd said so the other day but she wanted to check.

'No.'

'Do you want children?'

He looked up from what he was doing. 'Why do you ask?'

'I don't know. You seem sort of…disjointed.'

She'd used that word before when she'd been talking about her upbringing. He guessed that was why she could see it in him. 'Actually, Rayne, I *feel* disjointed, or perhaps disconnected is a better word.' He shook his head and returned his attention to his paper folding. 'I don't want to bore you.'

Rayne pulled up a chair and sat down. 'I'm not bored and we both need to wait for a while before we check on Damian. I'm a good listener.'

'I'll bet you are. Is that why you settled for becoming a GP?'

'One of the reasons.' She smiled. 'Don't get me wrong. I like being a GP. It's rewarding, it's encompassing, it's personal.'

'But does it give you the excitement you feel when you're in surgery?'

'No. I have to say it doesn't, but that doesn't mean that I want to throw away what I have here to go and study some more.'

'If you had the opportunity, though. Would you?'

Rayne shrugged. 'I don't know. I have Jasmine now and she's definitely filled a very large void in my life.'

'The void left by her parents' death?'

'Yes.'

'I know all about that void.'

'You do?'

'Yes.' He smoothed the paper but Rayne wasn't all that interested in what his fingers were doing. She was watching his expressions like a hawk, trying to decipher them. She could also feel him distancing himself and she knew it was time to let go.

'I think I'll go check on Jazzy and see if I can rustle us up a lift home.'

'Rayne. Wait.' Henry held out the paper he'd been folding. 'Here. This is for you.'

What he held out was a beautiful rose—an origami rose—perfectly made. Rayne took it, looking at the delicacy of it. Well, the man was a surgeon, which meant he was good with his hands.

She looked up. 'This is…' She shook her head, feeling a lump starting to form in her throat. 'It's…' she swallowed '…the nicest thing anyone has ever given me. Thank you.' She touched the petals. It was simple, it was elegant and he'd made it himself. She swallowed again. 'It's beautiful.'

Henry was completely taken aback at her reaction. He'd initially started to make the rose as a way of calming himself down because of the nature of the conversation they'd been having. He hadn't expected to see such overwhelming and raw emotion come into her eyes.

'I'm glad you like it.'

'Where did you learn to do this?'

He looked down at the desk for a moment before deciding to take a chance. He usually found it difficult to open up to new people and when he finally told them his sad little story, the pain and sympathy they offered sickened him. Taking a deep breath, he nodded.

'I used to have quite a bit of…extra time on my hands.'

'A surgeon? Really?'

'My…wife. She was sick. In a coma, actually. For two years. Six months ago she contracted an infection which her body couldn't fight.'

Rayne sat back down and just listened. He'd pulled out another sheet of paper and began folding again. She could tell he wasn't finished, that he had more to say, so she remained silent. Waiting for him to continue in his own time.

'I found a book. Taught myself the art of paper folding while I sat by her bedside every night when I wasn't working. It helped to pass the time.' He looked up at her, stared into her eyes. He saw sorrow and understanding there but no false sympathy. 'And that's where I learned to make the roses.'

Rayne smiled and touched the one he'd given her. 'They really are things of beauty. Thank you.'

'For sharing with you or for the rose?'

Her smile increased. 'Both.' His words now explained so much about him. Why he didn't seem to enjoy his job. Why he had needed to get away from his life in Sydney. Why he seemed to be searching for himself. Emotional trauma had a way of creeping up on a person and for most people it usually hit them about six months after the event when daily life started to settle down…settle down without the people you loved being there.

'I'll go see about that ride home.' She stood and headed off, and Henry watched her walk away. She really was an extraordinary woman.

The following Monday, Rayne had just returned from the airstrip and was in the supermarket, picking up some essentials.

'Hello,' a deep male voice said from behind her. Rayne's smile was automatic as she instantly recognised the voice as belonging to Henry. She turned.

'Hi, yourself.'

'How have you been?'

'Busy.'

'I figured as much. Haven't seen you about all that often.'

'Ah, well, people are starting to arrive for the festival, which begins this coming Sunday.'

'I know. I've been officially recruited onto Willard's team.'

Rayne laughed. 'Oh, you poor thing. Some holiday you're having.'

'Actually, it's been just what the doctor ordered, so to speak. I'd probably have gone mad just sitting around the pool all day long.'

'Need to keep the brain going, eh?'

'Something like that.' Henry couldn't help but look her over, his gaze drinking her in as though making sure his memory had remembered her accurately. Today she was wearing a black skirt, which came to mid-thigh, and a red knit top. Her hair was scooped up into a high ponytail on her head and she was even wearing a touch of lipstick. No, his memory hadn't been lax but it also hadn't done her natural, radiant beauty justice. 'You look nice.'

'Thanks. I've been consulting all day, have just picked Jasmine's grandparents up from the airstrip, and if I don't get this shopping done, I'll be late collecting Jaz from school.'

'Got your ute back, then?'

'Well…yes and no. I made Godfrey at least patch it up so I could get around but he'll still need to do more work on it once the festival's over.' She picked up some coffee from the shelf and put it in her trolley. 'Want to shop with me?'

'Uh…sure.' Henry only carried a basket which contained a few pieces of fruit, a litre of milk and a bottle of juice.

Rayne hadn't taken two steps before her phone rang. She shook her head as she pulled it from her waistband and checked the caller ID. 'Some days…'

'Wish you could ignore it?'

'Exactly. Hi, Brian. What's up?' She listened intently then looked at her watch. 'I can be out there around four-thirty.' Another pause. 'That's the best I can do, Brian.' She smiled. 'OK. See you then.' She shut her phone and clipped it back in place. 'Feel like spending some more time with me?'

'House call?'

'Yes. Patient's been having recurring abdominal pain and although I've run test after test, I can't seem to find what's wrong. We've tried different strains of antibiotics but nothing seems to be working.'

'Why not refer him to a specialist?'

'Tried that. He refuses to leave his house. Makes it difficult to X-ray him and I can't really ask a specialist from Wagga to come and take a look.'

'But as I'm here in town…'

'And you've offered to help…'

'I did. It's no problem, Rayne.' In fact, he was secretly delighted at the opportunity to spend more time with her. Since they'd operated together on Damian Simmons last Wednesday, Rayne had been constantly on his mind. It was as though the instant he'd told her about his wife, even though he'd only given her the briefest of outlines, a weight had been lifted from his shoulders. Perhaps it was also the people of Deniliquin, who had embraced him as one of their own, getting him to help out, chatting with him, inviting him for dinner in the evenings. Country hospitality was well and truly alive in this small town and he was loving every minute of it. He could see quite well why Rayne liked it here. She'd once called it her sanctuary and he understood that completely as that was exactly how he was coming to see things.

'So you said Jasmine's grandparents are here now?'

'Yes. Earlene likes to get here early enough to enter the cake-baking and decorating competition. She and Jazzy are supposed to do a test run as soon as school's out.' Rayne held up the shopping list. 'Hence this trip to the supermarket.' She continued to fill the list as they walked around, Henry telling her about some of the things he'd done during the past few days.

'It really does seem as though you've been having a great time,' she said after they'd been through the checkout and were wheeling the wayward trolley towards her ute. The trolley, however, seemed to have a life of its own, its wheels turning one way when she wanted them to turn another.

'Whoa.' Henry came around her to lend a hand to slow it down and Rayne skidded slightly. In the next instant both of Henry's arms were around her, his hands firm on the trolley, bringing it to a stop right next to her ute... But he didn't move.

His chest pressed against her back, bringing warmth, bringing tingles and bringing far too much awareness. Rayne's throat went dry, her breathing became shallow and she parted her lips, unsure what was going to happen next.

CHAPTER FOUR

WHAT was this sensation?

Henry found himself unable to move, unable to think clearly and rationally as he stood there with his arms on either side of Rayne, her back pressing electrifying warmth against his chest. Neither of them moved for a moment and he heard her breathing increase before belatedly realising his own had done the same.

He was attracted to her. How could any man *not* be? She was incredibly beautiful, incredibly smart and incredibly funny. What he hadn't planned had been to do anything about it. His life had changed. He'd accepted that years ago when Natalia had slipped into a coma, taking away his hopes and dreams, and he'd spent the past couple of years letting go.

Now, though, standing here, feeling those dormant emotions come zinging to life, telling him that what was happening here wasn't at all ordinary, he had no idea how to proceed.

'Henry?' His name on her lips was a breathless whisper.

'Hmm?' He angled his head to look down at her, still trying to recover from the shock of just how perfectly she seemed to fit against him.

Slowly her head turned, tilting slightly, her eyes flicking up to briefly meet his. They were so close. She could feel his breath mingling with hers and she swallowed, trying to calm her nerves and a sense of anticipation. She looked at his mouth for a second before closing her eyes, trying desperately to gain some sort of control over the situation.

'Uh…you can…uh…let go now.'

He could hear the lie in her words, knew that she was only saying them out loud from necessity. And she was right. They couldn't stand here like this, thinking what they were both obviously thinking.

'Right.' He said the word out loud and it was a fraction of a second later that his mind actually acted on that command. He let go of the trolley and took three huge steps away from Rayne.

She looked at him, not sure what to do or say next.

'I'm sorry, Rayne.' He shook his head, as though trying to clear it, as though trying to get it back on track. 'I don't know what came over me.'

'It's all right, Henry.' She tried to think of something funny to say in order to lighten the atmosphere but nothing came quickly to mind. She indicated to her ute. 'We'd better get a move on or we'll be late to pick up Jazzy.'

'And that would never do.'

'No,' she agreed.

Neither of them said a word as they drove the short distance to the school, both of them immensely relieved when Jasmine started chattering on about her day, filling the silent void.

'And then something really funny happened. Russell was drinking his milk and Julie told a joke and Russell

laughed and tried to swallow at the same time and...'
Jasmine started laughing again, her infectious giggle making both adults in the front seat smile '...milk came out his nose!'

Jasmine continued to laugh and as Rayne looked over at Henry, their eyes bright with mirth, she felt things shift back onto that even track they'd been running on before. By the time they reached her house, she felt calm and comfortable with Henry again, just so long as she didn't think about how wonderful it had felt to have his arms securely around her.

The little girl let out a squeal of joy as she spotted her grandmother coming out of the house as they pulled into the driveway.

'Wait until I've stopped the car,' Rayne cautioned, and the instant she had, Jasmine had unbuckled her seat belt and was out of the ute in a flash, dashing across the dry front grass and into Earlene's waiting arms.

Jarvis came out to see his granddaughter and to lend a hand bringing the groceries into the house, only to find Henry already had most of the bags in his hands.

Rayne introduced everyone and they went inside, Henry taking stock of his surroundings, interested to see what Rayne's house was like. There were photographs and books everywhere and pictures on the fridge which could only have been created by Jasmine.

They didn't get to stay long this time around as Rayne was eager to get the visit to Brian over and done with so she wasn't too late getting home.

'So tell me some more about Brian,' Henry said as she drove out of town, turning onto the road that led to Conargo.

'He's a farmer, a man of the land, and he's been on the land now for close on seventy years. A few months ago he started complaining of stomach pains. I've run a few tests, basic stool and blood tests, but the results were inconclusive. I wanted him to come into the hospital so I could do some more tests but he refuses to leave the farm.'

'And what are your suspicions telling you it might be?'

'Crohn's disease.'

'Right. In that case, how do you want to play this? Do you want to be the bad cop or shall I?'

'What do you mean?'

'Well, whether or not you're on the right track, Brian will need further testing. Right?'

'Yes.'

'And to do that, you need him in hospital. Right?'

'Yes.'

'So, what if I take the role of bad cop, saying things like if he doesn't agree to go to Deni, he might well end up in Wagga Base hospital or even in Sydney?'

Rayne shook her head. 'Poor Brian would have a fit if he had to go to Sydney. He's not a man who does well in big cities.'

'Which is probably his main fear for not wanting to come to the hospital in the first place. If it *is* Crohn's disease then there's so much that can be done for him and it can be done in Deni. If he leaves it, however, Wagga may be the best option.'

Rayne made a right-hand turn onto a long dirt driveway that led to the homestead. 'All right. So I'm good cop?'

'Yes. I'm new. Let me be the villain.'

As they climbed from the car, they were met by a multitude of dogs, all quite friendly as they tried to jump up, eager to be patted.

'All right, all right.' Rayne spoke to them brightly. 'Settle down, you crazy lot. It's only me.' She patted a few of them. 'Where's Brian?' she asked, as though cooing at them. Henry smiled at the way she was treating them. 'Where's Brian?' she repeated, before making her way up the old wooden porch steps onto the front verandah. 'Brian?' she called out as she rapped twice on the screen door before opening it and heading inside. Henry followed her, feeling a little intrusive, as he was walking into a stranger's house intending to convince the man to go to hospital for further testing.

'That you, Rayne?' An old croaky voice came from the direction of the bedroom and Rayne headed towards it.

'It's me, Brian. How are you doing? Any better?' As they entered the bedroom, Henry saw an old man lying back on the pillows, a haggard and scared look on his face. Perhaps it wouldn't take too much convincing to get Brian to the hospital after all.

'Where's Connie?' Rayne asked, as she placed her medical bag down next to the bed.

'Off shopping. She'll be back soon.' He gestured to Henry. 'Who's this, then?'

'This is Dr Henry Harcourt, general surgeon. Come all the way from Sydney to see you.'

'City slicker.' Brian curled his lip up in disgust but Rayne only laughed.

'Relax. He's actually here on vacation and has been helping Willard get everything ready for the festival.'

Brian relaxed a little. 'Willard trusts you, eh? Well, that's something, I guess.'

'Let me just wash my hands and then we'll get your examination under way.' Rayne walked back down the hall to the bathroom and thoroughly washed her hands. Henry came in and did the same. 'How's it going, bad cop?' She grinned up at him as she shook her hands dry.

Henry rolled his eyes. 'You made me believe Brian was some pit bull. He's just a frightened little lamb instead.'

'Very frightened. Do you think I should order the ambulance now?'

'The sooner he's in, the sooner he can be correctly diagnosed and home with the proper treatment.'

'Coo-ee, Rayne?'

'Connie?' Henry asked, and Rayne nodded, heading back into the main part of the house.

'Hi, there.'

'How's Brian doing?'

'Not sure yet. Just washing my hands.' She headed into the kitchen and opened a cupboard with her elbow before taking out a clean and ironed hand towel. She passed it to Henry as she introduced him.

'Ah, so this is the dashing doctor half the ladies in town are in love with.'

Rayne laughed at Henry's astonished expression. 'Only half?'

'The other half are married.' Connie winked at Henry. 'You're safe, mate. Anyway, Rayne, just wanted to let you know that Brian hasn't had a particularly good couple of days. I had to force him to call you today.'

'Symptoms getting worse?'

'Yes. Fatigue, stomach pains, loss of bowel motions. It's all just as you said it would be.'

'What about fever?' Henry asked.

'No fever as yet.'

'Could be ulcerative colitis,' Rayne offered.

'No. I think your original diagnosis of Crohn's is the line we follow.'

'All right. Connie, call the ambulance for me.'

'You're that sure?' Brian's wife asked anxiously.

'He needs further investigation and treatment. Now, if I have to give him a sedative so we can at least get him into hospital without putting further stress on his body, I will, but he needs treatment, Con.'

Henry watched the other woman blanch and for a second he thought she was going to pass out.

'It's that serious?'

'It's become that serious.'

Slowly her colour returned as she nodded. 'All right. I'll get everything sorted out.'

Rayne looked at Henry. 'Ready?'

Henry squared his shoulders and nodded. 'Ready.'

'Remember, you're the bad cop. I'm the nice one,' she whispered as they walked back to the bedroom.

'Got it.'

Rayne greeted her patient brightly and went through the motions of doing her observations. After she'd taken Brian's temperature, she handed the thermometer to Henry so he could see the reading. Brian may not have had a temperature that morning but he certainly had one now. Not excessive but, still, it was another piece of the puzzle which pointed towards Crohn's disease.

She explained to Brian that it was a non-specific inflammatory bowel disorder which could affect any part of the gastrointestinal tract.

'So I really need to go to hospital?' Brian's eyes were wider than saucers as he spoke and if Rayne thought he'd looked scared before, it was nothing compared to now.

'You do.' She took his hand in hers and gave it a little squeeze.

'Once you're there, I can run further tests,' Henry added. 'The sooner we have you on a treatment plan, the sooner you can come back home.'

'You'll be looking after me?' Brian asked the question of Henry, who nodded.

'You're rather fortunate he's here. If he weren't, I would have needed to send you to Wagga for treatment.'

Brian pondered this, then looked directly at Henry. 'How long are you gonna be in town, boy?'

Henry smiled. If that wasn't a sign of acceptance, he didn't know what was. 'At least until after the festival.'

'All right. Then I'll go now.' The words were said softly and again Rayne could feel the man's anxiety.

'I know you don't like hospitals, Brian, but we're going to do everything we can to make this as easy and as painless as we can.'

'Do I need to get Connie to bring the car round?'

Rayne smiled as Brian's wife came into the room. She'd been listening just outside the door for the past few minutes but now took her husband's withered old hand in hers. 'The ambulance is coming, love.'

'Already? That quick?' Anger flashed into Brian's eyes. 'You all weren't gonna take no for an answer.'

'It's because we care about you, love,' Connie persisted. 'Rayne can give you something so you don't feel so worried.'

Brian opened his mouth and for an instant Henry thought he would really be called on to play the bad cop after all. Instead, Brian looked at each one of them in turn, then he sighed, as though the fight had just gone out of him, that it was too much effort, that he realised how sick he really was.

It was another hour before Brian was settled in at Deniliquin hospital, Henry already having taken a few samples and sent them away to the Wagga medical science laboratories for priority analysis. Brian was also scheduled to have X-rays and colonoscopy to begin with, but Henry was sure he'd also need an ultrasound and barium uptake.

'Whew,' Rayne said as they left the hospital. 'That was a little exhausting.'

'But at least he's here now.'

'Yes. Thanks again for your help.'

'Glad to be of service.' Again, being here in this small community, helping Rayne out, had brought Henry a sense of accomplishment—more so than he'd ever received from having successfully completed the most intricate of surgeries.

'So? Hungry?' Rayne asked as she drove past his hotel.

'Uh…yes, actually.'

'Good, because Earlene will no doubt have some delicious meal cooked and it's the least I can do to really show my appreciation.'

Henry considered her words for a moment and secretly hoped that it wasn't merely appreciation Rayne wanted to show him but to prolong the time they spent together. 'Thank you,' he heard himself agreeing. 'I'd like that.'

Dinner was a joyous affair, with everyone talking over the top of everyone else. Rayne seemed very comfortable with Jasmine's grandparents, as though she'd always known them. Well, she had told him that Jasmine's mother had been like a sister to her so he guessed that accounted for their close familiarity.

It had been a long time since he'd enjoyed such a relaxed family evening, and after the superb meal had been eaten and praised, he offered to help do the dishes.

'Oh, no. Get along with you,' Earlene stated. 'Jarvis and I can do them quite well enough. It's quality time we enjoy spending together, isn't it, darling?'

'Quite,' Jarvis answered. 'The only time of night when you don't get bothered by pesky children.' He wagged a finger at Rayne as he spoke. 'The girls always left us alone to do the dishes because they knew if they came near us, they'd be given a dish towel and instructed to help out.' He chuckled and Earlene joined in.

'Why don't you take Jazzy for a walk in the park before bed?' Earlene suggested. 'It's still fairly light out and it'll help her work off some of that excitement which is still buzzing around her.'

Rayne nodded. 'Good idea. Henry? Would you care to join us? After all, we never did get that walk through the park last week when we had dinner together.'

'True.' Henry stood. 'I'd love to.'

Jasmine, who had been watching this turn of events with delighted interest, clapped her hands.

'Go and get a coat,' Rayne instructed. 'It'll get chilly soon.'

Jasmine raced off to do as she had been bidden and soon Rayne found herself walking to the nearby park, holding Jasmine's hand, Henry on the other side of the girl.

'Swing me!' she begged, and waited for the two adults to swing her back and forth between them. As they crossed the road and went onto the bark-chipped area that surrounded the play equipment, Jasmine broke free and ran off, leaving the adults to follow at a more sedate pace.

'She's a gorgeous girl,' Henry told Rayne.

'Yes, she is. She continually surprises me and it only makes me love her all the more.'

There was a pause before Henry asked softly, 'What happened to her parents?'

'Car crash. Janey and Jarrod were at a work function in Melbourne. They were coming home at around one o'clock in the morning and…' Rayne sighed sadly. 'They never made it. Janey was killed instantly and Jarrod died at the hospital.'

'You haven't seen a hospital report?'

Rayne shook her head. 'What good would it do? It wouldn't bring either one of them back.'

'True. And you said you were like sisters?'

'Yes. Janey and I…' Rayne stopped speaking for a moment, forcing herself to remember with happiness rather than with sadness. She took a steadying breath.

'If it's too painful, Rayne, you don't have to tell me.' Henry could see it in her eyes, see the pain and bewilderment that always went hand in hand with grief.

'It's not that.' She forced a watery smile. 'I like talking about Janey.'

'Makes you feel closer?'

'Exactly. I guess you know what that's like.' She was thinking of what he'd told her about his wife.

'I do.'

'You don't talk about her much.'

Henry shrugged. 'Never sure exactly what to say.'

'Well, I'll talk and you can be totally bored with my memories.' She laughed half-heartedly and was surprised when Henry took her hand in his.

'I would never be bored, Rayne.'

'I know. Sorry. I was being…uh…flippant. Defence mechanism.' She glanced down at their hands, feeling the warmth, the compassion, the understanding, and realised they had a lot in common.

After another second he let her hand go and she put it into her pocket, sudden feeling cool. 'OK. Janey. Now, where to begin? I guess you could say that she was my saving grace. So were her parents.'

'I can see that you're close.'

'Very. My mother used to move around a lot, going from one house to the next. I never seemed to be in one place longer than a year.'

'Was it her job?'

'Ha.' The laugh was sarcastic and totally without humour. 'My mum didn't work. No, she kept falling in love with different men. She'd move in with them and drag me along with her. The relationships would be all brilliant and wonderful and the best thing that had ever happened to her, and then after about six months things would start to fall apart. They'd fight, they'd argue and then they'd break up and we'd move again.'

'What about your father?'

'What about him? He left Mum when I was about two years old, I think.'

'Look at me!' Jasmine called as she ran over to the slippery-dip and went down headfirst.

'Very clever. Be careful, though.' Rayne clapped, watching as Jasmine headed for the swings. 'She's so much like Janey.'

'In looks?'

'In looks. In personality. A daredevil. Janey was the one who always pushed me out of my comfort zone. I'd never have dared to go down a slippery-dip headfirst if Janey hadn't done it about six times over to prove to me that it was safe, that I wasn't going to get hurt.'

Henry chuckled. 'A cautious child, were you?'

'With my upbringing? Oh, yes. When I was about ten I started to think that if I did everything right, if I was the model child, then perhaps Mum would be happy, that she wouldn't fight with whoever was her current boyfriend and that he'd like us so much that we'd be able to stay.'

'It wasn't your fault.'

'I know that. Janey's parents helped me to understand that. They're as wonderful as their daughter was.' Rayne shook her head, watching Jasmine. 'I want to make sure that Jazzy's love of life, the one she inherited from her mother, is preserved, that she has a part of her parents within her for ever. I don't want to do anything to quash that.'

'I'm sure that's why Janey left her in your care.'

Rayne smiled. 'When Janey and Jarrod asked me to be their child's godmother…I…well, I cried. Janey and I are both only children.' She paused. '*Were* only children,' she corrected herself, and turned away, her eyes filling with tears. 'It's so amazingly difficult to talk about her in the past tense. It just seems...wrong.'

'I know.' He watched as she dabbed at the corners of her eyes with a handkerchief. 'Go on,' he urged softly. 'Sometimes it's good to relive happy memories, even if they make you cry.'

'OK. Well, Janey and I met in high school, became friends instantly and stayed that way. By some miracle, my mother's relationship at that time lasted a whole two years but when that ended and she told me we were moving to Sydney, I kicked up a stink. I'd been dragged around for too long and wasn't going to leave.' Rayne smiled and shook her head. 'I don't know where I was planning on living or how I'd have the money to survive. Fourteen-year-olds don't think like that. I just knew I wasn't going with her. That was when Janey's parents offered to let me stay with them. They called it boarding—which would ordinarily mean that my mother would pay them a weekly amount to cover my food and clothing and everything else. I was overjoyed at this arrangement and moved in. I was amazed that I could stay in one place, amazed that I could have a normal life with loving parents looking after me, treating me no different from the way they treated their own daughter.

'I discovered years later, when I was in medical school, that my mother hadn't paid them a cent. Jarvis and Earlene had paid for everything. They cared for me. They loved me. They gave me stability, and although I've tried for so long to pay them back, they've refused to accept anything. They only insisted that I make the best out of my life. I hope I haven't disappointed them.'

A lone tear slid down Rayne's cheek and she sniffed.

'No fear of that.' Henry's words were full of meaning as Rayne blew her nose and laughed.

'Look at me. I'm a mess.' She shook her head, a lock of hair coming loose from her band and falling across her face.

'No.' He gently tucked it behind her ear. 'Not a mess at all.' His hand lingered on her cheek, caressing it lightly, and Rayne gasped at the touch, her eyes meeting his. There was something between them, something new and exciting. He looked at her lips, watching them part to allow the pent-up air to escape. 'You're very beautiful,' he whispered, his tone filled with intimacy.

CHAPTER FIVE

RAYNE swallowed, unsure what to do or say. Her heart was pounding wildly against her ribs and her breathing was erratic. Henry made her feel so gentle, so nurtured, so tender, so undoubtedly feminine. Her insides had turned to mush and even as he removed his hand and stepped back, putting a bit of distance between them, Rayne still found it difficult to get control over her body.

'Rayne. Rayne!' Jasmine called out, laughing. Both adults turned to watch the child, who was on the swings, going high in the air and giggling loudly.

'Wow. You're so good at that,' Henry praised.

'Not too high, petal,' Rayne cautioned, her mind visualising all sorts of scenarios of the girl falling off at such a height.

'Spoken like a true mother,' Henry remarked with a smile before heading over to Jasmine. 'Would you like a push?'

'Yes. Push me. Push me. Higher, Henry.'

It was on the tip of Rayne's tongue to declare she didn't think that was a good idea when she realised that although Henry was pushing the swing, he was also controlling the height, and within a few seconds Jasmine was actually swinging lower than previously but still enjoying herself immensely.

He was so good with children and she began to wonder why. Did he have nieces or nephews? Had he had children but they, too, had died? She hoped that wasn't the case because it appeared that he'd already lost so much and, in doing so, had lost himself in the process.

Again she was struck with the realisation that she knew next to nothing about this man—nothing at all about the man who was turning her legs to jelly and tying her stomach in knots simply by gazing intently into her eyes or caressing her cheek.

When Jasmine had had enough of the swing, she grabbed hold of Henry's hand and dragged him towards the sandpit.

'It might be a bit cold,' Rayne suggested, but followed them over, very happy at seeing Jasmine behaving more like her normal self. Rayne had visited Janey and Jarrod at least every three months to spend time with them, even if it had only been for a weekend. Melbourne was only five hours—a day's drive on very good roads—from Deniliquin so whenever Rayne had had a few days off, to Janey's house she'd go.

During the past five months she'd scheduled some time away from her clinic so that she and Jasmine could spend time with Jarvis and Earlene, the four of them finding solace in each other as they'd grieved together.

'You're all we have left now,' Earlene had said on the last visit. 'You've always been like a daughter to us, Rayne. You know that, don't you? We love you as though you're our own flesh and blood, so don't you go thinking you have to face the future alone. Jarvis and I want to move to Deniliquin with you to help you raise Jasmine.'

Rayne had been stunned but had also realised she shouldn't have been surprised. They were the type of people who would do that, who'd change their life to help others. 'It won't be immediate but we plan to be there by Christmas and, of course, we'll be there for the festival. There's no way I'm missing that.'

And now they hadn't been here even one whole day and Rayne already felt as though a weight had been lifted from her shoulders. For the past few months Rayne had sat in the dark of her house at night while Jasmine had been sleeping and had pondered what on earth she was supposed to do. How was she supposed to raise a child on her own?

She knew she had the support of the town as well. That's what they did—supported each other—but there was only so much they could do. They couldn't help with the loneliness she felt at night. They couldn't help her need to hide her real self in a little room, too scared to take a chance on a relationship because she was terrified of ending up like her mother—never being able to really commit. Besides, what man would really want her? That was the question she'd asked herself time and time again and although there were quite a few men in the town who had shown an interest in her, she just hadn't been interested…not in a romantic light.

And now Henry had come her way. It was undeniable that there had been a mutual instant attraction between them but attractions could wane just as quickly as they started—once you got to know the person better. Of this she'd had years of proof, thanks to her mother.

'Earth to Rayne,' Henry called, and she smiled at him. 'Penny for them?'

'Hmm. They're worth more than a penny.'

'What's a penny?' Jasmine asked, and Henry quickly explained what a penny was and also the context in which he'd meant his comment. Jasmine's eyes widened. 'You can *buy* people's thoughts?'

Both adults laughed. 'No, sweetheart. It's just an expression, a saying,' Rayne said, running her hands down Jasmine's arms. 'Ooh. You're feeling quite cold. Here, put your coat on. It's time to get you home and settled into bed.'

'Aw, come on, Rayne. I'm not even tired,' Jasmine protested, yawning as she spoke.

Rayne bundled her into her coat and zipped it up. 'No. Not tired at all.' Her tone was full of loving disbelief.

'How about a shoulder ride?' Henry asked, standing up and brushing the sand off himself.

'Yay! My daddy used to give me them all the time,' she declared. 'I love shoulder rides.'

They walked back towards Rayne's house, Jasmine sitting on Henry's shoulders as though she were queen of all she surveyed. Rayne directed Henry a different way, taking them through the edge of the nature reserve.

'Wasn't sure if you'd managed to explore this part of town yet.'

'No. I haven't. Willard's kept me quite busy and, combined with the odd house call with you, I haven't had as much of a chance to explore as I'd hoped.'

Rayne sighed and spread her hands wide. 'Well you know what that means…you'll just have to stay longer.'

Henry looked over at her, their eyes clashing, his words deep. 'I might just do that.'

It was there again, that amazing connection they seemed to have, and this time Rayne forced herself to go with it, rather than backing away from it.

'Sounds like a good idea.'

'I could help you on your house calls, if you like.'

'I would like that very much. You could also help out at the hospital now and then if you wanted to. They'd be more than happy to accommodate a surgeon with your skills.'

'Hmm. Of course, both of these ways would be terrific in getting to know more people in the district.'

Rayne's smile increased. 'It would be the perfect opportunity. Everyone you've already met sings your praises.'

'That's promising. I could also help with the aftermath of the festival.'

'No one would say no to an extra pair of hands.' Both were silent for a moment and, apart from Jasmine singing softly to herself, the only other noises were those of the nocturnal animals slowly waking up. 'You fit in perfectly here,' Rayne said quietly, and Henry stopped walking for a moment to look at her.

'I do, don't I?' He nodded as though only just now realising it himself. He breathed in deeply. 'That's so odd because for quite a few years now I haven't felt as though I'd ever fit in anywhere again.'

'Hey,' Jasmine protested from atop her perch. 'Giddy up, horsy.'

'A thousand humble apologies, Your Majesty,' Henry said, and started walking again.

'It must have been difficult when your wife passed

away,' Rayne said after a moment. It wasn't until she'd said the words aloud that she wondered whether the subject of Henry's wife was a taboo one. He was silent for what seemed like ages but which in reality was only about a minute.

'It's always difficult when someone you're close to dies, as you well know.'

'Yes.' They walked on for a bit before Rayne ventured, 'I'm sorry, Henry. I wasn't trying to pry.'

'It's all right. Natalia just isn't a topic I discuss or really have had no need to discuss because until I came here, everyone around me knew the story of what happened.'

His words only piqued Rayne's interest further but she kept her mouth zipped. She'd meant what she'd said. She *hadn't* meant to pry and although she was highly curious about his story, he obviously wasn't ready to tell it. Not yet. She looked ahead of her, trying to think of a new topic, one that would put them back onto a more even footing, and noticed a little bump on the side of the road not far from the glow of the streetlamps, which had just come on.

'What's that?' She headed over to investigate. Henry hung back but was watching with interest as Rayne gasped. 'It's a baby possum.'

'Out this early?'

'It's hurt.' Rayne's heart went out to the little thing as she quickly scanned the area for the possum's mother. 'I can't see the mother. Can you?'

Henry and Jasmine looked around, helping her to look. 'There's nothing.'

'I can't see a mummy possum.' Jasmine shook her head for emphasis.

'I need something to pick it up with. Henry, you don't happen to have a handkerchief, do you? I've blubbered all over mine.'

'Actually, I do.' He took it from his pocket and handed it over. 'My mother always made me carry at least two clean handkerchiefs.'

'Good ol' mums and the habits they instil,' Rayne murmured, not wanting to contemplate the habits her own mother had passed on. She opened the handkerchief and very carefully picked up the baby possum. It squeaked at her and tried to bite but Rayne wasn't bothered in the slightest. 'Oh, honey.' She held it carefully and pointed up the street. 'There's a wildlife habitat rescue centre just up here, but I'm not sure if anyone's there.'

'Let me see. Let me see,' Jasmine was demanding, and Rayne peeled away the largest corner of the handkerchief so Jasmine could see the possum. 'He's bleeding.'

'Yes.'

'Let's get him help.' Henry headed off in the direction Rayne had pointed and when they arrived at the centre it was to find it in darkness. Rayne took out her cellphone, dialled a number and a moment later was telling Carmel what they'd found.

'She's coming right over,' Rayne reported after she'd finished the call. 'She doesn't live far away. Just around the corner.'

'I like Carmel,' Jasmine told Henry as he took her from his shoulders. 'She lets me come and see the animals she looks after. I helped her feed a joey once.' Jasmine's eyes were wide with excitement as she reported this news.

'Wow. I don't think I've ever seen a joey up close, let alone fed one.'

'Really?' Rayne was a little surprised. 'You've never seen a kangaroo up close?'

'Nope.'

'Never went to the zoo as a child?'

'Nope.'

'I thought you'd visited our wildlife park here?'

'Nope. I've walked past it but haven't actually had the time to go through it yet.'

Rayne and Jasmine looked at each other before Jasmine nodded emphatically. 'We need to edjumacate him, Rayne.'

'We most certainly do need to educate him. How about Friday after school?'

'What?' Henry looked between the two of them, both wearing identical smiles.

'We'll take you through the wildlife park here. You'll not only be able to see animals close up but you can feed them, too.'

'Actually, that sounds kind of cool.'

'It *really* is.' Jasmine nodded again.

Their conversation was cut short as a woman came running around the corner in their direction. Rayne looked down at the bundle in her hands. 'Help's coming,' she whispered. 'Hang in there, little one.'

Carmel quickly introduced herself to Henry before opening the centre and leading them inside.

'You're the local vet?' Henry asked as he surveyed the set-up. They'd come through a waiting area into a more medical environment. Carmel turned on a bright light before putting a filter over the lens.

'No. I'm the local wildlife officer,' she told him. 'But I *am* a trained vet if that puts your mind at rest.'

'Wildlife officers are like specialists,' Rayne informed him, and Henry watched in awe as Carmel took the little possum from Rayne and began to examine it, not at all bothered at the animal's reaction. She cooed and she whispered sweetly to it, much as Rayne had done, but this time the possum seemed to understand her.

'A real-life Dr Doolittle?' he asked Rayne softly.

Rayne nodded. 'She has a gift and she's using it.'

Carmel was able to pinpoint the problem and set to work. She cleaned the wound site and gave the possum an injection, all the while answering Jasmine's one hundred and one questions.

'What's that? What does that do? Is it going to be OK? Can I hold him? Can I help? Will that make him better?'

'It's an antibiotic and, yes, it will help to make him better.' When she was done, she put a little bandage on the possum before wrapping him in a warm towel and handing him back to Rayne. 'Want to keep him for a few nights?'

Jasmine's eyes almost bulged out of her head. 'Really? We get to keep him?'

'Look after him,' Rayne corrected her, and Carmel nodded in agreement before going to a cupboard and pulling out the smallest little milking bottle Henry had ever seen.

'Hey, I have a bottle like that at home but it's just a plastic one I got with my doll.'

'Well, this one is real and I'll show you how to feed the baby.'

'What are we going to call him?' Jasmine asked as she watched Carmel's actions, keen to learn.

Rayne thought for a moment. 'How about...Poss?'

Jasmine pondered this. 'I like the name Ethel, but Poss is good, too.'

'Ethel?' Henry raised his eyebrows. 'Where did Ethel come from?'

Jasmine shrugged. 'I don't know. I just like it.'

'Then Ethel the possum she is,' Carmel said. She gave them some further instructions, where to make Ethel's bed, how to keep her safe, what else to feed her, and soon they were headed away from the centre and back towards Rayne's house.

Jasmine had asked to go back up on Henry's shoulders, given that she wasn't allowed to actually carry Ethel home, but as they got near Rayne's house, Henry said softly, 'Check Jasmine.'

Rayne looked up to find the little girl almost slumped over Henry's head, her eyes struggling to stay open.

'Almost asleep. I guess it's been too much for her tonight, what with her grandparents arriving, going to the park and now being able to look after a possum.'

'Ethel,' Henry corrected.

'Apologies. Looking after Ethel,' Rayne repeated.

Henry carefully lifted Jasmine off his shoulders, shushing her quietly when she protested. He shifted her into his arms and within another moment she had her head on his shoulder and her arms about his neck. She sighed and her breathing settled.

They made an alluring picture—man and child. Rayne couldn't help but notice the way he held her protectively in his arms, and she realised there was a true bond forming between the two of them. Was this something she

should be worried about? After all, Henry wasn't a
resident of Deniliquin and one day he would leave. Then
again, she recalled their earlier conversation and wondered if he ever would.

They were walking across Rayne's front yard when
Henry said softly, 'You go and open the door, get her bed
ready and I'll carry her in.'

Rayne placed the wrapped, drowsy possum into a card-
board box then went to prepare Jasmine's bed. Once the child
was settled, Rayne went in search of the man who was slowly
becoming very important to her. As she walked through the
kitchen, she glanced at the whiteboard on her fridge, which
had a message from Earlene and Jarvis. She filled the kettle
and switched it on before heading into the lounge room.

Henry was standing next to her bookshelf, a framed
photograph in his hand. When he saw her, he didn't automatically put it back, as though he'd been caught red-
handed. Instead, he pointed with his free hand to the couple
depicted in the photograph.

'Jarrod and Janey?'

'Yes. That was taken about a month before they died.'
She pointed to another photograph of the four of them and
then one that included Jarvis and Earlene. The photograph
was next to a small red vase—empty of water—which held
the paper rose Henry had given her. Henry was secretly
pleased that the rose was in such an honoured place, among
the photographs of the people Rayne loved most.

'Uh…would you like a cup of tea? I've just put the
kettle on.'

'That sounds great.'

Rayne nodded, suddenly feeling a little aware that the

two of them were, for all intents and purposes, alone in the house. 'Jarvis and Earlene have just gone next door to say hello to my neighbours.'

Henry nodded at this information as he returned the photograph to its rightful place. He continued to look at the books on the shelf. 'You're widely read.'

'I like reading. Relaxes me.'

He smiled at her over his shoulder. 'Me, too.'

'Although since Jazzy came to live with me I have considerably less leisure time than previously, but I'm not complaining.'

'She's wonderful.'

'That she most certainly is.' Rayne's gaze flicked over him, taking in his relaxed posture, and the transformation from the man she'd met a week and a half ago was obvious. His hair was slightly mussed, his shirt was a little unkempt and wrinkled from carrying Jasmine, and his dark denim jeans were starting to get a lived-in look to them. She knew he'd wear suits to the Sydney hospital, it would be expected of him, yet if he were to work here in Deniliquin, that wouldn't be the case at all. People out here didn't tend to go for appearances, they went on genuine feelings, and Henry was proving to have those in abundance.

'What?' he asked, and she realised she'd been caught staring.

'Um...' She smiled shyly and shrugged. 'I was just thinking how much more relaxed you are.'

'I feel it.'

'I mean even since I met you. The stress and worry have almost disappeared from your face.'

He raised an eyebrow. 'Almost?'

She smiled. 'Deni isn't finished with you yet.'

'So you've pointed out before.'

'It's true. This place has a natural healing quality.'

'Seems to have worked for you and Jasmine.'

'I guess so.'

'No, Rayne, I mean *really* worked. That little girl has been through the wringer—losing both parents, becoming an orphan. I know she's only five and that children bounce back, especially when they have people who honestly love them stepping up to fill the void, but what's happened to her is still *huge*.'

'Yes. And I'm not under the misapprehension that she's over it. As she gets older, she'll understand more, will start to process what happened. There's still a lot of healing to be done.'

'So you'll be staying in Deniliquin?'

'Yes. It's my home.'

'And what about surgery?'

Rayne sighed. 'That's another dream. Perhaps for another day.'

'You don't deny you love it?'

'Not at all. As far as work goes, it would be highly rewarding but so is being a GP. That said, Jasmine is far more important than anything else.'

'I totally agree, which only makes me admire you even more, Rayne Hudson.' He shifted and raked a hand through his hair. 'You've had motherhood thrust on you overnight and you've stepped up to the plate. That's a rare quality in a person.'

'I've had help and when Jarvis and Earlene move permanently to Deni, I'll have even more.'

'You'll form a family unit.'

'Yes.' Rayne was watching him carefully. He seemed on the brink of saying something, something she could see was causing a conflict within him. She heard the kettle automatically switch itself off but instantly discarded the thought of making tea. Not now. Not when Henry was about to open up to her.

'A family.' The words were spoken softly. 'Something else that was taken away from me.'

Her heart ached for him and when he lifted his eyes to meet hers, they were filled with repressed pain.

'When my wife...' He cleared his throat. 'When Natalia had the accident, she was six months pregnant.'

Rayne gasped and covered her mouth with her hand before shaking her head. 'Oh, Henry.'

'They delivered the baby—emergency C-section. A little boy. I named him Tucker.' He shook his head, a small sad smile touching his lips. 'I hated the name. Can you believe that? Yet it was the name Natalia really wanted if we had a boy.' He exhaled harshly. 'We'd argued about it the night before the crash.' He shook his head again, the smile gone. 'Stupid.'

Rayne didn't know what to say but she felt his pain. Deeply.

'Tucker had emergency surgery to stop internal bleeding and for a while there it looked as though he'd pull through.' His voice was dry, raspy. 'He died a week later.'

A tear slid down Rayne's cheek and Henry reached out to tenderly wipe it away.

'My family was taken from me, Rayne. Piece by piece. And there was nothing I could do.'

CHAPTER SIX

RAYNE put down the phone and quickly wrote something in Billie's notes before looking at her patient. 'The pathology results have just come in and I'm pleased to say the test was negative. You do not have glandular fever.'

Billie heaved a huge sigh of relief. 'You have no idea how good that is. I was very worried.'

'You and me both.' Rayne wrote out a script and handed it to her patient. 'Here you go. This should help with the sore throat and I can highly recommend this herbal tea. It does wonders for sore throats, although it tastes disgusting. Drink it with lots of honey. Mae has some in the health-food shop.' Rayne's phone began to ring again and Billie said goodbye as Rayne picked up the receiver.

'Dr Hudson.'

'Rayne.'

There was no mistaking that deep, resonating voice. It was the one she'd started dreaming about, the one she'd longed to hear, and it belonged to the man she'd been quite worried about since he'd abruptly left two nights ago. 'Henry.' Why was he calling her? Was he sick? Worried? Had there been an accident? She knew he was still helping out on Willard's crew. Did he need her help in some way? 'Everything all right?'

'Yes. Er…I'm sorry to disturb you at work but Willard mentioned you were headed out to Donna's place this afternoon to check on little DT and I was wondering if you wouldn't mind some company.'

The tingles, which usually started in her stomach before spreading to the rest of her body, flooded her instantly.

'If that's OK. I don't want to intrude.'

'Uh…no. That's fine. I'll be finished consulting here in about an hour, then I was going to grab a bite of lunch before heading out on my house calls. Donna's last on the list. Is that all right?'

'Sure. Sounds good. I'm heading over to see how Brian's doing soon so I'll be able to give you an update when I see you.'

'OK. Looking forward to it.' She went to ring off but had the feeling there was more he wanted to say so she waited with mounting expectation.

'Rayne. I've, um…had a thought.'

'Really? Just one?' Rayne couldn't help teasing and she heard Henry chuckle. She breathed a mental sigh of relief. She'd been quite worried about him.

'Why don't we have lunch together?'

'Oh.' She was surprised by the invitation. 'Uh…all right. That would be lovely.'

'Really?'

'Sure. Where? I can't promise I'll be on time.'

'That's fine. I understand completely.'

'Of course you do.' She closed her eyes and hit herself on the head. 'Well, how do you want to play this?'

'Why don't I call by for you in about an hour and wait until you're done?'

'You'll wait in the waiting room?'

'That's what they're for, Rayne.' It was obviously his turn to tease her.

'I guess it is. All right. It's a date. I'll see you then.'

'Date?' Henry asked his reflection after he'd hung up the phone. It had been absolutely years since he'd had a date. In fact, the last person he'd dated had been his wife…well, obviously, *before* she had been his wife. Henry lay back on the bed and hooked his hands behind his head, recalling how he'd met Natalia at university. She hadn't liked him at first, calling him obnoxious, but she'd later revealed that she'd been smitten since the moment they'd met but hadn't wanted to let him know it.

And then she'd been taken from him. At first not in a physical sense but mentally. He'd known that even if she'd come out of the coma, there would have been significant brain damage…but she hadn't. His life with her was over. He'd accepted that over a year ago and these past six months since her death had seen him hibernate inside his cave, trying to figure out how to cope with his new life.

Was it too soon to start dating?

He shook his head and stood, crossing to the bathroom to take a shower and get ready. He'd already been out with Willard that morning and the scent of sawdust might not be all that appealing to Rayne.

He smiled when he thought about her, about the woman who was so dynamic, so vivacious, yet he could still see the questions and sadness behind her eyes. She'd come to

Deniliquin to heal herself and she had, but the true sadness hadn't disappeared. Every time she spoke of her childhood, of her mother and now about Jasmine's mother, Janey, the sadness was there. Rayne was still broken and the overwhelming urge to help her was too much for him to continue fighting it.

He wanted to see her, to be with her, to listen to her talk, to hear her laugh. He liked spending time with Rayne and he didn't care what anyone else thought—he was going to date her.

Rayne found it nigh on impossible to concentrate properly for the rest of the morning, glancing at the clock and then her remaining patient list and then back to the clock again, all the time wondering whether Henry was out there, sitting in the waiting room.

Her first clue came when Margy Innes waddled into her consulting room, fanning her face.

'Woo-ee, Rayne. That is one gorgeous man ya got out there, hon. Snap him up. This one's a keeper.'

'Henry?'

'Of course. Who else do ya think I'd be talking about?' She rubbed her belly, caressing the child inside. 'There's a shortage of good-lookin' fellas out here. Gotta snap up the good ones while you can.'

'Just like you did.'

'Yep. My Josh is one of the better ones, I'll give ya that.'

'So how have you been feeling? No swelling in the slightly higher temperatures we've been enjoying?'

'Nah. This isn't hot, hon. Not even thirty degrees outside. I'll be fine.'

'I'm sure you will be but let's get your check-up under way.' Rayne looked at the clock again.

'Ah…pining to see him. That's always a good sign. I can go and come back another day. Don't want to stand in the way of true love.'

Rayne smiled, brushing Margy's words away. True love? No. Impossible. As far as Rayne was concerned, it didn't exist. Well…it *did* but for people like Earlene and Jarvis, Janey and Jarrod or Donna and Janic. Not for her. She had her mother's genes and from the few relationships she'd had in the past, true love most certainly wasn't on the menu.

When the check-up was finished, Rayne walked Margy out into the waiting room to find Henry chatting with the receptionist. Thankfully, there appeared to be no other patients waiting to see her, which meant she was finished.

'Won't be a moment. I'll just get my things.'

'Take your time,' he called as she headed back into her consulting room. Rayne closed the door and quickly checked she had the files and medications she'd need for the house calls. When she'd done that, she crossed to the mirror to check her reflection and nearly squeaked with dismay. Her hair was all messy, her ponytail all loose and floppy and her face was as pale as though she'd just seen a ghost. Why hadn't she thought to check her reflection before going out just now?

Quickly, she set to work, finger-combing her hair and searching through her bag looking for a lipstick or lipgloss. She couldn't find anything and made a mental note to put some make-up in her bag from then on. Instead, she bit her lips and pinched her cheeks to give them a bit more colour.

'That's the best you can do,' she told her reflection, then rolled her eyes and shook her head, unable to believe the tizz Henry had her in. He'd already seen her while she'd been delivering a baby; dressed in theatre scrubs with theatre mask and hat on; walking around the town bribing people with cupcakes! What did it matter how she looked?

But for the first time in a long time Rayne *wanted* to look nice for someone…and that someone was Henry.

This time, Henry drove. Not in her ute but in his highly comfortable and luxurious Jaguar.

'You don't mind your car getting a little dirty?'

'It's a car, Rayne.'

She raised her eyebrows at that. 'Not a big revhead, like most men?'

He laughed. 'Well, I appreciate the car, if that's what you mean, but the roads we'll be going on aren't too bad. Correct?'

She smiled. 'Too late now if they are.' They were headed away from town and curiosity started getting the better of her. 'So…where are we going for lunch?' She'd half expected him to take her to one of the numerous cafés around town but it appeared he had plans of another kind.

'Ah…somewhere special.'

'But you're not going to tell me?'

'Correct. Not much further to go.'

'You seem to know your way around.'

'Actually, Willard told me about this place and gave me directions.'

'Willard?'

'Problem?'

'No. No. It just means the whole town will know we've gone off to have a secret rendezvous lunch together.'

'They already have us matched. I heard Gladys talking to the minister the other day about reserving a date for us to come and see him for pre-marriage counselling.'

'She didn't!' Rayne was horrified but Henry only laughed. 'Oh, I'm so sorry.'

'For what?' He looked over at her for a moment. 'It's fine, Rayne. I'm used to being talked about.'

'At the hospital?'

'Yes.'

'Sure, but not right in front of your face and *not* about such a topic as *that*.'

'No.' He chuckled. 'The gossip around the hospital was more centred on the "poor Henry" aspect.'

Rayne shook her head. 'I hate that.'

'The pity party attitude?'

'Exactly.'

'So do I.'

'Is that why you left?'

'Taken a sabbatical, you mean.'

'No, I mean left.' She shifted in her seat, adjusting the seat belt so she could look at him a little better. 'You may have officially applied for leave but in your mind you were leaving.'

'Are you accusing me of running away?'

She pondered that for a moment. 'Sort of but not quite.'

'Well, I'm glad that's clear.' He chuckled. It was good to talk to her, to exchange banter with her, to laugh with her. He breathed in, her scent winding itself around him…and he liked it.

'You can hardly run away from yourself, Henry.'

'Good point.' They were almost at Conargo now and he

slowed the car, indicating a left turn, but all Rayne could see on the left was a wide-open field. Her curiosity was definitely piqued.

'So…what else makes you think I've left my job at the hospital?'

'For a start, the sentence you've just uttered because I never said you'd actually left *your job* but perhaps mentally you have. Since you arrived in town—'

'Almost two weeks ago,' he interjected.

'Almost two weeks ago,' she acknowledged, then continued. 'You've changed. You smile more. Your stride is less hurried and far more casual.'

'My stride?' She'd been watching him walk? The knowledge pleased him because it meant that whatever this thing was between them, it was mutual. It was certainly more than friendship, even though neither of them had said that out loud—yet.

'Sure. When you first arrived you were a little wary of the way people were accepting you and now you just accept them right back, taking them at face value. Plus you willingly volunteered for Willard's crew! Usually he's conning and bribing people to sign up.'

'It's for a good cause and I must say it also helps to build the excitement for the actual festival next week. I'm totally pumped.'

'And that's another thing. Even your vocabulary is more relaxed. "Totally pumped"?' She laughed. 'Jazzy says that.'

Henry gave her a quirky smile. 'Where do you think I got it from? In fact, very remiss of me—how is Miss Jasmine today?'

'Probably going to be a little peeved when she discovers we've had lunch together, but apart from that she's no doubt enjoying a class party for the last day of term. She had poor Earlene up bright and early this morning making little cakes for her to take to school today.'

'I'll bet Earlene loved every minute of it. And what about Ethel? How is Ethel the possum faring?'

'She'd doing quite nicely. We've made a home for her in an old fleece-lined boot, which is nice and warm inside. This morning she actually let us hold her and feed her at the same time. Before that, we had to just put little pieces of apple on the floor and she'd pick them up and run back to her nice warm home and munch away. Jarvis has taken so many photographs.'

'Sounds as though you're all doting on her.'

'We are.' Rayne sighed. 'I'm not sure how we're supposed to give her back once she's better.'

'Jasmine *does* know she can't keep Ethel, right?' Henry had no idea how practical the five-year-old was but from his limited experience of five-year-olds they tended to bond with toys and animals and people rather quickly.

'Oh, she knows. She calls herself Ethel's aunty, not her mother, because she has to go back to the wildlife park.'

'And the fact that you were able to hold Ethel while she ate? Is that not… Oh, I don't know…domesticating her a little?'

Rayne smiled. 'Perhaps, but she'll only be going back to the wildlife park and most of the animals there are used to humans…well, as used to humans as they can be.'

'Well, I sincerely hope everything turns out for the best on that front.'

'Thanks. Me, too.'

Henry was slowing the car down now and swinging onto a dirt car park.

'Where are we?'

'You've never been here before?'

'No. Not that I can remember, at any rate.'

'Good.' He stopped the car and turned the key to switch the engine off.

'Good?'

'Yes. I was hoping to give you a new experience, just as you've given me plenty of new ones during my time in your town. Now, out you get.'

'Are we having bush tucker?' Rayne looked at her surroundings. The ground was mostly flat and surrounded by quite a few gumtrees. Scrubland, some would call it, but it had a natural beauty all of its own that she loved. She could hear birds chirping and for a moment caught a glimpse of colour as one flew across the small clearing.

'Don't tell me Willard give you a quick lesson in how to find yams and roast a goanna over a spit?' Rayne stretched her legs and walked around the area, looking interested. There was a small path leading around a bend and she realised they were going on a little walk. Deciding to not ask questions and simply enjoy it, she turned to look at Henry, now not surprised to find him carrying a picnic basket, a blanket slung over his arm.

'Shall we?' Henry held out his hand to her and Rayne willingly took it, delighted that he'd offered and enjoying the thrill of having his warm skin against hers. They followed the path but didn't have to follow it for long before they came to a slightly bigger clearing and Rayne gasped at the view before her. A little billabong, unfortu-

nately with hardly any water in it but still highly pictur-
esque, was spread in front of them as though put there just
for this moment. There were rocks around the billabong
and the backdrop featured beautiful eucalyptus trees with
their unique shade of green visible all year around.

'Henry. It's beautiful here.'

Henry, too, was taking in the scenery. 'Yes, it is. Willard
was right.'

'I'm glad you listened to him.' She turned to smile at him
and Henry was struck for a moment by the natural beauty
that radiated from her. It was even better than the setting
they were in and he realised he was a lucky man to be able
to share this moment with her. Wonderful view, wonderful woman and, if Darren's cupcakes were anything to go
on, a basket full of good food, made by Darren himself.

Henry spread the blanket and they were soon enjoying
themselves immensely. He gave her a highly positive
update on Brian's condition and she was glad to hear he
was responding well to treatment.

'So…tell me about yourself,' she said as she lay back,
her stomach full, and shielded her eyes from the sun.

'Why? That's sort of a boring topic.'

'I beg to differ. Come on.'

'You already know a lot about me.'

'I know you're a brilliant surgeon.'

'Thank you.'

'That you're a widower. That you've lost a child.' Her
words were soft and filled with compassion. 'I know that
you're looking for something. Do you know what it is?'

Henry thought about it for a few seconds and Rayne
didn't push him for an answer.

'Peace.'

'That's a good place to start. Once you have some peace you can begin to think clearly.'

'Are you looking for peace, too?'

'Find me someone who isn't.' She smiled as she spoke and Henry shifted, lying down next to her, their hands touching slightly.

'I'm coming to the conclusion,' he said after a while, 'that life isn't made up the way I thought it was.'

'And how's that?' she asked.

'With little snatches of perfect memories.'

'Yes.'

He could hear the understanding in that one little word. Here was a woman who seemed to somehow *know* him and though it was hard to believe, it was true.

'Snatches of perfect memories,' she repeated. 'I really like that, Henry, and it's so true. Sometimes I sit outside at night when Jazzy's asleep and think about the times I had with Janey. Some when we were kids, some after she met Jarrod, some after Jasmine was born. I can even recall a few nice snatches of memories with my mother—albeit few and far between all of the bad ones, but there *are* good ones.'

'Isn't it funny how when someone first dies, all you can think of is all the things you'd wished you'd said to them? After that, you regret all of the horrible things you might have said and then…' Henry linked his fingers with hers and held her hand tightly. 'And then you can start to remember the good times, those perfect little memories, and you can put them in a box and take them out when you need them.'

'Life is like that.' Rayne turned her head to look at him. 'You're quite the philosopher, Dr Harcourt.'

Henry smiled as he levered himself up onto his elbow and looked down at her, still holding her hand. 'I appear to be today.'

And in that moment, as they looked at each other, Rayne knew they were both making another perfect memory. They were getting to know each other but it didn't have anything to do with their pasts. Of course their pasts were important. After all, they'd sculpted them into the people they were today, but they were getting to know each other as they were now. It was like moving to a new world and starting afresh.

'If you want to know about me, Rayne, I'll tell you.' Then before she could say a word, he continued. 'I'm a conservative man by nature. I was raised by conservative parents, went to good schools, never wanted for anything. I met the woman I thought I'd spend the rest of my life with and then had not only her but my child taken from me. I never thought I'd heal. I never thought I'd be able to face reality again so I locked myself away. For the two years Natalia was in the coma I operated on autopilot, losing a touch of hope with each new dawning day.

'I immersed myself in work and shunned almost all social contact. I was as polite as I'd been raised to be, I'd never intentionally be rude to anyone but all of my emotions were neatly locked away and that's where I'd planned to leave them.'

Rayne sighed. 'It must have been such a terrible time for you. I may not have had the best upbringing but good things always came out of the bad. That's one thing Earlene and Jarvis have helped me to realise. Out of the badness of my upbringing, I became part of Janey's family. Out of

Janey's death, I became Jasmine's mother.' Rayne paused and swallowed, her breathing becoming shallow and her mouth going dry as she dared to say what she was about to say. A moment of indecision was pushed aside because she knew…she just *knew* she had to say the words out loud. 'And because of coming to Deniliquin, I met you.'

'You have.' Henry squeezed her hand, then impulsively brought it to his lips and kissed it, his breath fanning over her skin, warming her through and through. 'I never thought I'd find a friend again—a *real* friend—but you've proved they do exist and I can't thank you enough, Rayne.'

'I get a lot out of it, too.'

Henry chuckled and the sound washed over her. 'It doesn't feel like you do from where I'm standing. I feel as though you're helping me but I'm not doing all that much for you.'

'You're restoring my faith in men.'

'Wow.' His eyes widened at this admission. 'I had no idea I was doing such a grand and noble thing.'

'Well, you are.'

'What…if I may be so bold as to ask…destroyed your faith in men?'

Rayne paused, knowing where it had all started but wondering if she had the courage to say it out loud. 'From the different men my mother dated, I guess.'

Henry could see the wall she'd obviously built around herself for protection slip into place. She wasn't ready and he respected that more than she could know. He smiled down at her, seeing the worry on her face, seeing the concern, and wanting to instantly remove it. He patted her hand. 'Do you think if we go for a little walk, we'll get lost?'

Rayne sat up, disengaging her hand from his. 'You're

not going to ask me anything else? You can. You can pry because I pried into your life and you told me.'

Henry packed away the rest of the food into the basket before standing and holding his hand out to her yet again. 'I guess I was ready to talk. I didn't realise it until the moment came on me, but it's out now and I feel much better for it. However, I can see that you're still not quite ready, not quite there, and that's fine, Rayne. We have all the time in the world.'

'We have house calls very soon.' She went to check her watch but he snatched her hand so she couldn't see the time.

'That's not what I meant and you know it. Come.' He gently pulled her to her feet. 'Let me continue to restore your faith in men. There really is plenty of time.'

And in that moment he fully realised the truth of his words. There was time. There was now time in his life to really get to know someone special, and that someone special was Rayne.

CHAPTER SEVEN

THEY went for a walk around half of the billabong, pointing out different things to each other and just generally exploring. Rayne could feel her stresses in life starting to ease and she had Henry to thank for that. He seemed to know just what she needed. It was uncanny.

She also found it hard to concentrate, especially when he was so near, so close. His masculine scent made her feel light-headed. Or was it his touch, the way he held her hand with such tenderness and care, as though she were the most precious thing in the world?

When they arrived back at the car, Rayne helped him put the blanket and basket into the boot then turned to thank him.

'I really needed this. It's been great.'

'All work and no play can make—' He stopped. 'Actually, that saying doesn't really apply here because even if you did work and didn't play, it still wouldn't make you a very dull person. Usually it applies to *me* but not to you.'

'Oh, I don't know about that. I'd hardly classify myself as the life and soul of the party.'

'Two peas in a pod, eh?' Before she could reply he walked around and opened the car door for her. 'We'd best get these house calls under way before the patients start calling up to see where their doctor has got to.'

'True.' Rayne watched as he came round the car before climbing in beside her. She liked the way he walked, the way he moved, the way he smelt, the way he made her feel when he looked at her the way he'd done when they'd been lying on the blanket. It had been a totally romantic picnic and she hadn't even realised until now. Was Henry trying to tell her something?

They drove out to the first patient's place with Henry's car handling the dirt roads beautifully. 'I guess it helps that the car has four-wheel drive, although I've never had to use it until now.'

'You'll need to clean it as well. All this dust will make it filthy.'

'It'll make me look like a local, though.'

'True. Very true.' They pulled up outside Mrs Eddington's house and Rayne collected her medical bag. 'This shouldn't be too long. Just need to change a dressing. June has a bad ulcer on her leg,' she explained as she opened the front door and walked right in. 'Hello?' she called, and Henry wondered whether he'd ever get used to seeing her do that—just walking in and making herself at home.

'Is that you, Rayne?' came a female voice. 'I'm in the bedroom at the back. Watch out for the washing baskets and don't trip over the books. They're for the jumble sale at the festival, if you wouldn't mind taking them back to town for me.' June continued talking as Rayne made her way through the house towards the bedroom.

'I've brought another doctor, June,' Rayne announced from the doorway, now that she could get a word in edgeways. 'Dr Henry Harcourt.'

'Ooh, is this that handsome doctor from Sydney Gladys has been telling me about? Well, come on, then, boy. Into the room. Let me look at you.'

Henry raised his eyebrows at this…unique welcome and looked at Rayne, who sidestepped out of the way and swept her arm out to indicate he should pass in front of her.

'Ooh, you are a looker. This one's good, Rayne. See if we can keep him.'

'He'll be for sale at the festival, June, so if you're so inclined you can purchase him yourself.'

'What?' Henry turned to look at her and both women laughed.

'She's just pullin' your leg, matey. Don't go sweatin' it.'

'Oh. OK. Right. Outback humour. I'll get there one day.'

Again, it was another positive comment, as though Henry was considering actually staying out here. Rayne pushed the hope aside and concentrated on changing June's dressing while Henry kept her entertained.

'The district nurse comes most days but Rayne likes to check up on me and make sure things are going along swimmingly, don't ya, darl'?'

'Yes, I do, and things most certainly are going along swimmingly. Two more weeks and things should be back to normal.'

'Ah. That's good news.'

'Will you be at the festival?' Henry asked.

'Try and keep me away. Rayne's already organised a

wheelchair for me, haven't ya, darl'? So there's no reason for me not to be there. But if you wouldn't mind taking those books, I'd much appreciate it.'

'No problem.' Rayne had taken off her gloves and packed up her bag. 'Come on, Henry. Let's go load up the car. See you next week, June.'

'Byebye, deary.' She waved to Rayne then smiled at Henry. 'I'll see you at the festival, right?'

'I'm sure there's a good possibility of that. Until then, Mrs Eddington.' And he made a little bow.

'Ooh, a charmer and a looker. Definitely a good catch. And call me June!'

Rayne couldn't help but smile as they made their way to the next house call, the books safely stowed in the boot of Henry's car. By the time they were on their way to Donna's place, Henry's boot was almost full with other bits and pieces people wanted Rayne to deliver back to town.

'You didn't mention you'd also be a courier service today,' Henry grumbled good-naturedly as he followed her directions to Donna's place.

'I didn't know.'

'Really?'

'Well…' she added sheepishly. 'I wasn't sure. It happened last year but that wasn't to say it was going to happen this year.'

'You're a soft touch, Dr Hudson.' Henry glanced over at her, a sweet smile on his face and one that melted Rayne's bones. Why did he have to be so incredibly good-looking and why did he have to have such an effect on her?

When they arrived at Donna's it was to find JJ and CC running around in the front garden…or front dirt, due to the drought, laughing and playing happily. Or they were until JJ knocked CC's hat off.

'Stop it!' she yelled at her big brother. 'Dat's not funny. Mummy says hats on or no playing.'

'Hi, kids,' Rayne said as she walked towards them. They both squealed with delight and ran towards her at full pelt. A moment later it was impossible for her to walk as she had a child wrapped around each leg, her hands on their heads. 'Hey, it's good to see you, too.'

They both looked up and started talking at once and somehow she was able to follow the conversation, answering their questions and asking her own. Henry watched the entire scene, totally amazed at how brilliant this woman was with children. In fact, she appeared to be brilliant with everyone she met. She really was suited to the outback GP job but she'd also shown amazing competence and aptitude in Theatre.

'Quite a woman,' he murmured softly to himself as he followed her into the house. He walked right in, not bothering to knock and trying not to feel strange about it. Donna was in the kitchen. Little DT was in a baby sling strapped to her mother.

'Ah, there he is. My knight in shining armour.' Donna crossed to his side then leaned up and gave him a kiss on the cheek, being careful not to squash DT.

'Aw, look.' Rayne pointed to Henry. 'You've made him blush.'

'I do not blush,' he declared, fixing Rayne with a firm stare, but his words and actions only made both women chuckle.

'Take a load off, Henry. I've just put the kettle on.' Donna busied herself in the kitchen, fixing a plate of homemade biscuits and putting it in the centre of the big wooden country table. 'Janic made the table,' she told him proudly. 'In fact, he made most of the furniture you see around the place.'

Henry was impressed. 'Quite the handyman.'

'Oh, yes. My Janic is a genius when it comes to working with wood. Could have been a sculptor but his love for the land is greater than that of sitting in a studio, whittling away.'

'He's out at the moment?' Henry asked.

'Yes.' The baby stirred a little and Donna patted the sling, shushing DT softly. There was a loud crash from outside and she rolled her eyes before heading to the door to see what was going on.

'I can't believe she's up and about like this.' Henry was amazed.

'She's from hardy stock is Donna. She can handle managing this farm, four children under the age of five and helping her husband whenever he needs it. Personally, I have no idea how she does it but she does and therefore serves as an inspiration to me.'

'Why? You're doing a terrific job of juggling the different aspects of your life.'

Rayne smiled. 'It's nice of you to say so but at the moment I feel like a duck on a pond. All calm and controlled on the surface but beneath…'

'Your feet are paddling like crazy.'

'Yes.'

'In that case, you're doing an excellent job of staying afloat.'

'Thank you.'

When Donna returned, she sat down for whole two

seconds before JR woke up from his afternoon nap. Finally, she was able to sit down and enjoy her cup of lukewarm tea and chat with both doctors.

'Let's get your check-up out of the way,' Rayne said, as she stood. Donna agreed and tenderly took little DT from the sling and held her out to Henry. Rayne watched an expression of surprise flit across his face for a moment before he took the baby and held her close. DT settled in his arms, snuggled down and continued to sleep.

'Fourth children are always so easygoing,' Donna said. 'I should know. I am one!' With that, Henry was left, literally, holding the baby.

It was the first time he'd held a baby since his son and all of the old yearnings, the old desires to settle down with a wonderful woman and have a family of his own came rushing to the fore. A picture of himself and Rayne, walking along the shore of the Edward River, a brood of their own about them, as well as Jasmine, came to mind. The image was so vivid he felt he could almost reach out and touch it.

'I never knew I was a daydreamer,' he whispered softly to DT as he pressed a kiss to her soft, downy head. 'Apparently, I am.'

As they drove back into Deniliquin, Rayne noted that Henry was rather quiet. Pensive. She hoped there was nothing wrong, that *she* hadn't done anything wrong, but as she thought back over the near-perfect afternoon they'd shared, she really couldn't put her finger on anything.

When he pulled up outside her house, she turned to him. 'Would you like to come in for dinner?'

'I'm not expected,' he said.

'I doubt anyone's going to mind. Besides, Jazzy would love to see you. Hey, and aren't we supposed to have our wildlife tour? Get you to pat a kangaroo? We can make it a nocturnal one if you like.'

'Uh…sure. Are you sure Earlene and Jarvis won't mind me gatecrashing for dinner again? I hate to intrude on their limited time with the two of you.'

Rayne waved his words away. 'They won't mind at all.'

'If you're sure,' he checked again, and when she nodded, he gave in. He wanted to continue to be in her presence, to just *be* there to see her interact with the family she'd pulled around her.

As they walked into the house, Rayne said quickly, 'Oh, and Jasmine wants you to show her how to make the paper rose. She's quite taken with it. In fact, she's commandeered mine and put it in her bedroom so she can look at it as she falls asleep.'

'Oh. OK, then.' He'd had no idea such a simple little thing as folding a piece of paper could have such a dramatic effect on them. He recalled Rayne's reaction when he'd presented it to her and now Jasmine's. Did it mean something? He pushed the thought aside as Jasmine came running towards him, her arms wide.

'Henry! You're here!' He scooped her up and hugged her close, pleased with her welcome.

'There you two are,' Earlene said cheerfully. 'Dinner's almost ready. Go and wash your hands, please.'

Henry glanced at Rayne and she shrugged. 'Apparently you were expected for dinner.' They did as they were told and then sat around Rayne's table, all squashed in a little bit because of its small size.

'You need to get Janic to build you a new dining-room table,' Henry quipped, and she smiled.

'Not a bad idea,' Earlene said as she began to clear the dishes away. 'With Jarvis and I planning to move here soon, we're going to be having more family dinners, Rayne.'

'True. I'll ask Janic after the festival,' she promised.

'When are you planning to move here?' Henry asked Jarvis.

'In the next month or so. We'll no doubt buy a place while we're here, or at least get a good look at what's available. It's a good financial investment, too. A place like Deni.'

'Hmm.' Henry nodded and Rayne saw that same thoughtful expression he'd had when they'd been driving home. After dinner, Henry patiently taught Jasmine how to make the origami rose and when she finally triumphed, she brought it over to Rayne for her inspection.

'That's fantastic, darling.' Even though the folding wasn't as precise as Henry's, she'd certainly done a very good job.

Next they collected their coats and walked the short distance to the wildlife park, Rayne taking photographs of Henry as he fed and patted his first kangaroo. Jasmine enjoyed herself immensely and when the sun had gone down, they spotted a few of the nocturnal animals who were coming out to feed.

When they returned to Rayne's house, Jasmine sitting on Henry's shoulders once more, the little girl showed Henry the habitat they'd made for Ethel the possum and how to feed her. Again Rayne took photographs, secretly delighted with the fact that she had the excuse to capture some of those special memories they were making together.

When Jasmine began yawning, Henry took that as his

cue to leave and thanked Earlene for the meal. Naturally, she waved his thanks away.

'Come on, pumpkin,' Jarvis said as he picked Jasmine up. 'Time to get ready for bed. Say good night to Henry.'

Jasmine did as she was told and went with her grandpa to brush her teeth.

'I'll be in to tuck you in soon,' Rayne called. 'I'll just walk Henry to his car.'

'What am I supposed to do with all the stuff in my boot?' he asked as they walked outside.

'Give it to Willard in the morning. He'll know what to do with it.'

'Right-o.'

Rayne smiled at the expression.

'What?'

'You're really starting to sound as though you belong here, Henry.'

He breathed in deeply. 'I do.' Then he slowly shook his head. 'I don't know what it is, Rayne. The air, the people, the atmosphere, the fact that no one knows me, that they just accept me. I don't know what it is but I feel like...*me* here.'

'And you didn't know who *me* was before?'

'Exactly.'

She nodded. 'That's how I felt when I first moved here.'

'It's a great place to live.'

'And work,' she offered.

'Here.' He held out the paper rose he'd made that evening while he'd been teaching Jasmine. 'This is for you, just in case you don't get the original one back.'

Rayne took the paper rose from him then looked up,

watched him intently for a moment, knowing if she stood there for too long she was in grave danger of becoming hypnotised by those amazing dark eyes. They were enticing her, drawing her in, making her want to throw caution and reason to the wind and explore anything and everything he was offering.

The chemistry was there, and it was becoming more potent the longer they stood, simply staring at each other. It was as though their souls were calling out, wanting to cling to each other in the hope that somehow, somewhere along the line, sense would be made from their lives.

When he spoke, his voice was deep and sensual. 'We may not know much about each other, Rayne, but right now that doesn't mean a thing. You've lived your life doing the right thing, for Janey, for her parents, for your mother and now for Jasmine. I know how that feels.' When she looked at him, she saw acceptance in his eyes.

Henry reached out and touched his fingers to hers. 'We have something between us. Something neither of us expected.'

His words were spoken with such an overwhelming tenderness that Rayne felt her throat constrict with emotion. She opened her mouth to speak but found it impossible.

There was a moment's silence between them when they both seemed to be breathing the other one in, absorbing the essence of who the other was and how they made something powerful and new when they were combined.

'Thank you for lunch.' The words were an intimate whisper and she cleared her throat. 'I needed that little escape.'

'Me, too.' Henry looked down at their linked hands and

the rose she held tenderly in her other one. 'Rayne, I'd really like to see you some time tomorrow.'

'I'm helping at the hall.'

'I'll be there too but that's not what I meant. I guess what I'm trying to say is that I'd like it if I could call on you more often.'

'While you're in town?'

'While I'm in town,' he repeated. 'And after that.'

'After that? Henry? What's happening here? You have a life in Sydney.'

'Do I? Do I, Rayne? Because it certainly doesn't feel like it.'

'Well, you at least have responsibilities and, despite whatever you decide to do with your life, you still have unfinished business in Sydney.'

'True.'

'Also, I don't want any decision you make to be based on what is…you know…between us. You need to be doing things, making changes, whatever they might be—you need to be doing them for *you* and no one else.'

'No one else,' he repeated, and shook his head slightly. 'For years I've done everything for everyone else. Getting away, coming here, it's the first thing I've done for *me* since Natalia's accident.'

'And I can't—in fact, I *won't*—influence any decisions you face.'

'But you're a part of the change, a part of the new me. I feel as though I belong here.'

'I understand. Believe me, I totally understand, but—'

Henry placed a finger across her lips. 'Shh.'

Rayne instantly trembled at his intimate touch. The way

he was looking at her, she knew he wanted to kiss her. She'd known he'd wanted to kiss her for some time now and it was also what she wanted, to feel his lips against hers. She'd dreamt about it, woken with the imagined taste of him on her lips, but now that the moment was really here, she wasn't sure she could go through with it.

Her lips parted, her eyes wild with questions. What did he expect from her? What would happen if she just gave in to her instincts and let him kiss her? As though he could feel her inner turmoil, he dropped his hand but maintained eye contact.

'I like spending time with you, Rayne. It's not something I do.'

'Spend time with me?' she asked breathlessly, slightly puzzled.

'Spend time with a beautiful woman without being on call, or up to my eyes in paperwork, or having to deal with other...responsibilities.'

She could completely understand that. 'So...uh... what do we do?'

'Well, the way I see it is that anything but friendship could drastically complicate things—for both of us right now.'

'Friends.'

'*Good* friends,' he stated, then frowned as though he wasn't really sure where this conversation was going either.

'And you like spending time with me?' Why was it that his words made her feel so special? With the simplest of words, touches, gestures Henry had the ability to make her knees go weak, make her stomach fill with butterflies and her breathing become shallow in anticipation.

'I do.' He smiled at her. 'You're interesting and smart

and beautiful and funny. You're on my wavelength and it's not often you meet people you instantly bond with.'

'Agreed.'

He shifted, coming a little closer than before. 'Rayne, you're an amazing woman, and for the record I am *very* attracted to you, but if we could just spend time together without adding extra complications then I think that might be the best way to proceed. For now.'

She smiled and shook her head, astounded at how his words made her feel. Her insides were buzzing with tingles, sparking new and dormant emotions back to life. 'You sound as though you're outlining a surgical procedure.'

Henry exhaled and closed his eyes for a moment. 'I do, don't I? Sorry. It's been a long time since I've courted a woman.'

'Courted?' Her eyes widened again in total surprise. She'd *never* been courted before.

'Yes. I guess that's what I'm really asking to do, although I'm doing it rather badly.'

'You want to court me?'

'I want to spend time with you, with Jazzy. I want the two of us to get to know each other. You have questions. I have questions. No doubt Jazzy has questions.' He paused. 'That sounds like a lot of questions but you know what I mean and agreeing that during the time I'm here we can see each other will take away a certain...'

'Awkwardness?'

'Exactly.'

'You don't feel as though we'd be...leading each other on?'

'I don't know, Rayne. All I'm certain of right now is that

I need to see you tomorrow, even if it's only across a crowded hall as we prepare for the festival. I'd also like to take you to the festival, to the various events. Jazzy, too. Earlene and Jarvis. I've never had that real inclusive family atmosphere before.'

'When you get a taste of it, it becomes something you crave.'

'Yes. See? You understand me. Do you have any idea how rare that is? For people who haven't known each other above a fortnight to actually connect on such a deep and emotional level?' His tone had dropped to a whisper, a highly intimate whisper, and when his gaze flicked from her eyes to caress her lips for a moment, the flood of tingles that had consumed her earlier returned for an encore.

'I do.' She looked down at the rose, down at their linked fingers, then back to his rich, deep gaze. 'Platonic,' she whispered.

'Platonic,' he agreed, although both of them knew it was a lie. Neither of them moved.

'I have to go inside now.'

'Yes, you do.'

Still neither of them moved.

'You're not moving,' he pointed out.

'Neither are you.'

'I'm not the one who has a five-year-old waiting for a cuddle.'

'I have to go.' Her words were just as soft, her eyes just as fixed on his. She now knew what a kangaroo felt like when it was trapped in the headlights of an oncoming car. She knew she should turn around and go back into the house, but she wasn't quite sure that her legs were ready to obey a simple instruction to walk after an intense moment like that.

'Good night, Henry,' she said softly, and gave his hand a little squeeze, but he still didn't let go.

'Good night, Rayne.' Then, before he knew what he was doing, he leaned down and brushed a light good-night kiss across her lips.

CHAPTER EIGHT

'WHAT…was…that?'

'Sorry. I'm so sorry. It just sort of…'

'Happened?'

'Yes. It's insane, Rayne, but honestly I feel as though we've been together for ever. Kissing you just then seemed like the most natural thing in the world.'

'I know. I feel it too, but what happened to platonic?'

'It was a…platonic kiss?'

'Hmm.' Rayne smiled at him.

'In fact, I'd hardly classify that as a kiss per se. It was more like a peck, or not even that. A light, feathery brush of my lips against yours. See? That's not even a peck—it's just a light brush of—'

'Will you stop talking about kissing?' She was trying very hard to keep her equilibrium under control. Henry wasn't making it at all easy.

'Why?'

'Because it flusters me.' Beneath the front house light, couldn't he see the colour in her cheeks? The desire in her eyes? At that thought, she looked away.

'I like it when you're flustered.'

His voice was like silk—smooth and sexy. 'Henry!' She closed her eyes. 'You were the one who didn't want to make things complicated.'

'I know. I said I was sorry but I actually don't think that I am.' He lifted her chin up and she opened her eyes. 'I'll see you tomorrow?'

'Yes.'

'OK.' He gave her hand a little squeeze then dropped all contact with her and quickly walked round to the driver's side of the car. 'Sleep sweet, Rayne.'

As he drove the short distance back to Sylvia's, Henry shook his head in astonishment. He'd kissed Rayne. He'd kissed Rayne! He honestly couldn't say what had come over him in that instant, only that, as he'd told Rayne, it had felt so natural, as though it had been completely the right thing to do—to quickly kiss her good night. It was what he'd done with his wife every time he'd left for work. It had been natural and real and as Henry parked his car, switching off the engine and staring out into the night, he realised a deep and meaningful truth.

He'd moved on.

Rayne had just finished getting ready for bed and headed into the kitchen to get a glass of water. Earlene was sitting at the bench, drinking her final cup of tea for the evening.

'Ready to turn in, love?'

'Yes. I'm exhausted.'

'Busy day?'

Rayne thought for a moment. 'No more than usual, I guess.'

'So that begs the question, why are you more exhausted today than other days?'

'You know, I'm not sure.'

'Oh, toffle. Of course you're sure. Your poor body, your poor hormones are working in overdrive, trying to figure out what's going on between you and Henry.'

Rayne concentrated on getting her glass of water. 'Is that so?'

'You know it is, dear. Come and sit down and tell me all about it.'

'There really isn't that much to…' Rayne stopped and looked at Earlene. There was no use trying to deny it, not to the woman who'd taken her in and helped her through the most trying times in her life. No, this woman could read her like a book and Rayne realised it was time for the next chapter.

'All right.' She sat down.

'Good. Now, tell me how Henry makes you feel.'

'Special,' Rayne said after a moment of reflection.

Earlene's eyebrows went up. 'We're going to go straight to "special", eh? Well, well, well. I hadn't quite expected that.'

'Why? Is there something wrong with that?'

'No. Oh, no, dear, not at all.' Earlene touched her cheek. 'I just hadn't expected it so soon. You've always been so careful, Rayne, so detached as far as men go. Jarvis and I quite despaired of you finding a man you could trust—really trust, Rayne—but thankfully you seem to have found him.'

'He's a nice man and yet he's been through so much already, so much pain and loss.'

'And I'm sure you're helping him out. That's a rare gift you have and it's great that you use it to help those around you, but don't forget to also use the gift on yourself. You need to heal from what happened to you in the past and really make the effort to work through it.' Earlene paused. 'Have you told Henry yet?'

'Why I'm so wary of men?' She shrugged. 'Sort of. Well, not quite. I told him he was restoring my faith in men.'

Earlene laughed. 'That would have made him feel fit to crow.'

Rayne smiled. 'You know, I think it did.'

'Go to bed, dear. Dream and find your answers.'

Rayne stood and gave Earlene a hug before collecting her drink. She made it to the door before turning to face her again. 'Earlene, what does it equate to when I say Henry makes me feel special?'

Earlene laughed again. 'Let yourself go and the answer will come to you. When it does, trust it.'

Rayne shook her head. 'Just what I need. More cryptic messages to decipher. 'Night.'

When the festival started a few days later, the town seemed to come to life. Fairy-lights hung in the streets, children laughed and played all day long, visitors from all over the country came to their little town to celebrate with them, and life was very merry.

At Henry's hotel, Sylvia had actually changed her books to allow him to stay for as long as he needed and he was beginning to realise that the entire town had matched him up with their very pretty general practitioner and seemed to be doing everything in their power to ensure they stayed matched.

'Didn't have much of a good childhood, from what I hear,' Willard had said.

'Her mother didn't do much. Poor Rayne was the one who looked after everything and from a very young age, too,' Gladys had added.

'She's very special is our Rayne and we're fiercely protective of her,' Carmel said, putting her two cents' worth in.

Henry had thanked them all for their concerns and had taken their warnings to heart. He had the notion that if he were to hurt Rayne, he'd be hung, drawn and quartered—and he loved the people of Deniliquin even more for their loyalty to such an incredible woman. Besides, he had no intention of hurting her. In fact, he was beginning to hope that things would turn out to be quite the opposite.

On Tuesday night, as they walked through the town after having an early dinner at Darren's café, Jasmine between them, Rayne breathed in deeply and sighed.

'You all right?' Henry asked, glancing over at her. She looked incredible tonight, dressed in strappy leather sandals, a white sundress and a burgundy cardigan Earlene had knitted for her. Her hair was loose and her eyes were sparkling with happiness. 'My word, you're beautiful,' he murmured before he could stop himself. Her smile was a small one and she looked away shyly for a moment before thanking him.

'It's such a lovely night. The weather is perfect, the breeze just warm enough not to be sticky, the stars shining brightly and the town shining its brilliance. It all seems to fit as though it were meant to be.'

'It does.' They were headed to the hall to see the exhibitions. The cake judging had taken place earlier that day and Earlene had won a prize for her cake, which was a typical Australian 'outhouse', complete with an old man reading the paper and a red-back spider on the toilet seat. It had made people laugh and completely captured the spirit of the outback.

'It's in here,' Jasmine said, tugging them both along. 'And the picture I drew at school last week is up, too.'

'I know, darling, we've already seen it,' Rayne pointed out.

'But you have to see it *again.*' And they did, standing before it and admiring it for all its brilliance, just as an art critic would do with a painting at a gallery. They oohed and ahhed over the cakes and made their way around the photographic and other exhibitions.

Then they walked towards Darren's café where they were going to have a quiet dessert before checking out the jumble-sale stalls. The town seemed to be filled with people and getting a seat at Darren's was difficult.

'It's so good for the town,' Rayne murmured as they sat down with their iced cupcakes and chocolate milkshakes.

'I can't believe the transformation.' Henry shook his head.

'Even though you helped with most of it?'

'I don't mean that. I guess having all the visitors come is what makes the real difference. It's great.'

Rayne smiled at his words. He sounded just like a local and she wondered if that was exactly how he saw himself. He'd helped get this town ready for the festival and now he was reaping the benefits just as much as people like Willard and Gladys.

People continually stopped by to say hello and chat, some patients, some friends and some both. Quite a few of them commented on what a happy family picture the three of them made, to which Henry and Rayne merely smiled politely and nodded.

'Jazzy, you're getting that everywhere,' Rayne remarked, reaching for some more napkins to wipe the little girl's face. 'Why did you choose to wear white?' she asked rhetorically.

'So I'd look pretty for Henry,' came the answer.

'Of course. I should have known.'

'Logical reasoning.' Henry nodded and winked at Jasmine.

'She has it in abundance,' Rayne agreed. When Jasmine had finished getting her cupcake icing all over her, they decided to go for a walk by the Edward River. The sun had almost set but the lights were on to ensure they could see where they were walking.

'I can't get over how perfect the weather is,' Rayne murmured as Henry carried Jasmine on his shoulders.

'Very.'

'Look at those colours, Jazzy. Aren't they amazing?'

'I'm gonna do a special painting tomorrow and I'm gonna paint the sky eggsactly as it is now.'

Rayne smiled at Jasmine's words and Henry chuckled. 'I look forward to seeing it. A beautiful sky on a beautiful night with two beautiful girls. I'm beginning to think I'm the luckiest man on the face of the earth.'

'You are, Henry,' Jasmine declared. 'This is just like when Mummy and Daddy and me used to go for a walk sometimes. Daddy would put me on his shoulders and Mummy would hold his hand. Now all you and Rayne need to do is hold hands and then it will be just the same.'

'Can't argue with that,' Henry said quickly, and before Rayne could utter a word, he took her hand in his, linking their fingers together. Rayne smiled shyly and he gave her hand a little squeeze. 'Relax,' he said softly. 'I won't bite.' Then he winked at her. 'Not unless you want me to.'

'Henry!'

He laughed, a deep rumbling laugh that echoed around the area, warming its way through Rayne, and she realised that she should do as he'd suggested. She should just relax and enjoy this moment. Life was very short. She'd learned that the hard way but she'd also learned that letting go of the tight rein she held over her life was nowhere near as easy to do as it seemed for others.

If someone were to ask her what love was, she wasn't sure she could tell them. Oh, sure, she knew what it was like to love like a friend because she'd loved Janey. She loved Jarvis and Earlene but that was more out of gratitude than anything else. She loved Jasmine but that was a maternal love.

Now Henry was forcing her out of the comfort zone she'd created for herself and it wasn't the first time he'd done it. First with that tantalising brush of his lips on hers and now by holding her hand in public. He made her feel nervous and excited as well as filled with anticipation that something special and really important was about to happen, although she had no clue what it might be.

Rayne had no real knowledge of what real love was. The love between a man and woman. She'd seen her best friend fall in love and run towards it with no fear at all, only complete happiness. Was that what it could be like for her? If she let go, would she be able to have that freedom of embracing love when it came along?

Ever since he'd kissed her the other night, every time she'd seen him since, her stomach had churned, her knees had become weak and she'd felt extremely light-headed, as though she had been about to faint. It was ridiculous and she'd tried her best to ignore it but the fact of the matter was that Henry really did make her feel special…and she didn't know how to handle that.

'Ooh! Look at the ducks.' Jasmine wriggled around on Henry's shoulders. 'Let me down, Henry.'

'Please,' Rayne reminded her.

'Please,' Jasmine said quickly, and when Henry let go of Rayne's hand to lift Jasmine down, Rayne felt a cold chill swirl around her. She shivered a little, even though it wasn't that cool, and rubbed her hands together. The instant Jasmine's feet hit the ground, she was off running towards the waterfowl, scattering them from the edge of the path back into the water.

'Don't get too—' She'd been about to say 'close' when Henry took her hand back, linking their fingers together once more.

'Close,' he finished for her.

'I won't,' Jasmine promised, and headed off towards a park with a swing set which she knew was just down the path.

'She's a bundle of energy tonight,' Henry commented.

'Yes.' That was all the answer Rayne could manage, her body once more warming at the simple touch of his hand holding hers.

'Let your stress go, Rayne.'

She looked up at him, surprised. 'You can read minds now?'

'I can feel your tension.'

'By holding my hand?'

'Yes.' He chuckled. 'Just enjoy this for what it is.'

'And what is it?'

Henry shrugged. 'Who knows? But I'm enjoying finding out. You should, too.'

They walked on in silence and slowly but surely Rayne started to feel less uncomfortable. 'This is nice,' she finally said.

'You're starting to relax. Good.'

'It's not easy. I'm working really hard at it.'

'And I appreciate that.'

Rayne gave his hand a little squeeze as they headed over to a bench so they could watch Jasmine play. 'Life gets so hectic sometimes and if I turn my head too much, if I take my eyes off all those balls I'm currently trying to juggle, I'll drop the lot.'

Henry nodded. 'I know the feeling. Although in my picture I'm not only juggling but I'm stuck on a merry-go-round.'

'That wouldn't make juggling all that easy.'

'It makes it nigh impossible at times.' He rubbed his thumb gently over the back of her hand, content simply to sit there with her. 'When are you planning to take Jazzy to the ute muster?' Henry asked.

'Probably Saturday afternoon. Until Friday, I'll be doing a shift at the hospital every day but I'm rostered on for Saturday morning so should definitely be free in the latter part of the afternoon.'

'Sounds good. Why don't we plan on going around four o'clock? It'll just be until…say…six? Just a couple of hours.'

'We?'

'Yes. I'm courting you, remember?' He held up their linked hands, as though that proved his point.

'Oh, that's right.' Why did his words have the ability to make her all tingly inside? 'I've never been courted before.'

'So you've said.' Henry paused, then decided to test the waters a bit. 'Why not?'

'Why not?' Rayne repeated, then thought. 'Never the time. Never the right man.' She shrugged. 'I don't know.'

'Yes, you do. You mentioned the other day I was helping to restore your faith in men.' Henry shifted so he could see her better. 'What happened, Rayne? Who hurt you?'

Rayne looked up at the sky and knew it was time. Knew she had to tell Henry. She owed it to him, especially after he'd been so open with her. 'It's nothing…just fuss and nonsense really.'

Henry nodded, encouraging her to go on, waiting patiently. Whatever she was about to say, she needed his understanding and support and she was going to get it. When he'd realised he'd moved on, he'd also realised he was moving towards Rayne. She'd become so incredibly dear to him and he wasn't about to jeopardise that for all the tea in China.

'Uh…well…' Rayne looked at Jasmine, hoping for a distraction, but she was playing happily with a few of her schoolfriends in the sandpit. She cleared her throat and looked at Henry. 'I told you how my mother had lots of boyfriends, how she would move from one place the next, following one man after another?'

'Yes.'

'Well…when I was about fourteen, we'd moved across Sydney so she could live with her latest boyfriend and one day after school, when Mum was still at work, well…' Rayne looked away and Henry suddenly had an awful feeling in his stomach. He tried not to tense at what he could guess she was about to say. 'I'd *developed* rather early and had a rather full figure at fourteen. He…' Rayne breathed out, forcing herself to say the words she'd only ever spoken to Janey's family and a therapist, and that had been at the time of the incident. 'He…uh…tried to…he came on to me.'

'Did he—?' Henry ground out angrily between clenched teeth.

'No. No. He kissed me and that was enough to make me want to be sick. I shoved him away as hard as I could and I got out of the house. I ran and I ran. I ended up at Janey's house and told Earlene what had happened. Then I promptly burst into tears.' She looked at Henry again. 'I never went back there. Jarvis and Earlene stepped in and just took me out of that situation. Gave me a different life.'

Henry bent forward and gently stroked her cheek as though he was helping her to heal the wound. 'Thank you for telling me,' he whispered, before straightening. 'You are one amazing woman, Rayne Hudson. I hope you realise that.'

'Some days I do. Most days I don't.'

'Then I'll have to keep reminding you.'

'Will you now?'

'Yes.' Henry let go of her hands and tenderly cupped her face. 'I want to kiss you, Rayne. So desperately. But especially after what you've just told me, there's no way I want to do anything to rush you or push you. You are in control of what happens between us and when. You have become very important to me these past weeks and you've stood by me while I've made some tough decisions about my life. You've been there for me and I want you to know that I am here for you. One hundred per cent. I want to be your friend—first and foremost—but I also want more. As I've said, it's your decision and I'll be as patient as a saint.'

Rayne raised an eyebrow at that and smiled.

'Well…*almost* as patient as a saint.'

She chuckled, amazed at how he could make her feel so warm and secure and special. Her Henry. Making her feel special. He leaned forward and kissed her forehead before dropping his hands, showing her he really did respect her.

Later, as they walked home, Jasmine back on her perch on Henry's shoulders, Rayne couldn't stop her thoughts from wondering what it would be like to have Henry hold her in his arms and feel his lips on hers. She'd dreamt about it enough and now, to her utter astonishment, he was leaving the decision entirely to her. He was a man of honour, of morals and ethics, and she not only trusted him but knew he'd keep her safe, that he wouldn't hurt her.

As they crossed the front garden, Jasmine asked to be let down, remembering she still had to give Ethel her night-time bottle.

'I won't come in,' Henry said at the front door.

'Tea? Coffee?'

He smiled and took her hand in his. 'Not tonight but thanks for the offer.' He lifted her hand to his lips and kissed it. 'I think you need an early night.'

'Are you saying that I look like a hag?'

'Hardly.' He kissed her hand again. 'Good night. I'll see you tomorrow.' He took a few steps away but Rayne wasn't ready to let him go just yet. She held on to his hand and he looked at her with puzzlement for a second before peering more closely into her eyes. 'Rayne?'

'Henry.' She urged him even closer then dropped his hand and placed both of her hands at his waist. Still he didn't move, waiting for her, and she appreciated his self-control. 'Henry?'

'Yes?'

'Kiss me.' She looked into his eyes and realised she'd been waiting for ever for this moment. '*Please*, kiss me.'

CHAPTER NINE

HENRY paused, his heart stopping for a second as he looked at Rayne to make sure this was what she really wanted. When he saw the truth of her words, the truth of her need for him to do exactly as she'd asked, he drew her closer.

She came willingly, filled with anticipatory excitement. She wasn't quite sure what to do or think so instead she decided to feel and, boy, oh, boy, did Henry feel good. Her eyelids fluttered closed and she sighed as the pressure that had been building since the first time she'd laid eyes on him, since the first time his deep and sexy voice had washed over her, since the first time he'd touched her, was released.

She'd wanted Henry to kiss her for so long—*really* kiss her. Even before he'd teased his lips across hers, giving her the smallest inkling of what it would be like, she'd wanted it. She'd dreamt about it, about him, night after night. Now, with his mouth firmly on hers, their breath mingling together, their bodies close with mounting heat and passion, Rayne couldn't believe how perfect everything was.

More than happy to let Henry lead, Rayne went willingly. It appeared that he certainly had more control over his faculties than she did as he took his time in exploring this exquisiteness that existed between them. Slowly, he parted her lips. Slowly, the tip of his tongue touched hers. Slowly, he caressed her mouth with his, showing her just how much he treasured this moment. His hands were at her back, not moving but simply holding her steady, holding her near him. She placed her hands on his upper arms, wanting this moment to last for ever.

His mouth was still exploring hers as though he wanted to take the time to memorise every minute part of her. With the utmost tenderness, he kissed the edge of her mouth on each side, then kissed her cheeks. Rayne was about to open her eyes, to look up at him, when she felt his breath on her face and realised he wanted to commit to memory more than just her mouth. He kissed her eyelids, then her nose, which made her smile.

Opening her eyes, she looked up at him, unable to believe the happiness welling inside her. Had there ever been a time in her life when she'd felt this happy? This secure? This…complete?

Henry kissed her mouth once more, unable to believe just how incredibly beautiful she was, how sweet she tasted and how addicted he'd become in such a short time. Nothing in the world existed except the two of them. He could hear her breathing increasing along with his and was glad both of them were in the same place, enjoying the amazing experience as he dared to deepen the kiss just a little bit more.

She opened her mouth, eager for more, eager to taste and tease him as much as he was doing to her. Feeling her capitulation, Henry wondered if he'd ever be able to *stop* kissing her. Now that he'd started, he wanted more—a lot more. Her scent was intoxicating.

Forcing himself to keep the pace nice and sedate yet still taking every opportunity of exploring every little part of her luscious lips, he was rewarded by a sighed moan emanating from the woman who was pliant in his arms.

The atmosphere was starting to become more intense, the emotions between the two of them rising, and it was incredibly difficult for Henry to keep control over the situation as he deepened the kiss, bringing her body even closer against his own. He was trying hard not to rush, telling himself not to lose control, but how was he supposed to do that when the woman was *everything* he'd been searching for? He'd waited for far too long to find someone else he connected with. To find a woman who understood him, who was on his wavelength, who felt the same way he did. Now that he'd found her, he knew in that split second that he couldn't let her go, and the knowledge rocked him.

What was flowing between them was perfect—the most perfect kiss in the world—and Rayne couldn't believe how incredibly sensual he made her feel. Even though the intensity had changed, Henry seemed in no rush. He was taking his time, eager to learn the exact contours of her mouth, her face, her entire being, and it made her feel so…cherished. She was special to him. There was no way she could doubt that.

When he broke away to press butterfly kisses across her cheek and round to her ear, Rayne breathed out with a deep, satisfied sigh. There was no way she could stand upright and so took advantage of leaning against him, more than content to let him support her. As he continued to nibble at her neck, she smiled, starting to squirm a little as his lips tickled her some more.

'Henry.' His name was a caress on her lips and when she licked her lips, they tasted of him. That in itself was intoxicating enough to raise her heartbeat, which had only just started to settle to a normal rhythm.

'Mmm,' he murmured against her neck, and she giggled as his breath fanned her skin, giving her goose-bumps.

'I'm ticklish there.'

'Really?' He pressed two more kisses to her neck then slowly drew back, his passion flaring to life once more when he saw the deep emerald green of her eyes. They were filled with desire, with need and longing.

He wondered what *she* saw as they continued to look into each other's eyes. Could she see how necessary she'd become to him? Could she see how he didn't want to leave Deniliquin if it meant leaving her? Could she see how he'd come to care so deeply for her in such a short time?

'Ticklish around the neck. I'll remember that.'

'Remember?'

'Yes. For next time.'

'Next time?' Rayne's heart rate picked up again as he caressed her cheek once more.

'The next time I kiss you. The next time I hold you in my arms. Because I'll tell you something, my pretty lady, now that the drought has finally broken, it's going rain for a very long time.'

As he spoke, he leaned forward and took her lips in a firm and promising kiss. He edged back, putting distance between them but still finding it necessary to hold her hands, unable to break all contact.

'Sweet dreams...and I mean that. They must be *very* sweet and preferably of me.'

Rayne laughed, loving the way he made her feel. 'Ditto,' she said with a nod. It seemed to be enough for him, enough to help him to disengage their hands so that he could leave.

She watched until the lights of his car had disappeared down the street before heading inside. And that night she did exactly as Henry had suggested, but this time she didn't need to fantasise about what it would be like to kiss him because she knew, and she hugged the knowledge close to her in delight.

On Saturday afternoon Rayne couldn't believe the way she was fussing in front of the mirror, pulling at her clothes, wondering whether or not she should change into something more formal-casual or casual-formal. Jasmine came in, dressed in a pair of denim jeans, cowboy boots, which Earlene had bought for her, and a navy-blue singlet. Her hair was in pigtails and an Akubra sat atop her head.

'How do I look?' she asked Rayne, edging her aside to admire her reflection.

'Perfect. How do I look?'

Jasmine peeled her gaze away from the mirror to look at Rayne. 'Why are you wearing a skirt? Should I wear a skirt?'

'No. You're right. I need to lose the skirt.'

'You should go dressed like me!' Jasmine's blue eyes were bright with excitement. 'Mummy and me used to dress the same sometimes. It was really superfun.'

'Superfun?'

'Yeah. Go on, Rayne. Please?' Jasmine was tugging at her hand, looking up at her with pleading eyes. 'Please? Please?'

Rayne couldn't help but smile as she lifted the little girl

into her arms and hugged her close. 'It sounds like an excellent plan to me.' She kissed her cheek then put her down
again. 'My goodness, you're getting heavy. Did you grow
last night?'

Jasmine giggled as Rayne changed her clothes yet again
and when the doorbell rang, Jasmine squealed, 'He's here.
Henry's here!' And raced for the door.

'My, my, my,' Rayne heard Henry say as Jasmine
opened the door. 'Don't you look gorgeous?'

'Wait till you see Rayne. We're dressed the same.'

'Really?' No sooner had he said the word than he looked
up as Rayne came into view. It was true. She was wearing
cowboy boots, jeans and the obligatory Deni ute muster
navy-blue singlet top. Her arms were bare, the singlet
hugging her curves to perfection, and he was having a difficult time trying to stop his eyes from popping out of his head.
With her hair plaited like Jasmine's, she looked even cuter.
The only thing missing was her hat. 'Wow,' he breathed.

Jasmine walked over to where Rayne stood and struck
a pose. 'Don't we look gorgeous?'

'Absolutely.' Henry couldn't believe just how much.
The moment seemed to last for ever but eventually he
cleared his throat and gestured to the door. 'Your chariot
awaits, my ladies.' He bowed and Jasmine squealed with
excitement.

'We're going in a *chariot*?' She jumped up and down
and clapped her hands, then stopped suddenly and looked
up at Rayne. 'What's a chariot?'

Rayne and Henry laughed, the amazingly intense
moment broken as Rayne collected her bag and her hat.
She couldn't believe the way Henry had looked at her. He

hadn't tried to hide the growing attraction he obviously felt. Henry led Jasmine out to the car, explaining what a chariot was and how it was also a figure of speech.

They'd seen him at least once every day this week and both Earlene and Jarvis were as taken with him as everyone else in Deni seemed to be. He was an incredible man and she felt so privileged that he'd come into their lives and enriched them beyond her wildest dreams. And speaking of dreams, they'd been getting wilder and more urgent. That was possibly because Henry would kiss her good night whenever he left and the feel of his mouth against hers, the way her body molded perfectly to his, the overpowering sensations he evoked were what made her feel so…right.

Rayne had to keep reminding herself to continue letting go of her tension, that spending time with Henry was good for her, good for Jasmine, and when Henry left to return to his life in Sydney, *then* she'd pick up the pieces of her life and get things back on track. For now, though, it was as though they were on vacation.

Once at the muster, with all the dust, heat, flies and people—most of whom were sporting navy-blue singlets—they headed for the family amusement section. The weather was scorching, even at this time of the evening, and Rayne was sure the temperature must be somewhere in the high thirties. It was a typical outback event and she loved it.

'What a night.' Rayne took off her hat and fanned herself as Jasmine went from one activity to the next, doing some woodcraft, completing a giant jig-saw puzzle and then having her face painted. 'That paint's going to melt off her face.'

'Must be almost one hundred Fahrenheit,' Henry agreed, as Jasmine came over to ask him to help her walk on a pair of stilts.

Next they fought the flies and went to the patting paddock, Rayne using her cellphone to snap pictures of the extremely happy child. It was perfect. Having Henry with them, joining in the fun, was perfect as well, and for people who had no idea who they were, they looked just like a family. One mother, one father, one very happy five-year-old.

As Rayne smiled up at Henry, for that moment she wanted it to come true.

They stayed at the muster for another hour or so but even though the moon was out, bright and full, the heat wasn't abating. There was, however, the smell of rain in the air. It had been announced to the masses through loudspeakers and by word of mouth that there was a storm coming and for people to pack away any unnecessary items and prepare wet-weather gear.

'I hope the concert doesn't get rained out,' Henry said as they headed back to his car, Jasmine on his shoulders.

Rayne looked at the cloudless sky. 'Looks as though it'll hold for a few more hours at least. I, on the other hand, need to get one very tired girl home, wash her face and get her into bed because I don't think *she'll* last much longer. It's been one very busy week.'

Jasmine wasn't about to argue, yawning widely as Henry lifted her down from his shoulders and helped her into the car. When they arrived back at Rayne's house, Henry walked them to the door.

'I'll leave you to it,' he said, looking down at her lips, his gaze lingering on them for a moment then meeting her eyes once more.

Rayne welcomed the tingles, the pounding of her heart in her chest, the way she wanted to feel his arms about her, crushing her body to his as their lips became intimately acquainted again and again.

Henry saw her desire, as potent and as real as his own. Leaning forward, he kissed her lips with such sweet softness she almost melted. He could hear Jasmine starting to whinge a little in the background and knew now wasn't the time.

'Rayne.' He brushed the back of his hand across her cheek as he looked down into her eyes. 'We need to talk, and soon.'

'I know.' She placed a finger on his lips and he kissed it. 'We'll talk.'

Jasmine started to cry from tiredness and Rayne smiled up at Henry. 'I'd better—'

'Go.' He nodded. 'I'll call you later.'

'OK. Are you going to go back to the muster? Earlene and Jarvis are still there and it's not as though you haven't made any other friends since you've been in town. You should go. Enjoy it. It's something not to be missed.'

Henry didn't want to be anywhere she wasn't but he shrugged. 'I'll think about it. Go. Deal with Jazzy.'

'OK,' she repeated, and, smiling up at him, she leaned up and pressed a quick kiss to his lips. 'See you tomorrow. I'll go deal with my tired five-year-old, who still has a large butterfly painted on her face.'

He nodded and kissed her again. It was as though neither of them wanted to part. That was a good thing, right? Rayne promised herself time to think about it once Jasmine was settled for the night.

'Finally,' Rayne muttered as she sat down on the lounge and picked up a soothing cup of tea. Jasmine was bathed and asleep and Rayne could put her feet up and think. The first thought that came to mind was Henry.

He seemed to be on her mind a lot. When she wasn't with him, she was thinking about him. When she *was* with him, she couldn't think of anything else. He was starting to cloud her ability to think logically, and she wasn't at all comfortable with that.

Rayne thought back to when Janey had first met Jarrod and the discussions they'd had.

'But how do you know this is the real thing?' Rayne had asked as the two of them had sat around in Janey's room, painting their nails.

'Because I feel it.'

'But how do you know?'

'I don't know.' Janey had laughed. 'I just do. Jarrod is…' She'd sighed. 'Jarrod is *everything*. I want to tell him my deepest, darkest secrets. I want him to be there for every little event in my life, whether that's buying a new pair of shoes…'

Rayne had rolled her eyes at this. 'You already have every pair of shoes known to man.'

'Shh. Don't interrupt. From buying a new pair of shoes and the excitement it brings me,' she'd continued, 'to the moment I find out whether I got that new promotion at work. The highs and the lows, the bigs and the smalls. I want him to be there with me for all of them. I want to share them with him. I want to see him every day and I want to be just as important in his life as he is in mine.'

'And is that how he feels?' Rayne had been highly sceptical but Janey had understood her friend completely.

'Yes. Amazingly, it is, and I think that's how you know. If he's as into you as you are into him. When he can't bear to spend a day without seeing you, without calling you.'

'Is that why the two of you spend hours on the phone?'

'Yes. We can spend all day together and then he still calls me at night, simply because he misses me. That is, I guess, how you know, Rayne. When you can't stop thinking about him, when you have news and he's the first person you want to tell. When you get all tingly when he looks at you and you lose yourself in his eyes.' Janey sighed, put down the bright orange nail polish she'd been applying to her toes and turned to look at Rayne. 'I know where you're coming from, honey, and you can't judge any relationship you might eventually have on how your mum behaved with her multitude of boyfriends. I know it has scared you away from commitment but there will come a day when you'll find Mr Right. I just know it.'

Rayne shook her head, not so sure at all. 'Mum would swear blind each time that it was different. With Greg, she'd say she was searching for security. With Brad, she'd say it was fun she needed. With William, she said it was knowledge. With every guy, she'd look for something else, something which she thought was missing from her life, so why didn't she ever find what she was looking for? She never found happiness, that I'm certain of. I do think she reached a certain level of contentment near the end, but by then it was all too late.'

'True love is out there, Rayne. It does happen. It does exist. My parents are proof of that, and Jarrod and I will be the same. We'll be together for ever.'

When the phone shrilled to life, Rayne jumped out of her chair and quickly snatched up the receiver, sniffing. Until that moment she hadn't realised tears had started sliding down her cheeks and she wiped them away as she answered the call.

'Rayne?'

'Henry.' She sniffed again.

'Are you all right? Do you want me to come round?'

She smiled at his words. 'I'm all right. I was just thinking about Janey.' She held the receiver away as she blew her nose. 'There. Much better now. So, to what do I owe the pleasure of this call?'

'It's a pleasure, eh?'

'Of course.'

'I'm not bothering you at all?'

'No.' Rayne settled back against the cushions, tucking her feet up. 'There's nothing wrong at your end, is there?' She glanced at the clock. 'I'm taking it you didn't stay for the concert.'

'No. Too noisy.'

Rayne laughed. 'You're getting old, Henry.'

'Or maybe I was just lonely.'

'Lonely? You would have been in a crowd of thousands.'

'And you don't think a person can be lonely when they're surrounded by people?' His voice was quiet and she could hear the underlying meaning in his words.

'That's usually when loneliness is at its worst.' She knew that feeling all too well.

'You sound as though you know what you're talking about.'

'So do you.' There was a pause with neither of them willing to say anything more for the moment. 'Just out of curiosity and not that I mind the call at all, but was there a reason for it?'

'Nope. I just wanted to hear your voice.'

'Even after spending so much time with us?'

'I went back to the muster but it wasn't the same. All I could think about was you. So I came back to Sylvia's and decided to call you.'

'Because you just needed to hear my voice?' Butterflies started doing somersaults inside her stomach. It was just as Janey had said it should be. That the man of her dreams would be the one who wanted to spend time with her, who *chose* to spend time with her. Who couldn't stop thinking about her, who wanted to talk to her at every available opportunity.

'Yes.' He paused. 'Is that all right?'

Rayne sighed and smiled into the receiver. 'It's perfect.' Because at that moment she realised the truth of the matter, and that truth was that she was one hundred per cent in love with Henry Harcourt.

CHAPTER TEN

THE phone shrilled to life and Rayne almost bolted out of the bed as her hand shot out to snatch up the receiver before it woke Jasmine. 'Rayne here.'

'It's Tanya.'

Rayne recognised her friend's voice. Tanya was obviously the triage nurse at the hospital tonight. 'Problem?'

'Yes. We've just received word from Bordertown that the rain we were expecting is more like a full-blown storm with hail. Bordertown's been hit quite badly and there's a lot of damage. Roofs have come off houses and shops, windows have been smashed. Their emergency services are fully stretched.'

'We'd be expecting the storm in about…what? An hour?'

'Or less. There are going to be casualties.'

Rayne rubbed her eyes, forcing herself to wake up properly and her brain to work. 'OK. I'll get ready and come in. I'm presuming people still out at the muster site have been informed?'

'The police are out there now, telling people to pack up their tents and seek shelter, but with that many people and so little time…' Tanya left the sentence hanging and Rayne could imagine far too well what sort of situation they might be expecting.

'OK. I'll see you soon.' She was about to hang up when she remembered Henry's offer to help out. 'I'll contact Henry to let him know we might be needing him.'

'That would be great. I wasn't sure whether to call him in or not, but we really could use all the help we can get.'

'I'll call him now.' Rayne hung up and quickly dialled Henry's direct room number at Sylvia's. 'Henry,' she said when he answered. He sounded all tousled and sleepy and totally yummy. An image of him, lying with the sheet half over his gorgeous body, came instantly to mind but she pushed it away, shaking her head to clear it a little and get her thoughts back on track.

'Rayne.' Her name was a sigh, a caress and she couldn't have been happier. 'I was just thinking about you.'

'You were?' Did that mean he'd been dreaming of her? The excitement she'd been working on controlling returned. 'That's nice.' She closed her eyes and made herself refocus. 'Uh...now's not the time. The hospital's just called. They need all hands on deck for the storm we're expecting. I sort of volunteered your services.'

'And rightly so.' She could tell he was now instantly awake. An occupational hazard they both knew all too well. Rayne continued to fill him in on the details.

'I'll come by and get you,' he said.

'Thanks. All right, then, I'll see you soon.' Rayne climbed out of her bed, pulling on clothes before heading to the kitchen to drink a cold glass of juice. Earlene came into the kitchen and switched on the light, momentarily startling Rayne.

'I heard the phone. Emergency?'

'Yes. The storm is apparently far worse than we'd imagined. You may want to wake Jarvis, get him to batten down the hatches, so to speak. It probably wouldn't even hurt to cover the windows with blankets in case they break, make sure all Jazzy's outside toys are stowed away.'

'We know what to do, dear. Don't worry about that. Go to the hospital and don't worry about Jazzy or us. We'll be fine.' Earlene held out Rayne's car keys.

'Uh…actually, Henry's going to come and get me.'

'Good idea. The less traffic on the roads, the better. He's such a thoughtful man.'

Rayne's smile was instant. 'Yes. Yes, he is.'

Earlene put the keys down and walked towards her, looking at her intently. 'You love him,' she stated firmly and without hesitation.

'Is it that obvious?'

'Only to me, dear.' She stroked Rayne's hair. 'You are so important to us—you know that, don't you, Rayne?'

'I do.'

'We love you dearly.' Earlene hugged her close. 'It's only right that you find happiness with a man after everything you've been through.'

'But I don't know what's going to happen. What do I say to Henry? Do I tell him how I feel?' Rayne hugged Earlene back. 'I'm even more confused than before.'

Earlene chuckled and let her go. 'Sounds about right. Love tends to do that to us women. Jarvis had me in a right royal tizz for quite some time before we sorted things out. You and Henry are only at the beginning. Take your time. Don't rush it but don't hide from it either.'

'Right.' Rayne took a few deep, cleansing breaths. 'I'd better go.' Earlene walked her to the door, both of them remarking on the stillness of the weather.

'The calm before the storm.'

'Yes, and it'll change faster than a snap of the fingers.' When Henry's car pulled into the driveway, Earlene kissed her cheek. 'Go. We'll take care of everything here.'

'Thanks. I'm so glad you're here.'

'Me, too.' Earlene's eyes sparkled in the early morning light with the love a mother had for her child.

Rayne headed out and climbed into the passenger seat of Henry's car. 'Morning,' she said.

'And what a morning it's turning out to be.' He stopped and stared at her for a moment. 'Your hair's loose.'

'I didn't have time to pull it back.' Rayne raked her fingers through the brown locks, hoping she didn't have really bad bed hair. Now, *that* would be embarrassing.

'I like it when it's loose.'

'You do?' They were caught up in each other's eyes again and Rayne forced herself to look away. 'Have you heard anything else about the storm?'

'Yes.' He pulled himself together long enough to drag his gaze away from her face and set the car in motion. 'Sylvia and her husband were up, getting the motel secured, and they'd heard from Willard that the muster site is in a right state. People everywhere are trying to pack things away, others are just up and leaving, heading to Wagga rather than sleeping in the back of their cars for the night. Apparently, the winds are starting to pick up.'

No sooner had he spoke then the trees on the side of the road started to sway.

Henry couldn't resist looking again at her hair. 'Your hair… It's…' He almost swerved into the kerb because he was looking at her rather than the road.

'Watch it. We don't need extra casualties.' She twirled her hair around with her fingers, wishing she'd grabbed a band, but there would be plenty at the hospital. 'It's probably really messy.'

'It's…beautiful.'

He brought the car to a stop in the hospital car park and, unable to resist, unable to control himself, Henry reached out and touched the silky strands. It was a light touch at first but when it appeared Rayne wasn't going to object, he sifted his fingers through the gorgeous tresses.

'*You're* beautiful,' he said softly, his deep voice sounding a little husky.

Rayne was mesmerised by him, by the way he was touching her in such an intimate fashion, one she found she liked—a lot.

The sound of a police siren pierced the air, breaking the atmosphere between them. This wasn't the time or the place. Rayne quickly climbed out of the vehicle, her hair whipped around by the mounting winds, almost blinding her.

As they walked into the hospital, it was to find the A and E department crowded with people who'd come to help. Tanya greeted them thankfully, noting they'd arrived together. A few police officers walked in and a moment later they were all called for an update.

Simon, head of the Deniliquin police, explained the situation, giving details of what had been reported at Bordertown and what sort of mess they could expect.

'The rain will be hard. Sixty millimetres was dumped on Bordertown in eleven minutes. Generators need checking.' He pointed to people as he spoke. 'There'll be a definite loss of power for most of the area. The first-aid and ambulance services out at the site will be bringing you the worst cases. We can't fly the chopper anywhere until after the storm has passed.'

'Where do the casualties from Bordertown go?' Henry asked.

'Emergency cases from Bordertown go to Adelaide as it's far closer. Wagga Base hospital is on standby and the weather bureau has informed us that the storm is headed towards Melbourne, rather than up towards Wagga, so they'll take any extra cases as necessary.' Simon finished his briefing and gave out jobs. Eventually everyone was allowed to go.

'Rayne,' Tanya said, 'can you check the blood supplies?'

'Sure.' Rayne pulled a rubber band out of a drawer and started to tie her hair back, trying not to remember the way Henry had made her feel when he'd been touching it.

'I'll go check the blood supplies.' She glanced over her shoulder at Henry as she walked away, only to find him watching her go. When their eyes met, he winked at her and she quickly looked away, feeling a blush engulf her from the roots of her hair to the pink nail polish Jasmine had put on her toes the day before.

As she rounded the corner, out of his sight, she stopped and leaned against the wall for a moment, closing her eyes and forcing herself to breathe deeply. Could he see that she was in love with him? Was it obvious? She hoped not but in the same breath she hoped it was. If he could see how she felt, it would mean she wouldn't need to actually come out and say the words because saying 'I love you' to a man was something she never thought she'd do. Her heart was supposed to be locked away for ever, never to be hurt, but somehow Henry had not only found the key but had unlocked her heart, for it now firmly belonged to him.

Squaring her shoulders, she headed off to check the bloods, deciding that whatever was destined to happen between Henry and herself it would need to wait until after their present crisis had passed.

Inside the hospital it was definitely the calm before the storm as they all waited, checking and rechecking things. Stocking the shelves with extra bandages and syringes. Ensuring their equipment was working, that the generators were primed, that everything would work like clockwork when the casualties started to arrive.

When the real storm did finally hit, it was worse than they'd expected. Hail the size of golfballs poured down on them, pelting through the night at strange angles. There was a smash of glass from a nearby room and Tanya sent one of the orderlies to check the situation.

Rayne's mind began to work through a mental list of what sort of injuries they might expect as everyone continued to keep busy, some of them sticking blankets over the windows, which were exposed to the elements.

'You all right?' Henry asked, coming up to stand beside her.

'Fine. You?'

'Trying to run through every possible scenario from here to Timbuktu.'

She smiled. 'Me, too.'

Henry leaned in closer. 'See how much we have in common?' His voice was deep, husky and intimate, and when she looked at him she caught a glimpse of the desire that had been there when he'd dropped herself and Jasmine home from the muster.

'Stop it,' she whispered, her words barely audible.

'Stop what?' Henry raised an eyebrow. 'Letting you know how drawn I am to you?'

'In a platonic way?' she questioned, trying to lighten the atmosphere.

'Who cares about platonic when you look at me like that?'

All his words accomplished was to make Rayne's heart beat faster. He had a point, though. She was looking at him as though she wanted to taste him, savour him and then devour him.

The sound of sirens made them both turn, made them both switch instantly into professional mode and made them both silently promise to themselves that this conversation would have an ending...later.

Tanya was an excellent triage nurse and once the patients had been seen and prioritised, they received treatment. Not only were they getting people brought in via ambulance but also people either driving themselves or being brought in by loved ones.

Rayne and Henry hardly had room to breathe as they debrided wounds, sent people off for X-rays, applied casts or bandages. After a steady two hours of a constant flow of patients, an ambulance arrived, carrying a patient with a thick wooden tent peg impaled in his abdomen. Henry came looking for Rayne.

'I'll need you with me on this.'

'How did it happen?' Rayne asked after they'd reviewed their patient. 'Who uses tent pegs that big and wooden?'

'It's a peg from one of the marquees. The wind pulled it from the ground and sent it flying. It landed in poor Rocky here. Give me four units of O-negative, plasma, saline and immediate X-ray. Where's Stuie Rhodes?'

'Right here,' Stuie said, and immediately began to question their latest patient. 'He'll be fine to anaesthetise,' he reported. 'It's good that he's still conscious and, thank God, stopped drinking at lunchtime.'

Henry nodded, already knowing that. 'He'd planned on driving back to Melbourne as soon as the concert was over but instead stayed to help out.'

'You go and scrub,' Rayne said to Henry. 'I'll take care of everything and see you in Theatre.'

'Right.' Henry went off and Rayne went to check on Rocky once more.

'How are you holding up?' she asked the twenty-eight-year-old. Why did he look so young, lying there?

'Am I gonna die, Rayne?' The question was asked in a quivering voice and her heart instantly went out to him.

'Not if Henry has anything to do with it, and as he *does*, I'd take that as a clear-cut no. You aren't going to die, Rocky. We refuse to let you.'

The man breathed in this knowledge and closed his eyes as Rayne and the orderlies took him off to Theatre. The radiographer was there, ready to take X-rays of the area so Henry could have a clearer picture of what was happening. The wound had been expertly bound with ring bandages, securing the impaled piece of wood in place, ensuring it didn't move around and cause more damage, especially while they'd been transporting him.

When the theatre was set up and Rocky was ready to be anaesthetised, Rayne went to the scrub sink.

'X-rays are ready,' she told Henry.

'Thanks.' He was almost fully gowned. 'Scans would have been preferable but we don't have the time. As soon as you're ready, Rayne.' He gave her a brisk nod and stalked into Theatre. He was in the zone.

'Rayne?'

She turned to find the theatre nurse waiting to help her gown and so forced herself to do the same and forget everything and everyone—except what she'd been trained to do so she could help Henry save Rocky's life.

'Once we're ready to remove the tent peg, things will move very quickly,' Henry told his staff. He wouldn't be lying if he said he wanted his trained staff and equipment around him at a time like this, but thankfully the radiographs had shown him the situation wasn't as bad as it had first looked.

'Rocky's large and small intestines have both been ruptured, but the liver, spleen and kidneys remain intact. We'll need peritoneal lavage as the stomach has ruptured, and as Rocky has voided, we can also add a bladder tear to the list.' He paused for a moment and looked around the room. 'If you have questions, make them clear and concise and I will answer them. Don't forge ahead if you're not one hundred per cent sure of what you're doing.' He looked at everyone, leaving Rayne till last. When she met his eyes and nodded, he said firmly, 'Let's begin.'

No sooner had he said the words than the lights flickered then cut out.

'Generator?' he asked.

'Give it a second,' Rayne responded, and a moment later the lights came back on.

'Stuie?'

'Everything's still fine. You're good to go,' Stuie reported, checking his dials.

The hail seemed to have passed but the wind and rain were still lashing the building. No one noticed this as they concentrated on the long and methodical operation they were performing to save Rocky's life. Rayne continued to listen to Henry's instructions, assisting him and doing exactly as he asked.

When the tent peg was removed, Rayne couldn't believe how quickly they worked, suturing off areas, using the suction and gauze pads, but gradually Henry brought the situation under control, making sure Stuie was also satisfied with Rocky's vitals.

'Everything's still good,' Stuie reported over two hours later.

It was four hours before the drains had been put in, the skin stapled back together and the anaesthetic reversed. And still the rain was hitting the roof of the hospital. When it rained in this part of the outback, it *rained*.

Rayne walked wearily out of Theatre, surprised she felt like a million dollars on the inside. 'That was…amazing,' she said as she degowned.

'You're not too exhausted?' Henry was surprised.

'Totally.' She nodded for emphasis. 'But it was still amazing. How do you do it? Day in, day out?'

'Do you mean standing in one place for so long or the work?' He was secretly pleased that he'd managed to impress her.

'Both.'

'The standing you get used to fairly quickly. The other is lots of study and hard work.' He watched her closely. 'Why don't you really consider doing further study?'

Rayne smiled. 'I can't leave Deni.'

'You may not have to.'

'I can't study surgery here, Henry.'

'Why not? You could do the training at Wagga and they have a university there that offers the required courses.'

Her eyes widened. 'You've looked into it?'

'I've looked into a lot of things.'

Rayne was astounded. Was it possible? Could she study surgery while still being a GP? No. It would be too much work, too much pressure on Jasmine, but perhaps in the future… The hope that had flared at Henry's words settled down to a more reasonable level. 'I'd never even considered staying in Deni and studying surgery. Of course, I can't do it now, but perhaps later…when Jazzy's more settled.'

'It's something to consider.'

'Actually, I can't. I can't be on call for Wagga Base hospital as a surgical registrar. I'd have to do night shifts and all sorts of odd hours. That wouldn't fit in with my clinics and house calls and the rest of my life.'

'You do know that you *can* study surgery part time?'

'No. Really?'

'Of course. And as to the actual practical hours, you could work here at Deni.'

She shook her head. 'We don't have a surgeon here to supervise.'

'Rayne!' Tanya's call came from down the corridor.

'In here,' she called back, and both she and Henry turned to face the harassed triage sister. 'How are things going? Do you need us?'

Tanya sighed heavily. 'Things have settled but I do still need help. Henry, there's a case in treatment room one. If you wouldn't mind taking a look, I'd appreciate it. Now that the rain isn't so hard, we can use the helicopter, but only if you think it's necessary.'

'Right-o. Lead the way.'

'What do you want me to do?' Rayne asked.

'We're out of 0-negative. Could you get some more brought up?'

'Sure.'

Henry watched as Rayne walked off before he followed Tanya. He still wasn't used to everyone pitching in like this. Rayne was a trained doctor yet she'd been sent off on an errand an orderly would do. Then again, perhaps all the orderlies were busy and there was no one else to do it. It was simply such a different, more relaxed and informal atmosphere than he was used to…but he definitely liked it. All around Deni he'd found the same sort of outlook. They were a community. Whether you were a retired headmaster in charge of building tables or the person who baked the best cupcakes in the world—everyone was still equal. And Henry realised that if Tanya had asked *him* to bring up some more blood, he most certainly would have done it.

In Sydney, he'd been the big cheese. The guy at the top. And everyone had bowed and scraped to him to the point where he'd become so used to it, he'd half expected it. Not here, though. He was Henry. He'd helped set things up for the festival, he'd hammered and sawed, he'd drunk luke-warm tea and chatted with people whose outlook on life was hardly complex. Happiness. That was the main thing he'd found here in Deniliquin—happiness. And he hadn't been happy in a very long time.

The wind outside started to pick up again and once more the lights flickered but held. As he walked into treat-ment room one, there was an almighty crack, like that of thunder, but it was followed by a loud rumble and the ground even shook a little.

'What was that?' Tanya whispered.

A moment later, someone came racing up the corridor. 'A tree's fallen on the storage area.'

Henry's mind processed the information as his feet started taking him in the direction of the area the young man had pointed to. The storage area. Where they kept the blood supplies. The area where Rayne had gone.

He started to run, heading down the corridors, fear and trepidation on his face. Other people were behind him, following to help out where it might be needed, but none of that meant anything to him. Rayne had been in that part of the hospital. The part that a tree had col-lapsed onto.

His heart was pounding wildly with anxiety and pain. This couldn't happen. It wasn't fair. He couldn't lose Rayne. He'd already lost one woman he'd loved and he wasn't going to lose another. He quickened his pace as he rounded a corner, his mind picturing many different sce-narios. His breathing was shallow and he forced himself to swallow, to calm down. If Rayne was indeed in any danger, he needed to have all his faculties to ensure he saved her.

He wanted her. He needed her. He loved her.

CHAPTER ELEVEN

EVERYTHING seemed to happen in slow motion when he finally came to the part of the hospital that had collapsed. There was debris everywhere and the people around him started to dig, started to clear it. Henry was stunned, unable to move for a few minutes as he took in his surroundings. If Rayne was beneath all that…

Henry's heart constricted with pain.

People were talking, moving things, working their way through and asking him questions. He blinked. 'What?' His daze began to clear.

'Henry? Are you all right? You're as white as a sheet.'

'Rayne. Has anyone seen Rayne?'

A few people said they hadn't seen her. Others just kept on working their way through, clearing piece after piece. A few orderlies were getting a tarpaulin set up to keep the rain off the area but it would all take time and they didn't have much of it, not if they were going to find Rayne.

Henry shifted, his gaze frantically searching the rubble as he stood there getting wet and not caring in the slightest. 'There.' He pointed and rushed to the place where he'd seen a glimpse of a foot beneath some plasterboard. People were beside him, helping him dig, moving things out of the way to get to the person trapped beneath.

As they shifted a larger piece, Henry noticed a belt buckle. He moved more stuff out of the way, his heart plummeting as he realised it wasn't Rayne. It was a police-woman he'd seen in the hospital earlier on that evening. It wasn't Rayne.

He continued to help get the woman out, still wondering what had happened to Rayne. Where was she? Was she trapped further back? If so, it would take them quite a bit of time to get to her, and if she was injured… bleeding… He closed his eyes for a second and blocked out the mental images.

'Henry?' Tanya asked. 'Are you sure you're all right?'

Henry nodded. As the policewoman was now almost ready to be moved, he needed to assess her first. He concentrated on his job but once she'd been taken to the A and E department, he stood up and desperately scanned the area.

'Henry?'

He turned as he heard his name called, heard it called by the one woman he was desperate to see. 'Rayne?' There she was. Perfectly fine. He picked his way back through the rubble and gathered her into his arms.

'Where were you? I thought you were in there. I thought I'd lost you.'

'I went to the ward first,' she told him, but her mouth was muffled against his shoulder so she wasn't sure he'd heard her properly. No one seemed to give them a second glance as they held each other close, as Henry pressed his lips to hers.

'Don't do that to me. Don't scare me like that again.'

'I'm sorry. I had no idea you thought I was in there.'

'How could I not? You'd gone to the supply area. This…' he swept his hand in the direction of the area '…is the supply area.'

'You're mad?'

'No. No. I'm so utterly relieved. I thought I'd lost you.'

'So you said.'

'No, Rayne. You don't understand.' He held her back a little so he could look intently into her eyes. 'I thought I'd lost you, like I lost Natalia. I thought you'd been taken from me just when I'd found you. Rayne, I love you.'

Rayne wasn't sure what to say. What to do. Henry… loved her? Was it true? Could it be true or was it simply adrenaline talking?

'Don't say anything now. I didn't tell you in order to pressure you or to have you say you love me too. That's not what this is about.' He held her close and tenderly kissed her head. 'I thought you were in there and you're not, and right now I feel like the luckiest man alive because you could well have been in there.'

'I heard there was a policewoman in there.'

'Yes. We got her out.'

'Do I need to assess her?'

'She had a fractured arm and leg. Blood pressure and neurological observations were fine. There was a loss of consciousness for only a few minutes. She was stable but I've sent her for X-rays to have everything checked.'

Rayne smiled up at him, her arms still firmly around him. 'You're quite a man, Henry Harcourt. Worried about me. Digging through debris. Treating patients on the fly.'

'That's what I've been trained to do. Well, the treating-patients part, not the digging part.'

'And the worrying-about-me part?' Rayne waited expectantly for his answer. Had she dreamed he'd told her he loved her? It was as though she needed to test it, to make sure it had been real and not just part of her fanciful daydreaming.

He smiled down at her. She was now almost as wet as him but neither of them seemed to care at all. 'I haven't been trained to do it per se, but it's something that is now a part of me.'

'Because you love me?'

'I do.' And as if to prove it, he kissed her soundly.

'Are you two gonna stand around kissing, or are you going to help?' Tanya asked. They smiled at each other before letting each other go.

'Sorry,' they said in unison.

'Ah, don't worry,' Tanya remarked with a grin. 'We all enjoyed the show. Just make sure you take good care of our Rayne. Although we might be inundated with the other kind at the moment, this Rayne is the only one we have and we really need her.'

'Noted,' Henry said with a nod, and winked at his Rayne.

She wasn't at all sure what to say so she said nothing and set to work. Thankfully, there was no one else trapped beneath the debris and once the tarps were up, they were able to close off that section of the hospital, salvaging what they could in the way of supplies.

Henry and Rayne treated more patients, although the stream was starting to thin out, but they all knew that once the sun was up, there would be more people wanting medical attention. The policewoman escaped with clean fractures, which would only require casts, and thankfully her temporary loss of consciousness appeared to have had no ill effects.

'How are things going?' Rayne asked Tanya a while later.

'Settled. For the moment. The smaller cases will start to come in now that the sun is up. The damage to the areas of the town that were worst hit will be assessed better but, from what I've heard, the muster site was the main one. People who didn't want to bother us during the immediate aftermath will all be in for checks. Why don't you head on home, have a shower and get refreshed? Spend some time with Jazzy and come back in a few hours' time?'

'All right. First, I want to check on Rocky. Has his transfer to Wagga been organised?'

'I just need Henry to sign off on some paperwork and then it will all be settled. How did the surgery go?'

'It was long…exciting but long.'

'You really enjoy surgery, don't you?' Tanya asked rhetorically. 'You should do surgery, Rayne. The afterglow definitely suits you…or is it the dashing surgeon who suits you?'

Rayne laughed, not sure what to say. The fact that Henry had confessed his love for her was still overwhelming, making her all happy and excited every time she thought of it. It also brought so many questions. Did that mean he wanted to stay here in Deni? Was he going to leave Sydney for good? Where exactly did she fit into his life? Did she really fit at all?

Questions. Doubt. Confusion. They all warred within her and she decided not to think about it until she'd at least left the hospital.

She went and checked on Rocky's situation, pleased

when he was able to talk for a few minutes even though he was still very groggy from the anaesthetic.

'Henry says I'll be fine.'

'Told you so,' Rayne remarked with a smile. 'We've done our bit—now you need to do yours.'

'Which is?'

'Stay still and do what the nurses tell you.'

Rocky started to laugh but then moaned in pain.

'Are you all right?' Rayne reached for his chart to see what analgesics Henry had prescribed.

'I'm fine. Just shouldn't laugh. Everything feels…I dunno…heavy down there.'

'Fair enough. Well, if you're sure you're not in pain, I'll leave you to rest. Your transfer to Wagga should be all organised soon so you'll be up, up and away in no time.'

'Thanks, Rayne.' Rocky tried to reach for her hand and Rayne immediately took his. 'Seriously—thanks.'

'It's Henry who deserves the thanks.'

'And I've already told him.'

Rayne patted his hand. 'Sleep.'

Rocky did as he was told and Rayne went to get changed out of her theatre scrubs. It had certainly been an adventure and one she was sure wasn't quite over yet.

As she walked out of the hospital, she stood in the early morning light and shook her head at the aftermath of the storm. Branches, twigs and leaves littered the streets, as though someone had dumped a huge bag of rubbish on the entire township. Paper and other litter added to the mess and yet, with the sun shining down through the clouds, giving it a clear golden glow, Rayne knew everything was going to be all right.

'What a mess,' Henry said softly as he came up behind her, slipping an arm about her waist.

'But still…pretty.' She indicated the sky, and Henry agreed.

'Looking at the sky, you'd have no idea what it looked like only a few hours earlier.'

'The world keeps turning,' she murmured softly.

Henry looked at her and she at him. 'That it does.' He took her hand in his. 'Let's go check on Jasmine.'

'No doubt she slept through the whole thing. She's such a heavy sleeper.' Rayne chatted happily about Jasmine as they navigated the streets. A water main had burst on the road so they had to take a detour to Rayne's house.

'You're here,' Jasmine squealed when they finally pulled into the driveway. 'Rayne, there was this big storm and I woke up at five o'clock in the morning and Granny and Grandpa were asleep on the lounge together so I woke them up because you weren't in your bed and they told me you'd gone to the hop-sital with Henry so I knew everything was going to be OK, and it is.'

'Yes, it is,' Rayne said as she held the little girl close. No sooner had Jasmine given Rayne a hug than she launched herself at Henry.

'Come inside. Granny's cooked up some bacon and eggs.'

'Mmm. Sounds good.' He gave Jasmine a kiss on her cheek. 'But you taste good, too. Maybe I'll have Jazzy for breakfast instead.'

She giggled. 'You can't eat me, Henry. If you did, you wouldn't be able to kiss me tomorrow.'

'Exactly right.' He gave her tummy a little tickle and headed inside. Rayne loved the way he loved Jasmine, the way he'd brought a light back into the little girl's eyes just by being himself. She closed her eyes for a moment and prayed he would stay here in Deni, that he would stay in her life. Sure, she had questions but surely they could work everything out. Couldn't they?

She had to keep brushing aside the feeling that Henry wasn't like all those men who had come and gone in her mother's life. He was one of the good guys, the ones you could trust. The ones you could bring home and let them become a part of you, of your life. He loved her. He'd told her so straight out and she also appreciated, given what he'd been through, that that would have been a difficult thing for him to say, but he'd said it. He'd found a way to move on with his life and she admired him for that. He wasn't looking back. Not any more.

'There's a lesson there, Rayne,' she murmured as she opened her eyes and headed into the house.

They ate breakfast together as a family and this time Rayne noticed Henry was more open, more animated in his discussions. It was as though in declaring his love for her a weight had been lifted from his shoulders and he was free to be exactly who he was. What you saw was what you got…and that meant she could trust him. There was no false dignity, no pretence whatsoever. He was her Henry, through and through, and as he laughed with Jarvis and received a mock scolding from Earlene, Rayne marvelled at the happiness he'd also helped to bring to her little family.

Everyone was smiling. Everyone was happy and healthy.

Another picture-perfect memory and one she hoped would last longer than a moment.

* * *

As they'd promised Tanya, the two of them returned to the hospital after Henry had gone back to Sylvia's for a quick shower to refresh himself. He'd insisted once again on collecting Rayne and when he did, he held her hand as they made their way back to the hospital.

The road workers had been hard at it and a considerable amount of debris had been cleared since they'd taken this route. The A and E was quite full when they arrived and so they set to work immediately, seeing patient after patient, but the numbers didn't appear to dwindle. As one left, another arrived.

At half past four that afternoon, it appeared they could soon think about going home, with only five or six people left to be seen. Thankfully, most of the cases in the past hour or so had been straightforward, with people wanting aches and pains checked out.

The doors to A and E swished open and in came a burly man, leaning on his mates. He looked feverish, and from the bandage around his right arm was not in good shape.

'Bring him through here,' Rayne said immediately, leading them into treatment room one. 'What happened?'

'Bart collapsed, Doc. We were gonna call for an ambulance when he came to and told us not to. Said he was fine.'

'We finally got him to agree to at least come here and get checked out before we leave,' the other man supplied. The two men hefted Bart onto the examination bed and then stepped to the side to allow Rayne and her team to do their work.

'Has he been drinking?'

'No, Doc. Bart's a teetotaller. He runs the petting zoo and says he has to keep his wits about him.'

'He's one of the carnival workers?'

'Yes, Doc. He's been doing the muster for a good four years now.'

She nodded, listening to the readings the nursing staff were giving her on the patient's vitals.

'BP is elevated.'

'Temperature is thirty-nine point two.'

'Get an IV set up to replace fluids. We need to get that temperature down.' Rayne had pulled on a protective gown and gloves and started to remove the bandage from Bart's right arm. 'How long has he had this bandage on?' It was dusty and bloodstained.

'Oh, I dunno, Doc. He gashed his arm before we got here. We were at Gunnedah before coming down to Deni.'

As Rayne removed the bandage, a stench filled the room and she wrinkled her nose. 'It's badly infected.' She looked over at one of the nurses. 'Call Henry. I'd rather he dealt with this.'

'Yes, Rayne. Uh…do you know where he is?'

'He should be around here somewhere. If he's not, check the ward or X-ray.'

Bart's two friends had been ushered from the room and asked to write down any details of what had happened to Bart during the last few days.

'Temperature still isn't dropping,' came the report two minutes later, when the next lot of neurological observations had been performed. They'd cut Bart's clothes off him, checking for other lacerations or tell-tale signs that might give them more of a clue of what they were dealing with. Was the infection causing his high temperature or was there something else?

Henry walked into the room and went directly to the

sink before pulling on a gown and gloves. 'What have you got for me?' he asked as he worked. Rayne couldn't believe she was having difficulty controlling her heart rate. Would there ever come a time when she wouldn't be instantly affected by this man?

During the report both she and her staff gave him, Rayne kept sneaking little glances at him. He was currently studying the wound beneath the bandage.

'I didn't want to debride it until you'd had a look. It appears rather deep.'

'No, that's fine. You've got him on fluids and IV penicillin so that's a start.' He looked up at her, their eyes meeting across the examination table, and for one blinding second it was just the two of them locked in a bubble in time. It wasn't the first time it had happened and it probably wouldn't be the last. Henry's eyes were intense, and she could see quite clearly that he was as aware of her as she was of him.

With a blink the bubble burst and the noises, the staff, the situation intruded into their minds, bringing them back to the present and the patient who was between them. 'I'll go get a theatre ready and we'll take care of that arm. Get Stuie in here to anaesthetise and tell me the instant Bart's temperature begins to drop.' With that, he walked from the room.

It was only a minute later that Rayne also left, throwing her gown and gloves into the appropriate bins as she went. Henry wasn't at the nurses' station so she headed around to Theatres to search him out. He wasn't in Theatres either, and as Rayne stood there for a second, wondering where he might have disappeared to so quickly, the door to the male change rooms opened and out he came.

'Gee, you move fast,' she said on seeing him.

Henry nodded but didn't say anything else.

'Henry?'

'Mmm?'

'Is something wrong?' Was he regretting telling her he loved her?

He stopped what he was doing and turned to face her. 'No. Just trying to concentrate, that's all. It's difficult to do when you're in the room,' he said, watching her expression. Her eyes widened at his words and Henry had to employ all his willpower not to close the gap between them and haul her into his arms. He pointed back towards the A and E department. 'I forgot there was a room full of people. I forgot there was a patient with an infected gash that stinks to high heaven. I forgot everything the moment I looked into your eyes.'

'I know.'

'That doesn't happen to me. Things…situations like that don't happen to me.'

'Or me,' she pointed out.

'But it did.'

'It did,' she confirmed. 'I feel it, too.'

Henry breathed in deeply and slowly exhaled. 'You do?' He'd told her hours ago that he loved her and while he'd also said he didn't want to force a declaration out of her, he also needed to know her emotions were as intense as his. 'That's good to know.' Then, as though to prove their points, they moved closer. Bit by bit the distance separating them disappeared and soon they were facing each other. He reached out and touched his hand to hers. Immediately her fingers linked with his. 'I knew once I'd started kissing you, I'd be unable to stop.'

'It's addictive. *You're* addictive.'

'Ditto.'

He was within kissing distance now and she wasn't quite sure how those last few centimetres had been bridged. 'I've missed you,' he murmured. 'I've been in the same hospital with you, working near you, but I've still missed you.'

'I missed you, too.'

'Sad.'

'Very,' she agreed, but all the while her mind kept urging him closer, needing him to follow through on the promise that was zinging all around them.

'I want to kiss you.'

'I want you to kiss me.'

'I can't.'

'Why not?'

'Because if I do I won't be able to stop, and I have surgery to perform.' Although his words weren't what she wanted to hear, she knew he'd needed to say them. He didn't, however, back away, seemingly content to torture both of them.

'Let's get Bart organised and out of the way and then I can clock off and we can have a great night together,' Rayne whispered.

'Yes.'

'Yes.' But before he let go of her hands, she couldn't resist and leaned forward to brush her mouth against his. 'Sustenance,' she murmured, and took three huge steps away.

'Tease.'

'Torturer.' She dragged in a big breath and let it out on a sigh. 'Do you need me in Theatre?'

'I need you everywhere.'

'Henry. Stop it.'

'You started it.'

Rayne merely smiled and shook her head, loving their banter.

'Hi, there,' Stuie said as he walked into the room. 'Henry, I've reviewed the patient and the antibiotics and extra fluids seem to be bringing his temperature down.'

'I'll go check on the staff,' Rayne said, leaving the two men alone. Henry couldn't help but watch her walk from the room and was again hit with the feeling that he couldn't let Rayne go. How had this happened? He hadn't planned to meet another woman. Hadn't planned to fall in love. But he had and now he wasn't exactly sure how to proceed. There were so many things that needed to be sorted out, so many questions he needed answers to, and so many new plans to make.

At least now, with Rayne out of the room, Henry was able to concentrate with more success, and even when Bart was wheeled into Theatre a while later, accompanied by Rayne, Henry still managed to maintain control. Realising they were taking this journey together was helping him not to lose concentration, even when she stood beside him to assist with the operation.

Once Bart was stable and settled in Recovery, it was close to six o'clock.

'Jazzy isn't going to like this,' Henry murmured as he headed for the change rooms.

'We'll make it up to her,' Rayne promised as she pushed open the door next to his.

'Change fast, Dr Hudson.'

'Likewise, Dr Harcourt.' Winking at him, she all but danced into the change rooms. It had been so much fun working with him in Theatre. The more he called on her to assist, the more she realised she was indeed selling herself short. She loved theatre work. She always had, and to be able to have that opportunity during Henry's visit had only made her realise just how much she'd missed it.

As she finished changing, pulling a hairbrush through her hair, Rayne stopped and looked at her reflection. What did Henry really see when he looked at her? Did he see a woman in control of her life? Did he see a brand-new mother, trying desperately to figure out what to do next? Did he see a woman who was madly in love with him but too afraid to admit it? She knew that once he learned of her feelings things would change... Things were already changing and she didn't know quite how to cope.

Could she put herself through such a big change? Allowing Henry into her life on a full-time basis? It was what she wanted, she knew that, but at the same time she was scared of it. Was this the real deal? She didn't want to end up like her mother. She didn't want to be incapable of giving and receiving real, honest, intimate love. She loved Henry, of that she was certain, but what if he hurt her? What if she sacrificed everything for him—the way her mother had time and time again—and what if he let her down?

Her mother had never recovered well from that sort of heartbreak. Could she?

CHAPTER TWELVE

BY THE time they returned to Rayne's house, Jasmine was in a very grumpy mood.

'Where have you been?' She stamped her foot and crossed her little arms over her chest. 'I've been waiting for ever!'

'Sorry, petal, but we had to help a sick man. He's going to get better now.'

'I don't care.' With that, Jasmine ran off. Rayne looked at Earlene in confusion.

'What's happened?'

'She has been out of sorts since you left this morning. She also has a slight temperature.'

'What?' Rayne's feelings switched from one of guilt at being away so long to one of caution. 'How long? Is it up by much?'

'Not by much, but it might account for her not feeling well.'

'She's sick? She can't be sick.' Rayne turned to Henry, who had just walked in the door. 'Jasmine has a temperature.'

'What? Where is she?'

'Mad at us.'

Henry shrugged and walked further into the house. 'She'll just have to be mad. Jasmine?' he called, but received no reply. 'Jazzy, we're sorry we took so long. We're both here now and we can't wait to spend time with you.'

'Go away!' Jasmine called, giving her hiding-place away. Henry headed over to where she was hiding behind the lounge, but didn't approach her. Rayne watched in awe at the way he dealt with the five-year-old's tantrum.

'Is that what you really want? Do you want Rayne and I to go away?'

'Yes,' came the answer, although all the adults could hear the wavering of the little voice.

'OK, then. We'll go away.' He turned and had taken two steps away when Jasmine flew at him, clinging to his leg.

'No. Don't go.'

Henry lifted the little girl into his arms and kissed her forehead, lingering a moment to try and gauge her temperature. 'She *is* a little warm,' he stated, looking at Rayne. 'Jazzy, are your ears sore?'

'This one is,' she said, pointing to the left one before burying her head into Henry's shoulder and bursting into tears.

'Medicine and sleep,' Earlene suggested.

'I'll get my bag,' Rayne murmured as Henry sat down with Jasmine. Rayne returned with the tympanic thermometer and an otoscope.

'You have an otoscope at home?' Henry seemed surprised.

'You don't?'

He smiled at her words and just that glorious sight was enough to help Rayne relax. As soon as Henry had confirmed that Jasmine had a raised temperature, Rayne felt the walls close in on her. Jasmine was sick! She couldn't be. Nothing could happen to that child. She was too precious, too necessary in her life. Jasmine was all she had left of Janey and therefore she wasn't allowed to be sick. Jasmine was sick! The words went round and round in her head like a stuck record and she desperately tried to control herself so she didn't panic. Medically she could handle anything, except Jasmine being sick.

Now Henry was here, taking control, remaining calm. Rayne had been ready to break into panic mode, to rush Jasmine up to the hospital, but Henry merely held the child close to him and cuddled her. The tears subsided and Jasmine was now lying on his torso, her arms about his neck, her eyes closed, her breathing regular.

'What's her temperature?' he asked as Rayne withdrew the thermometer.

'Thirty-eight point one.'

'Check her ears. You'll no doubt find that they're the culprit.'

She did as he'd suggested and agreed with him.

'No doubt Earlene's been keeping Jasmine's fluids up. We'll give her some medicine and sponge her down. She'll be fine. You'll see.'

'You've nursed children with temperatures before?'

'I looked after Natalia when she had a temperature.'

'Oh.' She'd forgotten he'd helped nurse his wife. 'It's just that you're so good with children...well, with Jazzy.'

'I've always liked kids.' He met Rayne's eyes. 'Always wanted a brood of my own.' He half expected her to shy away from his words, from what he was saying without really saying it, but she didn't. Instead, she took his hand in hers and brought it to her lips, kissing it tenderly. It was the perfect answer.

Together they sponged Jasmine down, pleased when the thermometer recorded a slightly lower temperature. Finally the fever broke and the child slipped into a deep, natural sleep. Rayne slumped down onto the lounge and sighed in relief. Slowly, the tension of the last few hours started to drain out of her, and as she remembered how scared she'd been for the little girl, tears started to prick behind her eyes. Valiantly, she tried to hold them back.

'Let it out, Rayne. It's OK to let go.' Henry's words were filled with healing and when she looked up at him and sniffed, he smiled and brushed the teardrop quivering on her eyelashes away with his thumb. 'Let it out, honey.'

She nodded and slowly the tears slid down her cheeks. Henry tightened his hold on her hand, wanting to let her know that she was incredibly special to him and that to share a moment like this was so intimate, so personal and so right.

When she'd finished, he held out his handkerchief to her, which she took with gratitude.

'Sorry, I'm overreacting, I know. Aren't you glad you came back with me tonight?' She laughed as she spoke. 'Sick children and crying women.'

Henry shifted so that he was facing her and reached out to touch her hair, sifting his fingers through it. 'It's OK. And you're beautiful.'

'What?' she scoffed. 'With a red nose and puffy eyes?'

'Yes.' He cupped her cheek. 'You're beautiful, Rayne, and I would far rather be here with you and Jazzy than anywhere in the world.'

'Oh.' His words were perfect, touching her deep within her soul. 'Really?'

'Yes.' He leaned forward and pressed his mouth to hers as though to prove his point. 'You're beautiful on the inside as well as on the outside, and that's an amazing quality to have.' He took her hands in his and looked into her eyes with complete tenderness. 'This thing between us, Rayne. You have to know it's just the beginning.'

'Beginning of what?'

'Of the next chapter of our lives.'

'*Our* lives?'

'Yes. I need you with me, Rayne. You and Jazzy.'

'Henry?'

'I want to move to Deniliquin. To be near you.'

'But you can't do it just for us. It needs to be the right thing for you, too.'

'It is. Believe me, it is. Rayne…' He shifted slightly, adjusting the way he was holding Jasmine, propping a pillow behind her head. 'Rayne…you've helped me in such an amazing way. You've brought me out of the past, out of my loneliness, and you've shown me that there's more of a future for me than just grinding away at that hospital. After Natalia's accident I despaired of ever being happy again. I was so alone. I had no one and that started to consume me. I started to tell myself I didn't *need* anyone, that work would be enough. I had to keep going, although I wasn't sure why.

'I knew after Natalia had been in the coma for about six months that she would never make a full recovery. The damage had been done and it was then I started to let go. Took a while, believe me, but deep down inside I knew I had to let go but, in doing so, I sank even deeper into that lonely void.'

'Oh, Henry.' She kissed his hand again, her heart wrenching for him. 'I know that void. I've been there.'

'I think that's why we connected so quickly. We sensed that about each other and you've helped me to climb out, helped me to let go and to start afresh.' He shook his head. 'When I heard that part of the building had collapsed, when I thought you were under all that rubble…' He stopped and closed his eyes. 'It was as though the loneliness was reaching out to grab me again.' He looked at her, his eyes intense. 'I can't lose you, Rayne. I love you so deeply, so passionately. I need you in my life, to fill it with joy and happiness and, hopefully, children. Brothers and sisters for Jasmine. More grandchildren for Earlene and Jarvis.'

'Are you asking me to—?' She stopped.

Henry smiled. 'By the scared look in your eyes, I think it best if I don't, but that is my intention, Rayne. I'll give you all the time in the world. I'll continue to restore your faith in men, to let you know that I am the one you can depend on, who's going to do everything in his power to protect you, to cherish you, to love you for ever.'

'Henry.' She couldn't help it and leaned forward, being careful not to squash Jasmine, and kissed him. She pulled back and looked into his eyes, her heart pounding wildly against her chest. 'I lo—' She stopped and swallowed.

'Shh.' He put a finger on her lips. 'It's all right. There's plenty of time. We'll sort it all out.'

'We will?'

'Yes.'

'I don't want you to think you don't mean anything to me. You do but—'

'I know.'

And she realised he truly did understand.

'Now, why don't we get Jazzy to bed and have a relaxing cup of tea?'

Rayne took Jasmine's temperature again, relieved when it was still down. Henry carried the girl to her bedroom and placed her gently on the bed. Rayne pulled up the covers and they stood there, just watching Jasmine sleep.

'You're doing a good job,' he told Rayne softly. 'Janey would be proud.'

'I hope so.'

'I wish I'd had the chance to meet her, and Jarrod.'

'I wish you had, too.' Rayne looked up at him. 'She would have liked you.'

'Really?'

'For sure.' They went into the kitchen where Earlene and Jarvis were playing a game of cards. Everyone chatted softly as they drank tea but slowly the day started catching up with Rayne and when she yawned, Henry stood, declaring it was time for him to go.

'I'll come by tomorrow and we can talk,' he told her as she walked him to the door.

'OK.' Rayne went willingly into his arms, closing her eyes and breathing in the scent of him. 'I love the way you smell,' she said.

'Yeah?' He smiled down at her. 'What else?'

Rayne swallowed and looked up at him. 'I love the way you love Jasmine.'

'She's so easy to love. Like you, Rayne.'

'That's not how I feel. I'm too insecure, for a start.'

Henry shrugged. 'You're working hard at overcoming

quite a few years of distrust. That's an amazing thing to accomplish, and you'll do it.'

'With your help,' she stated.

'With my help,' he confirmed, and kissed her. 'Sleep. Rest. Relax.'

'Yes, Doctor.' She smiled at him as he left then went inside to say good night to Earlene and Jarvis.

'Has he proposed yet?' Jarvis asked.

'Oh, shush.' Earlene sent him a look. 'Leave them alone, Jarvis. They'll sort things out in their own time.'

'I'm just saying that he's a good one, Raynie,' Jarvis said firmly. 'Good breeding. Good stock. Just like Jarrod. He'll look after you, girl, and it's quite clear to see he's mad in love with you.'

Rayne's smile was bright and uplifting. 'Yeah. He is.'

'And it's quite clear to see you're mad in love with him.'

Her smile grew. 'Yeah. I am.'

'Then what's stopping you?' Jarvis wanted to know. Rayne thought for a moment, *really* thought. Her life had changed all those years ago when she'd come to live with these wonderful people. She'd seen first-hand what a real family was like and she'd blossomed in it. She'd changed, she'd matured and she'd accepted the love she'd been offered. And she was no longer a scared fourteen-year-old but a woman who was loved by a very special man. What *was* stopping her from telling Henry how she felt?

'Nothing.'

The next morning when Henry came over to see Rayne, he was stunned when she opened the front door and planted a big kiss on his lips.

'Good morning, man of my dreams.'

'Uh…morning.' He was dazzled by the brightness in her eyes, by the happiness that seemed to surround her. 'Have a good night's sleep?'

'The best.'

'And Jasmine? How is she?'

'Putting Ethel to bed and doing just fine.'

'Good. Good.' Henry still had his arms about Rayne, her buoyant mood causing his hopes to rise. Was this the day? The day that would be the start of the rest of his life? 'Can I…er…come in?'

'Oh. Silly me. Of course.' She kissed him again before taking his hand in hers and leading him inside.

'Do you have clinic this morning?'

'Yes, but it always starts a little later on Monday mornings so I have some time.' They headed into the lounge room where there were paper and pencils all over the coffee-table.

'Jarvis and Earlene?'

'Earlene's baking. Jarvis is out in the backyard.'

'And you're happy.'

'I'm very happy.'

'May I ask why? Not that I'm complaining, you understand. I like it when you're happy.'

'Good. And, yes, you may ask.'

'OK. Why are you so happy?'

'Because I love you.'

Henry was stunned. Just like that. Just like that she'd said the words he desperately wanted to hear. Before he could respond, Jasmine came into the room, all but throwing herself at him.

'Henry. Henry. Henry.' She squeezed him tight around the neck and pressed three quick kisses to his cheek. 'Look what Rayne and I made.' She climbed off him as quickly as she'd arrived and ran to the table, picking up a 'chatterbox' she'd folded out of paper. 'Pick a colour,' she said, holding the little squares on her fingers.

'Uh…' Henry looked at the colours written on the top. 'Yellow.'

Jasmine spelt out the word, moving her fingers back and fourth as she did so, the 'chatterbox' revealing a set of numbers. 'Pick a number.'

He had to draw his attention away from looking at Rayne, still unable to believe she'd declared her love for him. 'Uh…six.'

'S—I—X,' Jasmine spelt out, moving the 'chatterbox' another three times. 'Pick another number.'

Henry looked at the new set of numbers. 'Five.'

Jasmine nodded and opened the paper up to read what message of wisdom was written behind number five. '"I love you." That's what it says. See, Henry?'

'Yes, and it's true. I do love you. What a clever "chatterbox" you've made.'

'I like it when you say that, Henry. It makes me all sparkly with love.' She jiggled as she spoke and both grown-ups smiled.

'You have a way with words, Jazzy.' Henry winked at her but caressed Rayne's hand while he spoke.

'She found a book in the library on origami,' Rayne supplied, feeling as though she should say something, but was totally surprised to hear her own voice sounding so husky. How could she be expected to help it when Henry wasn't letting go of her hand, was wanting her as close to him as she could get and was almost devouring her with his eyes every time he looked her way?

'Really?' He pointed to the other 'chatterbox', which was folded more neatly on the table. 'And who made that one?'

'I did.' Rayne leaned over to pick it up then looked down at the hand Henry still held. 'I'll need it back if I'm going to show you.'

Reluctantly he released her. She put her fingers into the little squares. 'All right. Pick a colour.'

Henry scanned the words written on each of the four corners but they all said 'white'. 'Uh…white?'

Rayne moved her fingers vertically and horizontally as she spelt out the word. When it landed open on the numbers, she said, 'Pick a number.'

Again they all said 'thirty-two'. 'Uh…thirty-two.'

Thankfully, Rayne didn't count out the number but instead lifted the flap to read what the message was beneath that number. '"Will you marry me?"'

'That's what it says, Henry. She's not making it up,' Jasmine said, pointing to the writing on the paper while she jumped up and down with excitement.

Henry looked at Rayne, then back at the words on the paper, then back at Rayne again. It was then he realised she was actually on one knee and he couldn't help the smile that came to his face.

She put the 'chatterbox' on the floor and took his hand in hers. 'I do love you so very much, Henry. I want to walk down the aisle in white in thirty-two days' time—as required by law—and I want to marry you. What do you say?'

It was the most courageous thing she'd ever done in her

life and when Henry glanced up at the doorway, he wasn't at all surprised to find Jarvis and Earlene watching and waiting along with Jasmine and Rayne.

He returned his attention to Rayne, seeing the love shining brightly in her eyes. 'You are amazing, Rayne. Just you try and stop me from marrying you.'

With mounting impatience, which was very unlike him, Henry tugged Rayne into his arms and covered her mouth with his, kissing her with such abandonment she instantly felt light-headed. His lips moved over hers in total possession and she surrendered to him one hundred per cent.

The power of the kiss was deep and extremely hungry. It was as though both of them had been crawling through the desert for far too long and now, finally, they could quench their thirst. Rayne matched his intensity, eager to show him just how much she loved him.

'Did he say yes?' Jasmine wanted to know. She turned to face her grandparents. 'Did he say yes?'

'I sure hope so,' Jarvis joked.

Henry pulled back, resting his forehead against Rayne's before looking at Jasmine. 'It is most definitely a big, fat yes.'

Whooping with joy, Jasmine threw herself at Henry, smothering him with kisses. 'You're going to be my daddy. I wanted you to be my daddy. I really did. I prayed every night that you'd be my daddy and now you will be.'

Henry and Rayne were both laughing at the exuberance of the five-year-old. Henry finally managed to shift and put one arm about Rayne and the other around Jasmine. He kissed his bride-to-be with love and then kissed Jasmine's cheek.

'My girls.'

EPILOGUE

THIRTY-TWO days later, Rayne was dressed in white and was ready to walk down the aisle of the historical Deniliquin church to her Prince Charming who was waiting for her. Willard, much to his delight, was best man and Stuie was groomsman.

Henry had returned to Sydney with both Jasmine and Rayne, shocking all the staff at his hospital by putting in for a transfer to Wagga Wagga Base hospital. Deniliquin had willingly accepted his services as a general surgical consultant and already he had a waiting list.

He assisted Rayne with her house calls on a weekly basis and she, in turn, was planning to go back to university the following year to complete her surgical training under the watchful eye of her husband-supervisor.

Earlene was nervously straightening her dress and Tanya was returning from taking Jasmine to the toilet.

'Are we ready?' Jarvis asked.

'Is everyone else ready?' Rayne questioned back.

Jarvis tut-tutted. 'You're the bride, dear. You're the one we wait for.'

'I'm ready, Grandpa,' Jasmine said, giving him another

twirl of her pink dress, her blonde hair up in ringlets with little pink rosebuds for decoration. 'I've got flowers in my hair! I've never had flowers in my hair before. I like it.' She paused then said, 'Rayne, why do Tanya and Grandma have flowers in their hair? They're not *flower* girls. Only I am.'

Jarvis laughed and patted the child's bottom. 'Time to start, pumpkin. Remember, nice and slow, like in rehearsal.'

'I know, Grandpa.' She nodded eagerly and took her place, ready to get this wedding under way As far as Jasmine was concerned, the sooner Henry was her new daddy, the better.

Jarvis held his arm out to Rayne, ready to walk her down the aisle. 'We're proud of you, Rayne. You know that, don't you?'

'I do. I can't thank you enough for everything you've done for me over the years. Taking me in. Giving me a home.' She kissed his cheek. 'You *are* my father in every possible way and I love you.'

'Ah, come on, girl. You're going to ruin your make-up if you keep this up.'

Rayne sniffed and nodded, dabbing at her eyes with the white lace handkerchief she'd initially given to Janey on her wedding day. Earlene had put it into her hands earlier and said, 'Here. This can be your "something borrowed", even though I want you to keep it.'

'I just wish Janey was here.'

Jarvis nodded and looked upwards at a ray of sunshine beaming down on them. 'She is, dear. She is.'

With that, Rayne was ready to walk down the aisle to Henry. When she arrived at his side, he lifted her veil and gasped with delight.

'You're…exquisite.' And then, unable to control himself, he leaned forward and kissed her.

The church erupted into a mass of wild cheers and wolf-whistles, with the minister clearing his throat and saying, 'I haven't got to that bit yet.'

Rayne blushed as Henry drew back and looked around sheepishly. 'Uh…sorry.'

After that, the ceremony proceeded as planned, with Henry accepting the rings from Willard and placing one on Rayne's finger and then one on Jasmine's.

'Are you my daddy now, Henry?' she asked.

'Absolutely,' he replied, and kissed her head.

Later, once the reception was over, Rayne and Henry headed out to the car they were taking on their honeymoon. They kissed Jasmine goodbye, knowing they'd see her the next day when she joined them in Echuca for the rest of the family honeymoon, but tonight Henry was determined to have Rayne all to himself.

Rayne stood back from the kerb and looked at the car she was supposed to leave in. 'A ute? We're leaving in a ute?' She shook her head and smiled. 'What happened to your snazzy car?'

'Hey. It's white. It's got wedding ribbons on it! It's also quite clean. No coat of dust.'

'Not *yet*. Well, I guess it's to be expected.' She shrugged, accepting fate. 'After all, Deni *is* the ute capital of the world.'

Henry held the door for her and helped her in then walked round to the driver's side, waving to everyone as he went. Once inside, he started the engine then leaned over to kiss his bride once more.

'I love you, Rayne.'

'I love you, Henry.'

And with that, he put the car into gear and drove off. A Just Married sign was on the tailgate along with a few tin cans and an old boot tied to the bumper—courtesy of the thriving Deniliquin community they were now a firm part of.

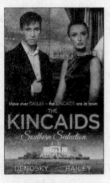